Addicted to
an Addict

Addicted to an Addict

Honey

www.urbanbooks.net

Urban Books, LLC
300 Farmingdale Road, NY-Route 109
Farmingdale, NY 11735

ISBN 13: 978-1-945855-92-4
ISBN 10: 1-945855-92-4

First Trade Paperback Printing Janaury 2019
Printed in the United States of America

10 9 8 7 6 5 4 3 2 1

This is a work of fiction. Any references or similarities to actual events, real people, living or dead, or to real locales are intended to give the novel a sense of reality. Any similarity in other names, characters, places, and incidents is entirely coincidental.

Distributed by Kensington Publishing Corp.
Submit Orders to:
Customer Service
400 Hahn Road
Westminster, MD 21157-4627
Phone: 1-800-733-3000
Fax: 1-800-659-2436

Addicted to an Addict

by

Honey

Chapter One

"The limo just pulled up, Mayor Bishop."

Josiah turned away from Gypsie, his trusted administrative assistant, and breathed a sigh of relief as he watched the midnight-blue stretch limousine roll to a stop. "I'll be back. I need to brief the girls. You know how shy they can be in front of large crowds."

"Of course, sir."

Almost sprinting, Josiah rushed to the car and opened the door. He smiled when he looked into the angelic faces of his daughters, 6-year-old Gem, and Treasure, who had just turned 4. Their mother was seated between them. One glance at her face caused Josiah's spirit to plummet. The sight of her glossy eyes with dilated pupils, blinking uncontrollably, caused him to curse under his breath. And that lopsided, lazy smile was always a dead giveaway.

"Move over, sweetheart," Josiah whispered to Gem, sliding onto the soft leather seat. He closed the door and reached across his daughter to grab his wife's arms and quickly rolled up her sleeves, one at a time. "Damn it, Mink! You're high *again!* Of all the days I needed you to stay clean, today was it. You knew how important this appearance was. Why, baby? Why?" he asked, wrapping his arm around her drooping shoulders.

He cringed when Mink giggled before her chin dropped forward to rest on her chest. He hated the raspy sound of her voice after she'd filled her veins with poison. And from the looks of it, she'd had one hell of a hit.

"I . . . I'm s-so s-sorry, JoJo. I-I didn't f-feel well. I h-hate this life we . . . we're living," she stuttered in a whiny voice.

Josiah checked his watch. The dedication ceremony for the new East Atlanta Community Center was scheduled to start in less than twenty minutes. Time was not his friend right now. Mink was going to be out of it for a while, so he would allow her to sleep it off. He and the girls would have to make yet another public appearance without her.

"Okay, Daddy's little princesses, you two are going to go inside of this nice new building. I want you to smile, look pretty, and wave at all of the people. And when it's time for Daddy to give his speech, you'll sit on the front row with Uncle J and Miss Gypsie and listen. After that, I want you to come on stage and help Daddy cut the ribbon with a *huge* pair of scissors. How does that sound?"

Gem smiled and nodded, causing her two long and thick ponytails—one on each side of her head—to swing back and forth. "I can do it, Daddy. I'm a big girl."

"Why can't Mommy come with us?" Treasure asked softly. "I want her to cut the ribbon with you too."

"Um . . . Mommy's sick again, sweetie pie. She needs to go home and rest."

"She's *always* sick, Treasure. You know that," a feisty Gem spat.

"Come on, you two." Josiah opened the door and exited the car. He helped his daughters get out as well. Then he looked around and spotted Gypsie talking to his identical twin brother, Jeremiah. With a frown on his face, Josiah waved the pair over.

"What's going on, JoJo?" Jeremiah asked when they approached.

"Mink is *sick* again. I'm going to make the appearance with just the girls. I'll ask Nelson to take Mink home." He kneeled down to meet his daughters at eye level. "You two go inside the center with Miss Gypsie and do everything Daddy just told you to do. I'll be inside shortly."

"Okay, Daddy," Treasure whispered.

"I'll wave like this." Gem showed off a perfect royal wave. Miss America couldn't have done it better.

Josiah stood to his full six-foot-three stature and smiled at Gypsie. "Thanks."

"It's not a problem, Mayor Bishop." She placed her body between the girls, took each by a hand, and led them inside the community center.

Josiah felt his brother burning holes through his flesh with his eyes as he walked around the limo to speak with Nelson, his driver. The older gentleman knew the routine. He had witnessed Mink's downward spiral in the world of heroin addiction over the last two years, so the conversation was brief. Josiah headed back over to Jeremiah, expecting his usual lecture.

"Now is not the time, J. I need to get inside, shake hands, and kiss babies before I make my speech."

"She's going to cause you to lose your reelection bid, dude. Make her ass disappear."

"What the hell am I supposed to do with her? Mink is my *wife*. I can't just walk away from her or ship her off someplace. What about our babies?"

"My beautiful nieces would be much better off without their junkie mother. Send Mink's strung-out ass back to her parents in Potomac. Let *them* deal with her. Hell, they created the selfish monster."

Josiah sighed. "I can stand here and argue with you and make all kinds of excuses about why I won't turn my back on Mink, but the truth is I love her, and I'm determined to help her. She ain't just some damn jumpoff or baby mama, J. The woman is my *wife* and the mother of my children, but you wouldn't know anything about that. You've never committed to a woman past two hours."

"Damn right, because I don't want to be like *you*."
Jeremiah sucked his teeth and ran his fingers through
his bundled locs. "You thought you had found a flawless
Siberian diamond when all you really got was a common,
worthless rock from the backyard."

"I love Mink, man. We've been married eight years, and
I'm committed to her. Can't you understand that?"

"I do, but I'm committed to *you*. You're a part of me,
JoJo. I was the first person you ever shared your dreams
with way before Mink came along. We got each other
through law school. I was by your side when you started
off as a city councilman, and it was *my* idea for you to run
for mayor. I'll be there when you become the first African
American governor of Georgia. And you better give me
my own bedroom and office in the White House when
you win the presidency. I want you to go all the way, but
it won't happen if things don't change. It'll all remain just
a big dream you had as a kid back in middle school unless
Mink gets the help she needs or you leave the marriage."

"I won't leave her."

Josiah walked away heavily burdened by his troubled
marriage and the stress of being an incumbent candidate who was currently only five points ahead of his
challenger in the polls. It was true that Mink's heroin
addiction was wreaking havoc on his career as well as
his campaign. She seldom accompanied him anywhere
anymore because she was high most of the time or falling
down from the clouds with terrible withdrawals.

His opponent, Attorney Dendrick Lomax, and his
trophy wife were zipping around Atlanta looking like a
power couple with their three children. They were all
over the news every day at one event or another. And
white people were more attracted to his candidacy than
Josiah's because he was one of those kiss-ass Uncle Tom
Negroes and a Republican. JoJo from Bankhead was all

about helping brothas and sistas all over the A get a fair shot at employment, education, and in the housing market. He wanted the city to give minority businesses the opportunity to bid for construction and infrastructure improvement projects too. People in black neighborhoods deserved the same law enforcement protection as those who lived in mansions tucked behind security gates. They didn't deserve to be shot and killed by the police without cause. Their voices need to be heard. And Mayor Josiah J. Bishop was *the* candidate to fight for all of that, and more, on their behalf.

He approached the entrance of the Woodrow S. Davidson Community Center a few steps ahead of Jeremiah and paused while the rest of his staff took their proper places in the procession line either in front, beside, or behind him. Lee, his chief of security, opened the double glass doors, and a round of applause and flashes of light from cameras greeted them.

Josiah felt sorry for his baby girl as he lifted her limp body from the bathtub and wrapped her in a towel. Treasure had fallen asleep as he bathed her after a long day on the campaign trail. Because Gem was a little bit older than her sister, she was able to take a bath and dress for bed on her own. Both girls were precious and dear to their daddy's heart, but it was becoming more difficult for him every day to effectively lead a major city and run a campaign while raising two young daughters alone. Yet, that's exactly what Josiah had been doing for the last several weeks because Mink couldn't seem to get the monkey off of her back. She was using more than ever.

As much as he hated the thought of it, he was going to have to confess to his parents and Mink's folks about her heroin addiction. He had been hiding it for two years by blatantly lying and making all kinds of excuses for her frequent absences from the public and her bizarre behavior. But now that the contest between him and his political opponent had heated up, he needed help with his girls. And just maybe his father, a Pentecostal pastor, and his mother could persuade Mink to seek substance abuse treatment. They had always been kind to her. Josiah wasn't sure what Mink's parents, retired Major and Mrs. Sinclair, could do to assist him and the girls from Maryland, but he was willing to reach out to them to find out.

In the princess-theme suite for two, Josiah dried Treasure's tiny body and dressed her in her frilly pink pajamas. Then he gently placed her in her bed with the tiara headboard that she adored. He looked over at Gem who was fast asleep in her bed of the same design. He kissed both princesses on the cheek before he turned off the light, left the room, and shut the door.

When Josiah entered the master suite, he was disgusted to find Mink sprawled across the bed in the same position she was in when he and their daughters had first arrived. She was still fully dressed in the red designer pantsuit she'd worn in the limousine along with the matching four-inch stiletto slingbacks. Her long, thick hair had covered her face as she lay on her stomach on top of the snow-white duvet comforter. He knew she wasn't dead because she was snoring softly.

Josiah removed the shoes from Mink's feet and covered her with the light blanket from the foot of the bed. Unable to resist, he brushed her hair away from her face and kissed her cheek. Then he left the room to go downstairs to his home office to catch up on some work.

Chapter Two

"Daddy, are you sure you can comb my hair just like Mommy?"

"Daddy's trying, princess, but if I fail, Nana will be here soon. Then she can redo it."

Josiah looked over at Gem who was sitting in the rocking chair watching TV. Her long, thick hair was loose and cascading over her shoulders and down her back. He didn't even know where to begin with taming her mane into a style. His mother needed to hurry, or he was going to be late for a breakfast meeting. He gathered the strands of Treasure's hair and pulled them as gently as he could into an elastic band.

"Ouch! Daddy, that hurts. Mommy *never* hurts me."

"He didn't mean to hurt you. Stop whining like a baby, Treasure. Mommy's in her bathroom throwing up again, so Daddy *has* to comb your hair."

Josiah was about to fuss at Gem for speaking so harshly to her sister, but the doorbell rang, interrupting him. "Gem, please go and let your nana inside the house while I check on your mom."

Without a word, father and daughter left the room, going in opposite directions. As Gem ran down the stairs, Josiah headed for the master suite. He rushed into the adjoining bathroom where he heard Mink retching and gasping. The pitiful sight of the woman he loved on her knees, facedown in the commode, pissed him off, but it also made his heart bleed. A part of him wanted to take her in his arms and love her dreadful addiction away. But he also felt like slapping the shit out of her for all of the heartaches she was causing their family. He saw her trembling and knew right away that she was experiencing withdrawals. She had stripped down to just a pair of black lace boys shorts because she often complained that clothes irritated her skin whenever she was crashing down from cloud nine.

"Let me help you, baby," Josiah said softly before he dropped to his knees. He gathered Mink's hot, sweat-drenched, shivering body in his arms.

She shoved him away. "Get away from me, JoJo! Get the hell away from me!"

"Baby, let me help you." He stood up and grabbed a towel from the shelf. He draped it over her shoulders and tried to rake her hair away from her face with his fingers.

"Don't freakin' touch me!" she screamed. "Just leave me the hell alone and run to your adoring fans at city hall! I don't need you!"

Josiah hated this reoccurring scene. He turned around, walked out of the bathroom, and closed the door only to come face-to-face with his mother in the master suite. Myrlie Bishop was a woman who didn't play checkers or the radio. She had been a no-nonsense disciplinarian since as far back as Josiah could remember. He swallowed hard when he saw the stern and daring look on her face. And she had her fists planted on her wide hips. He could tell she was about to give him "the business."

"What's wrong with Mink *this time,* JoJo? That girl is sick so often that she needs to pack up and move into a hospital permanently."

"Can I stop by the house this evening and talk with you and Rev? Right now, I have to get to a breakfast meeting. I need you to comb the girls' hair, feed them, and get them to school on time. I promise I'll tell you everything this evening."

"JoJo, don't play with me, boy. Something ain't right, and it hasn't been for a while. I'll let you off the hook for now, but you better have your behind at the house this evening. Rev and I will be waiting." Myrlie spun around quickly and stormed out of the room with her queen-size hips and ample ass swaying from left to right. She slammed the door behind her.

Josiah snatched off his bathrobe and started dressing. Earlier, he had taken out a gray, five-button suit, a crisp, white dress shirt, and a silver-and-black paisley print tie. It was Mink's favorite suit out of his wardrobe of many. She said she loved the way his rich mocha skin glistened against the fine fabric. He smiled when he recalled the many times Mink had told him that *he* was the sweetest chocolate she'd ever tasted. Then she would trace his mustache with her tongue down to his goatee and around again.

That was the charming and sexy Mink Isiana Sinclair that Josiah had fallen in love with his junior year in college at Tennessee State University in Nashville. She was only a freshman back then, but she was mature because of her world travels as an army brat. And she had an edge to her that made her zest for life appealing. She was fine as hell too with an ass that should've been bronzed and placed on display for men all over the world to see. That fat booty was an international treasure for real.

Josiah would never forget the first time he laid eyes on the feisty freshman who had just moved back to the States from Germany to attend college. Her sassiness and spunk had nearly brought a brotha to his knees! After putting the moves on her the entire fall semester, Josiah had willingly turned in his player's card and his pimp cup in exchange for the petite butterscotch freshman from Potomac, Maryland.

Neither his fellow Omega Psi Phi frat brothers nor his twin brother could believe that he had fallen prey to the old-fashioned pussy trap. But Josiah swore that wasn't how Mink had reeled him in. He blamed it on her copper, almond-shaped eyes, phat ass, and full soft lips. Pure ego had kept him from confessing to Jeremiah and his frat brothers that he hadn't even popped the panties yet. Mink had charisma and finesse. The chick was sexy with her clothes on, and she had sunk her hooks deep into him by *refusing* to give up the cookie. It wasn't until Christmas break after Josiah had saved up all of his money to rent a car to make the trip to Maryland that he and Mink finally consummated their relationship. And to him, it had been well worth the wait, and then some change. The memory of that night many years ago when he took Mink's virginity made his dick jump as he slid into his suit coat.

"That's my favorite suit on you," Mink said in a gravelly voice. "Which one of your whores do you plan to seduce today? Let me guess. It's that white slut in Human Resources, huh? Or is it Rita, the nappy-headed tar baby on your campaign committee? Who is it, JoJo? Tell me who you're screwing behind my back!"

Josiah turned to face the mirror and adjusted his tie, refusing to entertain yet another one of Mink's episodes of paranoia. She never ceased to accuse him of fooling around with other women whenever she was experiencing withdrawal symptoms. If any man had the right to have a side piece or two, surely, it was him. But he didn't. He had *never* cheated on Mink since the first night they'd made love. The truth of the matter was he wasn't attracted to any other woman because his heart belonged to his drug-addicted wife.

Josiah walked over to Mink with compassion in his eyes. "Mrs. Wilson is the driver for the afternoon carpool.

She'll drop the girls off at the regular time. Please try to be awake so you can let them in and help Gem with her homework. They'll need snacks and dinner too. You can order takeout if you don't feel like cooking. Miss Gladys will be here tomorrow." He lifted her chin and kissed her forehead. "I'll be home around eight o'clock. Mama and Rev are expecting me for a visit. Have a good day, baby."

"You're still a fucking mama's boy! You don't love me, JoJo! The only people you give a damn about are your controlling parents, Jeremiah, and the voters that put you in office. What about the girls and *me?*"

"No one comes before you and our daughters, Mink. You know that. Why don't you take a warm bubble bath to help you relax? I'm sure Mama will cook enough food for you and the girls. Eat something, sweetheart. You'll feel better." He hugged his wife as he fought back the tears. "I love you."

"Fuck you, JoJo," she growled, pushing him away before she stormed back into the bathroom and slammed the door shut.

"I cooked country fried steak smothered in brown gravy, mashed potatoes, and green beans just for you, JoJo, because it's your favorite. I made buttermilk corn bread muffins too. Come on and sit down, and I'll fix you a plate, baby."

"No, thank you. I'm still stuffed from a late lunch, Mama," Josiah said, taking a seat at the table. "Where's Rev?"

"He's in the den watching the news and talking to your brother."

"Yeah, I saw J's car in the driveway."

Myrlie laughed. "Your brother is here *most* evenings for dinner or picking up a carry-out plate. Where else is a 36-year-old bachelor with no plans to ever marry supposed to get a home-cooked meal? The boy has to eat, and his mama loves to feed him."

"He needs to stop acting like a pimp and find *one* good woman to settle down with. If he had a wife, he'd have a personal cook to prepare his meals, someone to clean his condo, and a body to birth your future grandbabies."

"You have a wife, but Miss Gladys is still at your house three times a week cleaning and cooking. Hell, the only good thing Mink has ever done for you is birth your daughters." Jeremiah walked farther into the den and took a seat next to his twin.

Josiah turned and frowned at the face that was identical to his. Hair type was the only physical feature he and Jeremiah did not share. Whereas Josiah sported a short and precise cut along with a neatly trimmed mustache and goatee, Jeremiah was a dread head with a clean baby face. His locs were usually secured in a bundle by an elastic band at the back of his head, which fell to rest midway down his back. But during his downtime, he allowed them to hang wild and loose.

"My marriage is far from perfect, J," Josiah finally admitted. "But Gem and Treasure are gifts from God."

"And Mink is Satan's daughter."

"Don't talk about my wife."

"Screw that b—"

"Watch your mouth, Jeremiah James! Rev and I don't allow filthy communication in this house! You know better!" Myrlie threw the dishrag she'd been holding on the counter. "And how come you hate Mink so much anyway?"

"Because she's going to ruin JoJo's life! She's nothing but a hindrance to him, and I'm sick of her!"

"JoJo, baby, what is your brother talking about? Tell me right now what's going on with Mink."

"That's why I'm here, Mama. I came by to tell you and Rev something that I should've told you two years ago. Mink is strung out on heroin. She's a real bad addict, and it's got my whole world spinning upside down."

Myrlie's jaw damn near dropped to the floor, but when she picked it up, she screamed, "Rev, you need to get your holy oil and bring it over here, honey!"

Chapter Three

Josiah honked his horn twice as he passed by the guard shack at the entrance of the exclusive gated community where he and his family lived. Tommy Lee, the night-shift security guard, was a talker, and he wasn't in the mood for his yapping tonight. Josiah was in a hurry to get home to read a bedtime story to his little princesses and tuck them in. They had called him while he was at his parents' house, asking for their assistance and support after he told them about Mink's drug habit. Gem wanted to know when he was coming home. Josiah had promised her that he'd be there in time to put her and her sister to bed. When he asked her how her mother was doing, Gem told him that she was fine. He was happy to hear that Mink had helped her with her homework and prepared dinner. The fact that she'd somehow managed to stay clean today gave Josiah hope.

He whipped his silver Mercedes GLS SUV into the three-car garage and killed the engine. He had exactly twenty-eight minutes to spend quality time with Gem and Treasure before their bedtime. Unfortunately, his job as mayor, along with his political campaign, often robbed him of precious moments with his family, and he hated it. Mink constantly threw up the lack of time he spent with the family in his face. But she had willingly signed on to be a political wife, so she should've expected Josiah to be missing in action sometimes. She had been a part of his dream to climb the ranks in law and politics.

In fact, she used to be his number one fan. Now it seemed like she had turned her back on his dreams, ambitions, and even their marriage for heroin.

Josiah entered the house with those thoughts in mind and found Mink in the kitchen. The second she turned around to face him, he noticed how clear and bright her eyes were. She was smiling too. His eyes lowered to take in the rest of her. For the first time in weeks, she bore some semblance to the old Mink—the healthy, sizzling-hot woman who he'd gladly give his life for. The smooth curves of her Coke-bottle figure were well defined underneath a form-fitting zebra print chemise. The mini hemline put her firm thighs on full display.

Josiah had always obsessed over her soft and taut butterscotch skin. And this particular night, he was especially drawn to it because of its eye-catching glow. Her long, naturally curly hair, spilling over her shoulders, was a complete turn-on. Josiah wanted his fingers to get lost in the wild, sandy tresses.

Mink smiled seductively with mischief in her bright, coppery eyes. "Are you hungry, or did you eat dinner with your parents?"

"I wasn't hungry."

"I cooked penne pasta with a tangy shrimp marinara sauce. Are you hungry now?"

Hell yeah, I'm hungry, but not for food, Josiah was tempted to tell Mink, but he suppressed his rising testosterone. "Yeah, I could eat a little bit, but let me go upstairs and spend some time with the girls first."

"Cool. You do that, but their mom wants a couple of hours tonight too."

Josiah dashed up the double marble staircase and rushed to the master suite. He changed out of his suit and put on a pair of sweats and a plain white tee. He heard the girls' voices floating from their room as he made his way down the hall. Treasure was laughing at something Gem was saying to her. The television was on the Disney Channel in the background.

"Daddy!" both girls shrieked when he crossed the threshold.

"I told you I'd be here before you went to sleep." He scooped up his baby girl in his arms.

"Mommy wasn't sick today," Gem announced. "She gave us apple slices, Nilla Wafers, and mango juice before she helped me with my math and spelling. Then she cooked pasta for dinner. I like it when she feels good."

"I do too, sweetheart."

Josiah walked over to the bookshelf and found the most recent book he'd purchased from the Chocolate Princess Collection by his friend and college mate, Tarashah Yokembe. He sat down in the rocking chair with Treasure in his arms. Gem climbed onto his lap also and wrapped an arm around his neck. He opened the vividly illustrated book and spent the next fifteen minutes casting a magic spell on his daughters with words.

"I loved that story, Daddy!"

"Me too," Treasure agreed.

"I'm glad you enjoyed it, but now it's time to say your prayers and get into bed."

He stood and led them to Treasure's bed. Then he knelt between his daughters and listened to them thank God for their family, friends, and a dozen other things. The list of blessings they asked for was even longer. The last thing Gem asked God to do was fix her mommy so that she would be well all the time.

It pricked Josiah's heart when he heard that request because he wanted the same thing. He had begged God many nights to remove Mink's craving for heroin from her body. There were times when he thought that his prayers had been answered because she would be clean and cognizant for several days. She would attend Narcotics Anonymous meetings daily and spend lots of time talking with her sponsor. Then just when Josiah believed she had turned the corner on her way to a drug-free life, she would crash and burn all over again. And each time she relapsed, her condition got progressively worse than the time before. Her heroin usage became more frequent, causing sporadic mood swings and surprise disappearing acts. Josiah and the girls didn't know what to expect from Mink at times. They were living in an ongoing nightmare. They had managed to hide it from most of the family for two years . . . until now.

Every expert in the field of substance abuse treatment that Josiah had sought professional advice from had recommended the same solutions. Mink needed to commit herself to an intensive in-patient drug rehabilitation facility and take methadone treatments regularly. She had done that a few times in the past at his insistence, but she always found an excuse to leave before the standard twenty-eight-day detox period and often refused the methadone injections. Most times she'd claim that she missed her girls and that she could do better in a day treatment program. Josiah had placed her in two or three of those before and spent thousands of dollars, hoping for a miracle. During one of those outpatient rehab stints, Mink had attended treatment sessions, including individual counseling and group therapy, every day from morning until afternoon like it was a job. She had even stayed clean and productive for a couple of weeks. Then one day, out of the blue, she went MIA for a few days, and the cycle started all over again. And now they were back to square one.

Josiah snatched his mind away from his thoughts as he tucked the girls in bed and kissed them good night. He thanked God that Mink was clean *today* as he closed the bedroom door. Maybe she was ready for long-term in-patient treatment and a methadone regimen to finally put an end to her heroin dependency once and for all. Josiah could only hope so.

He hurried downstairs and found Mink sitting at the kitchen table with the light from two candles flickering and slicing through the darkness. She smiled as Josiah walked closer to the table. The aroma of the pasta she'd prepared lingered in the air. He sat down across from her right in front of a place setting fit for a king. Steam rose from the tangy pasta and side serving of sautéed asparagus. And one look at the garden salad caused him to salivate.

Josiah picked up his fork. "This smells delicious, baby." He scooped up a forkful of food and placed it in his mouth. "You did good, girl. Thank you," he said softly as he savored the pasta.

"You're welcome."

For the next several minutes, Josiah ate in silence while Mink looked on, equally quiet. From the way she dressed, he was pretty sure how their night was going to end. It had been two weeks since the last time they'd made love. Tonight was as good as any to end their sex hiatus. They'd never had a problem connecting in the bedroom. It was only when Mink was using that Josiah was forced into celibacy. He wasn't exactly sexually attracted to a woman who was incoherent, moody, and puking or shitting all over the damn place. But he didn't have to worry about that tonight because the sexy lady sitting across from him now was looking all kinds of delicious in zebra print lingerie. *And* she wasn't high on the opiate she loved so dearly. The scent of her perfume was turning him on. So as soon as he finished eating, he was going to shower and take his wife to bed. He planned to make love to her until they both passed out from exhaustion.

***

Josiah didn't want to come too soon, but Mink's pussy was so tight, juicy, and hot that he was losing control. Plus, it had been two weeks since he had been inside of her, and she was fucking him like a seasoned porn star. Her energy level was through the roof, and she was working her coochie muscles like nobody's business. Josiah almost couldn't keep up with Mink's wild bucking and hip rolling. She was putting it *down,* pushing him closer and closer to the edge too soon. Josiah wanted their love-making session to last just a little while longer, but at the rate Mink was going, he knew he would explode too early. So he decided to end her wild cowgirl rodeo performance by flipping her over onto her back. A brotha had to regain control of the situation.

Now on top, Josiah shifted gears. He slowed down their fast-paced bumping and grinding to a smooth and lazy ride, but he plunged deeper into her sweet goodness on each stroke. Their tongues teased and twirled around each other's in a steamy salsa that was wet and out of control. Josiah couldn't tell whose moans were louder—his or Mink's. They were working magic on each other equally in their most intense sexcapade in many, many months. The reunion was sweeter than vanilla ice cream on a hot summer day. How the hell could the woman who continuously caused his heart so much pain also bring his body more pleasure than he could handle just when he needed it most?

Mink was Josiah's healing potion for whatever ailed him; yet, she was also the poison that was slowly choking the life out of him. She was a blessing and a curse at the same time. Josiah loved Mink, but he hated her habit. She loved him too, but not as much as she loved *heroin.* The sad reality of the matter was they both were addicts. Mink was addicted to heroin, and Josiah was addicted to

Mink. And in the middle of all of the dependency were their two innocent and precious daughters who deserved a stable family. But Mink's addiction to heroin was making that impossible.

At the moment, Josiah didn't care that his wife was a druggie. He was caught up in her sex trap, and that's exactly where he wanted to be. The feeling of being buried deep inside of her to the hilt made him forget every bad thing she had ever done to him and their children because of dope. Josiah was on the verge of busting a massive nut that had him delirious as hell. When Mink wrapped her legs around his waist and squeezed, causing him to slide deeper into her juicy walls, his heart flipped a few times.

"Damn, Mink! You're trying to kill me, girl!"

Her response was a bright smile and lots of hip action. Then she bucked underneath Josiah like she'd lost control of her body. "Yesss! That's my spot, JoJo! That's it, baby!"

Mink's climax triggered Josiah's. He released what seemed like gallons of semen inside of her. "Ah . . . shit . . . *Uuuuuugh!*"

The sound of their breathing into the darkness was faint. Josiah rolled over onto his back with Mink in his arms. He kissed her forehead as she lay on top of his body damp with sweat. "I love you, girl. I always have, and I always will, no matter what."

"I know, JoJo. I love you too, and I'm ready to get the help I need. I want to get well for you and the girls."

"I'm glad to hear that." He kissed her again. "We'll talk about it in the morning, baby."

Chapter Four

"Man, what's up with you? I noticed you smiling and bouncing around city hall this morning. You didn't yell at Conner one time throughout the entire staff meeting, even though he was asking all kinds of stupid-ass questions. What's the deal, JoJo?" Jeremiah took a sip of water and looked around the restaurant with a smile on his face. He knew his twin better than anyone else, including Mink. Something was going on with Josiah for sure, and he wanted to know the scoop.

"Man, Mink has been clean for *fourteen days*. She's never stayed on track this long without going into detox and getting methadone injections. I think she's going to make it this time."

Jeremiah leaned back in his chair. "If she's not in rehab and taking methadone, how is she doing it?"

"She's been going to Narcotics Anonymous six days a week and hanging out with her sponsor a lot. They talk on the phone all the time too. I'm proud of her, man. Life is good."

"I'm happy for you and the girls. I was about to put out a hit on Mink's ass for all of the bullshit she's been putting y'all through."

"Well, you can let her live now because I think she's kicked her habit for good."

"Do you . . . nah . . . nah . . ." Jeremiah shook his head. "Nah, I'm not going to say it."

"Say what, J? Go ahead. Say whatever you want to say."

"I don't want you to get your hopes up about Mink, only to have her disappoint you again. I ain't trying to rain on your parade, but I want you to be *realistic*. You've been through this enough times to know that Mink needs hard-core in-patient treatment. She can't stay clean on NA alone. She's too far gone for that. It ain't like she's smoking marijuana or popping Ecstasy tablets now and then. Your girl is on *heroin*. That's some powerful shit."

"Yeah, I know. That's why I've been trying to convince Mink to sign herself into a rehab center. I think a ninety-day program would change her life forever."

"Why won't she go?"

"She doesn't think she needs to go. She's never stayed clean this long before on the outside. The progress she's made so far has given her hope."

"I pray that she'll stick with it this time around, but we'll have to wait and see." Jeremiah looked toward the front of the restaurant. "We're going to have to finish this conversation later, JoJo. Senator Day and his entourage just walked in," he said, standing. He buttoned his suit coat and smiled.

Josiah stood as well. The Bishop twins waited for Emmanuel Day, Georgia's first African American United States senator, to reach their table. Staffers flanked him. They were about to have a very important lunch meeting that could give Josiah a much-needed boost in the polls. Jeremiah hoped that everything would go according to plan.

Senator Day had a great sense of humor. Everyone at the table was cracking up over a story that he'd just told about an out-of-control female who once stalked him while he was dating his wife-to-be, Jazz.

The server walked over and handed Josiah the check for everyone's meals. He skimmed over the nearly four-digit bill before he removed his platinum Visa card from his wallet. He inserted it inside the slot on the brown leather folder, handed it to the server, and continued laughing at the senator's story.

"Thanks for your support, Senator Day," Jeremiah said after everyone had settled down. "My brother has done some great things in the city of Atlanta. The citizens need him to serve another term so he can finish what he's started. With your endorsement and hefty financial contribution, he'll be able to seal the deal in November. We sincerely appreciate your support."

Senator Day smiled. "It's the very—"

"I'm sorry, Mayor Bishop, but your card has been declined, sir," a man who was the restaurant's manager announced the moment he arrived at the table. "Do you have another form of payment?"

"Of course," Josiah said, removing the card from the snooty man's hand. He was so damn embarrassed. Without even looking up, he knew that all eyes at the table were trained on him. He pulled his Black American Express Card from his wallet and handed it to the man.

A side glance at Jeremiah proved to be the wrong damn move. The look on his face was *lethal*. They had just conducted a productive meeting over scrumptious food at Nova Bella's, one of Atlanta's finest upscale restaurants. They weren't hanging out with their boys from Bankhead or Ridgewood. They were in the presence of political greatness. It was beyond embarrassing for the mayor of a major city to have his credit card declined, but it was even worse that it had happened in the company of Senator Day and his staff members. Josiah wanted to disappear into thin air. And he knew why Jeremiah was shooting him an ice grill. It had *everything* to do with his suspicions that Mink was somehow responsible for his present, shameful circumstances.

"I'm looking forward to meeting your wife, Senator," Josiah finally said, trying to move past his humiliation. "I'm sure that she and my Mink will hit it off just fine."

"I bet they will."

Just then, the manager returned to the table with a smile on his face and handed Josiah his Black Card and the receipt for his party's paid bill.

"I'm so sorry, JoJo. I was on a binge when I bought all of that crap with your card and sold it for the cash. It was because of me that your card was declined in front of a U.S. senator. I stole it and maxed it out. Oh God, I'm so sorry that I put you through that. Please forgive me," Mink pleaded with a pitiful sob.

"It's okay, baby." Josiah wrapped his arms around her and pulled her close. "I took care of everything. Don't worry about it. I forgive you."

Mink pulled back to look into her husband's eyes. The love and compassion she saw in his orbs made her feel terrible. She would never know why such a wonderful man like Josiah cared so deeply for her when all she ever did was hurt him. Mink knew she didn't deserve him, but he was committed to her even though she was a straight-up junkie.

No, she hadn't used in two weeks, but she was fighting cravings like crazy every day. Thank God for Lena, her faithful sponsor. Her no-nonsense attitude and strict guidance were the only reasons why Mink hadn't headed to her supplier early this morning to score a hit. She had dialed his number as soon as she dropped off the girls at school. Duke, Mink's loyal dealer, went on a bragging pitch telling her about the new shipment he'd just gotten in overnight. He said the shit was the purest anyone in the A could get their hands on. The mere thought of getting high again gave Mink the shakes. She wanted to escape reality and float away to her heroin fantasyland so bad that she ran a couple of red lights trying to make it to the spot. But Lena called while she was en route. It was like she knew that Mink was up to no good, so she insisted that she meet her at IHOP for breakfast. And she wouldn't take no for an answer.

Mink rested her cheek against Josiah's chest as he continued holding her in his arms. She was glad that she had stayed clean one more day, but she didn't know how much longer she would be able to handle the strong temptation on the outside without methadone. Her demons were on the prowl. Josiah was right. She *did* need to go and check herself into a rehab center, but she didn't want to. Mink couldn't stand to be separated from her girls. They were *her* children, and she didn't want anyone else to take care of them. She would continue going to NA meetings Monday through Saturday each week and attend her father-in-law's church every Sunday. Mink was determined to stay away from heroin by any means outside of rehab.

"Hello, everybody. My name is Mink, and I'm an addict."

"Hi, Mink," most of the other members of her NA group responded.

"What's up, Mink?"

"Welcome!"

Mink smiled, and it took Josiah's breath away. She looked gorgeous in a pair of faded jeans and a pink T-shirt.

She held up the orange plastic key in her hand. "Thirty days," she said softly as tears pooled in her eyes. She allowed them to fall freely down her cheeks.

Everyone in the room hopped to their feet and celebrated her accomplishment with a round of applause. Josiah joined them from his location in the very back of the room. He was so damn proud of Mink. He knew that it hadn't been easy for her to stay drug free over the past thirty days, but she had made it by the grace of God. And he had been with her every step of the way, doing whatever he could to help. He'd witnessed the tears, mood swings, and restlessness. They'd endured nights when he'd held her in his arms while her body shook with cravings, and she screamed and cursed through it. But she didn't throw in the towel, and Josiah was grateful.

"It was *not* easy," Mink continued. "But I made it with the help of Lena, the world's greatest sponsor, my husband, and God. I have a long road ahead of me, but I know I can do it one day at a time. I'm going to keep coming back because this program works as long as *I* work it."

Mink took her seat to more hand claps and cheers. Josiah slipped out of the back door and headed to his SUV. He wouldn't have missed Mink's big day for anything in the world. She had asked him to come, but she'd insisted that he play it safe and dress down in plain clothes and a baseball cap and arrive late. She believed it was best that he drive himself and sit in the very back of the room. It wasn't anyone's business who she was married to. Lena knew that Mink was the city's first lady because honesty was a requirement in the relationship between an addict and her sponsor. And confidentiality was also important. That's why Josiah wasn't worried about anyone else in the group finding out anything more about Mink than what they already knew.

He pulled out of the church's parking lot and headed for Mink's favorite Midtown boutique. He wanted to buy her something special to wear tonight for their celebration dinner date. Gypsie had planned every detail of their evening down to the appetizers at Masai's on Peachtree, his and Mink's favorite supper club. She'd even arranged for the girls to spend the night with Jeremiah at his bachelor pad in Buckhead. A sworn ladies' man for life, Uncle J was a sucker for his nieces. In his eyes, Gem and Treasure could do no wrong. So tonight, they would be able to eat junk food, play video games, and watch movies until they fell asleep. That was Jeremiah's style. Whatever the girls wanted, they would have.

Josiah gunned his engine and sped toward Sophisti-cations Boutique. He was sure that there was a sexy red dress somewhere inside with Mink's name on it. They always had whatever he needed to dress his wife for any occasion. Timia, the owner of the swanky shop, knew Mink's style and size. She would help him find the perfect cocktail dress in red and all of the accessories to set it off. Tonight was going to be a special night, and Josiah was looking forward to every minute of it.

Chapter Five

Just pick up the phone, Mink! Pick it up and call Lena! her conscience screamed. She closed her eyes tightly and shook her head frantically. There were too many voices inside her head, yanking her back and forth in a mental tug-of-war. Mink was confused and scared. The craving was too powerful. She wanted a quick fix more than she wanted to take her next breath. But she loved the new feeling of being drug free. She could think clearly and face herself in the mirror without guilt. And Josiah and the girls were so happy with her changes. How could she snatch their peace away from them? They didn't deserve that.

"*Nooo!*" she shouted above the evil voice inside her head and the sound of a baby crying pitifully, threatening to pull her under.

Just one last hit, Mink. . . . That's all you need, girl. It'll take the edge off. You'll be back home in time to get dressed for your hot date with the hubs. Thirty days is a looong time. You deserve a little taste. Go ahead and reward yourself. Miiink, you want it! You need it. You know you do, girl. Miiiiiink! Miiiiiink! Miiiiiink!

Mink unfolded her body from the fetal position on the floor inside the shower and crawled out of the bathroom. The heavy flow of tears that fell nonstop from her eyes blurred her vision. Beads of sweat covered her entire body. Perspiration saturated her hair and scalp. She was completely wet, although she'd never turned on the shower. And the loud wails of the invisible baby filled her ears. She made it to the nightstand where her cell phone sat connected to its charger. She reached up and grabbed it. Mink was in trouble, and she needed help. She licked her lips as she stared at the keypad. Her hand was shaking uncontrollably. She battled seconds of coldness followed by hot flashes alternately. She couldn't remember Lena's number or even the one digit she'd assigned to her on her speed dial because her brain was so damn scrambled.

Mink clamped her eyes shut and took long, deep breaths. She released them slowly like she'd been taught to do in her first admission to rehab. Meditation and visualization were effective, and both mental exercises had worked like a charm over the past thirty days. A clear vision of Josiah and the girls appeared in her mind's eye. It was so vivid that she felt like she could reach out and touch them. Mink smiled, and she felt her body beginning to relax. Memories of her first date with Josiah floated through her psyche. Then she saw glimpses of their wedding, the day each girl was born, and the night Josiah was elected mayor. Those were precious moments, and they gave her peace. Mink lowered her body from her knees onto her bottom as she continued reminiscing on happy times. Each memory gave her a reason to resist the temptation of going back to heroin and remain clean.

When her heartbeat returned to normal, and she felt like she could breathe normally again, she opened her eyes. Looking around her bedroom, she once again took in the lovely gifts that Josiah had surprised her with. The dress, sexy undergarments, and shoes had cost him a grip. He was such a romantic, and he loved her unconditionally. The scent of the red roses in the beautiful crystal vase on top of the dresser was heavenly. It wafted in the air, and Mink was just grateful that she could enjoy it.

There had been times when she couldn't even smell the foul odor coming from her body after going days without bathing while she binged on dope out on the streets. But today, she was alert and aware of everything around her. She had a good life with lots of people in it who loved her. She could stay clean another day by embracing her circumstances one day at a time.

Josiah hopped out of the limo the moment it rolled to a stop in front of the house. He'd spoken to Mink earlier, reminding her that he would pick her up at seven o'clock sharp. No doubt she was dressed and ready for a night out on the town because she'd told him how excited she was. And she'd gone on and on about how pretty she was going to look in her hot new dress.

"Mink, I'm home, baby. It's time to go." Josiah headed up the stairs.

The master suite's door was cracked, and a soft love ballad was flowing from the Bose system inside. It was just like Mink to try to slip in a quickie before they left, but it would have to wait because their reservation was at eight, and the downtown ATL traffic was insane on any given Friday night. Time wasn't on their side. Josiah pushed the door open all the way and was surprised to see the red cocktail dress and undergarments spread out on the bed exactly the way he had left them that afternoon. Even the roses were still in place on the dresser, which was unusual. Mink always moved the flowers to the nightstand on her side of her bed so she could enjoy their fragrance throughout the night.

Something was off. Josiah's instincts told him so as he walked farther into the room. He checked the bathroom, but Mink was nowhere to be found. He dreaded it, but he felt the need to check the safe where they kept their more expensive pieces of jewelry. One glance inside nearly caused him to punch the wall. One of the limited edition watches from his collection was missing, and so was a platinum and diamond bracelet that he had bought Mink for her birthday a few years back. He didn't care about the gold coins that he collected for the girls, but he wanted his Rolex back.

Josiah plopped down on the bed, totally defeated. He was furious, shocked, and *sad*. A few hours ago, Mink had picked up her thirty-day key from NA. Why the hell would she throw it all away? Josiah couldn't wrap his mind around it. He didn't understand why he, Gem, and Treasure weren't motivation enough to keep Mink off the needle. They loved her more than anything. So why couldn't she love them more than she loved heroin?

The tears that crept up on Josiah heightened his anger. Real men weren't supposed to cry. He had promised himself that he wasn't going to shed another damn tear over Mink and her drug foolishness ever again, but his heart was aching. He'd seriously thought she was on her way this time. The disappointment was the heaviest he'd ever felt. He didn't know what to do. Once again, heroin had taken over. No, he and the girls were back at the familiar place that he hated.

Josiah hung up the phone with Mink's mother. The call had been a complete waste of time. Mrs. Sinclair had told him that there was nothing that she and the major could do to help him with Mink. They did, however, offer to come and get the girls and keep them in Maryland. Josiah was totally against that. He wanted to raise his daughters, and he was willing to do it alone if he had to. Mink had been missing in action for a week now. No one had heard a word from her. A select group of officers

from the Atlanta Police Department had been searching
for her on the low, but the public had not been asked
to assist them. As Josiah's chief of staff, Jeremiah had
insisted that the search for Mink be kept top secret. The
news that the mayor's wife was MIA would cause major
problems for his career and his reelection campaign.

"What did Mink's parents say, JoJo?"

He released a frustrated breath. "They said there's
nothing they can do. Oh, but they volunteered to come
and take Gem and Treasure back to Maryland with them.
They must be crazy as hell. I would *never* uproot the girls
and ship them off, especially not in the middle of the
school year. I'm their daddy, and I'll take care of them,
even if I have to suspend my campaign."

"Oh, hell nah! You ain't about to do that. You've worked
too damn hard to get where you are. Since Senator Day's
endorsement, your numbers are up in the polls, and your
appearance at the skating rink last week pulled in some
young adult voters that we've been trying to reach."

"But my girls come *first*, J. They're more important
than my reelection. They've lost their mother to drugs.
Why should they lose their father also to his career? I
can't do that to them. If I can't work out some arrangement with Mama and Miss Gladys that'll maintain Gem
and Treasure's normal routine, I'll have to drop out of
the race."

"I've already worked things out for you," Jeremiah
announced, placing his hand on his brother's shoulder.
"Rev has to attend the spring ministerial conference in
Detroit next week. Then he'll be in revival in Akron the
following week. Of course, Mama is going with him, so
she won't be available for a while. But I spoke to Miss
Gladys, and she's agreed to come Monday through
Friday and even stay later than usual until Gypsie can
make it here."

"*Gypsie?*"

"Yeah. You know she's single with no crumb snatchers of her own. She doesn't have any family in Georgia, and she's not one of those club chicks."

"That doesn't mean she wants to be a nanny to Gem and Treasure after working for me all day long, J. I won't take advantage of her like that. Gypsie's a really sweet girl."

"I know. That's why she agreed to help her boss out. All you'll have to do is cut back on her evening hours. Let her do office work only. Conner or I will run around and make appearances with you. Sometimes we'll both be there."

"How did you talk Gypsie into it? What did you promise her, J? Please don't tell me you've been messing around with my assistant behind my back."

"Nope. But I've been tempted to, though, because she's fine as *hell*. Have you ever seen her ass jiggle when—"

"Stop it, J. She's a baby."

"I know, and that's why I didn't put the moves on her. It would've been too easy. Then she would be hooked on me. We don't need that in our close-knit work environment. But anyway, Gypsie will babysit my nieces any evening you need her, and she's cheap. Plus, Gem and Treasure already know her, and they like her, so everything will run smoothly."

"Okay. Adjust Gypsie's work schedule at the office and give her my itinerary for the next thirty days."

"She already has her new work schedule and your calendar. What else?"

Josiah stroked his goatee. "I guess *nothing*. You seemed to have handled everything."

"That's right. Your brother's got you, man."

"Because it's Friday night, they may stay up until ten o'clock, but not a minute longer, Gypsie."

"Yes, sir."

"Expect me back around one or two. But I'm sure you'll be asleep by then. I hope you'll find the guest room comfortable."

"It's a very beautiful room, and the bed is huge. I'm going to sleep like a baby, sir."

"Great. I'll see you in the morning." Josiah walked over to the sofa where the girls were sitting watching a movie in their pajamas. He knelt down to stare into their angelic faces. "Daddy is about to leave for a fundraising party. I want you two to be on your best behavior for Miss Gypsie, okay?"

"Yes, Daddy, we'll be good. Won't we, Treasure?"

"Yes."

Josiah kissed both girls and hugged them tightly. "I love you, my princesses."

"We love you too, Daddy," they returned in unison.

Chapter Six

Josiah tiptoed toward the bedroom door, careful not to wake the girls, and left the room. He closed the door quietly behind him. The fundraiser had been a big success. The Black Belles and Beaus had raised over $75,000 for his reelection campaign. Josiah felt like dancing even though he was tired. It had been a long night, and all he had the energy to do now was take a quick shower and hit the sack.

He entered the master suite and removed his shoes and suit coat before he sat down on the bed. Seconds after he slipped off his tie, shirt, and wife beater, the doorbell rang. Josiah frowned and glanced down at his watch. Who the hell would ring his doorbell minutes after two in the morning? As soon as the question formed in his head, he thought about Mink. He jumped up and ran swiftly down the stairs. After deactivating the security system, he snatched the door open. Lo and behold, it *was* Mink, but she wasn't alone. She was standing on wobbly legs, looking like hot ratchet shit between a pair of Atlanta's finest. The two officers were holding her body upright as it jerked and flopped. Her curly hair was matted to her head, and she smelled like a nasty farm animal. The white minidress with spaghetti straps she had on was filthy, and she was barefoot.

"We're sorry to ring your bell this time of the morning, Mr. Mayor, but—"

"I understand. Come in," Josiah said, stepping aside to give them a clear path into the house. He closed the front door before he headed toward the den.

The officers dragged Mink down the hall behind Josiah. She was rambling and shaking like a certified junkie. When they reached the den, the officers placed Mink on the sofa, and she toppled over on her side like a rag doll. Josiah looked at her, disgusted. He faced the two men and folded his arms across his bare chest.

"Where did you find her?"

"We got a call about a disturbance at a house on Spike Circle in Ridgewood. When we arrived on the scene, she and two other women were outside in the front yard fighting like Crips and Bloods. We separated them and tried to make sense of the situation. All we could make out was that Mrs. Bishop was trying to get a watch back from the women she believed had stolen from her."

"How did you know she was my wife?"

The younger officer smiled. "That was the first thing she told us when we put her in the back of the cruiser. Of course, we didn't believe her at first. But as she kept talking, it became clear that she knew you pretty well, especially when she gave us your private number at city hall. We dialed it, and sure enough, we heard your distinguished voice on the out-going message."

Josiah rubbed both hands down his face. "Look, I know you're supposed to file an incident report, but . . . um . . . I . . . um—"

The officers shook their heads, cutting him off.

"I got the biggest raise of my career when you became mayor," the older officer was quick to say. "I wouldn't dare file a report. As far as I'm concerned, there was no incident. We just gave Mrs. Bishop a safe ride home."

"That's right, Mr. Mayor," the other officer agreed.

"Thank you both so much. I'll walk you to the door." He led the way from the den.

At the door, Josiah thanked the officers again for bringing Mink home and for their discretion. They waved him off and wished him well. When he returned to the den, Mink was still slouched on the sofa trembling terribly. As he walked closer to her, he noticed a large puddle of liquid on the brown leather sofa. His belly rolled when he smelled the distinct odor of urine. Josiah frowned and shook his head. He was pissed! He was exhausted and wanted to go to bed, but he had to deal with Mink and her bullshit first. He considered leaving her ass right there in her own pee, but he couldn't risk having the girls find her in this condition in the morning. So, he turned to leave the den to get a towel and cleaning supplies. Imagine his shame when he found Gypsie standing at the entrance of the den looking at Mink like she was the monster from a horror movie.

By the time Josiah finished giving Mink a thorough shower, shampooing her hair, and putting her to bed, he was dog-tired. Her tremors and abrupt trips to the bathroom to vomit had made it almost impossible to blow-dry her hair, but he'd completed the job eventually. Now he had one more task to tackle before he could finally crash. He needed to disinfect the sofa in the den and air out the room. Gypsie had volunteered to do it for him, but he'd refused to let her. It was embarrassing enough that she had seen Mink high out of her mind and with such deplorable personal hygiene. He didn't want her to clean up behind her, so he'd insisted that she go back to bed.

Josiah trudged down the steps and entered the den. His body was so weary that he could hardly keep his eyes open. He forced himself to get to work, thoroughly disinfecting the entire sofa and spraying air freshener throughout the room. *Something's got to give,* an inner voice told him. Mink needed to go into rehab, and he was going to insist that she check herself into one in the morning—or else. Josiah was prepared for a tough fight with her, but he wasn't going to back down this time. It was past time for her to stop this madness. Couldn't she see that she was destroying herself and their family? If she was too blind to see the reality of the situation, Josiah had no problem pointing it out to her. He was fed up with Mink's bullshit. It was going to end in the morning.

"*Mommy!*" Treasure screamed with excitement and burst into the master suite. In a flash, her mother's two-week long disappearing act was forgotten. In Treasure's eyes, Mink could do no wrong.

"Hey, there, honey bunny!" She sat up in the bed and opened her arms to her baby girl.

Treasure ran and jumped into her mother's arms and rained kisses all over her face. Just a few hours ago, Josiah wouldn't have allowed Mink to touch either one of their daughters out fear that she would contaminate them with filth and body odor. And they would've been horrified by the very sight of her for sure.

"Where were you, Mommy? I missed you. Why did you leave us again?"

Each time Mink returned home after one of her drug binges, she was hit with that million-dollar question. And Josiah had to give her credit because she never failed to come up with an explanation that seemed to satisfy the girls. She was quite the creative liar. Josiah folded his arms across his chest and waited for her to come up with a new colorful tale. But sudden movement at the entrance of the room grabbed everyone's attention before Mink could speak. It was Gem, and she did *not* look happy to see her mother at all.

"Good morning, sweetheart," Mink whispered, extending a hand toward Gem. "I've missed you. Come hug me."

Gem twirled around fast like a destructive tornado and ran down the hall toward her bedroom. The sound of her door slamming shut boomed throughout the house. Josiah hurried out of the master suite and made his way down the hall. He turned the doorknob slowly to enter the room, but it didn't budge because Gem had locked the door.

"Gem, this is Daddy, sweetie. Please let me in so we can talk. I want to make sure you're okay."

He waited patiently, praying that she would let him in. She was just a little girl, but she had genuine feelings just like any adult. Mink's actions had caused the child so much pain and anger recently, and she was dealing with those emotions the only way a 6-year-old little girl knew how.

Josiah relaxed when he saw the doorknob turning. The door eased open slowly, and his firstborn appeared with a tearstained face. He immediately picked Gem up and squeezed her in a hug. Then he entered the room and threw a back kick to close the door. With his sweet daughter in his arms, he walked across the room and sat in the rocking chair.

"Why does she run away all the time, Daddy? Doesn't she love us?"

"Yes, she loves us, but Mommy is sick, baby. She has a disease that she has no control over. It's called *addiction*."

"Why can't the doctor give her medicine to make it go away forever?"

Josiah shifted uncomfortably in his seat as he went into deep thought, trying to choose his next words carefully. "The doctor can help make your mommy better, but she has to go to a special hospital and stay for a long time. There, she'll receive the treatment and medicine that she needs to control the disease. How will you and your sister feel about her going away? Won't you miss her?"

"If she goes, will she get better?"

"Yes, she'll get better if she stays and does everything the doctors tell her to do. They'll give her medicine that will help her."

"Then take her to the special hospital, Daddy. You've got to make her go and stay so she can get well. Treasure and I will go with you. I'm going to get dressed so we can leave soon. I'll help Treasure get dressed too." Gem got up from her father's lap and headed toward the walk-in closet.

"Mommy doesn't want to leave you and your sister," he told the child honestly. "I've been talking to her all morning about it. She told me she's not going to the special hospital, Gem. I'm sorry."

She turned around to face her father with tears streaming down her face. "I'll talk to her, and so will Treasure. She'll go to the special hospital if we beg her."

Chapter Seven

Mink sat up and snatched the bedsheets and extra blankets away from her sweaty body. She wasn't freezing anymore. A sneaky hot flash had hit her all of a sudden, and with it came another round of nausea. She bolted from the small bed with her head spinning. Weak and more nauseated than she'd ever been before in her life, she stumbled into the bathroom and fell to her knees.

"Dear God, help me!" she yelled at her blurry reflection in the water at the bottom of the commode. Her stomach rumbled and twisted before she heaved and huffed. Nothing came up except foul air from deep down in her gut. The stench caused her to gag and retch again, but her belly was empty and sore from vomiting and a terrible case of diarrhea she'd had all afternoon. She couldn't even hold water down, so food was definitely out of the question. And the quivering wouldn't stop no matter how tight she wrapped her arms around her body and prayed.

Mink wanted to fall asleep and never wake up again. A headache, queasiness, and convulsing had become unbearable. She needed relief in the worst way. Where was that fucking, mean nurse when she needed her? She was finally ready for the methadone injection that the woman had been trying to force on her since the moment she'd arrived. Mink crawled over to the wall with her bare ass peeping through the back slit of her blue hospital gown. She yanked on the string attached to the red emergency intercom on the wall.

"This is Laura. How may I help you, Mrs. Bishop?"

"I'm ready for the methadone injection. I can't take this shit anymore. I feel like I'm about to die in here. Please send somebody right away."

"Donna, your nurse, will be there as soon as she can. Hang in there, honey."

Mink couldn't help but cry. What the hell else could she do? She was a pathetic, worthless addict, and she hated herself. Her husband and children had persuaded her to sign into a drug treatment facility just across the Alabama state line. She didn't know a soul in Birmingham. Jeremiah had found the place online and made the arrangements for her admission. He hated Mink's guts, and he would do anything to get rid of her. She knew it was him who had hired Josiah's cute little assistant, Gypsie, to watch Gem and Treasure last night too. Jeremiah thought Mink was a damn fool, but he was wrong, and she would soon prove it.

"Mrs. Bishop, where are you, ma'am?"

Mink leaned on the commode and pushed to her feet. She was dizzy, and her stomach was still churning. She washed her hands and left the bathroom, walking slowly toward the voice in her room.

The nurse smirked. "So you decided to relieve your body of its misery, huh?"

Mink nodded, swallowing some choice words she had for the obnoxious woman. She had a personality better suited for dealing with animals rather than humans.

"Most heroin users prefer methadone therapy. It makes life a hell of a lot easier for them in detox. If you want to keep those shivers, the mood swings, and that nasty nausea away, you'll learn to get used to the injections."

Mink nodded but kept quiet as she offered the rude cow her shoulder for the injection. She was at the woman's mercy, so she didn't want to say anything that would piss her off while she had a needle in her hand. She closed her eyes as the nurse gently injected her with the methadone. The cool sensation of the healing potion trickling slowly into her bloodstream followed the sting of the sharp needle piercing her flesh.

"Thank you," Mink mumbled.

The nurse placed a Band-Aid over the injection site. "It wasn't a problem at all. Should I write a note in your chart for my replacement to give you a follow-up dose in eight hours if needed?"

"Yeah, I think that's a good idea."

"I'll take care of that right away."

Mink watched Donna take soft, measured steps out of the room. She was a tiny, young woman with a blond, pixie hairstyle and bright blue eyes. Although she was attractive, Mink didn't care for her razor-sharp tongue and snooty attitude that she'd unleashed on her when she'd first arrived. Thank God she had mellowed out some since then. Otherwise, they would've had major problems.

Mink took a seat on the edge of her bed as the methadone began to take effect on her body. She felt relaxed and less nauseated. And her mind seemed to have been expelling all of the jumbled thoughts that were swimming around earlier. The bad thing about that was it made room for fresh memories of some of the awful and unimaginable things she had done during her most recent disappearance act. Mink closed her eyes and covered her mouth with both hands when a vision of the fight she'd had with two other junkies floated through her psyche. And then she remembered the shameful ride in the back of the police cruiser. *Oh my God!* she screamed inwardly. The officers knew her true identity. Their respect for Josiah had surely flown out the window after that revelation. How could she have been so stupid? She was married to the mayor of Atlanta.

The salty taste of tears surprised Mink. She hadn't realized she was crying. She felt so numb. The trap of addiction was no joke. She didn't wish it on her worst enemy. She hugged herself and rocked back and forth as the face of the unknown thug that dangled the tiny vial of heroin in her face appeared in her memory. She could see his menacing glare and his tattooed body as he teased her with the drugs, but she couldn't remember his name. And what's worse is she had no recollection of what she'd done in that filthy house those few days to earn the multiple fixes that had kept her away from her husband and daughters. She wondered how long she'd been gone. It was hard even to determine what day it was.

Depressed and humiliated to her core, Mink got in bed and wrapped her body in the covers as tears continued to spill from her eyes. She wanted to die. After all, Gem and Treasure would be so much better off without her, and so would Josiah. Maybe if she were to end her life, he would be free to find the kind of woman he deserved. And because of her love for him, his new love interest would be a good mother to the girls. They needed a positive female influence in their lives because she was in no condition to be their role model. A devoted wife and a loving, drug-free stepmother would make them forget all about her, as if she'd never existed.

"Let me die, God. *Please* just let me die," Mink pleaded through loud sobs. "I can't be fixed, and I'm not fit to live. I've done too many terrible things. JoJo and the girls don't deserve the bullshit I continuously put them through. I'm no good for them, and I just can't do right anymore. So please strike me dead right now for their sake, God. Let me die."

Josiah didn't understand why he was nervous, but he was. He tightened his grip on Treasure's hand as they made their way down the hall. The linoleum floors were waxed to perfection, and the white walls were pristine. His nostrils detected the distinct smell of a pine-scented cleaner and bleach the moment they entered Lifeline Rehabilitation Center. He'd received his very first phone call from Mink two days ago, requesting that he and the girls come for a visit. She had described her three weeks at the facility as difficult but successful. According to her doctor, therapist, and sponsor, she had made great strides on her road to recovery, and Josiah couldn't have been happier.

There was a pep in his step as drew nearer to the visitation room. He would've been there by now, but Treasure had insisted that she carry the big bouquet of purple tulips, and it appeared to be weighing her down. Sadly, Gem had refused to make the trip to Birmingham with them. She was still a very angry and sad little girl who couldn't understand the terrible disease that plagued her mother. So when her father announced that Mink wanted the family to visit her, Gem adamantly declined. Her grandparents had tried to persuade her to go in every way possible, including *bribery,* but she'd stood her ground. She opted to hang out with her Uncle J for the day instead.

Josiah paused outside the double doors of the visitation room. He took a deep breath to steady the racing beat of his heart before he pushed one of the swinging doors and entered the wide open space. His eyes locked with Mink's right away. He could tell by the smile on her face and her jittery body language that she was excited to see them. Her smile faded slightly as she craned her neck to look behind Josiah and Treasure.

"Mommy!" Treasure squealed and took off in a sprint with the bundle of fresh flowers in her little hands.

Josiah froze in place as he watched Mink bend down and scoop up their baby girl into her arms. The series of hugs and kisses exchanged between the two warmed his heart. If Gem had come with them, their family circle would be complete, and Mink's eyes would have a full glow instead of the cloud of unspoken questions lingering in them. Her disappointment stole some of the glimmer from her orbs.

"Where is Gem Arianna?"

"She's with Uncle J, Mommy. I told her to come, but she said she didn't want to."

Josiah sighed and stroked his goatee. He closed the distance between himself and Mink. "I tried everything to persuade Gem to come here, but she's stubborn like you. I'm sorry, baby." He leaned in and pecked his wife's lips.

"Well, I'll just enjoy my visit with Daddy and Treasure Lorielle."

Josiah followed Mink to table in the corner with four vacant chairs around it. She had lost some weight, which had caused the junk in her trunk to downsize. But the absence of a few pounds looked good on her. His dick jumped, and he immediately chastised himself silently for allowing his thoughts to go there. Mink was in the hospital being treated for severe drug addiction. He had no business allowing lust to stir him up.

Mink sat down and placed Treasure on her lap. "So, do you miss me, honey bunny?"

"Yes, I miss you. When are you coming home?"

"I'll leave here when I'm all better, sweetie." Mink did a thorough inspection of Treasure's two long ponytails with bright red ribbons adorning them to match her romper. "Who styled your hair so pretty?"

"Nana did. Do I look cute, Mommy?"

"Nah, baby girl, you look *fabulous*!"

Josiah loved to see Mink healthy and drug free. She was a different woman. Hopefully, by the time of her discharge, she would be able to leave all of her demons behind and start life afresh with the family on the outside. He was willing to do anything to help her stay clean. But did she have the will and desire to help herself live a life without heroin? Only time would tell.

Chapter Eight

Josiah smiled at the sight of Treasure sleeping peacefully in Miss Gladys's arms. Gem was asleep also, sprawled out on the leather chaise lounge. Miss Gladys was so absorbed in what appeared to be a primetime drama on TV that she hadn't even noticed that her boss had entered the den.

Josiah crossed the den and stopped at the end of the sofa. "I'll take her up to bed."

"You scared me, chile," Miss Gladys said, patting her chest. "You shouldn't sneak up on an old woman like that."

"I'm sorry." He lifted Treasure from her arms and hoisted her over his shoulder. "I'll take her up first and come back for Gem. I'm sure you're going to finish your movie."

"I sure am, so be quiet."

Josiah hurried up the stairs to place Treasure in her bed and returned to the den for Gem. It had been a long and hectic day, and he was dog-tired. But he couldn't complain because his life seemed to have taken a turn for the better. He was up by eight points in the polls. Campaign contributions were steadily trickling in, and Mink had been clean for thirty-six days. The doctor and therapist were considering stepping down her level of care in the preparation of releasing her to a partial hospitalization program before finally allowing her to come home and reconnect with Narcotics Anonymous. What more could a brotha ask for? Maybe if Mink could stay clean, they could work on the son he'd always wanted. Josiah smiled at the thought of a tiny version of himself running around the house. Then he kissed Gem's forehead and left the bedroom.

Although it was late, he wanted to hear Mink's voice. They'd had an emotional reconnection since she had been in rehab working on her addiction and other mental health issues. It was true. God did work in mysterious ways. It had taken another relapse and an additional stay in rehab to draw them closer. Josiah missed his wife being home with him and the girls, though. He longed for the day when she would return clean, sober, and mentally healthy. He reached for the house phone on the nightstand as soon as he entered the master suite because his cell phone battery had died hours ago. He dialed Mink's direct number in her new private room at the facility and was happy when she answered on the second ring, sounding sexy.

"I couldn't go to bed without talking to you."

She laughed, and Josiah felt like flying to Birmingham at that moment just to kiss her good night. "I'm up reading and thinking about you and the girls."

"What are you reading this time of night?"

"I like to read stories from the Alcoholics Anonymous *Big Book* at night. It inspires me and keeps me focused. The doctor says I can come home in two weeks. He's already put in a referral to a day treatment program in Atlanta. If they accept me, I'll be back with you and the girls soon."

"Are you ready for that, baby?"

"Yes, I am. I know the program, and I have the mental tools I need to stay clean. I just have to use all I've learned and work the steps for the rest of my life. I can do it, JoJo. I know I can, and I really want to. Just promise that's you'll help me."

"I'm here, baby. I ain't going nowhere. We're in this together."

"Surprise!"

Mink took a quick backward step and covered her mouth with her hands. She leaned into Josiah for support. "Oh my goodness!"

"Welcome home, Mommy!" Treasure hurried over to her mother and handed her a bundle of balloons in an array of vibrant colors.

"Thank you, honey bunny," Mink whispered with tears in her eyes. She bent over and kissed her baby girl on the cheek. She watched as Gem slowly made her way over to her.

"Welcome home, Mommy. I hope you stay this time." She handed her mother a big brown teddy bear wearing a red ribbon across its chest, welcoming her home. Then she returned to her position between Uncle J and Miss Gypsie.

"Thank you, Gem."

"You're welcome."

"Yeah, the girls wanted to surprise you with a pizza party, so Gypsie and I threw something together," Jeremiah explained.

"Welcome home, Mrs. Bishop. You look wonderful." Gypsie touched her shoulder and smiled. "I'll leave you to spend time with your family. Good night."

"Thanks, Gypsie. I appreciate you helping out with the girls while I was away."

"It was my pleasure, ma'am."

"I'll walk you to the door," Jeremiah announced as he followed Gypsie.

"Well, if this is a pizza party, where is the food? The guest of honor is starving."

Treasure tugged at her mother's hand and led her to the kitchen, leaving Josiah and Gem alone in the den.

"You're going to have to forgive your mother someday, Gem. She's getting better, and she's sorry for leaving us all those times."

"I want her to promise me that she'll *never* leave us again."

"I, Mink Isiana Sinclair Bishop, promise to never, *ever* leave my family again," she declared softly, returning to the den. Mink wrapped her arm around Gem's shoulders and kissed the top of her head. "I'm so sorry for everything I've done to hurt you, your sister, and your father, Gem Arianna. But I can't change any of those things because they're in the past. All I can do is stay clean, sober, and healthy *now* so you can learn to trust me again. Pinky swear?" She hooked her pinky, inviting her daughter to take hold of it with hers.

Josiah held his breath as he waited for Gem's icy heart against her mother to melt. The poor child had been through hell over the past eight weeks her mother had been in rehab. The adjustment hadn't been easy for any of them, but they had weathered the storm, and Josiah was ready for his family to move on and start afresh.

"Okay," Gem finally agreed and hooked her pinky with Mink's to seal the deal.

Josiah exhaled and thanked God for new beginnings.

"You look beautiful, baby. Just continue to smile and wave."

Mink did as she was told like a good politician's wife. She and Josiah had attended nonstop events over the past two weeks since she had returned home. Her schedule was pretty much locked in. She took the girls to summer camp every morning before she went to day treatment from nine until one o'clock in the afternoon. Then she'd meet with her sponsor for an hour or so before heading home to start dinner. A couple of hours later, it would be time to pick up the girls from camp, feed them, and spend quality time with them before their baths. By that time, Josiah would make his evening appearance, and he and Mink would prepare to attend some party or fundraiser or political forum where she was expected to do exactly what she was doing now: smiling and waving like a trophy wife on display for strangers and snobs.

Mink hated her life. It was boring and without purpose, but she had signed on for it eight years ago, so she was trying her damnedest to play the part. It was much easier when Josiah was just a city councilman and a trial attorney, and they didn't have the girls. Things got crazy when she had the babies back to back, and he decided to run for mayor. It was too much, too soon, and she got lost in the mix somehow. Where was Mink, and what was her purpose in life? She wanted to be so much more than Mrs. Josiah Jacob Bishop, first lady of Atlanta and the mother of Gem and Treasure Bishop. She wanted her own identity and an important mission in life to fulfill.

After all, she'd earned her executive master's degree in business and had enjoyed some success in corporate America as a commercial real estate broker for a well-known Atlanta agency. Mink was climbing the ladder and making things shake in her company when Jeremiah convinced Josiah to run for mayor. She'd just discovered she was pregnant with Treasure, but her superiors had assured her that it wouldn't be a problem.

However, Mink's life became chaotic when she had to hit the campaign trail with a big belly, swollen feet, and a toddler in tow. It soon became impossible for her to work, so instead of taking a leave of absence from her

job as originally planned, she hit the campaign scene full
time. Her life was immediately benched from the game to
advance Josiah's dream, and she resented it wholeheart-
edly. Treasure was born in the middle of the campaign
and postpartum depression set in because she was a wife
stuck at home with two babies and no life.

After the inaugurals, Mink found herself even more
depressed, lonely, and burdened by the secrets of her
past. She felt like she was losing her damn mind. So she
weaned Treasure from nursing, hired Miss Gladys, and
took her place as the first lady of Atlanta, Georgia. But
sadly, it was the beginning of the worst days of her life. It
seemed just like yesterday when it all started.

*"Sweetheart, I'd like you to meet State Representative
Walter Fordham and his lovely wife, Gayla. Walter and
I have been trying to hook you two ladies up for a while,
but the time never seemed right before tonight."*

*"It's a pleasure to meet you, Mr. and Mrs. Fordham."
Mink offered them her hand.*

*"The pleasure is mine, Mrs. Bishop," Mr. Fordham
returned.*

*"I can't believe you have two small children. It took me
forever to lose my baby weight."*

*Mink smiled, flattered by Mrs. Fordham's compli-
ment. "Thank you."*

*"Let's go to the bar for drinks and let the men do what
they do best. You know they're dying to talk politics."*

*"Okay." Mink kissed Josiah's cheek before she followed
Gayla to the bar where they took seats.*

*"I'll have a double shot of Cîroc original," Gayla told
the bartender as soon as her butt hit the bar stool.*

*Mink was taken aback by Gayla's choice of drink. It
had been months since she'd had her occasional glass
of red wine. Even after she'd stopped nursing Treasure,
she hadn't indulged, but they were at a party, and she
was supposed to be relaxing and enjoying herself.*

"I'd like a glass of Merlot please," she finally requested.

The two ladies got acquainted over their beverages of choice. Gayla threw back three more double shots of Cîroc while Mink nursed her single glass of Merlot. After talking about husbands, children, and abandoned careers, the women realized they had a lot in common.

A tipsy Gayla stood abruptly. "I need to use the little girls' room."

Without a word, Mink followed Gayla to the ladies' lounge. She was surprised when her new friend locked the door once they entered and took a seat on the countertop. But she damn near blew her stack when Gayla removed a syringe and a tiny vial containing a clear liquid from her silver beaded evening bag. Mink watched in shock as Gayla tied an elastic band around her arm and tapped for a vein. Seconds later, she filled the syringe halfway and injected herself. Instantly, she smiled, and her entire body slumped, almost falling off of the countertop.

Mink jumped when someone knocked on the door. She spun around in circles for a few seconds wringing her hands, unsure what to do. Finally, she took the drug vial, syringe, and elastic band and stuffed it all back inside the evening bag. Then she helped Gayla into a stall, sat her on the commode, and shut the door. Trembling like crazy, Mink composed herself and went to unlock the bathroom door. She smiled politely at the three ladies as they filed in and powdered their noses and went into other stalls. Mink pretended that her hair and makeup needed retouching as she carefully rummaged through Gayla's evening bag for a comb and compact.

She was relieved when the ladies left to return to the party. Mink rushed into the stall. "What the hell is wrong with you? You just took drugs in a public restroom!"

"It's just a little taste of smack, honey," she slurred with a goofy grin on her pretty face. Her eyes were low and glossy. "A lot of political wives and politicians take a hit sometimes to help them deal with stress. Cocaine is played, sweetheart. Heroin is the shit. You should try it."

"I don't do drugs," Mink whispered through gritted teeth.

"Well, maybe you should. I see that desperate look in your eyes. You've got issues just like me. The mayor's wifey needs a hit to take the edge off. You've been home taking care of babies and standing by your man in public. When was the last time you had fun?"

"I don't know," Mink answered truthfully.

Gayla snatched her purse and removed the vial, the elastic band, and a new syringe. "Just chill and let me take you to a place you've never been before. Enjoy the flight. If you don't like it, so be it. If you do and you want some more, call me."

Chapter Nine

Mink's body stiffened as she forced her mind away from the past. She refused to relive that first time she'd ever felt heroin enter her veins and poison her blood-stream. Although it was one of the most euphoric feelings she had ever experienced in her life, it was the beginning of the endless chase of a high that she would *never* capture again. It had been a very costly chase that had nearly caused her to lose everything she loved. Mink rubbed her hands up and down her bare arms as a sudden chill washed over her.

"Are you okay, baby?"

"I'm fine," she lied, smiling at Josiah. "I'm kind of tired, though. Can we leave soon?"

"Yeah, baby. Just give me another fifteen minutes to work the crowd one last time."

Hand in hand, Atlanta's first couple strolled around the ballroom smiling, shaking hands, and making small talk. As they neared a section of tables in the middle of the ballroom, Mink decided to do the one thing that she'd made a conscious effort *not* to do all evening. She stole a quick glance at Charmaine Lomax, the wife of Josiah's opponent. For some unexplainable reason, the woman intimidated Mink. Josiah said he couldn't understand why. Yes, Charmaine was a pretty pecan-tan woman with light brown eyes. Her build was tall and slender, which most brothas would never prefer over Mink's curvy hour-glass figure. Plus, the first lady rocked beautiful sandy curls while the woman who wished to replace her on the political scene had invested in the most expensive auburn Brazilian wavy weave that money could buy.

According to the *Atlanta Journal Constitution* newspaper, the two women were equally educated; each with a master's degree. They'd come from similar middle-class backgrounds, and both were mothers who had placed their careers on hold to support their husbands' political aspirations. Seemingly, the two women were equal on all fronts. But Mink was willing to bet a million dollars that Charmaine Lomax wasn't a recovering addict. Sure, Gayla Fordham had convinced her that heroin and cocaine were prevalent amongst political figures and their spouses, but Mrs. Lomax didn't appear to be the type to snort, smoke a pipe, or shoot up.

Mink snuck another peek at Charmaine and admired how her bronze strapless cocktail dress fit smoothly over her thin frame. Her chandelier diamond earrings and matching necklace were exquisite. She looked gorgeous, and that made Mink feel self-conscious all of a sudden. She quickly adjusted the single strap on her lime-green sequin and chiffon sheath, which Josiah had told her appeared to have been painted on her body to perfection. He promised to waste no time stripping it off of her as soon as they got home.

Out of the blue, Charmaine turned and locked eyes with Mink. She smiled before she took a sip of champagne. It could've been a case of gross paranoia, but her smile didn't seem genuine. It was more like taunting, in Mink's opinion. Did Mrs. Lomax somehow know about her drug addiction? The thought of it made Mink lightheaded, causing her body to sway slightly.

"You're tired. Let me get you home," Josiah whispered in her ear and wrapped his arm protectively around her waist.

***

The late-summer sun shining through the blades of the venetian blinds kissed Josiah good morning the moment he flipped over onto his back in bed. He immediately reached for Mink, but her side of the bed was empty and cold. He sat up in a panic. She'd been clean and vigorously working her recovery for nearly ninety days now. Surely, she hadn't relapsed. She was too tired to make love last night after the party, so he wondered where she'd found the energy to rise so early in the morning.

Josiah's heart started beating so fast and hard in his chest that it was difficult to breathe. On instinct, he checked the safe and was relieved that everything was in place, including some money that he'd stashed inside that he needed to deposit in the bank. He stormed into the bathroom without knocking, but Mink wasn't in there. He left the master suite to check in the girls' room, but their mother was nowhere to be found. Thank God they were still asleep. Just as Josiah descended the stairs, he heard the alarm system chirp, and the front door shut. He jogged toward the front of the house and came face-to-face with Mink. She was carrying a few grocery bags. He removed them from her hands.

"Why didn't you wake me to tell me you were going to the store?"

"And why did I need to do that, JoJo? Am I not allowed to go to the damn grocery store without your permission?"

"It's not that, baby. It's . . . it's just that—"

"You thought that I had gone back out on the streets to use. Just say it! You don't trust me. You *expect* me to relapse, don't you? Thanks for the vote of confidence!" She brushed past him and stomped toward the kitchen in a huff with him trailing her.

"That's not fair, Mink, and you know it. You've put those girls and me through hell over the last two and a half years with your disappearing acts and erratic behavior. So when I woke up this morning, and you were gone, the thought that you may have relapsed again *did* cross my mind. I'm sorry." He placed the bags on the center island and reached for her.

Mink backed away from him. "No, JoJo! I need you to have faith in me. I'm doing everything I can to keep my promise to you and the girls. You have to believe in me and not assume the worst every time I walk out the door."

"I'm sorry, Mink. It won't happen again. But you've got to understand where I'm coming from too. Let me know when you're about to leave the house. I want to know where you're going. I worry about you because I love you. Don't you understand?" He opened his arms again and wasn't disappointed this time.

Mink walked into her husband's embrace. "I understand. Next time I'll leave you a note," she promised and rested her head on his chest.

"This is your second day in a row picking up the girls late from camp, Mrs. Bishop. One more time, and we'll have to suspend them for two days."

Mink ran her fingers through her unruly curls in aggravation and blinked a few times before she cast angry eyes on the camp employee. The young woman's warning pissed her, and her body was going through changes as a result of her addiction. "Are you threatening me?" she asked, snapping at the woman.

"No, ma'am, I'm not threatening you at all. I am simply reminding you about our camp attendance policy that's in your contract."

"Do you know who the hell I am?"

"Mommy, why are you yelling? What's wrong?" Gem asked.

"Be quiet, Gem!" Mink yelled over her shoulder at her daughter in the backseat of the car.

"But—"

"*Shut up!*"

Gem and Treasure immediately started crying.

"I had an important meeting today, and time slipped away from me. *That's* why I was late. It won't happen again." Dizziness and a hot flash had caused Mink to calm down and speak in a softer voice. "We will see you in the morning."

Mink peeled away from the building with tears blurring her vision and ran a stop sign. The car traveling perpendicular from the east had the right-of-way. The driver slammed on the breaks at the intersection to avoid what would've been a terrible accident. Then the driver blew his horn as Mink continued speeding recklessly toward the interstate.

"Mommy, are you okay? I think you're sick again."

"I am *not* sick! Mommy is just tired," she said, switching to a calmer tone. "I'll buy Chinese food for dinner. Then after your baths, we'll cuddle in my bed and watch TV until Daddy comes home."

"Yaaay!" Treasure shouted.

"Okay," Gem said quietly.

"I wanted strawberry jelly, not grape!"

"Just eat it and stop whining like a baby!"

Josiah placed his briefcase on the table in the foyer and rushed nervously into the kitchen. He thought his eyes were playing tricks on him when he saw Gem standing in a chair at the island with a butter knife in her hand preparing a peanut butter and jelly sandwich. Treasure was sitting at the table pouting with tears in her eyes.

"Where's your mother?"

"She went to get Chinese food. But we got hungry, so I made us a snack."

Treasure slid from her chair and walked slowly over to her father. "Daddy, I don't like grape jelly."

He picked her up. "Has Mommy been gone a long time?"

The child nodded her head and rubbed her eyes.

"But she'll be back soon," Gem rushed to say. "She promised."

Josiah knew something was off. Neither he nor Mink *ever* left the girls unsupervised for *any* reason whatsoever. Why hadn't she taken them with her to buy the food? Better yet, why didn't she just order takeout from Papa Chin's like they often did? An unsettling feeling stirred in the pit of his stomach.

He checked his watch and sighed at the time. It was after eight, and the girls were still wearing their camp uniforms. That meant they needed to take baths, but they hadn't eaten dinner yet. And Treasure had no business handling any knife at her age. Where the hell was Mink, and why had she left the children home alone? Deep in his heart, Josiah knew the answers to those questions, but he didn't want to accept the truth just yet. He wanted to trust Mink like she had asked him to, but tonight, it was difficult to keep that promise.

"I think we should hop in the car, roll to Chick Filet, and pick up some food. Then we'll bring everything back here so we can pig out in front of the TV. Hopefully, your mommy will be home by the time we return." *But I doubt it.*

Gem hopped down from the chair. "That's a good idea, Daddy."

"Can we buy Mommy something to eat too?" Treasure asked.

"Yeah, we'll get her the chicken salad with the fruit that she likes so much."

"She's going to be surprised when we come home with the salad. Right, Daddy?"

Josiah couldn't answer Treasure. He kissed her cheek and squeezed her tight before he headed for the door with Gem a few steps behind. Mink didn't have a problem lying to the girls, but *he* did. Being dishonest in the courtroom or on the campaign stump was normal, but Josiah would always be truthful to his daughters. Mink wouldn't be there when they returned, so he refused to tell them that she would.

Chapter Ten

Mink stumbled into the dark house and nearly fell flat on her face, but she caught herself. She giggled and immediately covered her mouth with both hands to muffle the sound. She reminded herself to be quiet as she slipped out of her shoes and tiptoed across the smooth marble floor. How she'd made it home safely was a story for the history books. Mink could hardly remember creeping along the streets with her high beams on in her inebriated state. Focused and determined, she had maintained as much control of the car as she could and avoided all accidents and the police.

"*Shit!*" she screamed when her bare foot connected with the corner of the center island.

She hopped clumsily on the other foot over to the table, snatched out a chair, and flopped down. As soon as she reached down to rub her injured foot, the light switched on, and brightness flooded the huge state-of-the-art kitchen. Even intoxicated, she realized that Josiah was pissed as he stood scowling at her in a pair of red boxers with his arms folded across his bare chest.

"I-it . . . it's . . . not what you t-think, JoJo," Mink stammered. She held out both arms to him so he could examine her veins. "See? I . . . did . . . did . . . *not* ssshhh . . . s-shoot up."

"You've been drinking, though. I can smell the alcohol from way over here."

"I only . . . had . . . had a few drinks . . . with s-some . . . old friends."

"Alcohol is a *drug,* Mink! Damn it! You are not supposed to drink or use any drugs!" Josiah rushed toward her, grabbed her by the shoulders, and shook her body with force. "What the hell were you thinking? You left the girls here alone to go get drunk!"

Mink looked up into a pair of eyes filled with fury, but she was unfazed. She managed to stand by some miracle and held Josiah's gaze. She spit in his face. "Fuck you!" she screamed before she wobbled away on unsteady legs.

"So you're still not speaking to me, huh? It's been a week now, JoJo. Get the fuck over it already. I made *one* mistake, and you're acting like I committed first-degree murder."

Josiah pushed past Mink and entered the walk-in closet to get his brown designer Monk Buckle shoes. He had an event to attend, and he didn't have time to duke it out with his dope fiend wife. Josiah cringed and cursed himself silently for thinking of the mother of his children in such a degrading manner, but he was tired as hell of Mink and her bullshit. Most men in his predicament would've divorced her ass and kicked her out by now, but he was still hanging in there, trying to honor his wedding vows and keep his family together. But at the moment, all kinds of thoughts were tumbling through his head. He wasn't sure if he could remain in a marriage with a temper-tantrum-throwing junkie no matter how much he loved her. Fuck that!

Josiah walked out of the closet and sat down on the bed to put on his shoes. He heard Mink sniffling in the corner of the room. She was having a pity party that he had no desire to attend. He was fed up with the apologies, the tears, and the damn dramatics. He wasn't down with any of that today. He was a damn good man, and he deserved a good woman who could hold him down and take care of his children. All Mink wanted to do was get high, and Josiah was sick of it.

"I told you I was sorry, JoJo. I was just having a really bad day. I needed to relax and have a good time, so I called an old girlfriend to meet me at Houston's to hang out. I only intended to chill with her for about an hour, but I lost track of time." Mink wiped her eyes and walked over to Josiah and wrapped her arms around his neck as he adjusted the knot in his tie. She tried to kiss him, but he turned his head and shoved her arms down to her sides.

"I'll be home in time to put the girls to bed," he announced dryly over his shoulder as he walked toward the door.

"Say what?"

"You heard me, J. After the election—win or lose—I'm filing for divorce."

Jeremiah chuckled. "Yeah . . . I'll believe that when I see the divorce decree. You ain't going nowhere, Negro. I don't know what kinds of tricks that woman is turning on you, but she's got your ass *sprung*, JoJo. That pussy must be flowing with milk and honey. I swear."

"That ain't cool, J."

"I'm sorry, but your love for Mink runs deep, and I don't believe you're ever going to let her go no matter how bad she continues to fuck up. You're just flapping your gums."

"Nah, man, I'm serious. The girls and I can't continue to live in dysfunction. They deserve better, and so do I."

"How high did she get this time?" Jeremiah walked across the room and placed his iPad on Josiah's desk.

"Is she still MIA, or did she come home looking crazy already?"

"I'd rather not talk about it. Just know that she has far exceeded her limit on my bullshit meter. I'm done, J. *For real.*"

"Well, I don't believe you. Act like your ass is from Missouri. *Show me.*"

"I will. You'll see."

"Aaaah, shit, Mink! Ugh . . . ugh . . . ugh . . . *Damn!*"

Mink's carefully, well-orchestrated mission she called *Operation Reconciliation* was going exactly how she had hoped. She had Josiah by the balls *literally* as she deep throated him into the fifth dimension. She enhanced his pleasure with a gentle massage on his manly jewels with her fingertips just the way he liked it. Josiah had tried like hell to resist Mink's sexual aggression, but she'd pounced on him the moment he stepped out of the shower all wet and exposed. She knew his desires and his weaknesses. So like a ho desperate for her next dollar, she was there on bended knees to swallow him whole in an attempt to make him forget about her most recent transgression. She was slurping, licking, and moaning on Josiah's dick unmercifully without the slightest gag like her life depended on it because . . . *It did.*

Josiah hadn't touched Mink in three weeks. He barely even looked at her. Most nights, he slept in one of the guest rooms. And his conversations with Mink were short, straight to the point, and usually about the girls. She was a dope addict, but she was a long way from stupid. The further she and Josiah drifted apart each passing day, she was losing him. That thought was more sobering than any addiction treatment. Mink could *not* lose her husband. She loved him too much, and living without him would *never* be an option, so she was trying to get her shit together. And the award-winning blow job she was performing on Josiah was the first move in her new game plan. But that was just the appetizer. An unlimited pussy buffet was on the menu, which included dessert. Mink was so desperate to repair her marriage that she was willing to do anything except stop drugging *totally*. She would simply monitor and control her usage.

She didn't know why she'd never thought of this idea before. But now that she'd experienced a few months of a drug-free lifestyle, she believed she could limit herself to a certain number of hits on specified days. She would not use during the week at all. Weekends would be her days to indulge. And even then, she would split her usual dosage in half. But if she had to make a public appearance with Josiah during the weekend, she would reward herself with a hit on Sunday evening to make up for her loss. *Brilliant plan.*

"Aaaah, shit! Aaaah, shit!"

Mink was thrilled, relieved, and completely satisfied when she felt thick, warm semen rain down her throat. She swallowed every damn drop. The delicious taste of Josiah's seed boosted her horniness to a brand-new level. She was ready to fuck him to outer space and back to earth again. She knew that would seal the deal and mend their broken marriage. Then she would be the perfect wife and mother by sticking to her plan to dial back on her drug use. But she had no plan to end her love affair with heroin completely.

Mink stood and looked into Josiah's eyes. They were low and twinkling with pure lust. *I've got him so damn weak,* she boasted silently. *I'm the drug that his ass can't shake, so he's just as much of an addict as I am,* she concluded without parting her lips. Mink reached down and stroked Josiah's moist dick, and it instantly returned to

Chapter Eleven

"Is Mink all right, JoJo? She's acting kind of strange. Look at her."

Josiah followed his mother's line of vision across the crowded fellowship hall and over to his wife. He had to admit that Mink was acting peculiar. She had way too much energy, like a hyperactive child. And she seemed very agitated. Her countenance appeared flat. "I think she's tired. She's been going to NA meetings every day, including the weekends now, trying to stay clean. I think she needs to rest."

Myrlie kept her eyes on Mink and frowned. "Mmmm . . . huuum . . . Well, take her home so she can sleep before she embarrasses you in front of the whole congregation."

Josiah wasn't ready to leave yet. It was homecoming at Fresh Anointing Pentecostal Church, and he was enjoying delicious food and fellowship with his family and church members. His campaign schedule didn't allow him to attend his home church very often. Most Sundays, he visited three or four churches with his entourage to connect with voters. He was glad to be at the church where his father had been a senior pastor for forty years.

"I'll send her home with the driver," Josiah finally said. "The girls and I will hang out here a little while longer. J can give us a lift home later on."

"Rev will like that."

"I'll be right back." Josiah stood from the table and kissed his mother's cheek. He patted his father's back on his way over to Mink and the girls. When he reached their table, he touched Mink's shoulder, and she visibly flinched. "Are you okay, baby? You seem offbeat."

"I'm fine. It's been a long day, and Gem is being Gem. You need to get her before I slap her little disrespectful behind into next week. She's getting on my nerves with her whining and temper tantrums, JoJo."

"Come here, Gem." He held out his arms to his daughter.

Gem stood from her chair and rushed into her daddy's arms. She buried her face into the crook of his neck when he picked her up. "Mommy is being mean to me. She pinched me because I didn't like the sweet potatoes."

"She *pinched* you?"

Gem lifted her head and looked at Josiah head-on. She nodded with tears in her eyes before she rolled up the right sleeve on her pretty lavender dress and showed her father a red mark.

Josiah kissed the small bruise. "I'm sorry, sweetie. Your mother shouldn't have pinched you, but you can't be sassy, baby. Respect your parents and all other adults. Okay?"

"Yes, Daddy."

Josiah looked down at Mink with anger bubbling in his blood. "Nelson is going to drive you home. The girls and I will chill here with Rev, Mama, and J. We'll see you later tonight."

Mink stood abruptly, gripping her designer clutch bag. Then without a word, she stormed toward the exit of the fellowship hall.

"Come on, Treasure," Josiah coaxed, placing Gem on her feet. He picked up his baby girl from her seat. "Let's go and talk to Nana and Papa."

***

"Are you sure about this, Mrs. Bishop?" Nelson, the driver asked. "Mayor Bishop expected me to take you home and not to this neighborhood. It doesn't look very safe in this neck of the woods. Let me take you home, ma'am."

Nelson had just parked on a street lined with abandoned houses and discarded trash. Young men wearing sagging pants on bodies covered with tattoos stood on every corner. A pimped-out car blasting loud gangsta rap sped past the limousine. The deafening bass line thumped so hard that it caused the luxury stretch to rock from side to side. A pack of stray dogs ran behind the car, howling into the early-evening air. The graffiti on the sides of outdated buildings was beyond vulgar.

"Please don't get out of the car, Mrs. Bishop. I want to take you home. I have a niece who's around your age, and I wouldn't want her hanging around here."

Mink sucked her teeth and waved the older man off. She licked her lips as she watched a stocky guy with cornrows slap hands with a young woman in the familiar secret handoff. She wanted a taste of whatever he'd given her so she could shush her demons. Mink exited the car all of a sudden.

"Mrs. Bishop, please—"

She slammed the car door and ran across the street in her platinum designer stilettos without looking back. "What's good, man?" Mink asked as she sashayed toward the stocky guy.

He turned and took her in, licking his lips. "What's up, ma? What can a nigga do for you, bae?"

Noticing the way the guy's eyes were roaming all over her body reminded Mink that she was wearing over two thousand dollars' worth of designer clothes and triple that amount in jewelry. But it wasn't her clothes the hustler was interested in at all. His eyes had already stripped her down to her flesh. She was virtually naked when he closed the gap between them and reached out to remove a wayward strand of hair from her face.

Mink shivered slightly. "What do you have?"

"You don't look like no rock star or a weedy. I bet you want some of that *H*. Yeah, you into that smack."

"You got some?" Mink's heartbeat accelerated five times over its normal rhythm just thinking about getting a hit. She hadn't used since last weekend because Josiah had dragged her and the girls from one event to another Saturday. Then he'd insisted that they join him for church service and dinner today. Mink needed a fix *right now* because the craving was driving her bat-shit crazy.

"Nah, I ain't got none, ma, but I can get my hands on some. You look like you rolling in dough and shit. I saw you hop outta that limo in your expensive gear and fancy pocketbook. Who are you, sexy thang?"

"That's not important. This is," Mink whispered, reaching inside her clutch. She pulled out a wad of cash. "Now, where can I get what I want? I need some of that good shit."

"Oooh snap! You got that paper! Let's roll out. I'ma take your fine ass to holla at my boy, Prince. Dude's got that fire."

"You were knocked out cold when the girls and I got in last night." Josiah wrapped his arms around Mink's waist and kissed the back of her neck. He immediately felt her back muscles tighten and contract against his chest. "What's wrong, Mink? Lately, every time I touch you, you tense up."

Mink dried her hands on a dish towel and turned around to face her husband. She'd been battling withdrawals since early morning. She was still nauseated and extremely irritable. Plus, her stomach was cramping like hell, more than likely signaling the onset of her cycle. "I'm tired. We had a full weekend, so I'm still trying to recover. I'll go back to bed after I take the girls to school."

"I'll take the girls to school, baby. Better yet, I'll help them finish getting dressed and feed them breakfast too. Go on back to bed now." Josiah kissed Mink's lips.

"Are you sure, JoJo?"

"Yeah, baby. I got this."

As soon as Mink heard the garage door close, she got up, ran to the dresser, and ransacked the bottom drawer. Her entire body was trembling violently with anticipation. She needed a hit in the worst way. It was Monday, so she wasn't supposed to be shooting up, but she was cold and nauseated as hell. There was no way around it. She was a sick woman, and heroin was her medicine. She looked at her left arm. It was sore and covered with dark bruises, so she decided to tap a vein on her right arm. With shaky hands, she secured the pink elastic band around her arm before she emptied the vial into the syringe. It had been nice of her new friend, Prince, to give her a parting gift before he put her in a cab home yesterday. She owed him big time.

Mink injected the needle into her vein, unleashing the drug she loved into her bloodstream. She welcomed the numbness before the airy, floating sensation. She was soaring, feeling like a dove in flight. All of her problems, insecurities, and troubling thoughts were back on earth as she ascended to her favorite place where everything was beautiful. The pitiful cries of the baby ceased too. Life after a dose of heroin was so refreshing, even though it was only for a while. Why couldn't it last forever?

Mink dropped to her knees and stared into space. She wanted to sleep so she could avoid the guilt that was soon to come. She would deal with it and a thousand regrets later on after the withdrawals and anger. So she gathered her dope paraphernalia and returned it all to its hiding place. She would discard the vial and syringe later, but before the girls arrived home from school. Right now, she needed to retire to her bed.

"That is why we need to keep guns out of the hands of repeat offenders and hold family members of the mentally ill accountable when their loved ones manage to get their hands on their firearms. If your spouse or your son or daughter or anyone in your household has mental health issues, it is *your* responsibility to secure your firearms and ammunition in a place where he or she is unable to access it. And if you fail to do so, you should face serious consequences."

Josiah paused when the audience applauded and verbally expressed their agreement with the content of his speech. He was grateful for a moment or two to catch his breath. He didn't feel well. The nagging burning sensation in his lower abdomen was stronger than it had been the last two days. Something was wrong. Josiah was sure of it each time he had to stuff his hand inside his front pocket behind the podium to scratch his dick and balls through his pants and underwear. This shit wasn't normal, and neither was the cloudiness he'd noticed in his urine this morning. And it stank like hell. The itching and burning below were annoying, and they were making it difficult for him to complete the final two points of his speech. But he would press his way to the end. Josiah gritted his teeth through the pain and secretly scratched his sensitive and very swollen penis and testicles through the remainder of his speech. At the conclusion, he received a boisterous round of applause.

"What's wrong, JoJo?" Jeremiah asked. He positioned his body to block a throng of people with questions from his brother the moment he ended his speech. "You don't look good."

"Something is wrong, J," he answered faintly, wincing through the pain. "I need to get to the emergency room."

"I'll tell Connor to have Nelson bring the car around."

"Nah nah nah . . . I need *you* to take me, J. But we can't go anywhere in Atlanta."

"What the hell do you mean?"

"Take me to your car. Then send Connor and Nelson home so that we can get out of here."

"What the hell am I supposed to tell all these damn people?" Jeremiah growled through clenched teeth.

"Tell them the truth. I'm under the weather."

Chapter Twelve

"Jeremiah?"

His head snapped toward the soft voice. He stood and hurried over to the nurse, anxious for an update on his brother. Jeremiah was exhausted and mad as hell. It was after one o'clock in the morning by the time he and Josiah arrived at the emergency room of the University of Alabama at Birmingham Hospital. And they were expected back in Atlanta for an interfaith prayer breakfast in just a few hours. Once again, Jeremiah sensed that Mink was dragging Josiah down into a rabbit hole.

"Is my brother okay?"

"He wants you to come in and speak with him and the doctor. Follow me, sir."

When Jeremiah and the nurse reached treatment room 9, he tapped on the door once and entered. The doctor was in the middle of giving Josiah instructions about one of three prescriptions he held in his hand. The word *chlamydia* almost caused Jeremiah to punch the wall, but he took a few cooling breaths to dial his anger back until the doctor finished his spiel and left the treatment room.

"I know, J, so you don't have to say anything. Just get me out of here. I need to settle the bill in cash and find a twenty-four-hour pharmacy somewhere around here so I can get these prescriptions filled. That transaction will have to be handled in cash too. My reputation will be at risk if I do it any other way. I feel a little bit better since the nurse gave me a shot, but I need these meds to pull through."

"This is it, JoJo! You get rid of Mink, and you better do it as soon as we get back to the A! I'm sick of this shit!" In a flash, Jeremiah's rage turned into sadness, and fear crashed down on him. He broke down in tears. Mink's actions were now affecting *him*. "I know you love her, JoJo," he whimpered over uncontrollable sobs from his soul. "But she is going to destroy you. It's chlamydia today, but it could be HIV or even AIDS next time. I can't lose you, man. I love you. Don't you get it? We're *one* for life, JoJo."

Josiah left the examining table and walked across the room to comfort his twin brother. He wrapped his arms around Jeremiah tightly and held on. Watching his brother cry for him had triggered his tears. They squeezed each other and cried silently as time slipped away.

"Promise me you're going to leave her."

"It's over, J. I swear."

"Where the hell have you been all night? It's seven fifteen in the morning. What's going on, JoJo?"

Josiah removed his suit coat and tossed it on the love seat and continued stripping out of his clothes. "It's funny that you should ask. You see, thanks to *you,* I was in a damn hospital in Birmingham being treated for *chlamydia!*"

"I don't have chlamydia! If you've got that nasty shit, one of the whores you've been dealing with behind my back gave it to you!" Mink sprang from the bed and rushed toward him.

He shoved her out of his face. "I'm sick and tired of your shit, so save your lies and drama for someone stupid, Mink. I have *never* cheated on you. You contracted chlamydia from some thug while you were out there drugging, and then you brought it home to me! Take your ass to the doctor today and get treated. Then come back here, pack your shit, and get the hell out of my damn house!"

"I'm not going *anywhere!* But if I do, Gem and Treasure are coming with me. You will not keep me from my children! *Never!*"

Josiah snapped like a madman, grabbing Mink by her neck with both hands and slamming her back against the wall. "You have kept yourself away from those girls more times than I can count. Every damn time you start feening, you leave and hit the streets like a typical junkie. And then you bring your ass back to this house like you've been away on a mercy mission overseas or deployed in Afghanistan. So don't play games with me, Mink. You don't care about our children, you selfish *bitch!* You don't even give a damn about yourself. *Heroin* is your life's priority, so go out there and shoot as much as you can into your veins. I don't give a damn anymore because I'm done with you. And if you go anywhere near Gem Ariana or Treasure Lorielle, I'll have your ass arrested."

"Hush now, Treasure. You're going to be fine."

"Mommy, don't leave!" The child wrapped her arms around her mother's legs, preventing her from moving.

Gem stood emotionless several feet away next to her father taking in the whole scene.

"Let me go, sweetie. As soon as I get settled, I'll call Daddy and set up a time for us to meet for a visit."

"*Noooo!* Mommy, stay here with me and Gem and Daddy."

Mink rolled her eyes sharply at Josiah as tears and snot poured down her face. He turned his head, seemingly unfazed that his baby girl was crying and pleading with her mother not to abandon her once again. The child didn't want Mink to leave, but unfortunately, she had no other choice. Josiah wanted her to leave the home they'd shared for most of their marriage because of her drug use and presumed infidelity.

As expected, Mink had tested positive for chlamydia, and she was now on three different medications to remedy the sexually transmitted disease. She had contracted it when she was out on one of her sneaky weekend visits to the streets a few weeks ago. She'd lied and told Josiah that she was at an NA meeting. The worst thing about the situation was that Mink had no idea who she'd gotten chlamydia from. The guy hadn't bothered to give her his name. Their interaction had been limited to dope and payment. The tall, lanky guy with a bald head and beady eyes had raped Mink after she'd gotten high off of his drugs and didn't have the money to pay him. She had offered him a handful of rare gold coins from the girls' collection and a diamond pinky ring that Jeremiah had given Josiah for his birthday a few years ago, but the dude didn't want those valuables. So he took what he wanted from Mink.

Josiah walked over and pried Treasure's tiny hands away from her mother's legs. "Mommy will see you soon, but she has to go now and get settled in her new place. The Uber car will be here any minute." He picked the child up as she cried, kicked, and screamed bloody murder at the top of her voice. He handed her to Jeremiah.

Uncle and nieces headed upstairs, leaving Mink and Josiah facing each other awkwardly in the foyer.

"I never cheated on you, JoJo. He *raped* me."

"I'm sure he did, Mink, but he couldn't have laid a finger on you if you had been home with your husband and daughters. You put those girls and me at risk every time you go back to the streets."

"Do you think I *want* to be an addict, JoJo, huh? Is *that* what you believe? Do you honestly think that as a child I dreamed of growing up one day to become a goddamn junkie?"

Josiah rubbed both hands down his face and sighed. "I know you didn't plan to become an addict, but you *did*, and I ain't able to handle it anymore. And I have to protect my children because I damn sure didn't protect myself. You've got me walking around here with my junk burning and itching like a damn fool. I won't give you the opportunity to bring physical harm to my girls, though."

"I would *never* hurt my babies."

"I can't take the risk. You've left them home alone before. Anything could've happened to them. You may never hurt them *intentionally,* but who knows what you'll do when you're high out of your mind on that stuff? That's why you've got to get out of here, Mink."

"JoJo, please don't put me out. Help me."

"I can't help you, Mink. You're going to have to help yourself. I'll pay your rent and all of your utilities at your apartment. I'll even buy your food and pay your cell phone bill. But what I will *not* do is give you money to use to buy drugs and alcohol."

"Okay." Mink nodded. "Why can't I take my car with me?"

"I don't trust you, girl," Josiah told her, laughing. "If you get a craving that's strong enough, you'll pawn the car for a fix in a heartbeat. I can't take that chance."

A car horn honked outside the house. Josiah looked out the window. "Your driver is here. I'll help you with your luggage."

"Take good care of my babies, JoJo."

"The girls will be taken care of. Between Mama, Miss Gladys, Gypsie, and J, I have more than enough reliable help. But, *I,* their father, will be their primary caretaker."

Josiah carried two large suitcases out to the car and went back inside for the third one. Mink followed him, balancing two duffle bags. After they loaded the car, they faced each other.

"No matter how terrible of a person I am and in spite of my substance abuse issues, I love you and those girls with all my heart, JoJo."

"We love you too, but you can't live with us anymore. Get yourself together and don't worry about us, Mink. We'll be just fine."

Mink reached out to hug Josiah, but he pulled back with his hands stuffed inside his pockets. She realized that he was still upset and hurt, so she didn't pressure him for his affection. She wiped her face with her palm and turned around to get in the backseat of the car. When the driver pulled away from the house, Mink looked back one last time, but Josiah was no longer standing in place. He had gone back inside of the house to start a new phase in life with their daughters that did not include her.

"Uuugh!" Josiah hurled the wedding album across the room and dropped to his knees in tears. He sobbed sorrowfully at the top of his lungs.

The fancy picture book hit the wall, causing some pages to separate from it. Glossy photographs of a happy couple on their wedding day eight years ago soared through the air before floating slowly to the carpet.

Jeremiah banged on the door from the outside. "Are you all right in there, JoJo?"

Josiah didn't have the will or energy to answer his brother. He just wanted to be quiet, alone, and still while he dealt with his heartache and disappointment. How could he still love Mink after all she'd done? He'd had to mentally wrestle with himself to keep from running behind the Uber car and pulling her out. Every fiber in his being had wanted her to stay, but his mind had warned him that he and the girls would be much better off if she was gone.

"JoJo, let me in, man!" Jeremiah banged on the door again. "I want to make sure you're okay. Open the damn door, JoJo!"

Josiah lay flat on his stomach on the floor, tuning out Jeremiah and the rest of the world. He needed peace so he could hear the voice of God speaking words of comfort to his heart and soul. He was a broken man who was deeply in love with a drug addict who had hurt him more than words could ever describe over and over again. But he desperately wanted her in his life. Without Mink, Josiah felt he had no life. He didn't know how to survive without her, and he wasn't sure if he even wanted to.

Chapter Thirteen

"Okay, girls, Daddy needs help picking out the right necktie for his new suit. Miss Gladys isn't here tonight, and neither is Uncle J, so you two will have to help me."

Josiah held up first tie against the sharp navy, single-breasted suit. Gypsie loved the combination on the spot. She appreciated how the plumb tie with a navy, gray, and mint-green plaid pattern brought out the richness of the dark fabric. But she kept her mouth shut because she didn't want to intrude on daddy-daughter time with her boss and his girls.

Neither girl liked the first tie very much, so Josiah moved on to a light blue one with a red, yellow, and gray paisley pattern. Gypsie *hated* it. She frowned and shook her head behind Gem and Treasure's backs after they gave their overwhelming approval of the ugly tie.

"Now this is the last one, so get ready to vote." Josiah showed them a red power tie. It was simple with navy polka dots.

"I like that one!" Treasure shrieked.

After the votes were tallied, there was a three-way tie; each person having voted for a different tie.

"Miss Gypsie didn't vote," Gem pointed out.

Josiah looked at his assistant-slash-part-time nanny. "Go ahead and break the tie, Gypsie. The debate will start in two hours, and your boss needs to be on point."

Hell, you stay on point, she wanted to tell him, but she wouldn't dare. He was her boss, and no matter how attracted she was to him, she would never cross that line—*ever*. Instead, she examined the ties more critically. "I love the plaid plumb one."

That was the tie that Josiah had chosen as well, so that would be the one he'd wear to the debate, which would be televised. Gypsie and the rest of the citizens of Atlanta would be watching attentively.

She was excited because she had assisted with the briefing process over all pertinent issues and even critiqued Josiah after the mock debate he'd had with Connor. With a bachelor's degree in political science from the University Georgia and a master's degree in public policy from Harvard's John F. Kennedy School of Government, Gypsie Robinson was a whiz in politics and law.

Josiah left the room to get dressed while Gypsie put the final touches on Gem's hair before she started on Treasure's. She was spending more time with the girls as the election drew nearer because Josiah's schedule was nonstop. So Gypsie took care of Gem and Treasure during the week for school, and they usually spent weekends with their grandparents if Miss Gladys wasn't available. But no matter what, Josiah made time for his daughters. He was a wonderful father, and Gypsie admired him for that.

"I want to talk to my mommy."

The sound of Treasure's faint voice pulled Gypsie away from her thoughts. "We've called her four times already and left a message each time, my most valuable Treasure. Let's wait and see if she'll call us back."

"Okay."

Mink turned the bottle of vodka up and gulped the cheap liquor down. A stream ran down the side of her face as she missed some drops in her haste to chug it down. She swallowed hard and coughed through the burning sensation in her chest. Then she closed her eyes and shook her head, fighting back the tears as she watched the debate. Josiah looked handsome standing behind the podium, exuding mad confidence. As far as Mink was concerned, his opponent didn't have shit on him. His black suit was off the rack, and his tie was drab as hell. Josiah's debate attire was smoking hot, especially the plumb tie with the unique plaid print. It looked sharp against the navy suit that Mink had never seen before. *It must be new,* she thought. Either way, he looked scrumptious enough to eat in a single serving. And she missed him.

Mink's cell phone rang, startling her. It was the kids again calling from the land line at her former home. Whoever was babysitting them was trying hard to allow them to speak to her, and Mink appreciated the gesture. But she was in no condition to talk to her girls. She was coming down from a major high, and she was attempting to minimize the effects with liquor. Of course, the vodka could only do so much, but it was better than crashing completely. At this point in her life, Mink needed some drug in her system at all times to drown out her pain.

She ignored the phone and concentrated on her good-looking husband. Now that she was out of the picture, Mink wondered who was taking care of Josiah's physical needs. He was a young, virile man with a healthy sexual appetite, and now that he no longer had chlamydia, there was no reason for him to suffer in celibacy. Mink picked up her phone and dialed the number to Josiah's house. She needed to speak with her girls after all. She could fish for information and get it from Treasure easily.

"This is the Bishop residence."

"Who the hell is this?" Mink slurred angrily.

"This is *Gypsie*, Mrs. Bishop. How are you?"

"How the hell do you think I am? JoJo put me out of our house. Tell me how *you* would feel if *your* husband did that to *you*." After several moments of silence with no reply, Mink asked, "Where's Treasure? I need to speak to her. That's my honey bunny."

"I'm sorry, but the girls are in bed, ma'am. We tried to call you before they said their prayers and a few other times earlier today."

"Yeah, I saw the missed calls. I was in meetings and with my sponsor all day. I just got home," she lied, slurring every word.

"I'll make sure they call you in the morning before they go to school."

In the morning? Why the hell are you going to be in my fucking house with my damn children in the morning? Instead of asking Gypsie the questions on her mind, Mink took another long gulp of the cheap alcohol. She watched the crowd's reaction to something Josiah had just said. Mr. Lomax, his tacky-ass opponent, looked flustered and frustrated.

"Mrs. Bishop, are you still there?"

"Yeah, I'm here. Have my girls call me in the morning and tell my husband I need to talk to him right away. There's something very important we need to discuss."

"Gem and Treasure will call you at seven forty-five sharp, and I'll give Mayor Bishop your message the moment he returns home this evening."

"Yeah, you do that." Mink ended the call.

Josiah entered the den with Jeremiah on his trail. "Gypsie, I didn't expect you to be up still this time of night."

She looked up from her iPad and placed it on the end table. "I couldn't sleep, so I decided to do some research on a few key issues."

"Did I screw up that bad tonight?" Josiah removed his suit coat and tossed it on the chair. Then he flopped down on the couch and loosened the knot in his tie.

"Oh no, you were great, sir. You won the debate by several points. I just want you to become more knowledgeable about local commerce and taxation, so I made a few notes for you."

"That's why I came inside," Jeremiah announced. "We were about to have a postdebate jam session, so I'm glad you're still up. I'll put on a pot of coffee. You two go ahead and get started on local commerce and taxes. I want to drill JoJo on law enforcement policies and procedures and training."

When Jeremiah left the room, Gypsie cleared her throat. "Your wife called just after eight thirty asking to speak with Gem and Treasure, sir."

"What did you say to her?"

"Well, I had just put them to bed, so I told her I'd have them call her in the morning before I drop them off at school."

"Good," Josiah said, nodding his approval. "You did the right thing. Mink knows the girls' bedtime. If she really wanted to speak to them, she would've called earlier."

"Also, she asked that I tell you that she needs to speak with you right away. She said it's important."

"I'll call her at some point tomorrow. Can you remind me to make the call before the senior citizens' luncheon?"

"Yes, sir, I sure can. Now let's get to work. As you know, Atlanta's current local sales tax is . . ."

Gypsie's words faded into the atmosphere the moment she crossed her legs. The floral print caftan was an appropriate length, but the hemline had crawled up her leg high enough to pique Josiah's interest. Her smooth brown skin with reddish overtones reminded him of spicy cinnamon. She had perfect legs, so Josiah wondered what her thighs looked like. The realization that his thoughts had had drifted underneath her loungewear made him sick. He blamed it on lust because he hadn't had sex in weeks. Heartbreak, more than likely, had contributed to it as well.

Josiah shifted his position on the sofa when he felt himself becoming aroused. He didn't understand why Gypsie's physical features suddenly turned him on. Jeremiah and Connor had been impressed by her exotic looks from the first day they laid eyes on her a little over a year ago during her job interview. Josiah had acknowledged that she was eye candy, but at age 24, she was much too young for any male on his staff to pursue romantically. So he swore the vultures off. But now as he watched Gypsie moisten her pouty lips with the tip of her tongue between sentences, he wanted to know the flavor of her kisses. He imagined that her jet-black hair, which fell down her back, was soft, and if he tangled his fingers in its tresses while he devoured her mouth with French kisses, she would purr. His dick jumped at the thought.

"So, in every speech, forum, and debate from this point forward, you *must* solidify your stance on this issue. It's imperative that you specify the difference between you and your opponent regarding this matter. Do you understand, sir?"

"Um . . . yeah, yeah . . . I understand," Josiah stuttered without a clue. He hadn't heard a damn thing Gypsie had said. "Can you forward me the notes so I can study them?"

"I already did."

"Thank you."

"Are we ready to talk about my law enforcement concerns yet?" Jeremiah entered the room carrying a tray topped with a carafe, coffee mugs, spoons, and beverage condiments.

"I think he's ready. I'll leave you two alone to tackle law enforcement. Good night." Gypsie stood and stretched her arms high above her head.

The simple, innocent gesture caused hot blood to rush to Josiah growing erection. The silhouette of her curvy figure was clearly visible because of the light from the lamp on the end table. She was petite in stature, but she was thick in all of the right places, especially her *ass*. Jeremiah often said she was too short and thin to carry all that junk in her trunk. Of course, Josiah hadn't paid his brother or his assistant's ass any attention all those times, but his masculine senses had awakened where Gypsie was concerned now. And in light of his newfound attraction, Josiah realized he probably needed to find another caretaker for his girls. Otherwise, he could end up in big trouble.

Chapter Fourteen

On the drive to his condo, Jeremiah's thoughts caused him to chuckle. If Josiah thought he had missed him gawking and lusting over Gypsie as she lectured him on her commerce and taxation concerns, his brain was on strike. The moment Jeremiah reached the entrance of the den, he smelled potent lust in the air. And then when he realized that Josiah was checking out Gypsie's curves instead of listening to her words, he became amused and *relieved*. The fact that his brother possibly had an appetite for a woman other than his estranged wife was a sign that he was on the mend. Hopefully, it meant that the spirit of Mink was being exorcised from his soul, and he would soon divorce her and move on in life with another woman. It was weird because Jeremiah had never entertained the possibility that the new woman in Josiah's life could be *Gypsie*. But the more he thought about it, the better he liked the idea.

Gypsie was gorgeous with flawless cinnamon skin and raven eyes. Her mother was Native American, and her father was a brotha from Madison, Wisconsin. The Robinsons had raised a very smart and tenacious daughter, and Jeremiah thought she might be just the kind of woman Josiah needed in his life. But before he started playing secret matchmaker, he needed to verify two important things. He had to make sure that Josiah was ready to cut his losses and end his disastrous marriage to Mink. And, somehow, he had to find out if Gypsie was the slightest bit attracted to her boss. The latter would be the harder task, but Jeremiah was willing to put in the work. He simply wanted to see his brother and nieces happy. And if Gypsie could bring them the joy they deserved, he was committed to doing anything to help make it happen.

Jeremiah didn't see Mink as an obstacle. She had pretty much excommunicated herself from her family. The longer she stayed away in her little drug world, the easier it would become for Josiah to fall for Gypsie. Jeremiah was so glad that he had suggested that she care for his nieces because it placed her in the perfect position. She was in Josiah's home spending time with him and the girls on a regular basis, and the other hours of the day she was her boss's right-hand chick. They were bound to become closer under the circumstances. Plus, Jeremiah believed if he could create the ideal atmosphere and place Josiah and Gypsie in the thick of it at just the right time, there would be a romantic explosion so hot and out of control that nothing or *no one* would be able to put it out.

Of course, things could go sideways and backfire if Mink were to return clean, sober, and born again suddenly. But Jeremiah couldn't allow the far-fetched possibility to deter him. As far as he was concerned, his plan to finish ripping Josiah's miserable marriage apart was already in motion. He would simply have to beg God for mercy for playing cupid to his married brother and much-younger administrative assistant. Hell, Jeremiah had committed many worst sins, and the Almighty had yet to strike him down. How bad could a little matchmaking be?

Jeremiah bobbed his head to the music and smiled, loving the idea more with each passing second. Yes, he was crazy enough to do something wrong that could turn out right, all for the sake of love.

***

"It's time to make that phone call, sir. Last night you asked me to remind you before the luncheon."

"Huh?" Josiah asked, totally confused with his eyes still focused on his iPad.

Gypsie leaned in and whispered, "Your wife wants you to call her. Remember?"

He looked up from his speech and gazed into Gypsie's slightly slanted eyes and got completely lost. "I'm changing the ending of my speech right now. Remind me to call her later."

"Yes, sir."

Josiah skimmed over his speech, but he didn't comprehend the words because Gypsie's perfume had launched a secret attack on his libido. And her black pencil skirt that put her svelte hourglass figure on full display was messing with his head in the worst way. It amazed Josiah that he'd never once looked at Gypsie with lustful eyes since she'd been his employee. His sense of focus had certainly changed since she'd *practically* moved in to care for the girls since his and Mink's separation. Now, he noticed every little thing about her, like her dazzling smile and the seductive way she tossed her hair over her shoulders whenever she was trying to make a point in a discussion. And every time she licked her full lips, Josiah became weak in the knees. More than anything, he loved the way she moved. She had a graceful stroll with her shoulders squared and her hips swaying from left to right rhythmically. It was almost like she was gliding on air to soul music. The woman was just plain damn sexy.

The other night when Josiah had found her asleep at the foot of Treasure's bed, he almost went into cardiac arrest. Sometime during their girls' movie night, they had all drifted off to sleep. When Josiah decided to check on them, he entered the room to turn off the TV. A simple glance at Gypsie proved to be a huge mistake. Her caftan and nightgown had eased up her legs and above her thighs as she lay on her right side. Josiah made every attempt to snatch his eyes away from Gypsie, but he lost the fight against temptation. The yellow cotton boy shorts that fit her perfectly round ass like a glove were more enticing than any Victoria's Secret lingerie. He had to sprint at full speed from the room to keep from touching her while she slept.

But Josiah's budding attraction to Gypsie wasn't just physical. He was drawn to her intellect and generous spirit. She was sweet and pleasant most of the time, but he had witnessed her firm, no-nonsense side when it came to dealing with a pouting Gem. Josiah was impressed with how Gypsie had stood her ground when his daughter had insisted that she wear the shoes of her choice to school instead of the pair that Gypsie had selected for her. From his hideout behind the bedroom door, he'd watched in awe as the incident unfolded. At the conclusion of the matter, Gem walked out of her bedroom wearing the shoes that Gypsie had chosen for her, and her funky attitude was nonexistent. And it hadn't taken a pinch on the arm or scolding to make it happen.

"We're here. Are you all right, JoJo?" Jeremiah asked from his brother's right side. "You've been reading the same paragraph for the past ten minutes."

"Yeah, I'm cool."

The door of the limo opened, and the trio filed out with Jeremiah leading the way.

"Connor's going to be with you this evening at the social, and Miss Gladys is on nanny duty. I figured since Gypsie has been spending so much time with the girls, she could use a break, so I'm going to take her out to dinner." *Wait for it. Wait for it,* Jeremiah told himself

silently with a smirk on his face. He waited patiently for
Josiah's response.

Josiah slowed his pace as they approached the elevator,
and Jeremiah followed suit. "So you asked Gypsie out on
a *date?* I thought I made it perfectly clear that you—"

"Yo, pump your brakes, JoJo." Jeremiah waved both
hands in front of his chest. "It ain't no *date.* I just want
to reward the girl for working so hard for you since
you obviously don't have the time to do it. If she keeps
hanging out at your crib watching Cartoon Network,
the Disney Channel, and Nickelodeon with Gem and
Treasure, she'll soon forget how to relate to adults."

"I guess Gypsie does need a break, although she never
complains," Josiah sighed. "Thanks, man. But no funny
business, J. Gypsie is the most efficient assistant I've ever
had at city hall and at the law practice. Don't mess with
her emotions."

"I have no romantic interest in Gypsie, man. The chick
is hotter than the July sun, but she's too much of a lady
for me. Plus, I'm not her type."

When the elevator doors opened, the Bishop twins
entered, and Jeremiah pressed the button to the private
garage.

"So what *is* Gypsie's type?" Josiah asked the moment
the doors closed.

Bingo! Josiah's interest was the confirmation Jeremiah
had been seeking before moving forward with his plan.
Now, all he had to do was cast the bait and reel his
brother in.

"Gypsie's attracted to older brothas, for sure," Jeremiah
explained after a pause. "But she likes the more reserved
and sophisticated type. . . . Kind of like *you.* We may
have the same DNA, degrees, and work together in two
capacities, but you've got to admit that *I'm* the wild twin.
There's nothing reserved about me. I'm not polished like

you. I consider myself a roughneck. Gypsie would never fall for a cat like me. If you weren't married, you would be the perfect catch for her."

"And you know that how?" Josiah exited the elevator.

"Gypsie and I have talked about her future and the type of man she hopes to marry. Yo, she loves kids, man. She wants to pop out a few someday. She's young, so she's got plenty of time. I just hope she finds a brotha that's worthy of her."

"Why doesn't she date?"

"How the hell is she supposed to date if she's always at your house?" Jeremiah walked Josiah to the limo where Nelson was waiting for him. He waved the older man off and opened the door for his brother. "I'll see you in the morning, man."

"Okay. Don't forget—Gypsie is off-limits."

"Get out of here, JoJo."

As soon as Josiah got settled in the limo, he threw his head back to relax. Although he trusted Jeremiah to keep his word and not put the moves on Gypsie, he was still jealous that they were going out. He had no right to be, but he was, and it disturbed him deeply. His phone rang just as a vision of Gypsie floated through his psyche. He appreciated the distraction, so he immediately sat up and removed his phone from his breast pocket.

"This is Josiah Bishop."

"JoJo, I want to come home. Please come and get me."

"*Mink?*"

"Yeah, it's me. Come and get me," she slurred again. "I'm hungry and lonely. I miss you and the girls."

"Mama bought groceries and delivered them to you last week. Where's the food, Mink?"

"Hell, I don't know. Somebody broke in here and stole it. I want to come home, JoJo. Come and get me. I'll do *anything* you say if you let me come home."

"You sound high right now, Mink. I don't want you around the girls until you get yourself together. Go to detox. You're still on my insurance. Use your card to sign yourself into a program."

"I don't want to go to no motherfucking detox! I need to be at home with my children. I'll stay clean for them."

"You need to get clean for *yourself*. Go to detox, *please*, Mink."

"If I go, will you let me come back home so you, Gem, Treasure, and I can be a family again?"

Josiah couldn't readily respond to Mink's question because he didn't know the answer. He wanted more than anything to have his wife back home with him and the girls, but she needed to be off of the needle and alcohol first. Josiah still loved Mink very much, and he missed her, but he didn't miss the drama of her addiction. He'd long since grown tired of the highs, lows, fears, and uncertainty. Josiah never wanted to experience any of that again. His home life was stable in Mink's absence despite the constant ache in his heart from missing her. He wasn't willing to give her another chance unless she went back to rehab and maintained a life free from drugs and alcohol for at least six months. And even then, he could make no guarantees that their marriage would be restored because he didn't trust her.

"JoJo, are you coming?"

"No, I'm not coming, Mink. Go to detox and call me when you complete the program."

"I'm glad Jeremiah invited me out tonight. A few hours away from the mayor's house will help me unscramble my brain."

Gypsie's longtime friend, Tianji, laughed softly. "You're *human*, girl. If I were joined at the hip with a man that damn sexy, successful, and fine for hours at a time, I would've jumped his bones by now. Stop beating yourself up because you're attracted to your boss, Blackbird."

"But it's not right, TiTi," Gypsie whined. "He's *married*, and I've been all up in his wife's face on many occasions. The woman trusts me. I shouldn't be tossing and turning in her guest room while I'm having erotic dreams about her husband. I feel like a skank."

"You're hardly a skank. You, my friend, are a young woman with needs and desires. Those natural feelings have intensified because of your circumstances. You're on mommy duty to two innocent, little girls with a missing mother and a daddy who is a politically powerful chocolate god. You didn't notice how smooth and handsome he was until now because you weren't in his personal space. Now that you're playing mommy to his daughters, your body wants to play house with *Daddy*."

"That's not funny, TiTi."

"But it's true, boo. Now get your ass off my line and go enjoy dinner with Jeremiah. Holla at me tomorrow. Bye, Blackbird."

"Goodbye."

Chapter Fifteen

"So, whenever I used to go outside to play on the block, Brianna, the little brat, would run over and pull my hair and call me Pocahontas. I used to cringe whenever she called me Blackbird, my Menominee tribal name, given to me by my grandmother. She only did it to mock me. Sometimes she'd have the nerve to dance around me in a circle, patting her mouth with her hand and making noises like she was doing some rain dance. I *hated* her. She made me feel like my Native American heritage was a disease."

Jeremiah laughed. "What did you do about it?"

"Nothing." Gypsie shrugged her shoulders. "I wasn't much of a fighter. Plus, I had tough skin and lots of friends. I didn't care that *one* jealous girl in the entire neighborhood didn't like me, so I ignored her insults and teasing. But my best friend, Tianji, stopped her from pulling my hair once and for all."

"How?"

"She punched her in the nose one day while we were on the block jumping rope. Brianna crept up on me, yanked my ponytail, and made me fall. I skinned my knee pretty badly. I was so embarrassed. I cried, and it made Tianji go off. She was *livid*. She dropped the rope and reached back ten years and punched Brianna square in the nose. Blood was everywhere! All of the other kids laughed and teased her before she ran home crying, but I felt sorry for her."

Jeremiah took a sip of his drink and placed the glass on the table. "You've got a soft heart, Gypsie. You remind me of my brother. No matter how many times his wife hurt him and my precious nieces, he always forgave her and gave her another chance. But not this time." Jeremiah shook his head slowly. "He's done with her. I wouldn't be surprised if he filed for divorce the day after the election. Nothing would make me happier. I want JoJo to move on and find a good woman to love him and hold him down. Of course, she'll have to love Gem and Treasure and treat them as if she gave birth to them too. My brother and his daughters are a package deal."

"The mayor is a good man and an exceptional father. And Gem and Treasure are as close to perfect as children can be. There're a lot of women in Atlanta and beyond who would jump at the opportunity to become the next Mrs. Josiah J. Bishop."

"Would *you?*"

"W-would . . . would I *w-what?*" Gypsie asked, stammering over the three words.

"If my brother were no longer married, would you toss your hat in the ring for a chance to become First Lady Bishop?"

"Have you lost your damn mind, Jeremiah? The mayor is my *boss*. And I'm too close to the situation. Mrs. Bishop trusts me. If Mayor Bishop and I got together, it would be the biggest scandal ever to hit Atlanta. What would people think of me? Do you realize how much older—"

"Whoooa, baby girl." Jeremiah reached across the table and took Gypsie's hand into his. "Take a deep breath and calm down. I just asked you a simple question. It wasn't a proposition. I didn't mean to upset you."

"I'm not upset," Gypsie snapped and snatched her hand free from Jeremiah's grip.

He smirked. "Oh, you're upset, sweetheart, and I think I know why."

"Why am I not surprised? You think you know every damn thing. Please tell me what you *think* you know about me."

"I know you've bonded with my brother on a more personal level since you've been spending the majority of your time in his home caring for my nieces." Jeremiah leaned across the table and pinned Gypsie in place with his eyes. "You've tossed and turned in his guest room bed many nights, wondering what it would feel like to be underneath JoJo in his big ole bed making nasty, buck wild love to him."

"You know what? You are even more disgusting than the women at city hall said."

Gypsie grabbed her purse and stood. "I can't believe you're Mayor Bishop's twin. The doctor obviously made a mistake. You're not a man, Jeremiah. *You are an animal!*" She threw a glass of water in his face and stormed out of the restaurant.

Jeremiah wiped his face with a cloth napkin and laughed from deep within his belly. He ignored the dozens of pairs of curious eyes trained on him. He laughed harder, satisfied that he'd caused Gypsie to reveal her true feelings for Josiah. And she was so pissed about it that she'd left the restaurant before their entrées were served. How could he not laugh?

"I may be an animal, sweetheart, but you want JoJo, and I'm going to help you get him."

Gypsie tiptoed past the den and hurried upstairs to the guest room. She was too emotional to face Gem, Treasure, and Miss Gladys. She heard them in the den laughing and talking with the TV blaring in the background, but she didn't want to greet them with a stank-ass attitude. Why ruin their good time just because Jeremiah had pissed on hers?

It didn't matter that his presumption of her feelings toward his brother was dead-on point. What bothered Gypsie more was that Jeremiah had suggested that she would act on her attraction. She wasn't a whore or a home wrecker. Hell, she despised married men who whipped out their charm and money on other women. Her brief relationship with NBA superstar point guard Tshambi Moore had come to a screeching halt the moment Gypsie discovered he was engaged. All attached men, whether they were married, engaged, or in a long-term relationship, were like poison. She stayed clear of them.

Gypsie sat down on the bed and removed her shoes. Her hands were still shaking from anger and shock. She wondered how Jeremiah knew she had a crush on Josiah. She had been extra careful not to show her feelings, or so she'd thought. And her attraction to the mayor was relatively new. She hadn't been chilling in the cut, praying for his marriage to fail or fantasizing about an affair with him. Sure, she realized that Mrs. Bishop was a drug addict many months ago. The indisputable evidence was there; even a blind man could've come to the same conclusion easily. But at the time, Gypsie's heart went out to the woman because drug addiction was a dreadful disease. It destroyed lives and tore families apart.

Not once since she'd discovered that Mrs. Bishop was a substance abuser had Gypsie thought of using the information to her advantage by trying to come on to her boss and ruin his marriage. Instead, she had done everything within her power to help the mayor, his wife, and their daughters through their hard times. And she prayed to God every day, asking Him to heal Mrs. Bishop from the awful disease that plagued her and to sustain the Bishop family. It was difficult to watch Gem and Treasure go through such an emotional ordeal at their tender ages. And although Josiah hid his feelings well from others, Gypsie could see through the façade. He was an emotional mess. She saw heartache in his beautiful eyes. He was suffering from the pain of being in love with a woman who was hooked on a powerful drug that had caused her to become emotionally detached from him and their children.

Gypsie removed her tan business suit and hung it in the closet. She avoided the mirror on the dresser because of guilt. Although she had no intention of *ever* acting on her blossoming affection for Josiah, she was ashamed of her attraction to him. Her heart had no right to hold romantic feelings for her married boss. She sat back down on the bed. Maybe it was time for her to resign from her position at city hall and help Jeremiah search for a new caretaker for Gem and Treasure in her departure. *Damn you, Jeremiah!* Gypsie screamed on the inside. This was *his* fault. It was his trifling ass that had confronted her about her feelings for her boss. She had never been angrier or more humiliated in her life. Jeremiah was now at the top of her shit list. She would never speak to him again. Gypsie decided to find the Bishop girls a new part-time nanny on her own. She would miss Gem and Treasure, but her actions were necessary.

"Miss Gypsie is home!" Treasure shouted.

Gem responded, "Yeah! Her light is on!"

"Knock be—"

Miss Gladys's attempted warning came too late. The girls burst through Gypsie's slightly cracked bedroom door and showered her with hugs and kisses, causing her to topple backward on the bed. She and the children giggled and exchanged open affection like they did all of the time. Gypsie's heart squeezed, thinking about leaving them. They had already been through enough insanity because of their mother. She didn't want to abandon them too.

"Where did you go, Miss Gypsie? Treasure and I missed you."

"Miss Gladys made us eat *spinach*. I liked the chicken and rice, but the spinach was yucky."

Gypsie giggled at Treasure's frowning face. "Spinach is very good for you, darling. It makes you healthy and strong. I think I'll have me some before I go to bed. I'm starving."

In her rush to get away from Jeremiah, Gypsie had forgotten to stop at a fast-food joint to grab something to eat. All she could think about was putting as much distance between him and her as possible. She could still see him smirking at her as he told her the truth about her lustful bedtime thoughts featuring Josiah in living color. Whew! The things they did to each other in her dreams were quadruple X-rated. Gypsie had to fan her face and lick her dry lips when a vision flashed through her mind. Overheated, she snatched her mind out of the gutter and sat up on the bed.

"I'm going to the kitchen to find something to eat. You two, my brightest Gem and most valuable Treasure, can wait for me in the den. Okay?"

"Okay," the girls answered in unison before they followed Gypsie out of the room.

Josiah paused outside the door with his heart racing, contemplating on whether he should knock or not. He couldn't come up with any good reason why he should except that he wanted to see Gypsie. And he wanted to know how her evening with Jeremiah had unfolded. He hadn't been able to reach his twin brother. It was Friday night, and there was no telling what kind of mischief he was up to. More than likely, he'd hooked up with one of his hotties immediately after he and Gypsie parted ways.

Unable to resist temptation, Josiah tapped lightly on the door. A moment or two later, the door opened slowly, and Gypsie appeared in a red University of Georgia tee and black oversized sweatpants. Her hair pulled up in a messy bun at the crown of her head made her appear even more youthful than 24. There wasn't a trace of makeup on her face, but she was a natural beauty who didn't need cosmetics anyway.

"Yes, Mayor Bishop?"

"I saw your light on when I pulled up. Why are you still awake?"

"I was responding to some of your emails. You've been invited to quite a few events. I carefully selected the ones that I think you should attend. Of course, you'll have the final say, but—"

"I'm sure the ones you chose are in my best political interest," he said, cutting her off.

Gypsie nodded. "I hope you don't mind that I told Miss Gladys she could go home. I returned from dinner early, and I didn't see a need for both of us to be here."

"It's cool. But why did you rush home?"

"I . . . um . . . I didn't. I was tired, and I had a feeling that Jeremiah had something more exciting to do on a Friday night than to babysit me. So I called it a night early and came home to hang out with my little divas. When they got sleepy, I put them to bed and decided to do some work."

"Well, put your laptop up. You shouldn't be working this time of night. I've got a vintage bottle of Merlot I want to pop. It's a 1997 Frescobaldi Merlot Lamaione to be exact. Come on," he insisted, pulling Gypsie by the hand.

They descended the stairs in silence and headed straight to the den.

"Get comfortable. I'll be right back." Josiah exited the den with a million thoughts about his sudden attraction to Gypsie tumbling through his head at once.

When he reached the kitchen to gather the wine, corkscrew, and wineglasses, he mentally told himself that he and Gypsie were about to enjoy an innocent nightcap while listening to some neosoul music. What would be the harm? Nothing was going to happen. An employer and his employee could chill together away from the office without crossing the line even if there was a one-sided attraction on his part. So Josiah uncorked the wine, grabbed the wineglasses, and returned to the den. Gypsie was sitting on the sofa flipping through an *Essence* magazine.

Without a word, he placed everything on the coffee table before he headed over to the Bose system, which sat on a handcrafted shelf on the other side of the room. He fired up the state-of-the-art stereo with the sounds of his favorite local artist and colleague. Deviny "CoCo" Love and the Bishop twins had attended the Emory University School of Law together. They were a tight trio back then, and they were still as thick as thieves today.

"Wow! She has a crystal clear voice, and it's filled with so much soul. Who is that, Mayor Bishop?"

Josiah smiled and picked up the wine and a glass. "I'll answer your question *if* you call me Josiah or JoJo. We're not at work or in the presence of any of our colleagues, so it's cool. Now try it. Ask me the question again." He poured a glass of wine and handed it to Gypsie.

"Thank you," she whispered.

"I'm waiting. Ask me the question again, Gypsie, but say my name this time."

Josiah watched her closely as she took a sip of wine. *Why is she so nervous?* His mind couldn't help but wonder. Her body language told him that she was scared to death, and that puzzled him. Finally, Gypsie looked up, and when their eyes met and locked, Josiah noticed something else. It struck him like an electric current. He wasn't an arrogant brotha by any means, but he knew when a woman wanted him, and Gypsie *did*. There was so much pent-up lust in her eyes that her raven orbs appeared glazed. Josiah panicked at the realization. Words abandoned him, and instantly he had a testosterone rush. The attraction was no longer one-sided. The feeling was now mutual.

"Who is the singer, *Josiah?*" Gypsie finally asked in a voice so sweet that it sounded like a seductive serenade.

"Her name is CoCo Love. She's a local artist. Jeremiah and I attended law school with her at Emory. We're still good friends today. She's a bad girl in the courtroom."

"Well, she has an amazing voice."

Josiah poured wine in the other glass and threw back a long sip before he took a seat on the leather chaise away from Gypsie. He quietly sipped more wine and vibed to the music, determined to get through the night a faithful, married man.

Chapter Sixteen

"I'm as comfortable on the Native American reservation with my mother's side of the family as I am kicking it with the Robinsons in Cedarburg and Milwaukee. My dad's mom still lives in Madison. I like it there too."

"Both sides of my family are from Atlanta, but I'm closer to my dad's folks, though. My mama came from a small family. The Bishops are like a whole village."

"I remember meeting some of your family members at your and Jeremiah's birthday party last year. They were really nice to the rest of your staff and me."

"Yeah, they're cool people." A lazy smile crept across Josiah's face, and Gypsie's heart fluttered.

It should've been against the law for one man to possess the sex appeal of an entire army of soldiers. The private, laid-back Josiah Bishop was more intriguing than the politician. He was smooth, impulsive, and funny too. Gypsie felt herself slowly falling under his spell, and it was scary. She couldn't . . . She *wouldn't* go there no matter how badly she wanted to. She wasn't built for the side-piece game.

"More wine, Gypsie?"

"Oh no, I've had too much already."

By now, Gypsie was enjoying a soothing, red-wine buzz. Another glass would push her over her limit, and she was afraid it would break her restraint. So she watched Josiah raise the wine bottle to his full, kissable lips and chug down the remainder of the vintage cocktail.

She covered her mouth with the back of her hand to stifle a yawn, but it also prevented a lustful moan from escaping her lips.

"You're sleepy. Let's call it a night." Josiah placed the empty bottle on the end table and stood.

Gypsie followed suit. Once on her feet, the full effect of the wine kicked in, and she stumbled a bit. Quickly, Josiah made his way to her side and placed an arm around her waist to steady her. His simple, caring gesture ignited an instant flicker of desire throughout her body that was more powerful than electricity. Gypsie shivered in response to his masculine heat.

"Are you okay?"

She laughed nervously. "I think I had one glass too many. I'm so embarrassed."

"Don't be. We were relaxing over a good bottle of wine and music. I enjoyed your company."

"I enjoyed yours too."

Without further conversation, Josiah released Gypsie and led the way from the den and up the stairs. When they reached the guest bedroom that had served as her temporary sleeping quarters for several weeks, they faced off.

"Sleep well, Gypsie. I'll see you in the morning."

"Good night, Josiah."

Gypsie, Gem, and Treasure were already seated at the table eating breakfast when Josiah entered the kitchen the next morning. The aroma of crispy, country bacon and freshly brewed coffee lingered in the air. Giggles mixed with animated chatter made him smile. Josiah embraced the peace and stability in his home, but he'd be lying if he said he didn't miss Mink. The intense chemistry he and Gypsie now shared wasn't strong enough to destroy the love buried deep inside his heart for his wife. Mink was the love of his life, and there wasn't a damn thing he could do about it.

"Good morning, Daddy. Miss Gypsie made cheese eggs, bacon, and toast for us. It tastes so *good!*"

"It smells good too, Gem." He kissed her on the cheek and pecked Treasure on hers as well. "You must've been hungry, baby girl. Your plate is almost empty."

"I like bacon and eggs, Daddy," Treasure replied.

"I can tell."

A heat wave swept through the room when Josiah looked at Gypsie for the first time this morning. She smiled at him, and he felt brand new. The look in her eyes told him that he hadn't imagined the connection between them last night. They definitely had a secret, reciprocal attraction.

"Good morning, Mayor Bishop. Would you like me to fix a plate of food for you?"

"Good morning. Yes, I would like that. Thank you."

Josiah sat down at his normal place at the head of the table. He was pleasantly surprised to find the newspaper, a thin stack of printed emails, and other correspondence next to it in front of him. As he flipped casually through the papers, he stole glances of Gypsie with his peripheral vision. She floated around the kitchen like she was in her normal environment, preparing his plate. He watched her pour coffee into his favorite mug before she added the perfect amount of his favorite French vanilla creamer and sugar. She knew him so well. Josiah diverted his eyes back to the emails when Gypsie approached the table carrying his food and coffee.

"Here you are," she said, placing the plate and mug on the placemat in front of Josiah.

"Thank you."

After a quick grace, Josiah started pigging out on the delicious food Gypsie had prepared while his daughters continued eating and talking. Gypsie sat quietly sipping coffee and scrolling through her iPad.

"I'm done," Treasure announced and slid from her chair.

"Me too."

The girls left the kitchen in a hurry, heading in the direction of the den. Instantly, Josiah felt an acute awareness that he was sitting across the table from a woman he had fresh feelings for who was *not* his wife. Life was so unpredictable. Nothing could've prepared him for Mink's drug addiction, their separation, or this present moment.

"I think we need to talk, Gypsie." Josiah placed his fork on the edge of his plate and wiped his mouth with a napkin.

"If it's regarding one of the events I selected for you to attend, you're not officially committed yet."

"I think you know that what you and I need to discuss has nothing to do with work."

"Did I do something wrong concerning the girls?"

"You haven't done anything wrong, but *I* may have. I brought you into a dangerous situation. It wasn't intentional, but I consider it dangerous, nonetheless."

"Mayor Bishop, I don't know what you're talking about, sir."

"This conversation is between *Josiah* and Gypsie," he clarified, pointing his finger back and forth between them. "And you damn well know what I'm talking about."

The phone rang before Gypsie had a chance to admit or deny that Josiah was right. They sat quietly looking into each other's eyes as the phone rang several times before it stopped. It immediately started another series of rings that Josiah soon found too annoying to ignore.

"Hold tight. I'll get rid of whoever it is quickly because we're going to have this conversation."

Gypsie nodded in agreement.

Josiah stood and hurried to the counter and removed the cordless phone from its cradle. "Hello?"

"JoJo, I want to see my children today. You've kept them from me ever since you kicked me out of the house. I want to see my girls *today*."

"You've kept yourself away from our daughters, Mink. I told you that I wouldn't allow you to see them while you're still using. I've encouraged you to get the help you need, but you refuse. So don't blame me because you haven't seen Gem and Treasure. You made the choice. Heroin *always* trumps everything else."

"I haven't shot up or drunk a drop of alcohol in a few days. And Lena's working on getting me in a detox program somewhere around here. She's sitting right next to me. You can ask her."

Josiah heard movement in the background seconds after Mink stopped talking. He peered over his shoulder at Gypsie who was still seated at the table watching him with an unreadable expression on her face.

"Mr. Bishop, this is Lena Avery."

"Good morning, Lena. How is she *honestly?*"

"Well, she's been staying at my house for the past three days. She called me over Wednesday while she was going through violent withdrawals. Her apartment was filthy, and there wasn't even a slice of bread in the kitchen to eat. So I brought her home with me, cleaned her up, and force-fed her. We've been like Siamese twins ever since."

"Do you think it'll be a good idea for the girls to see her today?"

"I seriously think it'll be great for Mink to see her children. She misses them. They're all she talks about. . . . And you too, of course."

"Where do you suggest we meet? Should we come to your place?"

"No, sir. I think a restaurant or the park would give the children more freedom to interact with their mother. It'll be more like a family outing instead of a supervised visit."

"Maybe we could meet at McDonald's on Cascade. What do you think?"

"Give me a time, and I'll have her there."

"The girls and I will be there at three o'clock sharp."

Gypsie entered her apartment, tossed the stack of mail on the coffee table, and walked directly over to the fish tank. Her neighbor, Mrs. Jefferson, had volunteered to feed her assortment of exotic fish and water her plants while she was away. But now that she was home for a few hours, she could tend to her pets, philodendrons, and African violets.

"Did you guys miss Mama, huh?" Gypsie sprinkled a small amount of food into the tank. Then she walked around her living room, inspecting all of her plants. They were as healthy as ever.

It felt weird returning to her lonely and quiet apartment after spending weeks with Josiah, Gem, and Treasure. The two environments were totally opposite. There wasn't a quiet or dull moment at the Bishop house until after everyone had retired for the night. And even then, Gypsie's dreams about Josiah brought her lots of excitement well into the night before she would finally drift off to sleep.

Gypsie grabbed the stack of mail from the table, kicked off her shoes, and settled in the recliner. Bills, magazines, and sales papers made up the bulk of the mail. She dropped it all on the end table and relaxed. Her mind shifted to the conversation that she and Josiah were about to get into before Mrs. Bishop called this morning. If he had intended to discuss the subject Gypsie suspected, she now considered herself saved by the bell.

Something magical had sparked between them last night. It was forbidden but still magical, just the same. No doubt, Josiah had sensed her true feelings for him, and he wanted to shut down all possibilities of an affair between them before it ever got a chance to start. That's what real men who loved their wives did. And everyone who truly knew Josiah was aware of how much he loved and cherished Mrs. Bishop in spite of her flaws. That's why he and his girls were spending time with her this afternoon. They were a family, and there was no room for another woman in the equation.

Chapter Seventeen

"Eat your french fries before they get cold, Treasure."

"But I want to save some for Mommy," the child whined.

"I'll buy your mother her own fries and anything else she wants when she gets here, so eat."

"Yes, Daddy."

"Daddy, may I have an ice-cream cone?" Gem asked.

"Sure. You two sit here while I get the ice cream." Josiah stood to walk away, but he paused when he saw Lena jogging toward the booth.

"I need to talk to you *in private,* sir." Lena patted her chest and took a few deep breaths.

Josiah noticed that she seemed upset. Sweat covered her brow, and her face was flushed. Josiah cupped Lena's elbow and led her away from the booth. They stood in the middle of the restaurant's floor several feet away from Gem and Treasure.

"She's not coming, Mr. Mayor. I'm so sorry."

"Damn it," Josiah growled through gritted teeth. "What the hell happened?"

"I left Mink in my living room while I was taking a shower. She was fully dressed and excited about seeing you and the girls, sir. When I stepped out of my bedroom ready to leave the house, she was gone. I found my purse on the kitchen table with everything scattered about. My wallet was on the floor, but every penny to my name was gone. I had to borrow money from my neighbor for gas so that I could make it here to tell you the bad news face-to-face."

"I'm so sorry, Lena. You didn't deserve that."

"It's okay, sir, but I feel sorry for you and them." She turned and looked at Gem and Treasure with tears in her eyes. "They're so precious. Promise me that you'll protect them from their mother."

"How?"

"Don't ever let Mink near them again until she's been clean from heroin, alcohol, and all other drugs for at least six months. Get a restraining order. Do whatever it takes to keep her from ruining their lives. I know firsthand how a parent's addiction can destroy their children. I have to face the results of my sins once a month when I visit my son, Montrez, in prison. He's there because of *me*, sir. I messed him up. He saw too much as a child. He was just 5 years old the first time he saw me crashing down from a high. He still remembers it like it happened yesterday."

Josiah reached out and drew Lena close for a hug. "Don't worry. I'll protect my girls by any means. Thank you so much for everything, Lena."

Gypsie ran downstairs when she heard Josiah and the girls enter the house. She met them in the kitchen. Gem walked over and hugged her. A sleeping Treasure was in her father's arms.

"Mink didn't show up. My baby girl cried herself to sleep on the way home."

"I'm so sorry. I'll take her upstairs and put her to bed," Gypsie told him in a hushed tone. She reached for Treasure.

"No!" Josiah snapped. "I'll do it."

Gypsie's body bristled at the sharp edge in his voice. She grabbed Gem's hand and backed away from Josiah. She stood in place, glaring at him before he disappeared from the kitchen. She held her breath and counted to ten before she took a timid step forward. The tiny hand inside of hers squeezed her fingers.

Gypsie looked down at Gem's frightened face. "Are you okay, darling?"

The child slowly nodded as tears streamed down her face.

"*Eeeeek!*" Gypsie covered her mouth over a screech when she collided with Josiah. She had just turned out the light in Gem and Treasure's room and closed the door. The moment she turned around, she came face-to-face with their father.

"I'm sorry. I didn't mean to scare you." He jiggled the set of keys in his hands nervously as if he was searching for the right words to say next. "Please forgive me for taking out my anger on you in the kitchen earlier. I apologize. I was wrong."

"I accept your apology." She stepped around Josiah and walked away.

He reached out and grabbed her arm and gently turned her around. "I'm about to leave and meet Jeremiah at a sports bar to watch a fight. He thought it might be a good idea for me to get out of the house to clear my head. Plus, there'll be a lot of male voters there I can connect with. I can kill two birds with one stone."

"Jeremiah is a smart man." Gypsie tried to walk away again, but Josiah wouldn't let her.

"We still need to talk. I'll see you in the morning. Sleep well."

Gypsie sat up in bed and looked around frantically. She checked the time on her cell phone on the nightstand. It was a few minutes past midnight. She wondered who in all of creation would have the nerve to ring the door-bell at this hour. *Could Josiah have lost his house key?* Gypsie hopped out of bed and slipped her favorite caftan over her nightgown. The persistent midnight mystery person was ringing the bell like crazy. She picked up her pace as she trotted down the stairs.

"I'm coming!" Gypsie yelled, entering the code to deac-tivate the security system.

"I want to see my damn children *right now!*"

Gypsie's body went completely still as the familiar voice yelling on the other side of the door registered. *Oh my God, it's Mrs. Bishop!* Anxiety swooshed through her veins. Gypsie still couldn't move even as the doorbell rang continuously, and the yelling grew louder.

"JoJo! JoJo! *JoooJooo!* I know you're in there! I want to see Gem and Treasure! I'm their mother, damn it!"

Gypsie inched toward the door and looked through the peephole. It was dark, but she was able to make out Mrs. Bishop's form. Gypsie turned on the outside light. The moment she did, she regretted it. Mrs. Bishop looked a hot mess. She was pencil thin, and her usually coiffed hair was all over her head. Her skin looked dark and very dry. An older model Cadillac bouncing on hydraulics with expensive rims was parked in front of the house.

"The girls are in bed, Mrs. Bishop," Gypsie said loud enough for her to hear through the door. "They've been asleep for a while. And your husband isn't home, ma'am."

"Who the hell are you? Where is Miss Gladys?"

"It's *Gypsie,* Mrs. Bishop. Miss Gladys isn't here."

"Let me see my girls, Gypsie. I miss them. Open the door."

"I don't want to wake them. Why don't you call Mayor Bishop and set up another visit."

Mink pressed the doorbell and held it. "You have no right to keep me from my children! Open this damn door, heifer!"

Gypsie ran into the den and grabbed the cordless phone. She dialed Josiah's cell phone number and hurried back to the door. The phone rang several times before the call rolled over to voicemail. Gypsie hung up but immediately dialed the number again. While she waited for her boss to pick up, his wife continued her rant and pressed the doorbell. Frustrated that Josiah had failed to answer the second time, she put her big girl panties on and dialed Jeremiah's number.

"This is Jeremiah Bishop," he greeted coolly.

"Jeremiah, this is Gypsie. Mrs. Bishop is outside on the stoop yelling like a hood rat, demanding to see the girls. And she won't stop ringing the damn doorbell. I'm afraid she's going to wake the neighbors. Jo . . . I meant *Mayor Bishop* doesn't need the negative attention. I called him, but he didn't answer his phone."

"Fuck! JoJo's phone is in his pocket on vibrate mode while he's working the room. Tell that fool, Mink, if she doesn't leave now, you're going to call the police on her ratchet ass. Tell her. I'll hold on."

"Okay." Gypsie looked through the peephole. "Mrs. Bishop, I can't allow you to see the girls because they're asleep. I'm sorry, but if you don't leave right now, I'm going to call the police."

"How the hell are you going to call the police on me for coming to *my* house to visit *my* children, you little red bitch?"

"I'm about to dial 911 right now, ma'am. You'll be arrested for criminal trespassing, disturbing the peace, and maybe a few other offenses. I'm sure you don't want that."

All of a sudden, the doorbell fell silent. Mrs. Bishop's screaming stopped too. Gypsie watched her closely through the peephole. Seconds ticked by before there was any movement on the other side of the door. Then in obvious defeat, Mrs. Bishop turned and walked away. She got into the car quickly, and it sped off.

"What's going on, Gypsie?"

"She left."

"Thank God. Well, JoJo is standing here with me now. I just told him everything. He'll be home shortly."

It had been a week since Mink had missed the visit at McDonald's with Josiah and their daughters. And her life had sunk even deeper into the hellhole of heroin. In the eyes of any *normal* human being, she had hit rock bottom. Her apartment, although well furnished, was nasty as hell and the stench from days' old trash was beyond foul. Mink was hungry too. She couldn't remember the last time she'd eaten a decent meal. Hell, she couldn't even recall her last shower. But even in the midst of living through the worst days of her life, the only thing she could think about was how she could score her next fix. What dealer could she sleep with in exchange for a taste? She didn't have any friends she could borrow money from because she'd burned too many bridges. Maybe she could steal a few things from the CVS Pharmacy around the corner and sell them to some strangers. It was hard to be a junkie incognito. No matter how much she hated Josiah at the moment for kicking her out of their home, she still loved him at the same time. So she didn't want to cause him any embarrassment.

Mink pulled herself from the bed that was covered with filthy, stinking linen, and went into the bathroom. She stripped out of the funky pajamas she'd been wearing for days and turned on the shower. When she stepped into the bathtub, she cringed at the thick ring of dirt around it. She was surprised when she reached for the soap, and there wasn't a bar there. Then she remembered that she had sold all sixteen bars to the single mother downstairs for seven dollars to buy a fifth of cheap vodka. With no soap or a washcloth, Mink showered, using her hand to rub warm water all over her body. Tears began to spill from her eyes as reality slapped her in the face. She was a serious addict, yet her sole goal for the day was to get high. And she would . . . somehow.

Chapter Eighteen

"So as you see, Mayor Bishop, this plan could advance Atlanta to the top of the list of World Cup host contenders. This city has just as much to offer as any other city around the globe. What do you say, sir?"

Josiah leaned back in his chair in deep thought. The idea of the city of Atlanta hosting soccer's biggest and most popular competition on the planet would be his greatest accomplishment. He couldn't even begin to calculate the tens of millions of dollars the city would rake in as a result.

"This could be *huge*, JoJo," Jeremiah whispered from his brother's right side.

Josiah looked around the conference table. Everyone, including Connor, who was always a skeptic, was nodding their approval.

"Prepare the proposal for city council, Brock."

All in attendance seemed to release a sigh of relief in unison after hearing the mayor's words. Everyone smiled and applauded. In the midst of the celebration, the intercom buzzed. Josiah frowned because he'd specifically told Gypsie and the clerical staff that he wasn't to be disturbed during the meeting. But then he realized that his dutiful administrative assistant would only go against his wishes in the event of an emergency. Josiah immediately thought about Gem and Treasure. He looked at Jeremiah and tilted his head toward his desk.

"Excuse me, everyone." Jeremiah left the conference table and walked over to his brother's desk.

Josiah returned his attention to the meeting, trying his best not to worry about the phone call Jeremiah was now on. He heard his muffled voice, but he couldn't make out his words. Whatever was going on, Jeremiah was more than capable of handling it. That's exactly why Josiah had ignored all of the criticism from his haters when he hired his twin to be his chief of staff. He would've been a fool not to have given the position to the one person in the world he trusted above everyone else.

"We've got a situation, JoJo. You're going to have to wrap this up."

His thoughts had so consumed Josiah as he tried to focus on the meeting that he didn't notice when Jeremiah ended the call and walked up behind his chair to whisper in his ear.

"What's going on?"

"Man, I can't get into it until you get these folks out of here. It's serious, bruh. It's *really, really* serious."

"Okay. Give me a minute."

"Time ain't our friend, man. Tell these people we have a family emergency so they can get the fuck up out of here."

Josiah nodded. "Ladies and gentlemen, a family emergency, which requires my immediate attention, has come up. I'm sorry, but I'm going to have to adjourn this meeting prematurely." He stood. "I'll have Miss Gypsie Robinson, my administrative assistant, contact each of you to schedule a follow-up meeting. Thank you all for coming. If you'll follow my senior aide, Connor Spivey, he'll walk you out."

Connor hopped up and stared at his boss with confusion clouding his countenance. His red eyebrows furrowed above his green, questioning eyes, but he didn't utter a word. He simply motioned for their guests to follow him out of the conference room.

The moment the door closed behind the group, Josiah turned and faced Jeremiah. "Is it one of the girls?"

"Hell nah! You and I would be halfway to the school by now if it were Gem or Treasure. It's *Mink,* bruh."

"What the hell did she do this time?"

"She owes this dude some money for drugs, and he ain't playing with her ass, man. Over the weekend, she went on a shooting-up binge for a grand and some change. Then she got up this morning and tried to haul ass without settling her debt. She's so fucking stupid!" Jeremiah slammed his fist on the conference table. "That dumb-ass trick told the hustler that she was your wife. So he had the balls to call here to speak to you, hoping to collect."

"And if I refuse to pay him?" Josiah stood up. He stuffed his hands inside his pockets and started pacing the floor.

"He said he'd put you and Mink on blast through the hood media."

"How much?"

"Thirteen hundred."

"Let's go. I'm sure he gave you an address."

"Yeah, I got the address, but *you* ain't going with me to make the drop. I've got it covered, bruh. Spud, Rob, and Tee are on their way here to scoop me up."

"You called *them?* Are you crazy, J? You know they don't have lids or filters."

"Nah, I ain't crazy, but *you* are if you think we can handle street business like gentlemen instead of real niggas from Bankhead. I have to come out of city hall and return to the hood on this one. I ain't about to even show that dude no money without making sure he keeps his mouth shut. Otherwise, he'll keep coming back for more. I can't let that happen, JoJo. Let our homeboys put the clamps on his ass."

"What's the plan?"

Jeremiah shook his head. "You don't need to know that, bruh. Just trust me."

"Okay. I'll stay out of it. But I have one request."

"Yeah?"

"Get Mink out of there safely and bring her home."

"What the fuck, JoJo? *Why?*"

"Don't ask me any questions. Just make sure my wife comes home unharmed, no matter what they have to do."

When the black Lincoln Navigator rolled to a stop in front of an abandoned house, Jeremiah checked the GPS on his cell phone. "Yo, this ain't the right house, y'all."

"We know. It's around the corner, J, but this is as far as you can roll."

"What the hell do you mean? I've got to make the drop because I'm the one with the money."

Rob and Tee started laughing and shaking their heads.

"Yeah, and you got JoJo's face too. So we can't let you get down with us, partna. You ain't 'bout this life. Me, Rob, and Tee gonna have to do this as a trio. We street niggas. What the hell do we have to lose?"

"Not a damn thang," Rob answered, laughing with his full gold grill shining under the sunlight.

Tee placed his hand on Jeremiah's shoulder. "Let us make it shake for y'all. You and JoJo are our heroes, J. We don't need your hands or his on this shit."

"That's right. 'Cause if you and JoJo go down for some bullshit, what's gonna happen to niggas like us?" Spud asked. "Black folks need y'all in the mayor's office, the state capitol, and the governor's mansion. So give me that damn money, hop in the driver's seat, and take my whip to my mama's house. My girl, Shequan, is there waiting for you. She'll take you anywhere you need to be."

"I don't know about this, y'all. JoJo thinks I'm going to make the drop and lay down the law on this punk while y'all kick his ass. Then we're supposed to get Mink out of there and deliver her trifling ass home."

Spud looked at Jeremiah sideways. "Yo, J, you don't trust us, man? We go all the way back to third grade when we were in the Sunshine Choir at your pop's church. . . . All five of us niggas. Remember when we thought we were the shit when we graduated to the youth choir, and all the girls wanted to get with us? Miss Allison was one mean bitch, but her fat ass sho' could direct the hell outta a choir. We used to be jammin' for Jesus. JoJo thought he was John P. Kee."

"I remember, man." Jeremiah laughed at the memories.

"I do too," Tee chimed in.

Rob nodded his head with a grin on his face.

"We were brothas way back then, and we still are today. We always had each other's backs. Me, Rob, and Tee got you and JoJo this time, just like y'all always had us."

Reluctantly, Jeremiah handed over the envelope filled with cash. His boys were right on all points, so there was no need to argue with their crazy asses. "Okay, man, y'all got it. But how're y'all going to roll out after it goes down?"

As if on cue, a navy Cadillac Escalade pulled up behind them.

Spud grinned and threw his head backward. "Deacon Hawkins's boys are still on the scene. They loyal as fuck too."

Spud, Rob, and Tee got out of the truck and looked back at their longtime friend.

Jeremiah slid over to the driver's seat and started the engine. He rolled down the window. "Keep it as clean as possible, y'all. I ain't playing. And don't forget to drag that piece of trash my brother married out of there."

"We gotcha, Chief." Spud saluted Jeremiah. "My baby is thicker than a Snicker, but you betta keep your hands to yourself. She's my ride or die for life."

"We're brothas, remember?"

"Damn right."

Chapter Nineteen

Mink shuddered when she heard the first knock at the door. Her eyes skidded over to the man she only knew as Lester. After a whole weekend of drugging and drinking on his tab, she still didn't know much of anything about him except he had a teeny-tiny Vienna sausage dick.

Lester grinned at Mink on his way to the door, and the sight of his platinum, diamond-encrusted grill caused her stomach to churn. She felt nauseated mainly from withdrawals, but the thought of their weekend fuck fest sickened her more. Mink changed positions on the lopsided sofa so she could be closer to the front door. She wanted to hear the conversation between Josiah and the low-life hustler.

"You Lester?" an unfamiliar raspy voice asked.

"Who wants to know?"

"Look, nigga, the only thing you need to know about me is I got what you want from a brotha you had no damn business fuckin' with."

"Bitch, this is *my*—"

The butt of a sawed-off shotgun came from over Spud's shoulder and crashed down on the left side of Lester's head. He dropped to the floor like a sack of potatoes. Mink screamed and jumped up from the sofa when she saw blood oozing from his ear. She took off running toward the back of the house, but she was too slow. Tee caught her easily and wrapped her up and covered her mouth to keep her from screaming again. Mink bit his palm as hard as she could, but he held on to her and pinched her lips together.

"Aye! She bit me, man!"

Rob cracked the hell up with the shotgun under his arm. He kicked Lester hard in his side to wake him up.

Spud kneeled down next to Lester and yanked him up in the sitting position by his collar. "From this day forward, you don't know her, her old man, or anybody else you see in this raggedy-ass shack. If you take your pussy ass to the badges, you's a dead motherfucka. The Atlanta Police Department has a boss, and you know who the fuck he is." Spud looked at Rob, and then Tee. "Should I pay this fake blackmailing son of a bitch this money?"

"Hell nah! His greedy ass is foul as shit. He'll try to come up on some more money later on. I don't trust him."

Rob shook his head, grinning. "Don't give his ass shit."

"Keep the money!" Lester told Spud with fear in his voice. "I don't want it. I won't bother her or her husband ever again. I swear, man!"

"Are we supposed to believe you? You callin' up big-time folks, threatenin' them, and makin' demands and shit. Who the fuck do you think you are?"

"I-I . . . I'm sorry, man. I'm *so* sorry. I shouldn't have done that shit."

"You damn right." Spud punched him hard in the face twice, and blood trickled from his nose and mouth. "Where's your cell phone, nigga?"

"What do you need with my phone?"

"You don't get to ask questions. Where is it, damn it?"

"It's in the kitchen."

Rob went to get Lester's phone, still holding on to the shotgun.

"Scroll through his contact list and find his mama's number or his baby mama's number. Hell, find *both* if you can."

"Why you gotta do that?"

"Didn't I tell your punk ass not to ask any damn questions?" Spud slammed the back of Lester's head against the floor and yanked him back up.

"I found his mama's number," Rob announced, grinning.

"What's your mama's name? And you betta not lie."

"Daisy Watson."

"Y'all got the same last name?"

"Yeah."

"Dial the number and put her on speakerphone, Rob." Spud glared at Lester. "Keep your fuckin' mouth shut."

"Hey, Lester. How're you doing, baby?" a cheerful voice greeted after the third ring.

"This ain't Lester, Miss Daisy. I'm John, his friend. He was just over here hanging out with me, and he made a mistake and left his phone when he took off. He told me he was on his way to your house to visit you. If you give me your address, I can bring it right over."

"That's so sweet of you, son. Do you know where the Prater Village Apartments are in Ridgewood?"

"Oh yes, ma'am. I sure do."

"Good. I live in apartment C45. It's a garden unit because I can't climb no stairs."

"I understand, Miss Daisy. Well, I'm on my way. Do you need me to stop by the store and get you anything?"

"No, thank you, but I appreciate the offer."

"I'll see you soon."

Rob disconnected the call.

Spud stood up and looked down at Lester. "I don't mess with sweet old ladies, but remember, I *do* know where she lives. You forget this shit ever happened and stay away from my people, and I'll do the same. Are we clear?"

"Yeah, man, we straight."

"Now, since my mama—God rest her soul—raised me to be an upstanding gentleman and shit, I'm gonna pay you what you *claim* she owes you to close out this little situation." He reached inside his pocket, removed the envelope, and tossed it on the floor. "I'm a man of my word, and you betta be one too—or else."

"My word is solid. I swear."

"Good. Go holla at your mama. Tell her you doubled back and got your phone before I left my house."

Gypsie still had an icy attitude toward Jeremiah, so she was keeping her distance from him. Because they were coworkers, it was necessary for them to communicate and interact throughout the day on the job. But now that they were alone at Josiah's house waiting for him to arrive with the girls, the iciness had returned. Gypsie was upstairs in her bedroom painting her toenails. She didn't give a damn where Jeremiah was or what he was doing. Just knowing that he was in the house with her made her very uncomfortable.

The situation involving Mrs. Bishop had stressed everyone's nerves. And according to Jeremiah, things were about to get even crazier. Gypsie's heart went out to Mrs. Bishop, but her loyalty was to her boss and the children. They had endured so much in a short amount of time. It was a miracle that they were still sane.

Gypsie rolled her eyes to the ceiling when Jeremiah knocked on her door. She had no words for him except maybe a few profane ones. She waddled like a duck on her bare heels to the door, trying not to smear the freshly applied polish. She snatched it open.

"What do you want?"

"Can I come in so we can talk?"

Without a word, she stepped aside to allow him into the room. Then she sat on the bed, leaving Jeremiah standing in the middle of the floor.

"I want to apologize for the other night. My words were kind of sharp."

"You think?"

"Yeah, I was dead wrong in my approach, but I believe there was some truth in what I said, though."

"Get out, Jeremiah!"

"Hold on, Gypsie." He held up his hands in surrender. "Just hear me out. I'm not a fool. You have feelings for my brother regardless of whether you care to admit it. And there's nothing wrong with that because you're only human. It's almost impossible for a woman to spend most of her time with a good-looking man she admires and respects without her eventually catching some type of feelings for him. JoJo is your work husband by day, and you care for his children from the time they come home from school until they leave the next morning. An attraction was bound to develop."

"And your point is?"

"Mink will *never* get her shit together. She's a hard-core drug addict, and I think she has some serious mental health issues also. And because she's too damn stubborn to dig down to the root of it all, she will die an addict."

Gypsie wiped a fresh flow of tears from her eyes. The thought of Gem and Treasure losing their mother broke her heart. "Those poor girls . . . They truly love their mom."

"My nieces will be fine as long as they have *you*." Jeremiah sat down on the bed and looked into Gypsie's eyes. "JoJo will be okay as long as he has you too."

"Stop it, Jeremiah! Just stop it, *please!*" She covered her ears with her hands and shook her head as tears poured heavily down her cheeks.

"He cares about you. I know him better than anyone else, Gypsie. When he hurts, I hurt. His happiness is my happiness. Every damn time he gets sick, it hits me too. We share the same heartbeat. I see the way he looks at you. The chemistry between you two could demolish an entire building. It's just that damn powerful."

"But I'm scared. This is too much for me. I didn't plan to fall for him."

"I know. Believe me, I know."

"What should I do?"

Jeremiah chuckled. "Nothing. It'll happen naturally and at the right time."

Gypsie looked down at her hands folded on her lap before she met Jeremiah's gaze again. "How can he have feelings for me when he's still in love with his wife?"

"I can't explain that. But I know JoJo's heart. There's a place in it for you. Be patient, and you'll see."

The doorbell rang, and Gypsie cocked her head to the side. "Why is Mayor Bishop ringing the doorbell?"

"It's not JoJo, but he and the girls should be here soon. Chill out for a while. I promise you'll understand everything before the night is over."

Chapter Twenty

"Give me a minute, y'all! I'm coming!" Jeremiah turned around and narrowed his eyes at Mink. "Go ahead and eat. I'll be right back. Don't touch *anything*. I mean it."

"Who the hell do you think you're talking to? This is *my* house, J! You have no right to treat me like a common criminal in my own home!"

"You're wrong. This is *my brother's* house. You ain't ever paid a bill up in here. And you forfeited your right to call this house your home the day you picked up the needle and put your family on the back burner. Now, I'm going to walk my friends to the door and thank them again for covering JoJo's ass on *your* bullshit. Then I'll come back and deal with you."

Jeremiah did an about-face and left the kitchen. Spud, Rob, and Tee were standing in the foyer talking smack and laughing. He smiled, appreciating the bond they shared. Their twenty-eight-year friendship had seen good times as well as bad. Regardless of the different paths they'd each taken in life, they were brothas until the casket.

Jeremiah dapped up his three friends and gave them each a man hug. "Yo, thank y'all for looking out. The moment I got the call, you three fools were the first people I thought about. I knew y'all would come through."

"As much as you, JoJo, Rev, and Miss Myrlie has done for all our asses, it was our duty to show up," Spud explained.

Rob, the quietest member of the crew from day one, nodded and flashed his signature smile.

"Well, I ain't gonna lie," Tee spoke up. "I want JoJo to throw a big-ass barbecue for us before it gets too cold so I can come over here and eat as much as I want and drink up all of his expensive liquor."

"You know he'll do it." Jeremiah laughed. "In fact, I'll set a date and make it happen. Y'all should hear from me next week."

"Cool. We 'bout to bounce, J. By the way, Shequan said you're cool."

"She's pretty cool too. Invite her to the barbecue."

"I will."

"Uncle J!" Gem and Treasure squealed at the same time, seemingly in musical harmony. They hugged their uncle around his long legs.

He bent down and kissed each niece on the forehead. "I've been waiting for you two. I want you to go and wash your hands for dinner. Your plates are already on the table."

"Okay." Treasure giggled as she skipped past her uncle.

"What's for dinner?" Gem wanted to know.

"Miss Gladys made some good ole fried chicken."

"Yesss!"

Jeremiah smiled and shook his head when the child ran off toward the bathroom. He walked in the opposite direction, en route to the den where he found Josiah massaging his temples.

"Where is she?"

"She's in the downstairs guestroom getting dressed."

"Does she know what's about to go down?"

"I didn't tell her a damn thing. I can barely look at her, JoJo. It was best that I say as little to her as possible."

"Where's Gypsie?"

"She's in her room." Jeremiah took a deep breath and released it slowly. "Yo, JoJo, Gypsie and I had a little talk. I think you need to know—"

"Now is not the time, J. I can't deal with *that* and the situation with Mink at the same time. It's too heavy."

"Wait a minute. So you know?"

Josiah nodded. "I'm a perceptive man, J, so, of course, I know. And, no, I did *not* encourage Gypsie in any way. I wouldn't do that to her."

"I know you better than that, man."

"Did Mama buy everything I asked for?"

Jeremiah laughed. "You know Mama. She bought everything, and then some. I threw everything in a suitcase. I packed an overnight bag for you too."

"Thank you."

"It's my life's purpose to take care of you, bruh," Jeremiah spoke sincerely. "That's why I can't settle down and get serious with a woman. I've got to be there for your ass."

Josiah and Jeremiah shared a laugh.

"I'm sorry I'm such a burden on you."

"You ain't a burden, man. I love you, and I don't mind taking care of you. Now go and eat dinner with the girls while I finish up a few things. Nelson will be here before you know it."

Josiah turned from the picture window in time to see Mink enter the room. He immediately noticed her drastic weight loss and darkened complexion. Her hair, pulled back in a loose ponytail, was brittle and dry. And although she was dressed in a brand-new designer ensemble, her overall appearance was less than average. For the first time ever, Josiah saw Mink for what she truly was from the depths of her soul—*an addict*. There was no denying that she was his wife and she'd given birth to his two daughters. But above those two very important, indisputable facts, she was a plain ole, typical, certified junkie. And that was all Josiah saw walking in his direction.

But then suddenly, like some unexplainable, supernatural phenomenon, Mink made a retransformation the moment she wrapped her arms around Josiah's neck. Every negative thought, painful memory, and horrible act she'd ever committed dissipated in the blink of an eye. Josiah couldn't fight it. He was a helpless prisoner of love, shackled and chained by his wedding vows. His arms snaked around Mink's waist and drew her so close that he could feel her racing heartbeat. The reunion was rapturous, and his love for her renewed. No matter where she had been or what she'd done, in his arms was where she belonged. Mink was his wife, and his love for her had no end.

Mink placed a palm on each side Josiah's face and pulled it down to hers. She pressed her lips gently against his and traced them with her tongue. She pulled back and looked into his eyes. "I love you so much, JoJo."

"I love you too, Mink."

She kissed him a second time but with more aggression, and he reciprocated her passion. Once again, Mink broke the kiss to gaze into Josiah's eyes. "Thank you for never giving up on me when most men would have. And thanks for letting me come back home, baby." She resumed kissing him, going in for the kill with her tongue.

Josiah broke the kiss abruptly and pushed Mink away. Her last words had zapped him back to reality. An unexpected bolt of rage sliced through him like a double-edged sword. After all she had put him through just *this day* was reason enough for him to have their marriage annulled if the law would allow it. He wiped his lips and drew in long, measured breaths, trying his damnedest not to go off on Mink. With his daughters in the kitchen and Gypsie upstairs, a knock-down, drag-out would not be a good look for him. So he dialed his anger back even as Mink glared at him as if *he* were the addict, missing parent, and unfaithful spouse in their marriage.

"You're not coming home, Mink," Josiah finally announced through pants for air.

"But you paid the guy the money and told your friends to bring me here. And what about the new clothes and shoes? If you didn't want me back home, why did you do all of that?"

"I had no choice but to pay off that dude and get you out of there! If I hadn't, pictures of you looking like home-made shit would be all over the damn internet. And what do you think that would've done to our daughters and me, Mink? Huh? Do you have *any* idea?"

Mink didn't respond. She simply covered her face with her hands and sobbed. It was exactly what Josiah had expected her to do. Every time she went back out to the streets and did something stupid, she would return home, crying and apologizing. Then she'd start lying and making bullshit promises that she knew she couldn't keep even if it would save her soul from hell. Josiah sat on the chaise lounge, waiting for the next phase of the all-too-familiar showdown. He probably could recite Mink's next words right along with her like a script. He waited for her next line.

"JoJo, I'm done this time. I'll call Lena tonight and start on step one again. Tomorrow, I'll go to every NA meeting in town. I promise."

Josiah laughed. "Do you *really* think Lena wants to talk to you? I know what you did to her. That was foul, Mink. . . . *Low-class* foul. But don't worry. I paid Lena back all of the bill money you stole from her wallet. You know I'm your pooper-scooper. I've always come behind you to clean up your shit. But I'm done. I can't do it anymore—and I won't."

"No, JoJo. Please, don't send me back to that apartment. Don't make me leave. I'll die out there on those streets. That's not where I belong. I need to be here with you and my babies."

"Nah," he said, shaking his head. "You can't stay here, baby. Do you think I'm stupid enough to let you come back up in here and put my children through another cycle of your insanity? Oh, hell nah!"

"But I'll do better this time. I swear. I can do it if I can see my babies every day. I miss them, JoJo, and I know they miss me."

"Yeah, they miss you. God knows those girls worship the ground you walk on. Treasure thinks the sun rises and sets on her mommy. That's why you've got to go, Mink. Each time you go out and come back, it becomes more difficult for them to heal and readjust. It's an unhealthy revolving process that I've got to put an end to. Hell, I've got to protect them from *you*," Josiah admitted through tears that he could no longer hold back.

Mink dropped down on the love seat. She doubled over and sobbed out loud pitifully. Although the kitchen door was closed and Jeremiah had been instructed to keep Gem and Treasure away from the den, Josiah rushed to shut the double doors. He didn't want to risk them hearing their mother crying.

He walked over and stood above Mink with tears still rolling down his cheeks. "If you love our daughters the way you say you do, and you're serious this time about kicking your drug habit, go to the guest room and pull yourself together. Then I want you to come back in here ready to go with me when Nelson arrives."

"Where are we going, JoJo?"

"Montana."

Mink's head popped up, and she looked at Josiah's tearstained face. "Why the hell are we going to *Montana?*"

"There's a substance abuse treatment center up in the mountains near White Sulphur Springs. It's one of the best in the country. Movie stars, professional athletes, and well-known politicians who've battled all kinds of addictions sing the facility's praises. I did the virtual tour online and spoke with representatives from their clinical and support staffs. And my insurance has already been approved. It's the perfect place for you, Mink."

"How long is the program?"

"That's up to you, but the standard time is six months minimum."

"*Six months?* Have you lost your damn mind, JoJo? You want to send me away like a convicted felon to some hellhole in the mountains way up in Montana for six fucking months?"

"Yeah, I do, because you need it, damn it!"

"What if I refuse to go?"

"You're an adult, Mink. I can't make you do anything you don't want to do. The choice is yours. You can go to treatment and get the help you need, or you can walk out of this house and never come back. Our marriage will end, and I'll file for sole custody of Gem and Treasure."

"Can I sleep on it?"

Josiah wiped his eyes and sniffled. He found it hard to fathom that Mink was being so resistant to going to treatment when it was evident that she needed it. "No. I have a short window period to inform the facility whether you're coming or not so they can refund me my full down payment of $12,000. What's your decision, Mink? I need to know right now. Nelson will be here in thirty minutes to pick us up and drive us to the airport to catch a ten o'clock flight. I've already packed our bags."

"I'll go." Mink reached out and grabbed Josiah's hand. "Can I please see my babies before we leave?"

"I don't think that's a good idea, Mink. They—"

"JoJo . . . *please*," she begged, dropping to her knees. She squeezed his hand. "Just give me five minutes with them. I promise not to say anything to upset them."

After a long pause, Josiah's heart softened. "All right. You can have five minutes with the girls. Then they'll go upstairs to Gypsie so that they can take their baths. Go to the bathroom and wipe your face. They're in the kitchen playing board games and cards with J. We'll meet you in here in a few minutes."

Chapter Twenty-one

"Mommy!" Treasure ran and threw herself into Mink's arms.

"Hey, honey bunny! How are you?" She pulled her baby girl onto her lap.

"I'm fine. I drew a picture of you and me and Daddy and Gem at school. It's so *pretty*. Miss Gladys taped it on the 'frigerator. Miss Hernandez, my teacher, gave me a gold star 'cause I knew all my sight words. I said the Solomon Grundy poem without messing up and . . ."

Treasure's endless chatter was more soothing to Mink's ears and heart than any love song, but it was muted by the cold look that she saw in Gem's eyes. The child stood at the entrance of the den staring at her mother and little sister, seemingly emotionless. Mink's heart shredded into a billion pieces. Her firstborn was clearly unhappy to see her. And it was her fault.

"Go on, Gem. Go and hug your mother," Josiah coaxed, pushing the child farther into the room.

Rigid and in slow motion, Gem crossed the den and stopped in front of Mink.

"It's so good to see you, sugar." Mink reached out and enfolded the child in her arms. She gave her a peck on the cheek. Staring into her cold eyes up close, she asked. "How are you, Gem Ariana?"

"I'm fine."

"How is school?"

"School is fine."

"Are you and Bella still BFFs?"

"No."

Mink decided to give Gem some emotional space. The mother-daughter bond they'd once shared had been broken by time and absence, which was a result of her drug addiction. It would be impossible to repair it in five minutes, so she wouldn't even try.

Mink returned her attention to the child she still had a bond with. "Who is your best friend, Treasure?"

"Leilani, Zion, and Karrington are my best friends. We play together, we eat lunch together, and we're all going to be just like Beyoncé and Michelle Obama when we grow up."

"Wow! That's a combination of two great women."

Josiah cleared his throat. Mink looked at him. He tapped his watch with his finger.

"Well, girls, it's getting late. Gypsie is upstairs waiting to help you with your baths."

"I want *you* to give me a bath, Mommy," Treasure whined.

"But Gypsie has been waiting all this time, so it's only fair that she help you." Mink placed her baby girl on her feet and stood. She gathered both of her daughters in a group hug and kissed each on the cheek as she fought back the tears with a vengeance. "Mommy loves her babies so much."

"I love you too, Mommy."

A lone tear fell when Gem failed to tell Mink she loved her, but she quickly wiped it away.

"Come on, princesses. Uncle J is waiting for you in the kitchen. He's going to take you upstairs to Miss Gypsie."

Mink broke down in a full-fledged sob as soon as Josiah and the girls left the room.

***

"Miss Gypsie, our mommy came back home. She's downstairs with Daddy."

Gypsie pulled the nightgown over Treasure's head and slid it down her body. "Yes, I know she's home, darling. I saw her."

It was true. Gypsie *had* seen Mrs. Bishop downstairs— in Josiah's arms kissing him passionately and declaring her love for him. And his reaction to her affection and the words he responded were heartfelt.

"I love you so much, JoJo."

"I love you too, Mink."

Gypsie swallowed the marble-size lump in her throat when the words resounded in her ears, and the vision replayed in her memory. The kiss Josiah and his wife had shared was hot and urgent. Gypsie regretted that she had witnessed it. But she'd accidentally stumbled upon the reunion when she went downstairs to check on Gem and Treasure after they didn't immediately come upstairs to greet her. She hadn't expected to find Josiah making out with the wife who had been out on the streets using drugs over the past several weeks. Gypsie was shocked that he wasn't angry with her for putting him in a position to be blackmailed and publically humiliated earlier today. But love was a powerful thing. It made strange things happen. That's exactly why Mrs. Bishop was back at home with her husband and daughters despite all of the pain she had caused them.

"Thank you for never giving up on me when most men would have. And thanks for letting me come back home, baby."

"Miss Gypsie!" Gem shrieked.

"Huh?"

"I just asked you which shoes you want me to wear tomorrow. Didn't you hear me?"

"No, darling, I didn't hear you. I'm sorry, Gem. My mind was somewhere else. Wear your white Nikes."

"Yes, ma'am."

Gypsie finished helping the girls dress for bed as she listened to them chat about everything under the sun. She noticed how happy Treasure was to have her mother back home. That's all the child kept talking about. Gem, on the other hand, made no comments about Mrs. Bishop's return. It seemed like a nonfactor to her. Treasure readily thanked God during her prayers for bringing her mommy home, but her sister didn't.

"Gem, aren't you glad that your mom came home?" Gypsie asked as she tucked her in.

"I don't know."

"Your mom loves you and Treasure very much, darling. She's just suffering from a very bad disease, and it's hard for her sometimes. She doesn't mean to go away and make you sad. Her addiction causes her to do that. Just pray for her every night so she'll get better."

"Why can't Mommy get well like the people on the TV commercial?"

"What are you talking about, my brightest Gem?"

"I see the commercial all the time. It says if you are suffering from *addiction,* you should call this number. Every time it comes on I run to find a pencil and a piece of paper so I can write down the phone number, but I keep missing it because I'm too slow. Can you help me find the number, Miss Gypsie?"

"I'll sure try."

"The people on the commercial said they went to the special doctor at the special hospital and got treatment to help with addiction. Now they feel better. If we find the number, we can give it to Mommy so she can call the special doctor and go to his special hospital so he can make her addiction go away too. Then she won't leave us again."

Gypsie kissed Gem's forehead. "We'll find that telephone number for your mommy, darling."

Josiah couldn't relax on the ride to the airport because his rushed decision to get Mink into the rehabilitation facility in Montana hadn't allowed him any time to speak with Gypsie. Jeremiah had promised that he would explain everything to her before he left her and the girls for the night. Josiah appreciated his brother having his back on some things, but he would've much rather preferred speaking to Gypsie about this particular situation himself. So he decided that he would call her once he and Mink arrived at their terminal. All he needed to do was come up with an excuse to step away to make the call without looking suspicious.

"JoJo, you're walking too fast," Mink said softly. "I'm not in good shape anymore. I haven't been eating healthy or exercising."

Josiah slowed his pace, reached back, and laced his fingers through Mink's to pull her along. Even at this time of night, Atlanta's Hartsfield-Jackson International Airport was popping. There were globs of people rushing in all directions, making their way to wherever they needed to be in the world's busiest airport. Josiah was sporting a fancy fedora, reading glasses, and casual attire, which included jeans and a sweatshirt. He was confident that his identity was undetectable to most. After a train ride, bypassing two concords, he and Mink arrived at their terminal and sat down.

"We have about twenty minutes before first-class passengers will start boarding the plane. I'm going to go and grab a magazine to read on the flight. Do you need anything, Mink?"

"Bring me a bottle of water please."

"Okay."

Josiah pulled out his cell phone and dialed Gypsie's number. He looked over his shoulder to make sure he had privacy. Mink was still sitting where he had left her. The phone rang several times without an answer before the call rolled over to voicemail. The matter was too important to be summarized in a message, so Josiah hung up and dialed the number again with the same results. This time he decided to leave a short message.

"Gypsie, this is Josiah. I need to talk to you. It's very important." He couldn't think of anything else to say, so he hung up and walked over to a magazine stand.

Gem burst into the guest room with Treasure right behind her carrying her baby doll. "Miss Gypsie! Miss Gypsie, wake up! You've got to get us ready for school. What are we going to eat for breakfast?"

Gypsie sat up slowly with her head pounding like a bass drum. It was the result of her taking a cheap over-the-counter sleep aid the night before. She was going to choke Susan, Josiah's internal affairs director, for giving her the two capsules and highly recommending that she take them whenever she had trouble falling asleep.

"Where are your mommy and daddy?"

"We don't know," Treasure whined. "We can't find them."

Gypsie checked the time on her cell phone and realized that she had overslept by thirty minutes. Usually, she would be up and halfway dressed by now and on her way down the hall to wake the girls. Although she'd had no intention to sleep past six o'clock, she had an excuse. But why were Josiah and wifey still locked up in their love nest when they knew their daughters needed to be dressed, fed, and taken to school?

Gypsie dragged herself out of bed and slid her signature caftan over her nightgown. She was groggy and had a bad case of the cotton mouth. How in the world could anyone get used to waking up to a hangover day after day?

"Look, Miss Gypsie." Gem bent down and picked up something from the floor. "You've got mail." She held up a white envelope.

"Thank you." Gypsie took the envelope and immediately saw her name scribbled on the front of it. She ripped it open and pulled out the single sheet of paper.

Gypsie,

I just knocked on your door, but you didn't answer. I guess you were snoring too loud to hear me. Josiah is on a flight to Montana, as I write this, on some personal business. That's why I needed to talk to you. He asked me to update you on what's going on. Things are a little screwed up right now. I warned you that it was coming. I'll run down the whole situation for you when you get to the office in the morning. Until then, take care of my nieces and tell them Uncle J loves them.

Jeremiah

Gypsie crumpled the note in her hand as she fought to maintain her composure in the presence of Gem and Treasure. Her feelings were crushed. How dare Josiah fly off to Montana with his wife on some marriage reunion retreat and leave her there to care for their children? Who the hell did they think she was? . . . *The help?* Gypsie never saw it coming, but the painful reality stabbed her in the heart like a sharp knife. *Yes, I'm the help, Mink is Josiah's wife, and Gem and Treasure are their children. There's no place for me in their world.*

Chapter Twenty-two

"We're ready to start the staff meeting, but we don't have the agenda."

Jeremiah looked up from his desktop screen. "Get it from Gypsie," he snapped, slightly annoyed.

"She's not here. Rebecca said she's out sick."

"*Sick?* Are you sure, Connor? Gypsie has never missed a day at work since she was hired. If anything, she's at this damn place more than she should be."

"Well, according to Rebecca, she came in briefly this morning and said she was going to take a few days off because she wasn't feeling well and needed to go to the doctor. Then she went into the mayor's office to put something important on his desk. She left the keys to her office and file cabinet with Rebecca before she left."

Jeremiah didn't like the sound of what he'd just heard, but he had to play it cool with Connor because he was such an aggravating drama king. "Have Rebecca send out a memo postponing the staff meeting until tomorrow morning at ten."

"What about the parks and recreation situation?"

"It can wait, damn it! What's going to happen in twenty-four hours, Connor? The Olympics?"

"I'll tell her right away," he mumbled, backing out of the office.

Jeremiah picked up the phone and dialed Gypsie's cell phone number. They spoke so often on a daily basis that he knew the number by heart. He was surprised when the call went directly to voicemail. He hung up and dialed the land line at Josiah's house. Jeremiah's gut told him that something was off, but he had no idea what it was. He had slipped the note under Gypsie's bedroom door telling her that he needed to talk to her. He hoped she'd seen it. If not, Josiah was going to go off! He hung up the phone when he heard his brother's voice asking him to leave a message after the beep.

"What's going on with you, Gypsie?" Jeremiah asked out loud. "This is so unlike you."

He left his office and headed straight to Josiah's corporate suite. He rushed inside, flipped on the light, and spotted an envelope lying on top of a neat pile of papers. As he got closer, he noticed Gypsie's elegant penmanship covering it. He didn't hesitate to open the letter. It was what Josiah would want him to do. There were no secrets between them. It had been that way since the womb. Jeremiah read the letter quickly before he doubled back for a slow and thorough read.

"Ah, shit!"

"I have one more question, Dr. Poindexter. When will my daughters and I be able to visit Mink?"

"If your wife completes the thirty-day detox program successfully and without incident, she will be rewarded with a family weekend pass."

"What's that?" Mink asked.

"Your husband and your little girls will be allowed to visit you here on the compound, but you won't be able to leave. We will assign you one of our very comfortable cabins for lodging and meals. You must report to your normal meetings and appointments at the hospital throughout the day, and you will be tested for drugs each evening. The good thing is that all of your leisure time will be spent in the cabin or somewhere on our beautiful property with your family."

Josiah reached over and placed his hand on top of Mink's and squeezed. She looked at him and gave him a half smile with tears in her eyes. She reminded him of a frightened child, but he refused to fall prey to his emotions. The choice he had made to bring her to the facility had been made in love. Josiah would never do anything to hurt Mink intentionally.

"Promise me that you'll come and bring my babies, JoJo."

"Today is September the twenty-second. Gem, Treasure, and I will see you on October the twenty-second. That's two weeks before the election, but I'm willing to make the sacrifice."

"Whew!" Gypsie dropped the box of shoes in the middle of the living room and ran back to close the front door.

She was officially back home and unfortunately, unemployed. Her resignation wasn't official yet, but it would be in exactly two weeks. Hopefully, city hall's human resources department, under Josiah's scrutiny, would find someone efficient to replace her. Gypsie was sure that there were thousands of qualified candidates in Metro Atlanta and beyond that would jump at the opportunity to serve the mayor. It was a great job with good benefits. It had given her the experience she needed to shoot for a higher-ranking position in other government offices. Gypsie's dream was to become the chief of staff or chief advisor to a governor or a member of congress. Hell, she felt confident enough to lead the staff of the president of the United States. But for now, a girl was going to chill, update her résumé, and live off of the vacation time she had accrued while working at city hall. It had been a smart move to maintain perfect attendance on the job for an entire fiscal year.

Josiah slid on the backseat of the limo, happy to be back in the Peach State. His twenty-four-hour turn-around trip to Montana had taken its toll on him. Visions of him taking a hot shower and slipping under the cool, crisp sheets on his bed filled his weary eyes. But first, he needed to kiss his daughters even though they were sleeping. He just needed to see them, and then his heart would be content.

After leaving a very tearful Mink at the Serenity Springs Rehabilitation and Mental Health Center, Josiah became emotionally drained. They'd only had a few hours to sleep in their separate rooms at the fancy bread and breakfast inn that the center's staff had recommended before it was time for them to rise and start their day. An official tour of the city by a local councilman after Mink's official admission had proven to be a great idea. Montana was beautiful and spacious. Its mountains and wide open ranges under a crystal blue sky made a man feel closer to God. By late afternoon, Josiah's faith in God had been renewed. Mink would make a full recovery, their marriage would be restored, and his political career would flourish beyond his childhood dreams.

"JoJo, I've been calling you forever. Why the hell didn't you pick up?"

"J, I'm tired, horny, and depressed. My phone was on silent because I was rolling with the president of White Sulphur Spring's city council all day. And you know I couldn't have my phone on in flight. I forgot to turn it on until just now. Is something wrong? What's up?"

"*What's up?* You no longer have an AA or childcare provider because Gypsie resigned from both jobs. And the parks and recreation director—"

"Whoooa! Whoooa! Whoooa! I need you to rewind. Who's looking after Gem and Treasure?"

"Miss Gladys is there tonight and tomorrow, but Gypsie isn't coming back, JoJo. I'll give the girl credit, though. She did make arrangements for your kids before she took off."

"What the hell happened, J? I haven't been gone a full twenty-four hours yet, but I'm returning home to an incomplete staff at the office and on the home front? I thought you were holding me down."

"I am on my belly for you, JoJo! But I ain't responsible for your fuckups, man! You're in love with your heroin-queen wife, but while she was out bingeing for the fucking trillionth time, you caught feelings for your cute little AA. And, naturally, she's crushing on you too because she was running your crib and taking care of your daughters like she was *Mrs. Bishop*. If I were to lock you and Gypsie up in a room and throw away the key, y'all would fuck each other's brains out like a couple of dogs in heat. I swear!"

"What the hell does that have to do with anything? You need to start making sense to me right now, J!"

"I don't know what happened! Hell, I'm just as confused as you are! I dropped Gypsie a note telling her we needed to talk, and the next thing I knew she had resigned. I'm guessing that her secret feelings for you got the best of her, and she bailed out. I can't say I blame her, JoJo. The girl has a right to protect her heart."

"I *never* touched Gypsie, and I had no intention to. Have I thought about it? Hell yeah! I would love to tap that ass. I'm a *man*. But I fight the temptation every time I look at her because I'm married, and I still love my wife."

"So you've never even come close to going for it?"

Josiah hesitated. He did *not* want to have this conversation with Jeremiah. And he would bet his annual salary that Nelson was listening. He sat up and pushed the button to raise the privacy window in the back of the limo.

"I'll admit that I've come pretty damn close a few times."

"I knew it!"

Jeremiah's rumbling laughter filled Josiah's ear, and it pissed him off. "Go to hell, J."

"Don't get mad with me because you have a wife and a fantasy boo." He cracked up all over again.

"That's not what I see when I look at Gypsie at all," Josiah told his brother with all sincerity. "She's a very smart, ambitious, gorgeous young woman who has a promising future ahead of her in politics. Her sense of humor is quirky, but I get it, and it makes me laugh— *hard*. I enjoy her cooking, and she fixes my coffee perfectly every time." Josiah felt his heartbeat accelerate. His palms became sweaty out of the blue. "One day she's going to be a wonderful mother, J. I can tell that by the way she takes care of my little princesses. I just hope that the man who'll father Gypsie's children will be worthy of her. She deserves a devoted husband who will love and cherish her for life."

"Whoever wins her heart will be one lucky man. Ain't no doubt about it."

"Do you know her address, J?"

"No. Why do you need it?"

"I want to talk to Gypsie face-to-face. She can be replaced at city hall, but I don't want anyone but her living in my house, taking care of Gem and Treasure. They need stability, and that's what Gypsie has given them."

"Okay. Give me ten minutes, and I'll text you her address."

Chapter Twenty-three

"I may just come home for a visit and surprise my mom and dad. It would be nice to see both of my grandmas too. You, Fatimah, my cousins, and I could hang out at the clubs and the casinos. *Oooh!* I think I'll look for flights in the morning, TiTi. Don't tell anyone, though. I want to roll into town like a tidal wave. They won't know what hit them."

"Don't play with me, Blackbird."

"Who's playing? I'm seriously thinking about coming home for a couple of weeks since I'm an unemployed, good-for-nothing bum now," Gypsie giggled.

"I can't wait to see you. It seems like you've been gone forever."

"I know. I've been so busy with—"

The sound of the doorbell interrupted Gypsie and threw her off of her game. She looked at her watch. It was almost ten o'clock. She didn't have any friends in Atlanta because she worked all of the damn time, and she never went out.

"Was that your doorbell, Blackbird?"

"Yeah." Gypsie bit down on her bottom lip.

"Girl, is there something you forgot to tell me?"

"Of course not. You know me better than that."

The bell rang again, and Gypsie just stared at the door.

"Well, go see who it is. I'll stay on the phone just in case it's a crazy stalker."

Gypsie walked to the door and looked through the peephole. She nearly choked on air when she saw Josiah standing there looking like a tall glass of rich, double chocolate milk. Her mind went completely blank for a few seconds until she heard Tianji screaming in her ear.

"Blackbird! Who's at the damn door, girl?"

"It's the *mayor*," Gypsie whispered in total shock. "Should I let him in?"

"Hell yeah! I'm about to hang up. Call me in the morning *if* you can." Tianji went into a fit of laughter before she ended the call.

Gypsie pulled her oversized T-shirt over her leggings and took a deep, calming breath before she released the chain and unlocked the door. Josiah smiled at her the moment the door swung open, and she felt the earth tilt on its axis.

"Josiah, what are you doing here?"

"May I come in?"

Gypsie nodded and stepped aside to allow him into the apartment. "Can I offer you something to drink?"

"No, thank you. I'm fine for now. Let's sit down and talk, Gypsie."

"Okay."

Gypsie took a seat on the sofa, and Josiah sat so close to her that she felt his body heat. His firm thigh pressed against hers made it hard to take in air. No man had the right to be this damn fine and dripping with pure swag.

"Why did you resign from city hall and your position as caretaker for Gem and Treasure?"

"I had allowed myself to become too emotionally invested in your life. It was a big mistake that I'd never intended to happen, but it did. So I had to make the best decision for *me*. That's why I chose to remove myself from the situation entirely. I hope you understand."

"Gypsie, I want you just as much as you want me, but because I have such great respect for you, I'm not going to act on those feelings. I care too much about you to reduce you to a side piece or a mistress. You're too special for that. The only way I would ever get involved with you is if I were free to have you and *only* you in my life. Do you understand?"

"Yes, Josiah, I understand."

"I'm glad you do."

"Jeremiah said you flew to Montana last night."

"Yeah, I took Mink to another rehab center in the mountains near White Sulphur Springs. She'll be there for six months."

"I'll pray that she'll make a full recovery."

"That's very sweet of you, Gypsie."

"Thank you."

"You know what would make you even sweeter?"

"What?"

"If you would rescind your resignation at city hall and come back and help me with my girls, I'd crown you the sugar queen." He gave Gypsie a sexy half grin.

"I don't know about that, Josiah."

"Please come back, Gypsie. I need you, and the girls do too. They've grown accustomed to you. And God knows you're the best AA on the planet. Are you really going to make me look for a replacement in the middle of my reelection campaign? That's just cruel."

"Okay. I'll come back."

"Thank you so much." He kissed Gypsie on the cheek.

"You're welcome."

Josiah stood. "I'm one tired man. The turnaround trip wore me out. I've got to get home so I can rest. Come walk me to the door, please."

Gypsie followed Josiah to her front door. He unlocked it and opened it wide. He turned to face her, and her

"Yes, I do understand. We have romantic feelings for each other. It wasn't planned on my part or yours. It just happened. We spend a lot of time together on the job, and you basically live in my home. It's easy to understand how we connected."

"I'm so ashamed of myself. You're *married*. I had no business going there."

"What about *me?* I'm the guy wearing the ring, yet I was so close to crossing the line."

Gypsie was stunned by Josiah's blatant honesty, but she didn't show it. "But you didn't cross the line. *We* didn't. And now that your wife is back home, we never will."

"Mink isn't home, Gypsie."

"But I saw her with you last night in the den." *Damn it! Why did I say that?*

"You saw Mink at the house last night? I thought you were upstairs the entire time she was there."

"I was. Then I came downstairs to the den to look for the girls and—"

"And you saw us arguing. Were we that loud?"

Gypsie looked at Josiah as if his head were spinning on his neck like the girl in the *Exorcist* movie. "No, you weren't loud at all, and you two definitely were *not arguing*."

"Oh, Gypsie, I'm so sorry that you saw that, but it wasn't what you think."

"Hey, it's okay. You don't have to apologize to me for kissing your wife. I'm just your former AA and ex-nanny. You owe me no explanation or apology for anything."

"Yes, I do," Josiah insisted, placing his hand on top of Gypsie's. "The moment I realized you had feelings for me, I should've addressed it, but the timing was always off."

"And what would that conversation have sounded like, Josiah?"

heart made an energetic hip-hop move, but she maintained her composure.

"Please go over your notes for the Lovely Ladies of Atlanta luncheon tomorrow. NeNe Leakes and Dr. Bernice King will be there. Your opponent is expected to show his face as well."

"I'll have a cram session in the morning. I've got to shut my eyes tonight. Will you quiz me?"

"Of course, I will. Don't I always?"

"Yeah, you always have my back."

"Your mother expects you to pick her up at eleven o'clock. She's your date for the luncheon."

"I'll have the hottest date there. Thanks for the reminder." Josiah reached out and pulled Gypsie in for a warm embrace.

Loving the feel of being in his arms, she rested her head on his chest. Mink was one damn lucky woman. She didn't deserve Josiah, but she had him hooked and on lockdown. Who couldn't respect a man for loving his wife and standing by her side through hard times?

"Good night, Josiah." Gypsie found her voice. She lifted her head from his chest and looked into his eyes.

Josiah released her. "Good night." He kissed her forehead before he turned and walked away.

"Mayor Bishop! Mayor Bishop, how are you, sir?" Charmaine Lomax greeted Josiah, approaching him with her hand extended.

"I'm well, Mrs. Lomax. How are you?" Josiah shook her offered hand.

"I'm fine. I was hoping that your lovely wife would be with you this afternoon. I haven't seen her since the Unity Gala."

"Mink isn't feeling well today, so I brought this beautiful lady with me as my date." Josiah wrapped his arm lovingly around his mother's shoulders. "This is my mother, Myrlie Bishop. Mama, meet Charmaine Lomax. She's the wife of Dendrick Lomax, my opponent."

"Hello."

"It's a pleasure to meet you, Mrs. Bishop."

"The pleasure is mine, dear."

The two women smiled at each other and shook hands.

Mrs. Lomax returned her attention to Josiah. "Will your wife and daughters attend the children's tea and art show next weekend?"

"Um . . . yes . . . Yes, they'll be there."

"Great. I look forward to seeing her and the girls. Please say hello to her for me and tell her to get well soon."

"I'll do that."

Charmaine walked away.

"She seems nice, but she's a little too nosy for my taste. Why is she so interested in Mink?"

"I don't know, Mama."

"And why did tell her that lie, JoJo? You know Mink will not attend that event next weekend."

Josiah shrugged his shoulders. "I don't know. She caught me off guard."

"Well, get ready to tell another lie next weekend when Miss Nosy asks about Mink again." Mrs. Bishop's jaw dropped suddenly. "Oh my goodness! There's NeNe Leakes! I'm going to say hello."

"Frances, there's something fishy going on with the mayor and his wife," Charmaine told her assistant.

"What do you mean, ma'am?"

"She seldom makes public appearances with him. The last time I saw them together was at the Unity Gala a couple of months ago. She's the first lady of Atlanta. She should be more visible, especially with the election right around the corner. It's just weird." Charmaine watched Josiah and his mother pose for a picture with NeNe Leakes. "I want you to do some snooping around. Ask Leon to help you. Find out what's up with Mink Bishop. I want to know why she's hiding out from the campaign trail."

"I'll get on the case right away, Mrs. Lomax."

Chapter Twenty-four

Gypsie rushed into the house behind Gem and Treasure carrying two grocery bags. She headed straight to the kitchen, dropped the bags on the center island, and grabbed the phone from its cradle.

"This is the Bishop residence."

"You sound like you've been running."

Gypsie smiled at the sound of Josiah's voice. "I was racing like Allyson Felix to catch the phone."

"Since I was in meetings all day long outside of the office, I only got to see you once in passing. Sooo . . . I decided to call and check up on you. How was your day?"

"It was long and stressful, but I won't complain. I'm about to check Gem's homework and quiz Treasure on her new sight words. After that, I'll prepare dinner."

"Don't bother to cook, Gypsie. Go ahead and study with the girls, and then I want the three of you to meet J and me for dinner. We have three hours before I'll have to make an appearance at a mixer at the Depot. I'm starving right now, so let's meet at Houston's on Peachtree in an hour. That's one of the girls' favorite restaurants."

"That sounds like a plan. We'll see you in a little while."

"Cool."

Gypsie replaced the phone in its cradle and went to find the girls. More than likely, they were upstairs in their bedroom changing from their school uniforms into the casual outfits she had placed on their beds this morning.

"I have a surprise for you," Gypsie announced with a big smile on her face as she entered the bedroom. "Your daddy and Uncle J want us to meet them at a restaurant for dinner."

"Are we going to McDonald's?"

"No, Treasure, we're not going to McDonald's, darling."

"I know! We're going to eat *pizza*."

"No, we're not going to a pizzeria either. Your dad thought that you two wouldn't mind eating at *Houston's* this evening."

"Yesss! We love Houston's! Don't we, Treasure?"

"Yeah!"

"Okay, let's go over your homework and sight words before we leave. Come on, little divas."

"Where's Uncle J, Daddy? I thought he was coming to eat dinner with us."

"He got stuck in traffic coming from Papa and Nana's house. He went to visit them after work, and now, he's having a hard time getting here."

Gem poked out her bottom lip and folded her arms across her chest, pouting.

"Don't be mad, darling," Gypsie whispered in her ear. "We can call him before you go to bed tonight."

"Okay."

"There's a new girl in my class," Treasure announced. "Her name is Tamalia, and she wants to be my BFF, but Zion and Karrington said no. They don't want any new friends. But Leilani likes her, and I do too. We want to be her friend."

"Then you should be her friend, sweetie. The more friends you have, the happier you'll be."

"Okay, Daddy. Tamalia is my new BFF, and when she grows up, she wants to be like Michelle Obama and

Beyoncé, just like me. She's going to be like Oprah and Simone Biles too because they rock!"

Josiah and Gypsie laughed at Treasure's excitement.

"When I grow up, I'm going to be like you, Miss Gypsie. You're smart and beautiful. And you wear pretty clothes too," Gem smiled.

"Aw, thanks, darling. I appreciate your kind words."

Josiah, Gypsie, Gem, and Treasure continue talking and laughing as they enjoyed their meals until it was time for them to part ways.

"Well, ladies, it's time for me to go. I have to attend an event in thirty minutes. Let me settle the check, and I'll walk you to the car."

After the server returned to the table with Josiah's debit card and receipt, he left the young woman a hefty tip. Then he guided Gypsie and his daughters toward the restaurant's exit. A cool stream of air wrapped around Gypsie out of the blue, and she shivered. She looked around at the many patrons scattered about. For some strange reason, she felt like she was being watched.

Frances ducked behind her upheld menu just when the mayor's young date scanned the area where she'd been seated comfortably watching them during their entire meal. His daughters seemed very fond of the cute little tenderoni. Was she a relative? And where was their mother? Mrs. Bishop was always missing in action. Mrs. Lomax was dead-on the money. Something *was* fishy between the mayor and his wife.

Frances couldn't believe her luck. She was just about to leave the restaurant after enjoying an appetizer platter and a strawberry daiquiri, when, lo and behold, Mayor Bishop entered the establishment to much fanfare. When she realized the hostess had seated him at a table for six,

Frances waited to leave, expecting him to be joined by his family. She was shocked when she saw the very attractive and much-younger woman approach the table with his daughters. If one didn't know better, one would've thought they were a family. They seemed quite familiar with one another.

Now, Frances was on a mission to identify the mystery woman, and then she needed to find out where Atlanta's first lady was hiding out, and why. She scanned the few pictures she'd snapped of the happy group with her cell phone. They'd been none the wiser as she snapped several shots of them while they laughed and chatted over their meals. The pictures would be a central part of the investigation, but she needed Leon to do the legwork for her. But first, Frances had to make her first official report to Mrs. Lomax and send her the secret pictures. She smirked as she sent the brief text message with the pictures attached before she dialed the number.

"Hello?"

"Mrs. Lomax, this is Frances. I just sent you a few pictures that you're going to find quite interesting."

"Mmm . . . I'll look at them as soon as I get home. I don't text or read text messages while I'm driving. I just left Lennox Square Mall doing a little retail therapy. Ugh! I'm so damn tired of this campaign. I don't care if Denny wins or not at this point. I just want my life back. Or I could hide out like Mink Bishop does," Charmaine laughed.

"I think she's doing more than just hiding out, ma'am. I believe she has left the scene. Once you see the pictures, you'll understand what I'm talking about. You'll call me later, I'm sure."

"Yes, I'll be in touch."

Frances ended her conversation with her boss feeling satisfied with her work. She was more determined now than ever before to crack the Mink Bishop case.

It was a rainy night in Georgia, and along with the heavy downpour came a feeling of melancholy descending upon Josiah. As the limo made its way through the city over the wet asphalt, he dreaded going home to a dark, quiet house. What he looked forward to even less was spending another night in a cold, lonely bed. Weeks of separation had forced him to adjust to celibacy and solitude in the bedroom, but Josiah would never get used to the lack of intimacy. There was a big difference between the two scenarios.

If sex was the only thing he wanted, he could've easily solved that problem by now. Women were willing to throw their panties at him every day, anytime of the day, anyplace, and anyway he wanted it. But that's not what Josiah wanted, and it damn sure wasn't what he needed. He needed some TLC in the worst way. And that didn't necessarily include *sex*. He craved a deep connection with someone he cared for who could reciprocate his feelings. He would gladly settle for a kind word or a soft gesture. Every good man deserved to be greeted with a caring, feminine touch and a toe-curling kiss when they returned home after a long day at the office. He also needed a listening ear to hear his concerns, fears, disappointments, and accomplishments at the end of the day. A delicious, home-cooked meal, a steamy shower, and wild, nut-busting sex would be the perfect way for any upstanding brotha to wind down at nightfall. But Josiah had only been privy to food and showers. And most nights, those showers were cold ones.

Josiah thanked Nelson for working late when the car stopped in front of the house. Then he ventured out into the rainy night without even opening his umbrella to protect him from the chilly raindrops. His thoughts drifted to Gypsie as he turned the key in the lock. If he were a low-down, two-timing dog, he would've propositioned her by now. And the way she looked at him sometimes was evidence that she would have no qualms about becoming his lover. But decency was more important than pleasure, so Josiah refused to go down that road.

"Good afternoon. Mayor Bishop's office. How may I help you?"

"Hello. My name is um . . . *Lisa Jones,* and I work for the *Atlanta Journal Constitution.* I'm trying to reach the first lady of Atlanta for an interview about her role as a political wife, mother, and her plans for her life after politics."

"If you'll give me your name and telephone number, I'll make sure that Mrs. Bishop receives your message," Gypsie lied smoother than whipped cream.

"Can't you just give me her direct number so that I can reach her right away?"

"I'm sorry. I can't do that, ma'am. The mayor and his wife have private telephone numbers, and I'm certain you know why. If you wish to speak with Mrs. Bishop, you'll have to leave your name, number, and a brief message with me or any other member of the mayor's staff. Then Mrs. Bishop will return your call at her earliest convenience *if* she's interested in sitting for an interview with you."

"You sound like a damn voicemail recording!" The woman ended the call abruptly.

Gypsie stared at the receiver in her hand, unable to believe how unprofessionally the woman had acted. But what disturbed her more than that was her interest in Mrs. Bishop. It was important that she alert Josiah right away, but he wasn't in his office. He wasn't expected to return to city hall until tomorrow morning. Gypsie stood quickly from her chair and rounded her desk.

"Cover me," she instructed Rebecca as she made a mad dash toward Jeremiah's office.

Without knocking, Gypsie burst inside his private work space.

Chapter Twenty-five

"Yeah, you know I'm going to tear that ass up tonight."

"Jeremiah!" Gypsie blurted out on a gasp and closed the door behind her.

"Whoooa!" He swiveled around in his chair with the phone pressed to his ear. "Um . . . Hey, let me hit you back later. Something just came up." Jeremiah ended the call. "What's up, baby girl? Sit down. You look like you just saw a zombie or something."

Gypsie dropped down in a chair like a ragdoll. "A reporter just called. She wants to interview *Mrs. Bishop*. I asked her to leave her name, number, and a message, but she got defensive and hung up. She sounded persistent. What if she—"

"She won't find out a damn thing, no matter what. I'll send out a memo to the entire staff, reminding everyone that all of JoJo's contact information, including his address, is confidential and should not be shared with the public. And I'll speak with the head of security in his community. No reporters or unfamiliar individuals will be allowed access to his house. Does that make you feel better?"

Gypsie nodded her head and closed her eyes, clearly shaken.

Her concern for Josiah blew Jeremiah's mind! She was in full protective mode. Only a woman in love would be so upset and ready to go to war to defend a man's privacy. Josiah didn't realize how lucky he was. He was still stuck on Mink's disloyal, strung-out ass.

"He needs to know about the phone call, Jeremiah," Gypsie whispered after some time.

"Yeah, we definitely have to put him on alert. Let *me* tell him, though. You can follow up with details later on, but I'll break the news to him this evening. Okay?"

"Okay."

"Hey, everybody. My name is Mink B., and I'm an addict."

"Hello, Mink B.," the small group of people seated in a circle responded in unison.

Mink took a deep breath as she studied the faces of her peers sitting around her. It was the first time she had ever spoken in a group session since she'd been a resident at the rehab facility. She had been fairly open and somewhat honest in her individual therapy sessions, but she'd chosen to be silent in the presence of the other residents until now.

"This is my fourth time in in-patient treatment in two and a half years. I don't know how many times I've gone to intensive outpatient treatment, but I'm the queen of Narcotics Anonymous. Hell, I can recite the twelve steps, twelve traditions, and half of AA's *Big Book* by heart."

Everyone, including the clinician, laughed.

"Yeah, I know the entire program like the back of my hand, but I haven't *really* been working it. I've been bullshitting my sponsors, fellow addicts, my husband, and myself. I was simply going through the motions and talking the talk, but I was never completely honest with anyone, including *Mink*. I didn't want anybody to know that I had been bullied and verbally abused as a child and teenager by my peers. Yeah, I was an army brat, and no matter where my father was stationed, I never seemed to fit in. I tried like hell to blend in, but I was always a misfit." Mink broke down in tears.

The clinician snatched a few tissues from a box on her desk and walked over to Mink. She offered them to her, and when she accepted them, the woman wrapped her arm around her drooping shoulders.

After she wiped away her tears, Mink took a few cleansing breaths and released them slowly. "In California, I was a country bumpkin. I was labeled a whore in South Carolina because of the way I dressed. Hell, who the fuck knew that wearing DKNY was against the law? Anyway, we moved to Texas next. Those motherfucking white kids called me a nigger to my face all day, every day! They considered me *too* black, but in Upstate New York, I wasn't black enough according to the African American army brats. And in Germany, I was treated like constipated shit because I was just as smart, if not *smarter,* than those kids were. Then I was betrayed by the one person who I *thought* truly cared about me, and it cost me a lot mentally. I really lost more than I was ready to lose. And my parents were a huge part of it. My dad's military career and his desire to climb the ranks were more important than me and what I wanted. After that, I had an emotional meltdown.

"By the time I returned to the States for college, I was *fucked up*. I didn't know who the hell I was, or where I belonged until I met my knight in shining armor. I attached myself to him for mental security and held on for dear life. I rode the tidal wave of love with him to help him fulfill his dreams while forgetting all about what I wanted to be. I didn't know how to get off of the wave to find myself. I felt trapped in his world, but I didn't have the heart to tell him. So the first opportunity I was offered to escape my unhappy existence, I took it. I used heroin for the first time in a public restroom, and I loved the brief getaway. Just for a little while, I wasn't a wife or a mother or a misfit. And my greatest sin wasn't dangling in my damn face, taunting me. I was free even though it was only temporary."

After a few moments of silence, members of the group thanked Mink for sharing her story. She felt a bit of relief for revealing a portion of her life, but the untold was still buried deep within her soul. As the meeting continued with more stories from other residents and readings from the clinician, Mink's thoughts drifted into the past.

"Mink, are you drunk, baby?" Josiah asked, approaching her at the bar.

"Just a little bit, JoJo." She giggled and took a small sip of Merlot. She wasn't really drinking the wine. Gayla had advised her to take a few sips so that the smell of alcohol on her breath would throw her husband off from the real source of her high.

Josiah removed the glass of wine from Mink's loose grip and placed it on the bar counter. "It's time to go, baby. You've thrown back one too many. You would get wasted on your first night out in a while." Josiah laughed and helped Mink stand from the bar stool. He grabbed her beaded evening bag and guided her away.

Mink looked back at Gayla Fordham who was even more smashed than she was. But she managed to raise her hand to her ear with a crooked smile on her face, gesturing for her new fellow druggie to give her a call. Mink nodded in response, assuring Gayla that she would reach out. And she would. . . . Many, many times.

The sound of chairs scraping against the floor and bodies moving zapped Mink back to the present. She blinked a few times and looked around. The other residents were up and joining hands to form the traditional circle to recite the Lord's Prayer, which would terminate the meeting. Mink got up and eased between two women she'd been relatively friendly with in passing. She closed her eyes and prayed with the rest of the group. As soon as the prayer ended, she made a beeline out of the room and headed down the hall to find her favorite orderly. She'd obviously spoken too much in the meeting because the baby whimpers had returned, and it made her anxious.

"*Pssst* . . . You looking for me?"

Mink whipped around quickly and smiled when she saw Greg, the orderly. She looked around to make sure they were alone before she rushed toward him. "Yeah, I was looking for you. You got something for me?"

"Maybe." He smirked and licked his lips.

"Don't fuck with me right now. I'm crashing. You know I'm good for it."

Greg scanned the area around them before he reached inside his pocket and removed a tiny plastic bag and stuffed it in Mink's cleavage. He grabbed his crotch and smiled. "I get off at five. I'll double back and see you at eight."

"But that's meditation time. I can't miss that or I'll lose privilege points."

"Sometimes you gotta make sacrifices to get what you want. You ain't new to this, baby. So, what's up?"

Mink blew air from her cheeks in frustration. "I'll be in my room pretending to be sick."

"Yeah, that's what I thought."

"Now unto Him that is able to keep you from falling and to present you faultless before the presence of His glory with exceeding joy. To the only wise God our Savior, be glory and majesty, dominion and power, both now and ever. Amen. Consider yourselves dismissed. Fellowship with your brothers and sisters before you depart from the house of God."

Myrlie watched her husband, Reverend Paul Bishop, as he made his way to the front doors of the church to greet his flock. Something was bothering him. The Holy Ghost had shown her during Bible study and prayer meeting. The good reverend had taught a wonderful Bible lesson, and the fifty or so church members in attendance had received it enthusiastically. But throughout his soul-stirring message, Myrlie saw something in her husband's eyes that troubled her spirit.

She had been in love with the boy, who everyone knew would become a preacher like his father, since she was 10 years old, and he was 13. They had courted all of their teen years and through college and then married shortly after that. He was her rock when their 3-month-old daughter died in her arms of respiratory failure two years before they celebrated the birth of their identical twin boys. Myrlie and her husband, whom she and her sons affectionately called Rev, were best friends and soul mates. That's why she knew by just looking at him that he was worried about something.

Myrlie handed the few Bibles she had gathered from the pews to a passing usher and walked slowly toward her husband. He looked at her and smiled before he turned to shake hands with one of his deacons and peck the man's wife on her cheek. Myrlie began to shake hands and hug members before they left the building alongside Rev. They chatted with their faithful Wednesday-night followers until the last soul had left. Myrlie watched Rev lock the double doors and secure the padlock.

She gently placed her hand on his back and immediately felt his muscles flex with tension under her touch. "What's the matter, honey? And before you lie and tell me *nothing,* remember we're in the house of the Lord. I'm not a weakling, you know. I'm tough, and I can handle anything. I whipped Peggy Finney's behind good when I was in the seventh grade after she kissed your cheek at the Sunday school picnic."

Myrlie and her husband of forty-two years laughed hysterically and embraced. She squeezed Rev tightly, silently praying that her strength would sustain him through whatever was bothering him.

"A spiritual storm is coming, Myrlie Anne. God didn't tell me when, but it *is* coming. Josiah is in trouble, but he doesn't even know it. He's a good boy. God knows he is. We love him and Jeremiah more than we love ourselves, but he made a bad mistake when he married Mink."

"I was never very fond of her either, but Josiah just had to have her." Myrlie dabbed at her tears with her fingertips. "What can I do to help my baby, honey?"

"Call Josiah and ask about the grandbabies and the reelection campaign. You can even ask about Mink, God bless her drug-addicted soul. Just talk to him, Myrlie Anne, but before you do, join your husband at the altar in prayer."

Chapter Twenty-six

After entering the dark house, Josiah dropped his briefcase carelessly on the floor and headed for the stairs. He was exhausted and slightly tipsy after a few too many shots of Don Julio tequila. Once his last political function of the night had ended, Jeremiah hit him with the news that a reporter was snooping for a scoop on Mink. Hearing some shit like that was enough to drive any sober man to drink. But thank God for Nelson Brown, his loyal driver. The man was a godsend. An ex-convicted armed robber, who was now a faithful member of Fresh Anointing Pentecostal Church, he'd insisted on working late so that he could deliver his boss home safely. Jeremiah had been in a hurry to get across town to spend time with one of his *playmates*.

Josiah pressed a series of numbers on the lighted keypad located on the wall at the bottom of the staircase, activating the security system. He planned to go straight to his girls' room to sneak a peek at them as they slept before retiring to the master suite for a quick shower. He was sure he wouldn't have a problem falling asleep after that.

Just as he placed his foot on the first stair on his way up, Gypsie appeared on the landing above. "Josiah!" she greeted him, running down the stairs.

Absentmindedly, he gathered Gypsie in an intimate embrace, lifting her off of her feet. Her soft curves, bearing a subtle floral scent, fit perfectly against his tired muscles. Their bodies locked together perfectly and securely like the final two pieces of an unfinished puzzle. When their lips first touched, Josiah felt his spirit take flight. Sweet Jesus! He felt born again the moment his tongue connected with Gypsie's. She moaned out her pleasure as their tongues indulged in a daring dance—exciting, enticing, and *erotic.*

Josiah instantly got caught up and was slowly losing control. The humongous bulge between his thighs was harder than Stone Mountain as it pressed into Gypsie's midsection. His hands found their way to her round bottom as he lowered her to her feet. He gently pressed her back against the wall and continued exploring her body with curious and greedy fingertips. Quickly, Josiah gathered the flowing skirt of Gypsie's caftan, lifting it inches above her knees. He caressed her inner thighs and spread them apart while still devouring her mouth with sizzling, juicy kisses. He took great joy in branding it thoroughly with his hungry tongue.

Muffled buzzing and a vibrating sensation robbed them of a very passionate exchange. Against his wishes, Josiah broke the kiss and took a backward step. His eyes never left Gypsie's as he struggled to regain control of his breathing. He touched his breast pocket, realizing his phone was ringing. He removed it and answered quickly.

"Hello?" he mumbled in a labored breath. Then he reached out and rubbed his thumb gently across Gypsie's swollen bottom lip.

"JoJo, did Mama wake you up, baby?"

"N-no . . . no . . . um . . . No, ma'am. I just walked in the door."

"Well, you were on my mind, so I decided to give you a call to check up on you and my grandbabies. How're y'all doing?"

"We're doing fine, Mama. How are you and Rev getting along?"

"Never mind us. We've got each other. I take care of Rev, and Rev takes care of me." Myrlie paused, and Josiah became agitated. "Mama is worried about you because you don't have anybody to take care of *you*."

"I'm okay. My schedule is full all of the time, so I'm always busy. The girls are in good hands with Gypsie, so there's no need to worry about them."

"How is *Mink?*"

Josiah allowed the question to float in the air unanswered for a few seconds as his gaze bore deeply into Gypsie's lust-filled eyes. Guilt hovered over him like a dark cloud after his mother mentioned his wife. There was no doubt that if she hadn't called, he and Gypsie would be upstairs in his bed butt-naked, saturated with sweat, and doing a slow, vertical dance under the sheets.

"JoJo, did you hear me, baby? How is Mink doing in rehab?"

"I'm not sure, Mama. I haven't spoken to her."

"And why not? Doesn't she call Gem and Treasure?"

Gypsie pushed her body away from the wall and brushed past Josiah. He reached out for her hand, but she pulled away and ran up the stairs.

"Mama," Josiah said, running behind Gypsie. He stumbled on his chase and fell. He winced in pain and rubbed his shin as he stood from his fall. "It's been a long day, and I'm really tired. I'll call you in the morning."

Josiah ended the call before his mother had a chance to respond. He hopped up the steps, missing a few on the way. He ran straight to Gypsie's bedroom and banged on the door hard several times.

"Go away, Josiah! I can't face you right now. I'm sorry about what just happened. Can we pretend like it never happened, *please?*"

Josiah rested his forehead against the closed door and exhaled. "But it *did* happen, Gypsie, and I'm not sorry about it. Just let me in so we can talk."

Deafening silence was Gypsie's reply, and it infuriated Josiah down to the bone. But he had no one to blame except himself. Lust was *powerful*. He had allowed his emotions and need for affection to weaken him. And above that, he already harbored genuine feelings for Gypsie in his heart, and they were growing stronger every day. He was in a complicated situation, and it would only get worse as long as Gypsie remained in his house. But he couldn't fire her because he needed her to take care of his daughters until Mink made a full recovery—*if* she ever made a full recovery.

Josiah left the hallway and headed for his bedroom. Once inside, he looked in the mirror and saw the face of one terribly distressed dude. Mink, her addiction, the care of his daughters, city hall, the reelection campaign, and his forbidden attraction to Gypsie—all of it was weighing him way down low. He was having a hard time keeping his head above water. He needed a breakthrough before he ended up having a *breakdown*.

His first order of business in the morning would be a long conversation with Gypsie. It was more than necessary for them to clear the air. Then he'd ask Jeremiah to book flights to Montana for him and the girls to visit Mink in two weeks. In the midst of his crazy schedule over the last few weeks, the conversation with Gypsie had fallen through the cracks, and he refused to ask her to book the flight for him now since they had come so close to falling overboard into dangerous, lust-filled waters tonight. His mother had saved him from destroying his life with an affair. Josiah knew beyond a shadow of a doubt that if he had made love to Gypsie tonight, he would make love to her every night for the rest of his life.

***

"So you were saved by the bell, huh, bruh?" Jeremiah replaced the dumbbell on the rack and sat down on the bench.

"Yep. Mama called in the nick of time. It was like she knew I was about to do something sinful and stupid."

Jeremiah smirked at his brother. "I bet you the *Lord* told Mama to call you so you wouldn't fall into temptation. You know how she and Rev are always praying and talking to Jesus. That's how we got caught leaving that motel prom night with Rasha Colson and Venus Bell. I'm glad they didn't get the revelation from the Lord until *after* we had done the deed."

"Well, I'm happy the Lord worked faster last night than he did prom night." Josiah raised his legs in a perfectly straight, horizontal line in front of him as he pumped iron on the thigh lift. "Man, it would've been the worst thing I could've ever done to Gypsie. I ain't going out like that."

"I understand. You're still keeping the light burning for your wife."

Josiah nodded and continued pumping his legs while sweat poured down his face.

"For your sake, in the end, I hope Mink is worth every sorrow she's ever caused you and all the blessings she's blocked from coming your way."

"Are these figures correct, Mayor Bishop?"

Every eye in the room zoomed to the head of the conference table as they waited for the reply of the man in charge.

"Why would you ask such a question, Connor? Jeremiah hired three independent accounting firms to crunch the numbers, and the results were almost identical. The numbers you see there are an average of the three, which is standard."

"Well, the figures look a little inflated to me."

"*Inflated?*" Jeremiah snapped. "I've never had to inflate anything in my damn life just to impress someone. I wouldn't risk the city's financial stability under my brother's leadership either, especially in the middle of a reelection campaign. Get a damn clue."

"The figures are fine, Connor. Trust me," Josiah interjected. "Compared to other cities the size of Atlanta with similar demographics and business makeup, the report is on the mark."

"If you say so. . . ."

Jeremiah threw lethal daggers at Connor with his eyes. "He *does* say so, and I do too."

Josiah looked around the conference table, trying to gauge the mood of his staff members. He paused when he looked at Gypsie, and she lowered her eyes to the iPad sitting on the table in front of her. "We will follow up on the convention and tourism report tomorrow and the airport project as well. If all minds are clear, this meeting is adjourned. Gypsie, I need you to stay, please. Thank you."

"This is not the time or place, Josiah," Gypsie whispered as soon as the last person had left the room and closed the door.

"I can't go through the rest of the day with this situation on my mind. What happened last night was wrong, but I have no regrets. It won't happen again, though. I promise."

"Didn't we have this same conversation before at my apartment? You promised that we wouldn't get involved unless you could be with me and *only* me."

"Yes, but we're not involved, Gypsie."

"Like hell we aren't! I felt it last night, Josiah. It was *real*. You can fool yourself if you want to, but I *never* lie to myself. Just remember wherever your heart, mind, and body go, so will your soul soon follow. Although we didn't commit *the act* last night, your body was fully committed to me, as were your heart and mind. But you've allowed your soul to be trapped where it doesn't belong for too long."

"Are you suggesting that my commitment to my wife and our daughters is a mistake, Gypsie? Do you believe that Mink's drug problem is justification for me to leave her for you?"

"No, I don't believe that you should leave your wife for me or any other woman because of her drug dependency. If you can walk away from your marriage to be with me, it'll be just a matter of time before you'll dump me for another woman."

Josiah frowned in confusion. "Then what do you want from me, Gypsie? Just tell me."

"It doesn't matter what I want from you, Josiah, because you can't give it to me. But I understand, and I accept it. Just stop sending me mixed signals."

"I'm sorry. I honestly didn't realize I was doing that."

"Well, you have, Josiah, but I've got the perfect solution for our situation. From here on out, everything will be *strictly business* between us. I will remain your administrative assistant until after the campaign, at which time I'll submit my resignation. I love Gem and Treasure very much, and they are attached to me. Therefore, I'll continue to take care of them in your home until Mrs. Bishop returns. In the meantime, I promise not ever to allow my feelings for you to cause me to act unladylike again."

Chapter Twenty-seven

Jeremiah did a double take and almost choked on the sip of cognac trickling down his throat. He would recognize the pretty smile on that flawless face anywhere. It was *her* all right, and Jeremiah was shocked shitless. He stood from his seat at the bar and crossed the restaurant, heading straight to the table for two so that he could be as nosy as hell and messy.

"Good evening, Miss Robinson. I thought you'd be working this evening since your boss is at the Manchester fashion show."

Gypsie took a sip of water after she looked at Jeremiah for a few seconds like he had three eyes. He could tell from her facial expression that she was embarrassed.

"Miss Gladys is covering my duties this evening while I enjoy some personal time off. Do you have a problem with that, Mr. Bishop?"

"Of course, I don't. I just thought—"

The gentleman who Gypsie was having dinner with coughed loudly, cutting Jeremiah off.

"You better drink some water for that cough, bruh."

"Jeremiah, this is Preston Collier."

"I know who he is. He's the dude from the accounting department at city hall."

"I'm the *manager* of the accounting department's division for city employees."

"Oh yeah? So I guess you know how much money I make, huh?"

"Jeremiah!" Gypsie snapped. "Is there anything else we need to discuss right now?"

"Nah, we're good. I'll see you at the office in the morning."

Jeremiah grinned at Gypsie and shook his head before he turned and left the table. He walked out of the restaurant, removed his cell phone from his pocket, and hit the number two on his speed dial list.

"What's up, J?"

"Guess who I just saw at Pappadeaux."

"Who?"

"Gypsie."

"So what? She asked for the evening off so she could do some personal stuff. Miss Gladys is holding down the fort for her."

"*Personal stuff,* you say?"

"Yeah. What's up, J? You know I'm at an event. It ain't cool for me to be on a phone call instead of mixing it up with the crowd."

"Gypsie is on a *date* with one of the managers in the accounting department at city hall. I think his name is Clowers or Collins or something like that."

"Are you taking about *Preston Collier?*"

"Yeah, that's the one." Jeremiah unlocked his car door and slid into the driver's seat.

"I had no idea Gypsie was seeing anyone, especially not some guy from city hall."

"Well, now you know."

Gypsie exited her office a couple of steps ahead of Preston and ran directly into Josiah. She broke her stride and stood like a statue in place with her heart racing. For a few seconds, she and Josiah stared each other down in silence. Gypsie lowered her eyes and noticed the thin stack of papers in his hand.

"I was about to go to lunch. Do you need to speak with me about something before I leave, Mayor Bishop?"

"Yes, I do. It'll only take a minute, though."

Gypsie turned around to face Preston. "I'll meet you in the waiting area in a few minutes."

"Okay." He looked at Josiah and extended his hand. "Mayor Bishop, how are you, sir?"

"I'm fine," he answered flatly, shaking the offered hand.

After Preston walked away, Josiah reached around Gypsie and opened her office door. Then he stepped aside and allowed her to enter first, and he followed her. Gypsie's body jerked involuntarily when the door slammed shut. She spun around swiftly and looked into a pair of dark eyes filled with anger. She swallowed hard.

"Why are you running around with that guy all of a sudden, Gypsie? You had dinner with him last night, and now you're about to go to lunch with him? What's going on?"

"What I do, and who I choose to do it with in my personal time is not your concern, *Mayor Bishop*. If you need to discuss something with me regarding work or your daughters, let's do it. If not, I'd like to go to lunch now."

Josiah wiped his hand down his face in what appeared to be frustration.

Gypsie smiled inwardly, totally amused by his jealousy. *I ain't your wife, buddy. Don't get it twisted.*

"I wanted to go over a purchasing proposal with you before I share it with the staff and city council. It can wait until after your lunch date with your *boyfriend*, I suppose."

"Okay. I'll be ready to look at it as soon as I get back."

Josiah nodded and stuffed his free hand inside his pocket.

Gypsie walked past him and left her office, strutting like a supermodel on a Parisian runway. *He has some damn nerve to question me about who I spend time with,* she thought. Josiah wasn't her father, and he damn sure wasn't her man. Therefore, he had no right to stick his nose into her private affairs. Besides, Preston was just a friend, although he wanted to be more. He had been begging Gypsie to go out with him for months, but she'd always turned him down because of her crazy schedule and lack of interest in him. But after a long conversation with her BFF, Tianji, she decided to step outside of her box and try something new. And she was happy about the choice she'd made. Of course, she didn't expect to make a love connection with Preston, and she had been totally honest from day one and told him as much. But she did enjoy the companionship and attention that he offered, so she would continue to go out with him as a friend.

"Daddy, why didn't Miss Gypsie come with us?"

"I gave her the day off, Gem."

"She's at home watching TV," Treasure clarified.

"That's right, sweetie. So it's just Daddy and his two princesses. We're going to go inside and sip tea, play games, and look at artwork with the other children and parents, okay?"

"Okay, Daddy." Gem grabbed Josiah's other hand.

The mayor and his daughters walked hand in hand toward the building's entrance. Judging by the many cars in the parking lot, a crowd had already assembled inside. Josiah and the girls were greeted by a throng of people the moment they stepped inside. They stopped and posed for several pictures. As they walked away, Josiah heard a female voice call his name.

"Mayor Bishop! Mayor Bishop!"

Josiah turned around and immediately cursed under his breath when he saw Charmaine Lomax making her way toward them. He looked down at Gem and Treasure and smiled before he faced his opponent's very pushy wife.

"Mrs. Lomax, it's nice to see you again," he fibbed.

"How are you, Mayor Bishop?"

"I'm fine. What about you?"

"Life is great. I was expecting to see your wife this afternoon."

Josiah looked around and noticed a clown nearby making animals out of balloons for the children. He kneeled down to speak to the girls. "Go and get in line so you can get a balloon animal from the clown. Daddy can see you from here. Go on now."

Gem and Treasure joined hands and hurried toward the line with their father watching them closely.

"Mink isn't coming today," he informed Mrs. Lomax. "She had a family emergency in Maryland, so she flew up the day before yesterday."

"I see. Well, please tell her that I asked about her, and I'm sorry I missed her *again*."

"I sure will."

"Well, I better go and find my husband and the kids. Goodbye."

Josiah waved and watched Mrs. Lomax sashay through the crowd in search of her family. An eerie feeling suddenly came over him, but he quickly shook it off. He went and joined Gem and Treasure in line.

After the Bishop girls received balloon animals from the clown, they got their faces painted by a woman dressed as a mermaid. Then they played musical chairs, watched a puppet show, and looked at all kinds of art. Afterward, they sat down for tea, crumpets, finger sandwiches, and an assortment of fresh fruit. While the children ate, the adults mingled. Josiah stood in the middle of a group of businessmen and a newspaper reporter discussing Atlanta's economic growth under his leadership. Though fully engaged in the conversation, he kept a sharp eye on his daughters the entire time. It wasn't easy, but his girls meant the world to him, so he would do anything to protect them.

Josiah realized that he had made a mistake by refusing Gypsie's help the moment Treasure got up from the table and walked toward him. His live-in nanny had offered to accompany him and the girls to the tea and art show, but his stubbornness had caused him to decline. Josiah was still in his feelings over her unexpected interest in Preston Collier, which was childish. Gypsie was a grown-ass woman, and she had every right to date any man she wanted to.

"Excuse me, everyone." Josiah stepped out of the huddle when Treasure approached them. He kneeled down. "What's the matter, princess?"

"I have to use the bathroom."

Damn it! Josiah looked around for a familiar face. The only person he recognized was Charmaine Lomax standing a few feet away sipping tea as she talked to one of the artists whose sculptures were on display. He walked over to her reluctantly. "Excuse me, Mrs. Lomax. I need a favor."

"Yes, of course, Mayor Bishop."

"Can you watch my daughter, Gem, over there while I take this little one to the restroom, please?"

"I'd be happy to."

Josiah, Treasure, and Mrs. Lomax walked over to the table where Gem sat talking, laughing, and coloring pictures with the other children around her.

"Gem, Daddy is about to take Treasure to the restroom. Do you need to go too?"

"No, Daddy."

"Well, Mrs. Lomax is going to watch you for me while I take your sister, so stay put until I get back, okay?"

"Okay."

"I really appreciate this."

"It's not a problem at all," Mrs. Lomax said with a bright smile on her face.

Chapter Twenty-eight

"Gem is a very pretty name."

"Thank you. My daddy gave me that name. He said I looked like a precious gem when he first saw me when I was a baby." Gem picked up a red crayon and started coloring an apple on the group mural.

"Did your *mommy* say that about you too?"

Gem nodded her head and smiled, but she continued coloring without a word.

"Do you miss your mommy while she's away?"

"Yes, ma'am. Well . . . *Sometimes* I do, but sometimes I don't. We're going to fly on an airplane to visit her soon."

Mrs. Lomax's perfectly arched eyebrows furrowed in confusion. "You're going to Maryland to visit your mommy?"

"She's not in Maryland." Gem giggled. "Mommy is in *Montana*. She's in the mountains."

"*Montana?* I thought . . . Anyway, what is your mommy doing in *Montana*, sugar?"

"She's very sick so she had to go to the special hospital in Montana to see the special doctor so he can give her medicine and stuff to make her disease go away forever."

"What kind of disease does your mommy have?"

"It's a bad disease called *addiction*."

"Oh my God!" Mrs. Lomax covered her bronze-painted lips and gasped.

"You know about addiction?"

"Yes, I sure do, sugar."

"It's really bad. It makes Mommy act weird sometimes. She screams a lot and throws up all the time."

Mrs. Lomax looked up in time to see Josiah and Treasure approaching the table. She smiled and picked up an orange crayon and pretended that she was helping Gem color her section of the mural. The wheels inside her head were spinning out of control. Her suspicion that there was trouble in the Bishop family's perfect little world had been confirmed, but she hadn't suspected that wifey was a *drug addict!* She wondered what her substance of choice was. She, Frances, and Leon would have to do some digging around to crack the case. The information could be invaluable.

God knew that Denny could use a boost in the polls because he was thirteen points behind Mayor Bishop. But if voters were to find out that the mayor's cute and curvy Barbie-doll wife was a crackhead or an alcoholic that he'd secretly shipped off to rehab, the political needle could move in the Lomax direction. Charmaine would love that because she didn't want all of her stompings on the campaign trail to be in vain.

"Thank you so much, Mrs. Lomax." Josiah had returned and touched her shoulder gently in a friendly gesture.

"You are most certainly welcome, Mayor Bishop."

Josiah bent down and picked Treasure up. "This little girl is getting sleepy. I'm going to take her home and lay her down for a nap."

Treasure rubbed her eyes and rested her head on her daddy's shoulder.

"Come on, Gem. We're going home, sweetie. Say goodbye to Mrs. Lomax and thank her for watching you while Daddy stepped away with your sister."

"Thank you for watching me. Bye-bye."

"Aren't you sweeter than molasses? May I have a hug?"

Gem nodded her head and threw her arms around Mrs. Lomax's neck before she stood up. She waved again and grabbed Josiah's hand. Then she allowed him to lead her away with Treasure in tow.

A wicked smile spread across Charmaine Lomax's expertly made-up face. All kinds of underhanded ideas began to unfold in her brain as she watched Josiah and his daughters leave the building. One question also came to mind. Who was the young lady that Frances had seen the mayor and his girls with at the restaurant last week? According to her very efficient assistant, they'd looked and interacted like a regular family. Was the mayor having an affair while his wife was up in Montana trying to exorcize her drug demons? Inquiring minds wanted to know and . . . soon they would.

"Babe, I was hit with the most shocking revelation today at the children's event. I didn't get a chance to tell you about it because you rushed off to your meeting."

Dendrick closed the book he'd been reading and placed it on the nightstand. He looked at his pretty wife as she walked closer to the bed in a sexy burgundy negligee. He smelled his favorite scented lotion on her skin as she rubbed her palms together. He wanted her tonight. He wanted her *bad*. Since the campaign had started, it had been difficult for him to spend time with his secret lover, Anastasia. *Good Lawd*, he missed her! But since it was impossible for him to be with the one he loved tonight, he would have to love the one he was with. It was cool, though, because Dendrick was still sexually attracted to his wife of twelve years. So, their random romps between the sheets were still satisfying. But Anastasia had that platinum pussy that made a man feel rich and famous after fucking her. Dendrick saw visions of Rolexes,

Ferraris, and Nottingham Palace after every nut he busted inside of Anastasia. Yeah, she had that platinum, prize-winning punanny. But unfortunately, tonight, he'd have to settle for silver sex.

"What are you talking about, Charmaine?" Dendrick asked after she'd teased him with a moment of silence.

Charmaine sat down on the bed, almost on his lap and ran her fingers through his hair. "I found out some information that might just turn the campaign around in your favor, babe."

"I'm listening."

"A very reliable source informed me that Atlanta's current first lady, Mink Bishop, is in a drug rehabilitation center in Montana. That's why we haven't seen her on the campaign trail with her hubby in months. Don't you find that interesting?"

"That's *gossip*, Charmaine. You know I don't deal in bullshit. I want to win the election on my own merit and my stance on the issues. I'm not into mudslinging and slanderous attacks."

"Ugh! But you're *losing*, Denny! I want to win! I would make a much-better first lady for Atlanta than some crack-rock-smoking, alcoholic, pill-popping addict! I deserve all the glitz and glamour that'll come along with the position."

Dendrick snatched the covers from his body and got up from the bed wearing only a pair of plaid, flannel pajama bottoms. "Leave it alone, Charmaine. I'm warning you. Forget about whatever you think you know about Bishop's wife."

Charmaine pursed her lips and rolled her eyes in response.

Dendrick stormed into their spacious walk-in closet and exited with a gray and black jogging suit in his hands. He quickly dressed before he went back into the closet to search for his white sneakers. He ignored his wife's juvenile pouting while he put on his shoes. She was such a snobbish, self-centered *bitch*. Their three children were far more mature than her childish ass. Did he want to kick Josiah Bishop's ass? Hell yeah! But he refused to do it by trashing the man's wife.

Dendrick picked up his keys and wallet from the dresser and headed for the door.

"Where the hell are you going?"

"I need a drink."

"We have a full, goddamn bar downstairs, so where are you *really* going, Denny? You must think I'm a fool!"

Dendrick shook his head and laughed. "Only fools plot to get what they don't deserve." He slammed the door and jogged down the stairs. It would be a platinum night after all.

"I got it, Mrs. Lomax!"

"You do?"

"Yes, ma'am. It's Serenity Springs Rehabilitation and Mental Health Center in White Sulphur Springs, Montana. That's the only facility of that kind in the mountains up there."

Charmaine Lomax took a long drag on her cigarette as she paced the floor in her home office. She blew out a stream of smoke before she gulped down a mouthful of brandy. "Do you have the Tracfone?"

"Yes."

"And you know what to say, right?"

"I sure do."

"Okay. Make the call."

Jeremiah slid onto the bench inside the booth across from his surprise lunch date. "What's up, stranger? I haven't seen you in three or four full moons. You're looking chocolatey delicious, girl. I may just have to lick you for dessert."

"You're still crazy as hell. But . . . um . . . You may owe me a good licking after I tell you why I called and asked you to meet me here."

"You've got my attention, baby."

"I received a strange phone call after my morning show. It was from some anonymous chick with a tip on a potential scoop. She was adamant about me looking into the story and reporting on it as soon as possible."

"Okay. I'm going to assume that this has something to do with my brother, right?"

"You're kind of right. The tip definitely involves your brother, but it focuses more on his *wife*, J."

Fuck! Even after he sends the bitch off to druggie boot camp, she's still causing problems! "Go ahead and give it to me straight, Quay. No chaser. No bullshit."

"The chick claims that your sister-in-law has been MIA on the campaign scene because she's on drugs. *And . . .* She swears that the mayor sent his wife away to Serenity Springs Rehabilitation and Mental Health Center up in the mountains of Montana."

"What if it's true? Are you going to run with the story?"

"If I was going to do that, I wouldn't have called you. I would be at the station with my team researching and writing. I came here to give you a head's-up so that you can protect your brother and his daughters."

Jeremiah nodded. "Thanks, Quay. I owe you big time."

She licked her lips. "You damn sure do owe me, Negro. This story would've been major for me. Shit, I could've been the next Tamron Hall or Joy Reid if I had run with the tip. But I started reminiscing about all the good times we used to have. My conscience wouldn't let me do it."

"We can have a good time *tonight* if you're down with it."

"You don't have time for me tonight, handsome. Just because *I* didn't pounce on the story, it doesn't mean that some other reporter at another station won't. You, your brother, and his crew better get ahead of this. If that heifer called me, I guarantee you she'll call someone else."

Jeremiah rubbed his temples. "How do you suggest we handle it?"

"Is it true, J? Is your sister-in-law in a drug rehab center in Montana?"

"You already know the answer."

"Okay. Mayor Bishop needs to have his publicist prepare and deliver a statement on his behalf right away. I don't want him to do a press conference because it needs to appear that he's too broken to talk about it or answer any questions. The statement has to be sincere and filled with emotional content and humility. Women like that kind of shit. Their hearts will bleed for him, and most of them will want to fuck him to sleep to comfort him. And men will respect him for being a loyal family man."

"Do you really think so?"

"Hell yeah! Mayor Josiah Bishop will be a hero in everybody's eyes. He's a political giant, running a major Southern city while seeking reelection. And he's doing it all alone while caring for his two little angelic daughters because his wife is away in a drug rehab center in Montana. Sympathy will pour in from all over the city. His poll numbers are going to shoot off of the meter."

"I hope so."

"Trust me on this." Quay reached across the table and placed her hand on top of his. "Just make sure the mayor gets his wife to sign a medical release consent form permitting him to air out her dirty laundry to the public. Those HIPPA laws ain't no joke. Do you think your sister-in-law will sign the form?"

"She better sign it because she owes JoJo *royally*. This shit that he's going through is *her* fault. If she weren't on drugs, my brother's life would be squeaky clean. I hate the day he ever met that b—"

"J!"

Jeremiah exhaled audibly. "I'm sorry, but that woman makes my ass itch."

"Just tell your brother to secure the medical consent release form, have his publicist compose a solid statement, and make sure it goes live as soon as possible."

Chapter Twenty-nine

"Good morning, everyone. My name is Geisel Arrington, and I serve as publicist and media consultant for the Honorable Josiah J. Bishop, mayor of the city of Atlanta. On behalf of Mayor Bishop, I would like to thank all of you for coming on such short notice. Each of you members of the press was invited here this morning at the request of the mayor for an important announcement that he deems necessary and urgent. In an effort to maintain transparency between the mayor and the citizens of Atlanta, as promised during his first bid for the office he now holds, he has decided to make some very personal, painful information public at this time. Thus I quote:

It is with a heavy heart and deep humility that I inform you, my fellow citizens of Atlanta, that as of September the twenty-second of this year, my beloved wife, Mrs. Mink Sinclair Bishop, was admitted to a long-term drug rehabilitation and mental health facility in an undisclosed location in the United States. The reason for this is due to her continuous, yet hard-fought battle with substance abuse. Although my family, close friends, and I are deeply concerned about my wife's illness, we are equally optimistic about her recovery because our faith sustains us. At this time, my family and I request privacy regarding my wife's health. We humbly solicit your prayers and well wishes. Thank you for your understanding.
Sincerely,
Mayor Josiah J. Bishop

"I decline questions at this time. Again, thank you all for coming. The press conference is now over."

"Mrs. Arrington! Mrs. Arrington!" a female reporter shouted with a microphone in her hand. "When will you take questions, ma'am?"

"Is Mrs. Bishop addicted to prescription drugs?"

An older male reporter snapped a picture of Geisel. "How long has the first lady been an addict?"

"Why didn't Mayor Bishop make the announcement?" Someone yelled out from the back of the room.

Geisel continued her brisk walk up the aisle of the atrium without a word, leaving a throng of media vultures yelling at her back. She was flanked protectively by Josiah's staffers and other employees with the exception of Jeremiah and Gypsie. They were with the mayor upstairs inside his office at city hall watching it all go down on TV like the rest of Atlantans. Rev and Myrlie were there also supporting their son. The small group watched in silence as reporters ran after Geisel firing questions at her until she entered an elevator and the doors close behind her.

Jeremiah picked up the remote control from Josiah's desk and turned off the television. No one spoke immediately. The quietness lingered, and everybody remained perfectly still. Finally, Rev stood from the love seat he'd been sharing with his wife. He walked over to Josiah who was sitting behind his massive cherry wood desk with his chin resting in the palm of his hand.

"Everything is going to be all right, JoJo." Rev gripped his son's shoulder.

Unable to respond verbally, Josiah buried his face in his father's side and wept. For the first time since Jeremiah had delivered him the shocking news that his darkest family secret had been discovered, he succumbed to his pain. Initially, he was livid and wanted to know who had violated his family's privacy and why. Then fear followed. He was afraid of how the publicity of Mink's drug addiction would affect Gem and Treasure. Children could be so cruel. No one knew that better than the Bishop twins. Josiah could recall many times that he and Jeremiah had been teased and picked on as young boys because they were preacher's kids, better known as PKs. He would bet his life that if Gem and Treasure had a choice between a preacher dad and a junkie mom, they'd quote Bible verses, speak in tongues, and beat tambourines all day long.

After Josiah was finally able to reel in his emotions, he raised his head and looked around the room. The first person in his line of vision was Gypsie. From the sad expression on her face and her bloodshot eyes, she appeared just as upset as he was. She was crying, and her body was trembling terribly. Josiah hated that he had pulled her into his crazy world. Although it had never been his intent, their hearts had somehow connected. But even in this low and uncertain moment in his life, Josiah was sure that his love and commitment for Mink remained intact.

Mink anxiously paced back and forth in her elaborately furnished and decorated private room at the rehab facility. Her thoughts were on her two babies. She figured that Josiah's publicist had done the press conference by now, and the entire city of Atlanta knew her secret. Tears pooled in her eyes just thinking about the noonday and evening TV news reports on all of the major local channels. The radio shows were probably popping off as well.

Quite naturally, Mink had signed the medical consent form, granting Josiah permission to go public with her condition, but she'd only done so because she felt she had no other choice. Like thousands of times in the past, she had agreed to do something she really hadn't wanted to do just to please someone else. Mink had truly believed that she owed it to Josiah because of the predicament her drug problem had placed him in politically. She was an addict for sure, but no one could ever call her selfish.

All her life she had made sacrifices and given up her will for the people she loved. So, yesterday, when Josiah called and told her about the situation involving the anonymous culprit that wished to expose her secret drug dependency to hurt his chances at being reelected, she did what had been expected of her, as usual. Without hesitation, she used her fingertip to scribble her electronic signature on a medical release consent form his office had sent via email in a PDF file. There was no way that she was going to allow someone to rob Josiah of his dream. So, she'd done what she had to do, all for the sake of love for her husband and her commitment to him.

Mink sat down on the bed and rubbed her hands up and down her arms against the chill in the room. She had been quite irritable for the last few days because she hadn't snorted any cocaine or popped any Ecstasy tablets in nearly a week. Hell, Greg hadn't even slipped her a sip of alcohol. He was a brick-wall motherfucker. Whenever he decided on something, he stuck with his plan. And his current plan was to keep her clean of all substances until after Josiah and the girls' visit this upcoming weekend. He didn't want to risk losing his job, but that's exactly what would happen if anyone were ever to discover that he had been supplying her with drugs and alcohol. So, he had cut off Mink's fixes several days ago to prepare her for her pending weekend visit with her family. She had to pass a drug screening before they arrived. Otherwise, the visit would not take place.

In previous weeks, Mink had only passed all of her *so-called* random drug screens because Greg was privy to each resident's clinical schedule. Therefore, he knew at the beginning of every month the exact days Mink would be required to submit a urine sample. *And* as a member of the staff, he also knew she would only be tested for heroin because she had identified that particular substance as her sole drug of choice. Therefore, it was the only substance the medical staff at the center had ever tested her for. So, all the coke she'd snorted, the E tabs she had popped, and gallons of liquor she'd guzzled down had gone undetected.

However, once Josiah and the girls arrived, the nurses would test Mink every single day for *all* substances. Additionally, the cabin she'd share with her family would be searched daily for drugs and alcohol. This was a policy that the center had implemented four and a half years ago after a resident had nearly died of a heart attack while bingeing on crystal meth and vodka that his daughter had smuggled into the facility during a family weekend visit.

Mink knew Josiah wouldn't sneak any drugs or alcohol onto the premises for her, so she had prepared her body and mind for a clean and sober weekend with her husband and daughters. She was honestly looking forward to it. But at the moment, she was experiencing a coke craving so powerful that she couldn't sit still. She had dumped her entire lunch of chicken quesadillas and Spanish rice in the trash can because her appetite for food was nonexistent. All Mink had a taste for was something . . . *anything* . . . to make her high.

Norm M.! The older gentleman's face instantly popped into her head clear out of left field. He always had a secret supply of some expensive, strong, dark liquor stashed away, and he'd been kind enough to share with her on a few occasions. Norm M. was a cool, white dude in his mid- to late fifties. He was pleasant, polite, and proper. And according to the rehab grapevine, the man was filthy rich. Mink had peeped his designer clothes and shoes, as well as his solid rose gold Omega Seamaster Aqua Terra watch the first day they met. It was Josiah's dream watch that he'd vowed to own someday. He actually drooled over pictures of the exquisite timepiece whenever he ran across one.

Norm M.'s overall appearance and demeanor reeked of money and power. His eloquent speech that was seasoned with an accent that reminded Mink of the late President John F. Kennedy's, also hinted that he had a fortune tucked away someplace. And instead of puffing on cigarettes out on the veranda and other designated smoking areas outside the building, he was often spotted with expensive-looking cigars wedged between his teeth as he read from some thick, hardback book. He was quite the distinguished gentleman in Mink's eyes, and he intrigued her enough to want to hear his story one day. But right now, she wanted to find him to see if he had any liquor to spare and if he'd be willing to share it with her. He had never asked for any *favors* in exchange for drinks before, and Mink hoped he'd be as generous today. However, there were no guarantees amongst addicts. They were just as unpredictable as the weather.

So, just in case Norm M. was feeling frisky this afternoon, Mink dabbed a little bit of perfume behind each ear, applied a soft shade of pink gloss to her lips, and popped a few spearmint Altoids in her mouth. Then, after a final glance in the mirror, she left her room. More than likely, her secret bartender was on the veranda smoking a cigar and making love to a book.

Chapter Thirty

"I think he should skip it." Connor took a sip from the Styrofoam cup in his hand and swallowed. "You and I can go in his place. Everyone will understand. The man just admitted yesterday to the entire city through his publicist that he's married to a goddamn *dopehead*. Surely, no one expects him to show up this evening to hand out food and clothes to a bunch of freeloaders the day after that. There'll be TV reporters and cameras everywhere. He doesn't need to show his face."

Jeremiah looked up briefly from packing files in Josiah's briefcase to stare at Connor. "I think this is the first time we've ever agreed on *anything*, dude. I'll tell Gypsie to call the mission and inform Mrs. Jeantine, the director, that the mayor won't be able to attend the event and that his chief of staff and a senior aide will represent him in his absence. I don't see a need for Gypsie to explain as long as we'll be delivering the food items JoJo promised to donate."

"There'll be no need for Gypsie to make an excuse about anything on my behalf because she's not going to make the phone call," Josiah announced, entering his brother's office without knocking. He plopped down in one of the chairs facing Jeremiah's desk. "I'm going to the mission this evening as scheduled. Keeping my promise, I'll be handing out whole chickens, hams, and dozens of sweet potato pies; compliments of Myrlie Bishop and the women of Fresh Anointing Pentecostal Church. It's cold outside, so people need those hundreds of coats we've collected."

Connor frowned, ran his fingers through his curly red hair, and blew out a gush of air. But he didn't utter a single syllable in protest.

"I don't think that's a good idea, JoJo. The local media will rip you a new asshole if you venture out so soon after the press conference. I'm against it, bruh."

"That's too bad, J, because I really thought you, of all people, would have my back."

"I *do* have your back. It's just that I think it's too much, too soon. Reporters can be vicious, man. I don't think I can stand there and watch them shoot for your heart without going off. You may be the mayor of the A, but you're my big brother. If they come at you sideways, I'll clap back."

"No, you won't because you're too smooth and professional to let a bunch of thirsty, kiss-ass, underpaid reporters set you off. Plus, JoJo with the git mo' can take care of himself. I ain't about to dip and hide like some little punk because my wife is on drugs. At least she's in treatment getting the help she needs and not out on the streets blooping."

"I just feel you're moving too fast, JoJo. Why don't you chill for a few days?"

"I-I . . . I . . . um . . . agree with Jeremiah, sir," Connor stammered, adding his unsolicited two cents.

"Thank you both for your concern. I sincerely appreciate it, but I don't need you two to protect me. No matter what, the media clowns are going to come hard for me whether I face them tonight or next week. So, I might as well get it over with, don't you think?"

Jeremiah couldn't respond because he knew Josiah was right. There was no need for him to avoid the media because, at some point, he would have to face them. What better time was there than the present? The sooner he answered a few questions from local reporters, the better. Then he could put yet another episode of his fucked-up life as the husband of a dope fiend behind him.

"Okay, JoJo, I get it. You want to split through the shit head-on today and hope the media will drop the issue after they drill you once."

"Correct." Josiah nodded and smiled.

"Cool. I'm down with it, but don't spend a lot of time answering questions. And say as little as possible without revealing too many details. All they need to know is Mink has a problem with dependency, and she's in treatment. Just confirm what Geisel said yesterday."

"That's my plan, bruh."

"But what if someone goes rogue and starts getting pushy?" Connor asked with genuine concern in his voice.

"Don't worry about it, dude. I'll arrange extra security to cover JoJo. You never know. A fight might break out over the last chicken or the fattest ham, and we'll have to get him out of there in a hurry," Jeremiah laughed.

Connor stood up, shaking his head. "I'm not worried about the people who'll be there for the food. It's the *news reporters*. Those are the bastards I want to punch in their faces."

"Take off your boxing gloves, champ. The extra security and I will have everything under control."

Gypsie entered Excellence Unlimited Preparatory Academy and blazed a path straight to the front office. Her heart was racing as she gripped her designer clutch bag with sweaty palms. Mrs. Scott, the school's secretary, had called Josiah thirty minutes ago out of concern for Gem. She had been quiet, distant, and even teary-eyed since art appreciation class earlier this morning. Gypsie had a hard time understanding that because the child was very happy, talkative, and full of laughter on the drive to school this morning. She and Treasure had even sung Andra Day's "Rise Up" loud, in perfect pitch, and with full voices between giggles and lively chatter all the way to school.

What the hell happened in art appreciation class? That question was on repeat inside Gypsie's head. The teacher and headmistress had said that Gem had refused to talk when they'd asked her why she was so upset. Gypsie hoped the child would confide in her because, unfortunately, her father wasn't available to tend to her right now. He didn't even have a clue that Gem was having a rough time at school because he was in the early stages of an all-day budget meeting at the time of the call. That's why as soon as Gypsie hung up the phone with Mrs. Scott, she asked Rebecca to cover her desk before she tore out of city hall en route to the school like a ho on a john. Josiah didn't need the stress of dealing with the situation with all he had going on. So, as the official, trusted caretaker of the Bishop girls in the absence of their parents, Gypsie decided to exercise her limited authority.

She opened the glass door to the office and walked in. Immediately, she was greeted with a warm smile from a woman standing behind the counter.

"Good morning and welcome to Excellence Unlimited Preparatory Academy. How may I help you, ma'am?"

"Hi. I'm Gypsie Robinson, administrative assistant to Mayor Josiah Bishop. I spoke to Mrs. Scott on his behalf about his daughter—"

"Gem," the woman said softly, finishing Gypsie's sentence. "Please follow me, ma'am. She's with our headmistress, Dr. Bah, in her office."

Without a word, Gypsie followed the woman down a short, narrow hallway to a set of double doors. The runaway beat of her heart caused her breathing to become labored.

After one hard knock, the woman opened the doors and waved her hand, gesturing for Gypsie to enter the office ahead of her. "Dr. Bah, this is Miss Robinson from the mayor's office. She's here regarding Gem."

"Thank you, Gilda. Please hold all my calls."

"Yes, ma'am," she replied before she left the room, closing the doors behind her.

"Please have a seat, Miss Robinson."

Gypsie had heard Dr. Bah's request for her to be seated, but she was momentarily paralyzed by the sight of a terribly upset Gem slouching in a chair on the side of the headmistress's desk. The poor child was sitting with her head hanging down and her arms folded across her chest. Gypsie stood motionless in shock with her heart crumbling to pieces.

"Gem, darling?" She inched slowly toward the little girl she loved with all her heart. "What's wrong, sweetie."

"Please sit down, Miss Robinson. I'd like to discuss something with you."

Gypsie ignored Dr. Bah again and made her way to Gem and kneeled down before her. She took the child by the hand. "My brightest Gem, please talk to me."

Slowly, Gem lifted her head and looked at Gypsie with tearful eyes. "I want to go home."

"Those are the first words she's spoken since the art teacher brought her in here. She's been awfully rude and stubborn. Nothing anyone did or said to comfort her made her explain why she started acting out in class."

Gypsie whipped her head around and stabbed the headmistress with her eyes. "*Acting out?* I was told she appeared sad and started crying all of a sudden. Mrs. Scott didn't tell me she was cursing, spitting, or fighting with other children in the class. Now, *that* would've been acting out."

Dr. Bah let out an audible sigh and rolled her eyes to the ceiling, unmistakably annoyed by Gypsie's words and attitude. The crooked frown on her face confirmed that she was offended. "It's a matter of public record now that there's a *situation* within the Bishop household, so—"

"Oh no, you didn't! How dare you!" Gypsie stood to her full five-foot-five stature. She grabbed Gem's hand and pulled her to her feet along with her. "This discussion should not take place while the child is present, and especially not with *me*. It's unprofessional, insensitive, and downright tacky. I'm going to take Gem and her sister home for the rest of the day. I would appreciate if you could arrange for them to be dismissed."

"I assume you're authorized to sign the girls out of school."

"I sure am."

"Very well." Dr. Bah stood from her chair and walked around her desk. She stopped in front of Gypsie and Gem. "Will the girls return to school tomorrow?"

"Mayor Bishop will decide that. I'm sure he'll be in touch."

On that note, Gypsie did a graceful twirl on her stilettos and guided Gem out of the office. She was 100 degrees emotionally hot, and nothing could cool her off better than a two-punch combination to Dr. Bah's smug face. She was a pretty woman with smooth brown skin, a short Afro, and dark eyes, but she was ugly on the inside.

After a brief wait in the school's busy front office, Treasure was escorted inside by her teacher, Mrs. Lawton, who reported that the younger Bishop daughter was one of her brightest and most well-behaved students.

"I'm happy to hear that, Mrs. Lawton," Gypsie responded and took Treasure by the hand.

The young teacher walked closer to Gypsie with compassion in her bright blue eyes. "Please let the mayor know he has my support," she whispered. "Anything I can do to help him, Treasure, or her sister during this difficult time would be my pleasure."

"I will deliver your message to Mayor Bishop, and I'm sure he'll appreciate your kindness and concern."

Chapter Thirty-one

Gypsie was relieved when she pulled in front of Josiah's house and spotted Jeremiah's car parked outside. She had sent him a text message right before she left the girls' school, begging him to meet her at his brother's house. Unable to go into details, she'd insisted that he not mention anything to Josiah, and he had willingly agreed.

"Come on, girls. Let's go inside. Your Uncle J is waiting for us."

Gypsie gathered the pizza and wings she'd purchased for lunch and followed Gem and Treasure up the walkway. Just as they reached the front door, it swung open.

"Uncle J! Uncle J!" Treasure wrapped her arms around Jeremiah's long legs and squeezed.

"Hey, precious." He picked his niece up, pecked her cheek, and lowered her feet back to the ground.

Gypsie found it strange that Gem didn't greet her uncle with the same enthusiasm as Treasure had. She simply waved her hand at him with an expressionless face and walked right past him to enter the house.

"What's up with her?" Jeremiah asked. "And why are they home from school so early?"

"That's why I asked you to meet me here. Gem had a crying spell at school."

"Why?"

"I'm not sure. I was hoping you could get her to tell you what happened. She hasn't said a word to me. Let's go inside so you can talk to her."

"I can't. I was on my way out. Rebecca called and said that JoJo is acting a hood-rat fool because I'm MIA. I've got to get back to city hall, baby girl."

"But I need you *here*, Jeremiah."

"I waited here for you over thirty minutes already."

"I know, but I had to stop and buy food for the girls because I signed them out of school before lunchtime. Can't you at least spend five minutes talking to Gem please?"

Jeremiah checked his watch and shook his head. "I'm sorry, but I can't. I'll call you as soon as I can. Take care of my nieces." He kissed Gypsie on the forehead and walked away, leaving her and Treasure standing on the stoop.

"Come on, little one. It's time for lunch." Gypsie entered the house with Treasure acting as her shadow. She went straight to the kitchen, washed her hands, and prepared a lunch plate for the child. Gem was nowhere in sight. "Go and wash your hands, sweetie," she said, placing the plate and a cup of apple juice on the table. "When you come back, say your grace and eat your food. I'm going to find your sister."

"Okay."

Gypsie left the kitchen and went to the den. It was dim and empty, so she headed upstairs to the girls' bedroom. She was thankful to find Gem lying on her bed on her side with her face turned toward the wall.

"My brightest Gem, I need you to tell me what happened this morning in art class that made you cry. Please talk to me, sweetie."

Like a robot, Gem's tiny body shot straight up in the bed. She narrowed cold eyes on Gypsie. "Is my mom a crackhead?"

"W-what . . . What? *Nooo!* Where on earth did you hear such a terrible thing?"

"Ryland! She said she doesn't want to be my friend anymore because my mom is a crackhead that takes bad drugs and gets high all the time! She told all of my friends that people on drugs steal, and they're dangerous, and they die all alone in raggedy, old houses." Gem broke out into a pitiful sob. "Why did she say those mean things to me, Miss Gypsie? *Why?*"

Gypsie rushed to the bed, sat down, and gathered Gem in her arms as the child wept from her soul. "It's okay, darling. It's okay."

Gem squirmed out of Gypsie's arms and leaned back to stare into her eyes. "Is my mom a crackhead? Does she take bad drugs, Miss Gypsie? Is she going to die?"

"Your mom is *not* a crackhead, darling." Gypsie drew in a deep breath and exhaled it slowly before she spoke again. "Your mom is sick, and that's why she's in the special hospital in Montana. She realized she needed help to control her disease. We've talked about this before, Gem. Your daddy has discussed it with you and Treasure too. You know all about your mom's addiction."

"Yeah, I know about the addiction disease, but does Mommy take drugs? Ryland said her auntie told her that people with addiction are addicts, and addicts are hooked on drugs. Is my mom on drugs, Miss Gypsie?"

Lord, please give me wisdom and strength. "Yes, sweetheart, your mom is on drugs, but—"

"You lied to me! And Daddy lied too! I hate you! I hate you!" Gem sprang from the bed and ran out the room crying hysterically.

With lightning speed, Gypsie ran and caught up with her in the middle of the hallway. Seconds before Gem reached the bathroom, Gypsie reached out and threw her arms gently around her.

"Get your hands off of me! Let me go! You and Daddy lied to me!"

Even as Gem resisted with flailing arms, screaming at the top of her lungs, Gypsie held on to her. The sound of the child's heart-wrenching cries broke the emotional dam. A heavy flow of tears began to spill down Gypsie's cheeks. The tighter she held on to Gem, the more violently her tiny body bucked against the embrace. All of her wiggling and twisting caused Gypsie to lose her balance, and the two of them collapsed to the plush taupe carpet. The drop to the floor must've shocked Gem because she instantly fell quiet and still. Gypsie rushed to seize the moment.

"I'm so sorry about what Ryland said to you, Gem. It was very mean of her." She paused and rocked the child in her arms. "I'm also sorry that I didn't tell you the whole truth about your mother's disease. Your daddy didn't think you would understand the part about the drugs. He thought you were too young to learn about that type of thing."

"I want to know about drugs, Miss Gypsie. I want you to make me understand why my mom has the addiction disease and why she takes drugs. Will you tell me?"

"I will tell you everything about drug addiction that I think you're old enough to understand. Deal?"

Gem nodded. "Deal."

"Okay, let's go and log on to the computer. There's a lot of information on the internet."

Gypsie released Gem, and they scrambled to their feet. They stood facing each other in silence for a brief moment.

"Miss Gypsie?"

"Yes, my brightest Gem?"

"Can you make me a promise?"

"What is it?"

"Promise me that you will never lie to me again."

"I promise."

"Pinky swear?" Gem extended her hand with her pinky finger curled.

"Pinky swear."

They hooked their pinky fingers together and smiled to make the promise official.

"Hello?"

"What took you so long to answer the phone?"

"I was in the den playing a game with your nieces, sir. What the hell took you so long to call me, Jeremiah? I had a little crisis going on with Gem."

"What's up?"

"Apparently, some grownups don't have a clue how great an impact their words can have on children. A little girl in Gem's art class named Ryland had a mouthful to say to her about Mrs. Bishop. Her auntie told her the ghetto version of Geisel's press conference yesterday."

"Fuck! What exactly did the little brat say to Gem?"

"In a nutshell, she doesn't want to be Gem's friend anymore because according to her auntie, Mrs. Bishop is a dangerous, thieving crackhead, and she's going to die in an abandoned house in the hood."

Jeremiah sucked his teeth. "I hate my sweet niece had to experience some shit like that. It's a damn shame how Mink's drug habit is still affecting her children even though she's almost two thousand miles away in treatment. JoJo is going to be pissed about the school incident. I hate to be the bearer of bad news once again."

"Don't tell him. Let him get through this day and the event at the mission this evening. I'll have a talk with him when he gets home. I need to tell him my thoughts on Dr. Bah, the headmistress at the school too. I don't like her very much. I was about five hot seconds away from snapping that chick's neck."

"*Damn!* She must've really pissed you off. I haven't heard you spit words with that much ice in your voice since that night at the restaurant when you gave me the business and threw a glass of water in my face." Jeremiah laughed, but only for a split second. "Yo, here comes JoJo now. I've got to go. Are you and the girls good?"

"Yeah, we're fine. I'll see you in the morning. And remember not to say anything to your brother about the mishap with Gem at school."

"I won't."

The moment Gypsie hung up the phone, it rang again.

"Hello?"

"What's up, Blackbird?"

Gypsie smiled at the sound of Tianji's voice. Her BFF always seemed to call at just the right time. After her day from hell, a venting and gossip session was exactly what Gypsie needed.

"Girl, you wouldn't believe what kind of day I've had. After the election, I'm going on a fourteen-day cruise on a luxury liner. Hell, I deserve it after working like an indentured servant and playing mommy all this time."

"Honey, you can't go on a vacation until the first lady completes treatment and comes back home. Those little girls need you."

"*Uuugh!* You're right. Gem needs me a lot. Let me tell you what happened to her at school today. This little girl named Ryland . . ."

Chapter Thirty-two

Josiah surveyed the last dozen or so people standing in line and looked down at the coolers filled with frozen chickens. "We'll make it with a few birds to spare," he whispered to Jeremiah. "Then I'll work the room and shake some more hands before I sneak out."

"Cool. I'll have time to swing by and play with a lucky member of the 'J Team' and give her a prize before sunrise." He grinned with a glint of mischief in his eyes.

"Well, I'm going home to kiss my two little angels, take a hot shower, and curl up in my bed with a good book."

"You have your life outside of politics, and I have mine, bruh."

The Bishop twins continued working side by side at the giveaway event along with members of the mission's staff. Josiah was distributing the chickens while Jeremiah handed out plump hams. The program had unfolded without any drama or glitch. Josiah's speech had been well-received, and the crowd had responded favorably.

As expected, reporters were lurking around outside the building before the event. But thanks to a special five-man security team that Jeremiah had contracted to back up the two uniformed officers from the city, no one from the media was allowed within five feet of the mayor. In fact, the group of reporters was served the okeydoke when the sleek, black Range Rover rolled to a stop in the side alley adjacent to the building instead of the mayor's official vehicle. By the time they realized Josiah was the mystery occupant riding in style, he was halfway inside the building.

But the media hogs weren't the only ones taken by surprise. Josiah was caught off his square when his childhood buddy, Spud, first arrived at city hall and announced that he would be driving him, Jeremiah, and Connor to the Agape Ministries Mission instead of Nelson. It was such a classic move for his twin brother to make an off-the-wall arrangement for him behind his back. Initially, Josiah was pissed to the max and had to fight the urge to kick Jeremiah's ass. But they had a rule to never argue in front of staff members or any city hall employees, especially not Connor with his supersensational self. So, Josiah just rolled with the flow. He figured that Jeremiah had a good reason for giving Nelson the evening off and arranging for Spud to chauffeur him to the mission in his place.

The moment they arrived at the mission and Josiah saw all the reporters and TV cameras, he clearly understood exactly why Jeremiah had changed their original plan. He smiled when he spotted Rob, Tee, and Deacon Hawkins's two sons all decked out in designer suits and shoes posted up in strategic locations around the building. As usual, his twin brother and ace in the hole had made moves to hold him down. He had called in the old hood cavalry to protect him from the enemy, which, on this particular night, was the local media.

"Thank you, Mayor Bishop," a young lady whispered. She took the chicken from Josiah and placed it in a cardboard box filled with other food items she held in her hands.

Her soft voice yanked Josiah from his thoughts before he gave the woman his full attention. She had three small children; two little boys who were around his daughters' ages and a sleeping baby girl secured in an old stroller.

"You're welcome, ma'am. Have a good evening," Josiah said, smiling at the woman and her children.

"We'll try." The woman stared at Josiah for a few seconds before she politely asked, "Will you please take a picture with my boys? They admire you so much. Keon, my oldest, even did a report about you in school. He says he wants to be just like you when he grows up. My boy wants to be the mayor of Atlanta one day."

As if on cue, Jeremiah took a break from ham duty and reached for the woman's cell phone. "Y'all get in close. Mama, you should get in the picture too."

"And I want this little angel to join us also," Josiah announced as he reached down and freed the adorable baby girl from the less-than-sturdy stroller. He grinned when her eyes popped wide open the moment he lifted her into his arms. "Hey, precious. My name is Josiah. What's your name?"

"That's Heavenly, my baby sister," the younger of the two boys blurted out. Then he covered his eyes shyly with his hands and giggled, displaying a snaggletoothed smile.

His mother pulled him and his older brother closer to her as she stood next to Josiah who was now in a cooing exchange with baby Heavenly.

"Okay, everyone, look this way and say cheese."

The group looked at Jeremiah and smiled. He snapped several pictures as everyone changed poses like professional models.

"Thank you, Mayor Bishop. It was very nice to meet you. Keon and Brent will never forget this day. "

"It was my pleasure. By the way, I want to invite you and your kids to a special dinner and children's party at my church on October thirty-first. It's a safe alternative to trick-or-treating on Halloween. What's your name, ma'am?"

"I'm Therria Mayes, sir."

"Miss Mayes, I want you to call my office at city hall tomorrow and leave your name, telephone number, and address with my administrative assistant, Gypsie Robinson. I'll contact you personally with the information about the dinner and party. I'll also make arrangements for you and your children to be picked up and returned home safely."

"Oh my, I don't know what to say! I'll call bright and early in the morning, sir. Thank you so much, Mayor Bishop."

"It's my pleasure." Josiah hugged Miss Mayes and handed Heavenly back over to her. Then he embraced both of her sons before they all walked away.

Within seconds, he resumed distributing chickens and greeting those in need with a warm smile and a handshake. As the line of people got shorter, mission employees started cleaning up and ushering the guests out the door. Connor entered the building from a side entrance, looking like he'd just escaped death. His face was a fiery shade of red, and his emerald eyes held a flash of anger.

"What's up, Connor?" Jeremiah placed a ham in a box for an elderly gentleman on a cane and his wife.

"There are reporters and television cameras at every exit." He raked his fingers through his hair nervously. "One broad, Korrie Kaufman, from Channel 5, is acting like a real bulldog. She and her stooges are camped out for the long haul, but those private security guards you hired are some bad dudes. They forced a couple of cameramen back inside their trucks."

Josiah glared at Jeremiah who quickly turned his head. Everyone knew that Spud and the gang were much too aggressive and lacked the training to be a part of the mayor's unofficial security detail. If the reporters became overly persistent for an interview, all hell would break loose.

"I'm not going to hide out in here all night. I plan to exit the same door I entered, and if anyone from the media approaches me *respectfully* to ask questions about Mink, I'll offer a few simple answers. And after I've said all I feel is necessary, I'm going to walk away and not look back."

"Don't you think the citizens of Atlanta have the right to know if their mayor's wife is addicted to prescription drugs or alcohol or illegal street drugs? There is a difference, sir. Some people want to know if Mrs. Bishop has broken the law by using crack cocaine, heroin, marijuana, crystal meth, or some other outlawed substance."

"I believe the fine people of Atlanta have already been informed about what is important about my wife's condition. She realized she had developed a substance dependency, and she made the conscious decision to enter treatment."

The aggressive, petite reporter tossed her golden curls over her shoulder in obvious frustration. Jeremiah noticed her bright baby blues darken as she sneered at Josiah. Connor had been dead-on point. She was a feisty bulldog.

"Is Mrs. Bishop in treatment in the state of Georgia?" Miss Kaufman pressed.

"My wife is in a very reputable drug rehabilitation and mental health facility receiving quality care. I ask that you and all of the citizens of Atlanta include her in your daily prayers and positive thoughts. Thank you." Josiah turned away from the microphones and stepped toward Jeremiah, Connor, and his loyal homeboys.

"So, I guess that means your wife is hooked on street drugs. If she were addicted to pain killers or alcohol, you would've said so. What is she strung out on? Crack? Smack? Or is she on that ice?"

"Yo, you need to back up, fool!"

Josiah raised his hand to silence Spud. Everyone in the small crowd huddled around the door seemed surprised at the young male reporter's tactless line of questioning. Even Korrie Kaufman appeared shocked shitless as she turned around clutching her microphone. But Josiah held his head high and walked past her and the rude young man and headed toward the SUV. Rob was sitting behind the wheel. Josiah, Jeremiah, and Connor piled inside quietly with the sound of the male reporter's voice echoing in the night air.

Chapter Thirty-three

Dendrick raised the remote control and turned off the TV. "Did you see that bullshit? Did you see it?"

"Yeah, I saw it." Anastasia rolled her eyes and waved her hand at the television. "It's a damn shame. I hope TV and newspaper reporters won't come after you like that once you become mayor, Daddy."

I won't ever become mayor, babe. Even though Bishop's wife is now a known dope fiend, he's still kicking my ass in the polls. "Yeah, hopefully, they won't ride my ass like that. Those reporters were like wild animals, especially that skinny Disney princess from Channel 5. And who the hell was that weird guy with that nappy beard, wearing a toboggan over dreadlocks? One of Bishop's bodyguards was about to kick his ass."

"He should have. Dude had no business trying to get all up in the mayor's personal business. That shit wasn't cool at all."

Dendrick rolled over on top of Anastasia and pinned her back to the mattress. He gripped her hips tightly with both hands and grinded his lower body into hers. "Since when did you become a fan of my opponent?"

"I'm not his fan, but he has been a good mayor. The park in my old neighborhood had been run down for years because the drug dealers and crackheads had taken it over. Now, look at it. The basketball court has been renovated, and the children have new swings, sliding boards, a merry-go-round, and jungle gyms to play on.

The lights around the park are so bright at night now, the
dope boys and junkies are scared to show their faces."

"And you give all the credit to *Mayor Bishop?* You
think he's doing a good job, huh?"

Anastasia met Dendrick's gaze, and he immediately
detected apprehension in her eyes. She had always been
honest with him from the first day they met at Spa Onyx
where she worked as a masseuse and reflexologist. It was
flammable lust at first touch. A foot massage had never,
ever been more arousing. Dendrick had been hooked on
Anastasia's hands, mouth, and sweet pussy ever since.
And she'd been the perfect side chick to him the entire
two years. She was loyal to a fault, considerate, and she
went above and beyond her duty to please him in any way
imaginable. If anyone had the right to be candid with
Dendrick, he believed it was Anastasia.

"Do you think Bishop is a good mayor, baby?" he asked
again.

"Yeah, I do. But I think you'll be just as good a mayor
as he is or even better." Anastasia reached up and framed
Dendrick's face with her palms. Her eyes bore directly
into his seconds before she kissed his lips softly. "Just
promise me that you won't forget about me . . . about *us*
when you get to city hall, Big Daddy."

"Nothing will ever make me forget about you, girl.
Daddy can't get enough of your sweet self."

Dendrick eased his tongue between Anastasia's lips as
his hand snaked down between their bodies. His fingers
found her sweet goodness warm and saturated. Her clit
was hard and pulsing under his magic touch.

"Aaaah, yesss, Daddy . . ."

Dendrick continued strumming Anastasia like his personal musical instrument as she squirmed and hummed
a melody of pure pleasure against his lips. With each
snaking motion of his tongue, feasting on hers in coor-

dination with the finger massage to her clit, he felt her soul soaring higher and higher above the earth. Nothing made him feel more like a man than to please his woman.

When Anastasia's body began to writhe and convulse underneath him as she climaxed under his touch, thoughts of Dendrick's failing campaign and his miserable marriage vanished from his mind. He had one thing on his brain. He wanted to sink his dick so deep inside of Anastasia and stroke away every worry, failure, and fear that was haunting him.

Dendrick entered her in one long and smooth thrust. Their bodies were so in sync that the physical connection was tighter than a bolt and screw. The warmth and wetness of her tight pussy felt so damn good, it made his heart float inside his chest. His entire body was ablaze from her fiery, drenched walls as he eased in and out of her with the sound of her sex honey sloshing in his ears. Dendrick swore before man and beast that no other woman on the planet could satisfy his sexual appetite like Anastasia. Her platinum pussy was the potion for his pain on any given day. On top of that, she knew just what to do to cater to his emotional needs as well.

If it hadn't been for his children, Dendrick would've packed up and left Charmaine for Anastasia the moment she started hounding him about running for mayor. It had been *her* dream to make a splash on the political scene, not his. Now, he was in too deep financially to drop out. Too many people had made commitments to his candidacy, and they were now working hard in his camp. It was a damn shame that their efforts would prove to be in vain. It didn't matter what kind of dirt anyone uncovered on Bishop, his wife, dog, or distant cousin. The people of Atlanta were crazy about him, and they were going to reelect him to city hall without a doubt.

But that wasn't important at the moment as Dendrick bumped and grinded his way closer and closer to a heart-stopping nut. His mounting release was spreading slowly through his body, kissing every inch with sweet sensations. And then, like fireworks, an orgasm blasted him into orbit, and he lingered there for several pleasurable seconds. When he landed from the stars, the aftershocks rocked him to a peaceful sleep like a newborn baby with Anastasia in his arms.

"I thought you'd be in bed by now." Josiah turned on the light in the den and walked farther into the room.

Gypsie tore her eyes away from the TV to stare at her boss. She smiled nervously for no other reason than to lighten the mood. After finally helping Gem come to terms with her mom's condition, preparing dinner, and feeding the girls, Gypsie was physically and emotionally drained. But she found enough energy to get Gem and Treasure in and out of the bathtub in time to catch Josiah being hammered by the local media on the evening news. After that, she had no reason to smile. And she knew that matters would only get worse once she told him about Gem's little "situation" at school.

"I waited up because there's something I need to discuss with you."

"Yeah?"

Gypsie sighed and nodded her head.

"Lay it on me. How much worse can it be than what I've already dealt with today?"

"Gem was teased at school today because of the announcement about Mrs. Bishop's substance abuse problem. A little girl named Ryland repeated some nonsense her auntie had said around the house, and it hurt Gem's feelings. The little brat even had the nerve to tell the other children not to play with her."

"Damn it! Some people are just plain stupid and cruel. I don't blame the little girl. I want to throw her aunt in jail and make her swallow the key."

Gypsie smacked her lips and made a fist. "I want to punch her in the face. The crap she fed her niece caused Gem to have a meltdown in art class. The school called you, but you were in the budget meeting, so I turned into the Incredible Caretaker and went to the school."

"You did? I'm so sorry, Gypsie. I don't pay you enough to do school visits."

"Honestly, I didn't mind. My only concern was Gem. When I arrived at the school and saw how upset she was, I almost fell apart. But I held it together long enough to give the headmistress a piece of my mind."

"Why? What the hell was her problem?"

"She attempted to bring up Mrs. Bishop's addiction in a conversation, but I cut her off. It was inappropriate for her to discuss the situation with me, especially in front of Gem."

"You're right. Dr. Bah was way out of line. I need to have a conference with her before Gem goes back to school."

"That's exactly what I told her before I signed both girls out of classes for the remainder of the day."

"Good." Josiah nodded. "Schedule a conference for Monday morning after the girls and I return from Montana. I want them to stay home for the next two days until we leave."

"Okay. I'll call Miss Gladys so she can watch them."

"Nah, don't call her. I'd rather you stay home with them."

"What about *work,* Josiah?"

"You can do anything that requires your immediate attention from my home office. And Rebecca can cover your other duties."

"Fine."

A few moments of silence floated between them. Gypsie's thoughts were running all over the place. Her heart was still tender for her brightest Gem, and she was worried about Josiah as he entered the final phase of the campaign with the news of his wife's drug issues hovering over him.

"I can't wait for this year to be over," he announced, breaking the silence. "It has been the worst year of my life. My marriage is on the rocks because my wife is hooked on drugs, and my children are suffering as a result. I don't give a damn how the election turns out. I just want peace in my life again. Mink's problem with heroin has robbed our girls and me of our peace, and I want it back. I hope she realizes how much her addiction has cost our family."

"I think she does. That's why she's working hard to kick the habit. She's been in treatment close to thirty days now, so she must be doing okay."

"I damn sure hope so. The girls and I will find out for sure in three days."

Chapter Thirty-four

Mink rested her chin in the palm of her hand as she lay in bed on her side. The damp and rumpled bedsheet was wrapped loosely around her naked body.

Norm M. picked up his red and black checkered boxers from the floor and turned around. He smiled at Mink. "I've got to get out of here and make it back to the other side before the shift changes."

"How do you expect to do that without getting caught?"

"Wealth has its privileges, my dear." He winked his eye. "The rich live in a totally different world than others. Limitless benefits are always within reach. There's nothing that some people won't do if the price is right. And because I have globs of money, I can pretty much have whatever I want and do anything I damn well please."

Mink laughed dryly. "If that's true, why are you stuck in a rehab center with common junkies and alcoholics like me, Mr. Moviemaker? Surely, all your millions could've bought off a doctor or a judge or two to spare you from living in druggie land amongst us paupers. What's your story?"

"It's my brothers' and cousins' fault. They were always jealous of me because I was the golden child in the family. Those bastards hated me when we were growing up because it was obvious that *I* was next in line to rule over the family empire."

"So, I guess you're the oldest. The oldest is always the successor, right?"

Norm M. shook his head. "No, I wasn't the oldest of my brothers or cousins. Clifford, my cousin, was. My brother, Irwin, was right behind him. But *I* was the most qualified."

"Of course, you were," Mink said with a smirk on her face and deliberate sarcasm in her tone.

"It's true, my dear. I was born with *the gift*. It's the same gift that Grandpa Abner had. Everyone knew very early on that I was a natural filmmaker. By the age of 10, I was fascinated with movies and all that it entailed to make them. I used to go to work with my father and uncles every chance I got. Medallion Studios and Production Company became my favorite place on earth."

"Wait a minute." Mink sat straight up in the bed with her mouth wide open. The sheet fell to her waist, exposing her bare breasts. "Your family owns *Medallion Studios?*"

Norm M. nodded with a cocky gleam in his eyes.

"So . . . So, you guys are responsible for that twisted movie called *Love's Maniac*, starring Asia Blair and Hugo Whitby?"

"Yes, my dear. I worked particularly hard on that Oscar and Golden Globe–winning masterpiece."

"Get the fuck out of here! Oooh! Oooh! Medallion Studios produced Denzel's most recent movie with Thandie Newton too," Mink said excitedly, snapping her fingers. "What was the name of that flick?"

"*Uncertain Matters.*"

"Yeah! That's it!" Mink's enthusiasm suddenly faded, and, once again, her curiosity was piqued. "I still don't understand why you're in drug rehab. You're *loaded*. Did you do some crazy shit, and your brothers had you legally committed to drug jail?"

"No, I didn't. You see, my two brothers and three cousins were jealous of my success in the family business even when we were just boys. While they were out doing normal things like baseball, Boy Scouts, surfing, and goofing off with their friends, I was on a movie set; sometimes even behind a camera. I used to hang around the directors and producers all the time. Entire crews and some of Hollywood's A-list actors knew me. I was a prodigy."

"So why didn't your brothers and cousins learn the family business like you did?"

"They didn't want to. The five of them thought the company would be handed over to them automatically by my father and uncles once they retired or died. Each of them wanted to sit behind desks and make business deals on behalf of the company, but they forgot about the artistic side."

"What happened when the time came to hand over the reins to the next in line?"

"Uncle Phillip died three years after I completed my master's degree in cinema and media production at the prestigious Boston University School of Theater. My siblings and cousins had all studied business. They didn't have any idea how to produce a movie or which projects or actors were suitable to star in Medallion productions. I was the only one who did. So, my father and uncles crowned me prince of the pack. And I served the company well. I brought in *billions*."

Mink noticed the sadness in Norm M.'s eyes as he took a seat on the bed and began putting on his socks.

"The money, the fame, and the glamour got to you, didn't it? You can tell me because I understand."

"Gorgeous, high-society women swarmed all around me like bumblebees. I was weak and unable to resist them all. After three childless, failed marriages due to my constant infidelities, I became terribly depressed. Something was missing from my life, but I had no idea what it was. On a whim, I snorted pure cocaine for the first time at a wrap party on the island of Viti Levu in Fiji. I was hooked immediately, although I was in great denial $2 million and three box office flops later." Norm M. sighed and closed his eyes. "My brothers, Irwin, and Ellis, led the group in my intervention when a few actors and an overzealous director started complaining. I stopped using cold turkey for three months. All was well until—"

"Until the cravings became too powerful for you to bear. That cocaine was calling your body like a horny lover, wasn't it? That shit had you feenin' like a weak little bitch, and your strung-out ass relapsed, right?"

Seemingly ashamed and defeated, Norm M. nodded his head.

"I know the deal. Without treatment and the desire to stop, we addicts can forget about recovery. It's impossible. People like us have to be treated by professionals and work a rigid rehab program. But hell, it's *hard!* Normal folks like my husband and his family just don't get it. Unless a person has experienced addiction, they'll never understand what we're battling against."

"You're right. My brothers and cousins refused to see how hard I was trying. Yes, I had messed up a few deals and cost the company millions of dollars, but I didn't do it intentionally. They were looking for a reason to get rid of me, and I gave them one."

"What did you do?" Mink grabbed his hand and squeezed it.

"I went over my budget on a film that we were shooting in Vegas, and I had already snorted half of the salaries for the two lead actors. But I was going to make up for it by using the advance investments for a movie that was scheduled to begin production in Monte Carlo in a few weeks. Irwin, that evil son of a bitch, had taken my name off of the company's accounts without my knowledge so that I couldn't make good on my mistake. The movie was never completed through production, so the actors, director, and the entire crew didn't get paid. They all sued Medallion, and for the first time in fifty years, the company's reputation took a hit."

"I'm sorry, Norman," Mink said sympathetically, calling him by his full first name. "I'm so sorry."

"My family settled with all of the plaintiffs and took legal action against me! I could've fixed the mess that I'd made, but *nooo* . . . Irwin and Clifford wouldn't let me. They went to court to try to oust me out of the family business, and the judge took their side. He ordered me to come here for ninety days or lose my place in the company and my financial share."

"So, you chose to come here."

"Of course, I did. My fiancée, Tawny, and I decided it was my only choice. So, here I am."

"Are you . . . I mean, did you . . ." Mink's question got twisted on her tongue.

"Did I really work the program? You want to know if I've recovered from my coke addiction."

Mink nodded.

"Well, I haven't used cocaine in ninety days. I'm not an alcoholic, but it did the trick most days when I needed to relax. But to answer your question, I don't know if I'm actually in recovery or not. I won't know until I leave and return to the real world next week. That will be my test."

"I hope you make it out there. It won't be easy, but you ought to give it an honest effort."

"I will, my dear. I owe it to myself, my fiancée, and Evan, our 4-year-old son. That woman has supported me tremendously. She brings out the very best in me, and Evan is my world." Norm M. raked his fingers through his tousled, gray hair. "What about you, Mink? Did you come to rehab to get clean or are you here under duress?"

"Both, I guess. I don't ever want to use heroin again, for sure. But I also came here to please my husband. I want my family back, Norm M. I love my man and my babies more than I love myself, but I'm a sick woman. I have five more months to go in this hellhole. I can endure without heroin. I'll just have to continue to use other substances to keep me settled."

"I'll take care of that. I'm going to make sure you have whatever you need once I leave."

"You will?"

"Of course, I will. I've walked in your shoes, so I know how difficult this disease is. I'll make arrangements with Shannon, the nurse. My buddy, Greg, will look out for you too. He's the tall African America orderly with all those gang tattoos."

"I know who he is." Mink didn't want to deal with Greg. He was one scandalous son of a bitch.

"Good. I'll make sure he maintains your alcohol supply."

"Coke too, please. I'm not hooked on that shit. It just keeps me calm and relaxed while I'm here like the liquor did for you. The way I see it, I'm clean as long as I don't use heroin. Everything else is like smoking a cigarette or drinking coffee. I can take it or leave it."

Fully dressed, Norm M. stood and handed Mink a business card. "You'll have phone privileges soon. Give me a call from time to time."

"Thanks. I'll hit you up now and then. I may even visit you in Hollywood for your next movie premiere. I would love to stroll down the red carpet and strike a pose or two."

"If all goes well in New York, you'll get your red carpet experience someday soon."

"Oh yeah?"

"You will indeed, my dear. You see, I'll be in the Big Apple after I'm discharged from here Monday. I have an apartment there on Park Avenue, and Medallion's casting office is there as well. I'm going to spend a few weeks in the city before I go home to LA. I have a few meetings lined up with some key players I'm trying to woo for my comeback project. If everything goes according to plan, I'll be back at the top of Medallion's totem pole again."

"I have my fingers crossed for you. You're a cool dude, Norm M. I wish we had hooked up earlier."

"So do I, Mink." He looked around the room. "Well, I better get going. Enjoy your visit with your husband and children this coming weekend."

"I will."

Chapter Thirty-five

"Daddy, look! That mountain is so *big*. It goes all the way up to the sky!"

Josiah looked out the window as the driver maneuvered the car slowly over the narrow, winding road up the mountain. The view was breathtakingly beautiful. He understood why Treasure's young and impressionable eyes were so amazed.

"I like the water. Is that a river or the ocean down there, Daddy?"

"It's a *lake*, Gem," he answered, chuckling.

"I bet there's a lot of fish swimming in it."

"I think you're right."

Just then, a massive, beige, stucco structure surrounded by smaller buildings and trees came into full view. The car slowed down on its approach, but Josiah's heartbeat went into express mode. It thumped rapidly and forcefully inside his chest with nervous anticipation. His excitement over seeing Mink clean and sober was like that of a child in a toy store. Josiah handed the driver his license when the car stopped at the guard shack right outside the brick and wrought iron gate. It only took the security guard a moment to verify that he was a pre-approved guest at the facility before he allowed the car entrance.

Josiah opened the car door as soon as the car stopped in front of the rehab center's main building. "Come on, princesses. Let's go see your mommy."

He helped the girls out of the car as the driver retrieved their luggage from the trunk. Josiah lifted Treasure into his arms and grabbed Gem by her hand. They followed the driver as he carried their bags toward the building's entrance.

"Does Mommy live in this mansion, Daddy?"

"It's not a mansion, Gem. It's a hospital. Remember?"

The child didn't respond. Josiah squeezed her hand gently as they entered the building.

"Thank you, sir," he said to the driver after he placed the two suitcases on the plush burgundy carpet. He then handed the man a hefty tip before he walked to the reception area.

"Welcome to Serenity Springs. How may I help you, sir?"

"My name is Josiah Bishop. My daughters and I are here for a weekend visit with my wife, one of your residents. Her name is Mink Bishop."

The woman smiled. "Oh, *you're* Mink's husband. She talks about you all the time. Have a seat in the waiting area, Mr. Bishop. Someone will come and escort you and your beautiful daughters to your cabin. Your wife will join you there after midday group session."

"Why are you still wasting that man's time, Blackbird? You don't want him. You're in love with *Josiah*."

"And where exactly is Josiah right now, TiTi?"

"He's in Montana visiting his wife."

"Now, where do I fit into his *married* life?"

Gypsie stared at Tianji through the computer screen, waiting for her smart comeback. Their FaceTime session had taken a turn into the serious zone. All the laughter and joking around had come to an abrupt halt. The pair of lifelong BFFs looked into each other's eyes as silent seconds ticked by.

"You're his administrative assistant and childcare provider *for now,*" Tianji finally answered, breaking through the awkward quietness. "But you love that man, and he's got the hots for you."

"I'll admit there's chemistry between Josiah and me, but I don't think it's *love.* Looking back on it, I believe I had an innocent crush on him for a minute, but I quickly came to my senses and shook it off."

"A *crush,* huh? Bye, Felecia!"

"*TiTi,*" Gypsie whined.

"You're in love with that man. I can hear it in your voice and see it in your eyes, Blackbird. Who knows you better than I do?"

"Nobody."

"Damn right! We've been tighter than cheap shoes on a bunion since we were 5 years old. I know you love Josiah, but I understand why you refuse to admit it. And I respect you for not acting on those feelings. *But—*"

"But *what,* TiTi? If you were me, you'd play home wrecker, seduce the man, and tear his family apart? I'm not built like you. I respect Josiah for standing by his wife, even though I don't believe she's worthy of his loyalty. As much as it breaks my heart, I'm cheering for him because I want him to be happy. And if reconnecting with his wife will bring him happiness, I hope God will make it happen."

"I can't argue with you because you're definitely correct, honey. I would be all over that sexy hunk of delicious fudge. He wouldn't even remember his cracked-out wife's name. Those little girls would be calling *me* Mommy by now." Tianji laughed like crazy. "But all jokes aside, I've got nothing but respect for you, Blackbird. You're a classy lady. I'm glad you're not like me."

"Yeah, you're like a male version of Jeremiah. I should box him up and send him to you special delivery."

"Hell yeah! Send his ass on up here, especially if he's a mocha god like his twin brother. I would train him to sit, roll over, and fetch my bedroom slippers, among *other things*."

Gypsie giggled and wrinkled her nose. "*Eeeew!* You're so *nasty!* You and Jeremiah are two of a kind for sure."

"Thanks for the compliment, darling."

"Well, I've got to go. Preston will be here in an hour."

"Okay, go ahead and get ready for your boring date with Mr. Accountant. He will *never* make your panties wet and drop to your ankles with just one touch like Josiah can."

"Oh, shut up, TiTi! I'm fine with dry panties up to my breasts as long as I can look at myself in the mirror without guilt. Besides, Preston is a nice guy, so I owe it to myself to see how far this thing between us can go."

"It won't even make it around the corner, honey, because he is *not* the man for you."

"Whatever. Bye, girl. I love you."

"I love you too."

Mink rushed out of group therapy with one thought in mind—she was about to see her husband and her babies. It felt like a million butterflies were fluttering around in her belly as she made her way to Shannon's office. She was the sweet nurse who had taken her urine and hair follicle samples early this morning. As expected, Mink had tested negative for heroin and all other drugs. All she needed from Shannon now was a copy of the official drug screen report to pass along to her case manager. After that, Mink would go to her room, grab the duffle bag she'd packed last night, and report to the security office. One of the guards would then transport her by golf cart to the cabin that had been assigned to her and her family for the weekend.

Anxious and on an adrenaline rush, Mink picked up her pace as she rounded the corner, leading to Shannon's office. As bad luck would have it, she came face-to-face with none other than *Greg*. She'd been avoiding him since her rendezvous with Norman M.

"What's up?"

"Hey, Greg."

He flashed a smile dripping with venom. "I see you're in a hurry to check out for your weekend pass with your family."

"You're damn right." Mink placed her hands on her hips and stared Greg down with disgust.

"You act like you don't know me no more since you hooked up with ole white dude. I bet when he leaves Monday, you're gonna be trying to ride my dick again for a treat."

"Bullshit."

"So, you've gone *legit* now? You're clean and sober all of a sudden?" He laughed and clapped his hands like he was on the front row at a Kevin Hart comedy show. "You're a dopie . . . a junkie . . . a plain ole addict who's wasting your husband's money, time, and emotions while you're up here in this expensive drug farm using, boozing, and snoozing with any man who'll throw you a bone."

"Shut the fuck up, you evil bastard," Mink hissed softly.

"Go ahead and call me whatever you want, but by five o'clock Monday evening, you'll be calling me *Big Daddy*."

Greg taunted Mink with laughter when she stormed past him madder than a rattlesnake. She was *pissed*. The truth hurt, but what could she do about it? She no doubt was faking her way through her treatment program instead of working toward genuine drug abstinence and sobriety. Mink was beginning to think maybe she was incapable of being clean. Her emotional wounds were deep and severely painful. She wanted to release them, but fear wouldn't allow her to. Her flaws were too ugly and shameful. No one could ever know what she had done in Germany, especially not Josiah. If he ever found out about her past, his love for her would dry up like a river in a drought. Therefore, her sin would forever remain a secret between her and the parties involved. And, unfortunately, the chains of bondage that enslaved her to heroin would never be broken.

Chapter Thirty-six

"Mmm . . ." Preston moaned against Gypsie's parted lips as his tongue indulged hers.

Most women would consider his kissing game mind-blowing. And his large, slow hands gently palming her ass should've been igniting tiny sparks all over her smooth cinnamon flesh. But Gypsie felt nothing. No sizzle. No tingles. *Zilch. Nada.* It was a damn shame too because he was making all the right moves, and he had been on his A-game the entire evening throughout dinner and the movie. But neither a physical nor an emotional connection was in the stars for them.

"Oooh . . ." Gypsie pushed against Preston's chest with her palms and took a giant backward step to break their connection abruptly. *Damn! He must have a daddy python down there! That thing is huge and harder than a sledgehammer.*

Preston smiled seductively, seemingly flattered that his protruding erection had gotten Gypsie's attention. There was a haze in his light brown eyes that were slightly shaded by long, curly lashes. His silky caramel complexion appeared heated with passion, evident by flecks of crimson. Preston was a handsome man, oozing with raw sex appeal. Gypsie couldn't deny that. His towering, muscular frame and confident gait were enough to make any girl do a double take, even in church. But although he was wrapped in masculine beauty, the clean-cut accountant missed the mark on Gypsie's companion must-have checklist. Sadly, he could not light her feminine fire.

"Come here, girl. I can't get enough of you." Preston reached out and pulled Gypsie's petite body snuggly against his again. Squeezing her tiny waist with his long arms, he went in for another kiss.

Gypsie turned her head, avoiding his lips. "It's getting late, Preston." She poked her chest with her index finger. "This girl has to hit the gym and make a grocery run in the morning."

"Yeah, but this guy can give you a *special* workout tonight, will gladly go grocery shopping for you tomorrow, and deliver all of your desired food items to your doorstep by noon. Let me spend the night, baby. I want to make love to you."

"Um . . . I . . . um . . . Preston . . ."

"What's the matter, Gypsie? We've been seeing each other for a while. I thought we were heading toward something serious and possibly permanent."

"I'm sorry if I've said or done something to make you believe our friendship was evolving into a romantic relationship. Please forgive me because that was *never* my intention. I thought you understood that from the very beginning."

"I heard what you said on our first date." He frowned and stuffed his hands inside his pockets. "But you can't blame a brotha for wishing. I'm a good man, Gypsie. You know that. I don't have any kids, ex-wives, diseases, or creditors. Give me a chance. Give *us* a chance. I'm willing to do anything to please you or die trying."

"I'm sorry, but my heart and head aren't ready for a commitment right now. It wouldn't be fair to you to get seriously involved with me when I'm unable to give you my all."

"Girl, I want you so badly that I'd gladly accept 20 percent of whatever you have to offer and still give you all of me, plus bonuses."

"You deserve better than that. And I'm sure there's a woman out there somewhere who'd be happy to give you exactly what you're looking for. I'm just not that woman, Preston."

Without another word, Gypsie opened her front door and instantly felt a cool fall breeze wisp around her body. Her heart ached for Preston because he was truly a great catch, but he wasn't the man for her. And because of her selfless spirit, Gypsie refused to keep him hanging on.

"So, I guess this is it, huh?"

"Yes, it is."

"Can we hang out now and then as *friends?*"

Gypsie shook her head. "That wouldn't be wise."

"I understand. I don't like it, but I'll respect your wishes." Preston kissed her cheek. "You're a special lady, Miss Robinson. The man who'll be lucky enough to make you his should be crowned king of the world. He better treat you like a queen too, or he'll have to deal with *me.*"

Josiah looked up from his laptop and stared at Mink when she closed the bedroom door.

"I didn't think Treasure would ever fall asleep. She kept begging me to read story after story until she could barely hold her eyelids up. It was like she thought if she drifted off, I'd disappear forever. My poor little girl . . ." Mink wiped away the tears trickling down her cheeks. "My insanity has scarred her emotionally."

"Come here, baby." Josiah closed the computer and placed it on the nightstand. Then he pulled back the covers and opened his arms to the love of his life.

"Oh, JoJo, I'm *sooo* sorry. I've made a big mess of our lives," she cried as she took a seat on his lap. "My baby girl thinks I'm some kind of phantom, and Gem looks at me like I'm a complete stranger. What have I done to our babies?"

Josiah wrapped his arms around Mink comfortingly and placed a kiss on her forehead. "The girls are going to be okay. I'll get them into individual counseling as soon as we get back to Atlanta. Hell, I'm thinking about seeing a shrink myself. And, of course, we'll do family therapy once you come home to us. Until then, just continue to do well in treatment and pray to God for strength."

Mink rested her cheek against Josiah's bare chest and listened to his heartbeat. It was a strong and steady cadence; the result of healthy living. The warmth of his touch as his hands caressed her back tenderly awakened her sexual hunger for him. The Almighty had created only *one* man who could make love to her entire body with total satisfaction while reviving her spirit and causing her heart to sing.

"There ain't no words to describe how much I love you, JoJo. God knows I don't deserve you, but you're still here. I have put you and our daughters through pure hell; yet, you never gave up on me."

"I promised to love you forever, and that's what I'm going to do." Josiah pulled back and held Mink at arm's length and looked into her eyes. "Just keep working toward becoming clean, sober, and mentally healthy for the rest of your life, and you'll never have to worry about me going anywhere. Can you promise me you'll continue to commit everything you've got to recovery?"

Hell no, I can't! And right now is the perfect moment to explain why. Tell him about the baby, Mink. Confess it, damn it! Look that man in his eyes and tell him what you've never told all of your sponsors, therapists, or doctors. He won't judge you because he loves you, and he's committed to your marriage. Reveal the one secret you've been hiding all these years. If you don't, it will continue to haunt you, and you will never be free. Heroin will kill you.

Mink's entire body shivered as her conscience continued screaming its appeal for her to tell Josiah her deep-
est, darkest, and damnedest secret. *I can't!* she mentally
shouted back in protest. Once again, fear and shame won
the battle. Her secret would remain buried deep within
her soul until death.

She forced a smile on her face and nodded. "I promise
to do everything in my power to complete the treatment
program here. Then I'm going to come home a brand-
new woman for you and our babies."

Mink solidified her phony promise with a passionate
kiss. It felt like heaven to be back in Josiah's arms again.
She found strength and security in his embrace. United,
they were invincible and powerful enough to take on
the world. With Josiah in her corner, Mink believed she
could conquer anything. But heroin was the single force
of evil standing in her way.

When the kiss deepened, and the primitive call of
nature enveloped them, Mink surrendered. Josiah
relaxed his back against the headboard and pulled her
on top of him in a forward straddle. The heat level spiked
from fifty to a thousand in a matter of seconds. Desirous
moans and the sound of the bed springs yielding to their
movements filled the room. Slowly and with great care,
Josiah slid the simple blue nightgown over Mink's head
and carelessly tossed it aside. Once again, their lips met
in a fiery kiss with so much tongue action that Mink's
heart did the Electric Slide in her chest.

She threw her head back and purred when Josiah's hot,
moist mouth left her lips and covered her right nipple
and suckled. His oral grip and the sensation of his tongue
circling the taut tip caused a feminine flood in Mink's
crotch. On instinct, she began to grind her wet goodness
rhythmically against Josiah's stiff penis. Their bodies
moved in perfect coordination as the kisses grew more
urgent and greedier.

Mink squealed with sheer delight when Josiah flipped
her over onto her back and hovered above her. She
offered no protest when he slid her drenched thong
from her bottom and down her legs, releasing the aroma
of pungent sex in the air. When he stood from the bed
with need in his eyes and a sexy half smile on his face,
Mink watched him in awe. Torturously unrushed, he
rid himself of his wife beater and loose-fitting boxers.
Magnificent! she mentally complimented as if she hadn't
been blessed with the honor of witnessing all his splen-
did nakedness countless times over the years.

But tonight was special. It was a long overdue reunion.
Everything about the moment seemed new and improved.
Josiah's body far exceeded the satisfaction of Mink's
memory, and his dick looked thicker, longer, and more
delicious than ever before. Unable to control herself, she
reached out both arms to him, ready to devour him from
head to toe.

"JoJo . . . *please* . . ."

Josiah smiled teasingly and turned away. He reached
into the nightstand for reasons unknown while the
pressure between Mink's thighs began to escalate. Every
inch of her anatomy was ablaze. She felt like she would
explode if she couldn't have him *now*. But in the blink of
an eye, the flame was doused like ice water on a flickering
candle when Josiah turned around with a condom in his
hand.

"JoJo?" Mink sat up straight in bed. "Why did you
bring condoms? You know I can't get pregnant. I had an
IUD inserted eight weeks after I gave birth to Treasure."

Josiah sat down on the bed next to her. "I know, but
we haven't been together in a while. And the last time . . ."

Mink remained quiet after Josiah's voice trailed off.
She knew what he'd failed to say. Why would he remind
her about the chlamydia incident at a moment like this?
At times, he could be so fucking insensitive.

"Mink, don't be mad, baby. I just think we should practice caution until you come home, and we both have physical exams and receive clearance from our doctors. You do understand, don't you?" He searched her eyes.

Mink smiled, but she was seething inside. "Yeah, I understand."

Chapter Thirty-seven

"Good morning, baby."

Mink smiled. "Good morning to you."

"The girls are in the living room watching TV. I came in here to make sure you were still breathing. I think you overexerted yourself last night." Josiah grinned sheepishly. "If you're sore, I apologize."

"I've never felt better. I'm hungry, though. I burned off all three meals from yesterday, thanks to you." Mink laughed out loud. "You need to feed me, Mayor Bishop."

"The kitchen attendant delivered breakfast nearly an hour ago. The girls and I have already eaten. The chef did his thing on the French toast. Your plate is in the microwave. Get up so your man can feed you."

"Okay." Mink sat up in bed, quietly staring at Josiah for a moment.

"What?"

"Have you been faithful to me, JoJo?"

"Mink, I—"

"Wait. I have to say this to you. We were separated for a while back home, and I've been here a month. You're a young, good-looking man with a healthy, sexual appetite. I bet women throw their panties at you all the time. Be honest with me. I can handle it. Have you been with another woman?"

Josiah shook his head. "No, Mink, I have not had sex of any kind with another woman. I've *never* cheated on you. I swear."

Images of that steamy night at the bottom of the staircase with Gypsie invaded his mind while Mink continued talking softly. *Hot damn!* His body was craving her like a starving man in search of bread that particular night. If his mother hadn't called, Josiah would've . . .

"*JoJo!*"

"Um . . . yeah, Mink?"

"I said if you've slept with another woman, I don't have a right to be upset." Mink lowered her eyes. "When I was out there, I did some things I'm not proud of. But it was all a part of the disease, you know. The insanity of my addiction caused me to lose control."

"That's all in the past, baby. Forget about all of that. I've already forgiven you for everything you did when you were using. Hey, you're in recovery now, though, right?"

Mink sniffled and wiped her tears away with her fingertips. "Right."

"So, things are going to be different when you come home. I promise to do whatever it'll take to make you happy and comfortable. You can even go back to work if you want to. I don't care as long as you're content."

"I can't wait." Mink smiled through more tears.

Josiah extended his hand to her. "Come on, baby. It's time for you to eat."

"Okay. After I finish, I want to take you and the girls for a walk on the nature trail. The scenery is so beautiful and relaxing. Treasure is going to go crazy over the ducks in the lake."

"Yeah, she'll like them."

Mink's face grew somber, and she began to cry again. "Nothing seems to excite Gem anymore whenever I'm around. I think I've lost her, JoJo. She stares at me like she hates me."

"Gem is so much like you." Josiah laughed lightly. "Hell, she's the spitting image of you, Mink. She didn't inherit a single physical trait from me. Her face, hair, complexion, and stature are exactly like yours. Even her stubbornness and smart mouth came from you. That's why you two have always butted heads."

"And my drug use only made it worse, huh?"

"Unfortunately, it did. But I don't want you to think about that right now. Let's get our day started and have some family fun."

Soulful music from the Bose system filled the small kitchen. The sound of the edge of a butcher knife hitting the chopping board as it sliced through celery stalks seemed to be keeping time. Gypsie, in her private world, threw her head back and belted out the song's lyrics and shimmied her hips.

"I can cast a spell of secrets you can't tell! Mix a special brew, put fire inside of you! But anytime you feel—"

The phone rang, interrupting Gypsie's loud and off-key crooning as she sang "I'm Every Woman" along with the legendary Chaka Khan. She frowned and stared at her cell phone, wondering who the hell was disturbing her Saturday afternoon solitude. She had already spoken to her parents, Tianji, and even her cousin, Clark. They all made up her regular gossip gang. No one else was supposed to be chiming in on her downtime away from city hall and nanny duty.

Gypsie dropped the knife and wiped her hands on the skirt of her apron before she reached for the phone. "Hello?"

"What's up, Miss Robinson?"

"What do you want, Jeremiah?" Gypsie giggled like a silly kid. "Don't you have something better to do on the weekend than harass me?"

"Yeah, I do, but my weekend life doesn't start until midnight. So, I figured I'd check up on you since JoJo and the girls are away. What's on your agenda today?"

"I'm keeping busy doing a little bit of this and a little bit of that."

"Yeah, right."

Gypsie took immediate offense. "What the hell is that supposed to mean? You don't think I have a life outside of work? Well, I do."

"So, I guess you're still kicking it with that buster from the accounting department."

"No, I'm not. I ended that last night." Gypsie pulled out a chair and sat down at the dinette. "Preston is a real cool dude, but I just couldn't connect with him romantically. Anyway, what're you up to this afternoon, *Mr. Midnight?*"

"Walk to your front door."

"Huh? What are you talking about, Jeremiah?"

"Just do it and stop lip hustling, girl."

Gypsie padded to the front door in her favorite red and white striped socks. Out of curiosity, she looked through the peephole and got the shock of her life. She disengaged the locks and snatched the door open.

"So, you thought it was a good idea to show up at my apartment unannounced on a Saturday afternoon? You think too highly of yourself, Mr. Bishop."

Jeremiah grinned and held up a bottle of Emmolo Merlot. "Now, how're you going to be salty at a brotha with a fine bottle of wine?"

"Bring your cocky behind on in here. I'm cooking stuffed chicken breasts in a curry roux and a vegetable-pasta casserole. That wine will go just right with my gourmet masterpiece. Plus, I'll get to kick your ass in Madden 15 while the food is cooking."

"I knew the wine would be my ticket in."

"Oh, shut up."

***

"Look at the ducks, Gem!"

"Wait a—"

Treasure took off running at full speed with her sister chasing behind her before their mother could object. Mink became a bundle of bad nerves as her daughters ran closer to the lake. Of all the people who could be outside enjoying the spectacular sights along the facility's nature trail, why the hell were Norm M. and Greg chilling around the campus today? A sudden, unsettling feeling in the pit of Mink's stomach caused her body to stiffen.

Josiah squeezed her hand. "Relax, baby. They'll be fine," he assured her, looking at the girls. "You said Treasure would be fascinated with the ducks. I think Gem is too. Look at her feeding them. It was nice of that guy to give her a handful of whatever she's tossing on the water."

Mink didn't respond because her words were lodged painfully in her throat. She wanted to scream for the girls to get away from Greg. They knew better than to talk to strangers. She and Josiah had taught them that rule very early on when they were barely able to speak. They obviously had no worries because their overprotective father was close by, and they had all the confidence in the world in him. The girls knew Josiah would never allow harm to come to them.

"I'm 6 and Treasure is 4. We live in Atlanta with our daddy and Miss Gypsie. Our mommy lives here."

"Is that right?" Greg asked, grinning like an evil villain from a horror movie.

"Yes."

"My wife tried to stop my daughters from bothering you, sir, but they ran off."

Greg eyed Mink and then Josiah. "These pretty little girls ain't doing me no harm, sir. They're just helping me feed the ducks."

"I'm Josiah." He extended his hand for a friendly shake. "You've already met my daughters, Gem and Treasure. We're here visiting my wife."

Greg released Josiah's hand and eyeballed Mink from head to toe. "Hello, Miss Mink. You look happier today than I've ever seen you. I can tell you're enjoying the visit with your husband and girls."

"I sure am," Mink responded bitterly.

She looked over at Norm M. who was sitting on a bench near the water's edge reading a book. *Thank God he's a gentleman and not an asshole like Greg. He knows how to separate what goes on in here from real life.* With that thought in mind, Mink decided to speak with Norm M. later on about her situation with Greg. She had a feeling he was going to make her life a living hell after Norm M. left the rehab center.

"Daddy, come and feed the ducks with us!" Gem shouted before running off.

"Excuse us." Josiah walked away from Greg, pulling Mink along with him.

On impulse, she looked over her shoulder and found Greg smirking at her. She felt like vomiting when he grabbed his crotch and rolled his eyes to the sky in a lewd gesture. Mink turned her head quickly and squeezed Josiah's hand as they followed their daughters to the other side of the lake.

Chapter Thirty-eight

"You're cheating, J!" Gypsie yelled over the ringing telephone. "*Gnac* is not a word, and you know it."

"Yeah, it is. Where I come from *gnac* is a strong and delicious dark liquor, baby girl. I'm the Scrabble King. Three points!"

"Whatever, Negro."

Gypsie reached for Jeremiah's cell phone on the end table and handed it to him, but not before she sneaked a peek at the ID screen. It was Josiah calling him. Gypsie stood from the couch and walked into the kitchen with her heart pounding madly inside her chest. She wanted to give Jeremiah some privacy while he talked to his brother.

All the dishes had been washed, dried, and put away. And Jeremiah had spooned all the leftovers that he wasn't taking home with him into bowls and placed them inside the refrigerator. Therefore, there was nothing for Gypsie to do in her small kitchen except kill time. She just didn't want to be in the room with Jeremiah while he spoke to Josiah. All thoughts of him had escaped her since he and the girls had been gone, and for that, Gypsie was grateful. Keeping busy had been the perfect way to avoid thinking about him. Having seen his picture pop up on Jeremiah's phone was threatening to unravel her emotions, and she couldn't have that.

No matter how much Gypsie cared about Josiah, she had accepted the fact that they would never be together.

His love for his wife was strong, and his commitment to their marriage was indestructible. Gypsie prayed that one day God would bless her with a man who would dedicate his life and heart to her the same way.

"He asked about you."

The sound of Jeremiah's voice startled Gypsie as he entered the kitchen without warning. She spun around to face him with a smile on her face. "I'm sure he and my little divas are enjoying their visit with Mrs. Bishop."

"I told him you were fine. He was glad to hear it."

"I hope the clothes I packed for the girls are warm enough. Gem is always cold when everyone else is fine."

"He asked when had I'd spoken to you last, and I told him we were hanging out now."

"I bet Treasure is talking nonstop about her BFFs and school. She loves those little girls in her clique."

"Damn it, Gypsie! Are you *really* going to ignore me and dance around my words? I'm trying to have a conversation with you! Tell me how you truly feel."

"I am *fine*, J! I'm not some emotionally fragile damsel in distress who's about to fall apart because your brother went to visit his wife! Please stop trying to make something out of nothing, okay?"

"You love him, Gypsie. I know you do."

"So what?" She folded her arms across her chest defensively. "Love has nothing to do with this situation. Your brother is married, and he and his wife are working toward rebuilding their family. Once Mrs. Bishop completes substance abuse treatment and comes home to Atlanta, everything will return to normal. And I, for one, will wish them well. End of story."

Jeremiah laughed and shook his head. "Is that *really* how you believe the situation between JoJo and Mink is going to play out?"

Gypsie nodded. "He loves her."

"Maybe he does love her, but Mink loves *heroin*."

"*Nooo!* I want my baby! Please don't make me! Don't make me do it! Nooo!"

Josiah sat up and turned on the lamp on the night-stand. He pulled Mink into his arms and rocked her. "It's okay, baby. It was just a bad dream. I'm here with you. I'm here."

Josiah replayed Mink's words in his head as he held her close, rocking her in his arms. Her body was trembling, and she was whimpering pitifully. *Why is she dreaming about a baby? And who is she pleading with?*

"I have to use the bathroom, JoJo."

Mink pulled away from him and left the bed. His senses were on high alert. Her dream about a baby was weird. Maybe she'd had a nightmare about someone trying to kidnap Gem or Treasure. But what was someone trying to make her do? And who was the person? Josiah's curiosity was off the chart. He relaxed on the pillow and stared at the ceiling while he waited for Mink to return.

"I'm sorry I woke you up, JoJo. I must've had a nightmare."

Josiah studied Mink for a moment. She seemed nervous and frightened. "You were screaming and begging somebody not to take your baby. Come back to bed and tell me about your bad dream, Mink." He patted the space next to him.

"I-I . . . can't. I don't remember what w-what . . . what it was about. Are you sure I said something about a *baby?*" Mink laughed and fidgeted with her fingers. "That's crazy as hell. Why would I be dreaming about a baby?"

"I don't know. That's why I want you to try to remember the dream, baby. Maybe you need to talk to your therapist. You may be recalling something from your past that you've suppressed. Can you remember anything from your childhood about a baby doll or an actual baby that traumatized you?"

Mink sat down on the bed next to Josiah and rubbed his chest. "The only babies I remember are those two little angels in the other bedroom. From the moment they came into the world, they brought me joy. My dream was just a dream, JoJo. It has nothing to do with my real life. That's why I can't even remember what it was about."

Josiah searched Mink's eyes for some sign that she was being honest with him. Something in his gut told him she wasn't telling him the truth. He had a feeling she was hiding something. He had felt her body shivering, and her pleas for the baby had come from her soul. How could she not remember a dream that had brought her to tears?

Mink kissed Josiah's lips. "This is our last night together, and I don't want to waste it worrying about a dream that has already vanished from my memory. Make love to me, JoJo."

Josiah's body wanted to grant Mink's request, but his mind was on an entirely different page. He relaxed and tried to rein in his thoughts to enjoy one last night of passion with the woman he loved, although he believed she was withholding something important from him.

Through a crack in the blinds, Greg watched Mink kiss her daughters goodbye and hug them tight. She covered her face with both hands when the little girls got inside the car. Then the dam broke when she turned and faced her husband. With tears streaming fast and heavily down her cheeks, she fell into his arms, and he lifted her off her feet. They passionately kissed as if they would never see each other again. Most people's hearts would've melted watching the emotional scene, but Greg saw it all as one big show.

Mink had outdone herself over the weekend by pretending to be the perfect wife and mother on the road to recovery. Bullshit! She was nowhere near becoming clean and sober. Greg had seen thousands of addicts in his eleven years at Serenity Springs, and he knew the different levels of recovery. It was easy to spot the residents who were really trying to beat their addictions and even easier to point out the ones who had no desire to let go of the drugs they worshipped. Mink, in his opinion, was one of the worst addicts he had ever come across. Her soul was deeply sinking in the sea of chronic addiction. She was the most dishonest and fundamentally deceptive junkie in the history of the facility.

Her beauty and innocent-like aura worked in her favor, though. And she could talk her way out of or into any situation. No one had better communication skills than Mink Bishop. It was hard to deny her anything. Her soft-spoken voice and bright coppery eyes could charm a hungry, great white shark. But if her words, exotic good looks, and bubbly personality couldn't earn her whatever she wanted, she'd whip out her most irresistible trick of all—*sex*. An addict like Mink had no shame when it came to exchanging her body for a fix. No one knew that better than Greg.

He turned away from the window when the car transporting Mink's family pulled off. She wrapped her arms around her body and walked slowly toward the building with her head hanging low. It was obvious that she was sad that her weekend with her husband and daughters had come to an end. Greg expected her to return to her regular room and cry herself to sleep. But tomorrow morning she would arise and resume her normal routine. The *real* Mink Bishop would return.

***

Gypsie heard Josiah and the girls enter the house. She was excited because she had missed them like crazy, but she decided to stay in her room. Gem and Treasure liked whenever their father helped them prepare for bed, so she would allow them some daddy-daughter time tonight.

"Is Miss Gypsie asleep, Daddy?" Gem asked.

"I think she is. Her door is closed."

"Let's wake her up," Treasure suggested.

Gypsie softly giggled when she heard the child running down the hall toward the guest bedroom.

"No, Treasure. Let Gypsie rest tonight, sweetheart, because she has to deal with you and your sister all day tomorrow. You two are going to stay home from school again while I go there to meet with the headmistress and your teachers."

Gem frowned and lowered her eyes to the floor. "I don't like our school anymore, Daddy. Ryland and the other kids were mean to me. They teased me because Mommy is sick."

"That's why I'm going to visit your school in the morning. Daddy will try to fix the situation, if I can. If I can't, I'll find you and Treasure a new school."

"But I don't want to go to a new school," Treasure whined with tears in her eyes. "I'll miss Leilani, Karrington, Zion, and Tamalia. We're best friends." The child went into a full pitiful sob.

Gypsie jumped up, yanked her bedroom door open, and ran into the hallway. She lifted a crying Treasure into her arms. "Hush now, my most valuable Treasure. Don't cry. Your daddy will straighten out everything at your school tomorrow."

"Miss Gypsie, you woke up." Gem hugged her around her waist. "I missed you."

"I missed you too, darling."

Gypsie closed her eyes and basked in the love and affection her little divas were pouring all over her. It felt good to be loved. Oh, how she adored the little girls. They meant the world to her. The fact that she hadn't given birth to them didn't diminish her love for them one bit.

All of a sudden, Gypsie felt like she was being watched. Her eyes popped wide open and skidded over to Josiah. As expected, he was standing quietly taking in the love fest between her and his daughters. Still, without a word, he smiled and walked away toward the master suite.

Chapter Thirty-nine

"I'm glad we were able to reach an understanding on this issue, Dr. Bah. Attorney Gutierrez was shocked and very disappointed that the anti-bullying policy here at EUPA hadn't been updated to include stricter punishments for verbal abuse and taunting. The board of trustees and the fundraising committee called for immediate action when I brought it to their attention."

"I know," she replied flatly with a roll of her eyes.

Josiah detected that the headmistress was quite pissed with him, but he didn't give a damn. No child should be subjected to cruel ridicule and teasing. And if he or she did experience verbal abuse from another student at the prestigious private school, the culprit deserved to be punished.

Josiah became livid when he learned the little girl who had been mean to Gem had not been reprimanded. So, even while he was in Montana visiting Mink, he'd made time to reach out to the chairman of the academy's trustee board and its chief fundraiser—both strong political supporters of his. Attorney Miguel Gutierrez and Professor Shanika Brown had assured him that they would handle the situation as expeditiously as possible, and they had.

"As I'm sure you're aware, words can often slice deeper than a razor to the wrist. Some people's tongues are so sharp that their victims would prefer a beating from them over a verbal assault."

"That's true, Mayor Bishop. Some psychologists say harsh words can be more hurtful and intimidating than a punch in the face."

"Well, *you* should know all about that. Your words regarding the *situation* in my household disturbed my administrative assistant a great deal the other day when she came here on my behalf to attend to Gem."

"But . . . but . . . I-I . . . I meant no harm, sir."

"Yet, you upset Miss Robinson terribly. Not only were you out of order for broaching the subject of *my* personal life with my employee, but you were also downright insensitive to make the statement in the presence of my already upset daughter. Professionalism definitely escaped you that day. But that's a subject Attorney Gutierrez and Professor Brown will take up with you later on today."

"Today?"

"Yes. They'll be here at one o'clock this afternoon with a few other board members to discuss the matter with you." Josiah checked the time on his watch. "I have an important lunch meeting to attend. Have a good day, Dr. Bah."

"What's up, J?" Josiah sat down in the chair across the table from his brother.

"You tell me. You're the one bouncing around smiling like a little boy on his birthday."

"Life is good, man. What can I say? I just left the girls' school handling business. Gem and Treasure will return to classes tomorrow."

"Did you go in on that snobbish headmistress?"

"The trustees and chief fundraiser promised me they'd take care of her." Josiah smiled at Jeremiah. "I saw the polling reports. We're looking good in the final stretch of the campaign, bruh. And donations are stacked high. I'll be able to help out fellow Democrats during the midterm elections with the surplus."

"Yep." Jeremiah nodded. "Tell me about your trip. How is Mink?"

"Mink is good, man. She's grinding her way through recovery one day at a time. The girls and I enjoyed spending time with her. I hated to leave my baby up there, but she needs to complete the program. I plan to visit her again right before Thanksgiving."

"Well, you know Mink and I have never been close, and we never will be. But I'm rooting for her to get her shit together."

"Yeah, I know you're not a fan of hers. And I get it. She's caused major damage in my life, and because we're identical twins, all those times she hurt me, it affected you as well."

"Correct."

"Well, that's all in the past, J. Mink will be a different woman when she leaves Montana and comes back to the A to the girls and me. You'll see."

I doubt it, big brother, but for the sake of your sanity, I hope you're right.

Jeremiah kept his opinion about Mink to himself for the remainder of lunch at Mama Fannie's Kitchen. It was his and Josiah's favorite soul food restaurant in Atlanta. The brothers focused on the last days of the campaign and the victory party that Gypsie and the rest of the staff were planning. They also brainstormed over some key points that would be included in his election-night speech as they devoured Southern fried chicken, collard greens, and baked macaroni and cheese. At the end of the meal, Josiah reached for his wallet, insisting that he treat Jeremiah for lunch. His face creased when he counted the thin stack of bills in his hand.

"What's wrong, JoJo?"

"I think I lost some money."

"Seriously? How did you do some careless shit like that?"

"I don't know. I didn't spend any money while I was in Montana because we never left the premises. All of our meals and activities were covered under my insurance and out-of-pocket payment plan."

"When did you last open your wallet?"

"I remember opening it Saturday afternoon in the facility's financial office when I put a lump sum on Mink's expense account. I can't have her walking around without her hair and nails done. And you know women need perfume, makeup, and girlie products."

"True." Jeremiah rubbed his chin. "Did you pay the cabdriver in cash after you and the girls arrived at the airport Sunday?"

"I did, but I paid him from the loose bills I had in my pocket. I didn't touch my wallet." Josiah exhaled. "Anyway, it's all good. Let's get out of here. Connor is probably clowning because we're MIA while he's running down the convention bureau's income report."

Mink looked around before she entered the supply room. She quickly closed the door behind her.

"So, now you know me again, huh?" Greg sneered. "Your old sugar daddy is gone bye-bye, so now, you're back in *my* face."

"Greg, I was just kicking it with Norm M. to get what I wanted. You know I wasn't trying to diss you."

"But you *did*. You hopped off my dick to ride his because he's rich. You didn't have any use for me no more. And then when your husband came, you really stuck your nose in the air. That was fucked up, Mink."

"I'm sorry."

"You ain't sorry. Your ass is *desperate*. You need a fix. That's how low-down dopeheads like you operate. You use people to get whatever you want."

"Okay, you're right, damn it! I'm in a bad way right now. I've been running on willpower, but that shit ain't working no more. What you got? Norm M. told me he was going to hook me up through you. Do you have some coke?"

"Yeah, I got some. What you got for me, though?"

"Hold up now. Norm M. said he would make sure you had whatever I needed and all I had to do was come and see you."

"As I said, I got the powder, but I ain't about to just give it to you for free."

"You evil bastard!"

Greg doubled over, laughing before his face turned as hard as granite. "*I'm* in control, bitch. If you want what I got, you gotta give me what *I* want."

"I'll give you $200 for a quarter ounce and a pint of liquor." Mink reached inside her cleavage and pulled out the $540 she'd stolen from Josiah's wallet. She peeled off two crisp hundred-dollar bills and tucked the rest away in her bra. "Take it," she said, offering Greg the money.

He snatched the cash and stuffed it in his pocket. "I'll take your husband's money, but you're gonna have to get on your knees too." Greg unzipped his pants. "You fucked with my pride. Money can't make up for that."

"Come on, Greg. I don't want to do that. Take another hundred dollars."

"Bitch, bow down."

Tears pooled in Mink's eyes, but she assumed the position because her body was craving cocaine. It wasn't heroin, but it was the next best thing inside the center. And she needed it like she needed air to breathe. The crying baby had kept her up most of the night before, and she needed the booze and coke to help her relax and eventually put her to sleep.

"Ouch!" Mink wailed when Greg grabbed a fistful of her hair and yanked her face toward his exposed crotch.

She opened her mouth, and he shoved his stiff dick down her throat. She slowly began to suck as tears spilled from her eyes. She didn't want to blow Greg after spending such a wonderful weekend making love to Josiah. Her husband had been faithful to her while she was jumping in and out of bed with different men for drugs. Mink had thought the arrangement Norm M. had made with Greg regarding her would put an end to her tricking days, but she'd been dead wrong. How had she been so fucking naïve?

"Ah, shit! Suck this dick, bitch. Suck it good, damn it. Aaaah . . ."

All of Greg's moaning and cussing made Mink's stomach churn. She was nauseated as hell and on the brink of throwing up all over his dick. Visions of getting high motivated her to finish the job, though, but it didn't overshadow an idea she had in the back of her head. In the middle of the blow job, Mink came to a split-second decision that this would be her last time ever dealing with Greg for as long as she lived.

Chapter Forty

"Are you okay, baby? You sound tired."

Mink released a frustrated breath. "I didn't sleep much last night because I miss you and the girls so much. I couldn't stop thinking about y'all. And today was a long day. There was a guest speaker in the afternoon group session, and I had a late appointment with the psychiatrist. So, I'm about tapped out."

"Why don't you take a long hot shower and turn in?"

"That sounds like a good idea, JoJo. I think I'll do that."

"What time will you be able to call tomorrow? I'm sure the girls would love to speak to you."

"I . . . I . . . I'm not sure right now. Just kiss my babies and squeeze them tight for me. Tell them that Mommy loves them deeper than the bottom of the ocean." Mink shivered from a cold flash as the salty taste of fallen tears settled on her tongue. "And I love you too, JoJo. I love you more than you'll ever know. Always remember that."

"I love you more, baby. No matter how rough things have been over the past two and a half years, I've never stopped loving you, and I never will. Go take your shower now. We'll talk tomorrow. Good night."

"Good night."

"Shannon, please don't scream," Mink pleaded in a soft and calm voice.

"*Uuugh!*"

The midsize car swerved over into the left lane and skidded back to the right one with a jerk. Drivers in both lanes honked their horns and flashed their lights as tires screeched. Shannon looked in her rearview mirror with eyes as wide and as round as a pair of compact discs. She couldn't believe that Mink was crouched on the floor in the back of her car. The sharp pain in her chest made her feel like she was in cardiac arrest. Warm urine saturated the driver's seat and cascaded down her thighs and legs as a result of pure shock.

"How the hell did you get in my car?"

"I sneaked in early this morning before your shift ended. I had to get out of there, Shannon. Greg was driving me crazy. He's an evil piece of stinking shit."

"How did you get past the security cameras?"

"I paid that fat-ass security guard to turn them off for two minutes and turn his head while I ran out and jumped in your car."

"Look, I don't want any trouble, Mink. I'm going to turn around and take you back to the center. I can sneak you back into the building before anyone even notices you left. Everyone should be on their way to the cafeteria for breakfast right now. They probably think you slept in. I'll turn around."

"No! I'm not going back!"

"And I'm not about to lose my fucking nurse's license because of *you!* I've worked too damn hard to get where I am. My children need me to keep a roof over their heads and food in their bellies. I need my job to do that, so I'm going to take you back right now."

"Wait, Shannon! Wait! Just wait a damn minute! Um . . . um . . . Okay! Don't take me back to Serenity Springs. It's too fucking corrupt there. I can't go back. Damn it!" Mink dropped her face into the palms of her hands. "Okay, take me to the airport. Yeah . . . um . . . Just drop me off and go. I swear I'll never tell a soul you drove me there. You have my word."

"Okay. I'll take you to the airport. It's over an hour away, but shit, I'll take you to save my ass. But if you ever mention—"

"I won't. I promise, Shannon. I won't tell anyone."

"In closing, I encourage each of you to reach up and grab your rightful portion of the vision of a stronger, more productive, and prosperous Atlanta." Josiah turned around and faced Gypsie with a twinkle in his eyes. He smiled at her as her fingers clicked away on her iPad. "And as we move forward together in solidarity, let us—"

The door opened, breaking Josiah's word flow. Jeremiah stepped into his brother's office and closed the door behind him. "You know I wouldn't have interrupted y'all if it wasn't important, bruh."

"What's going on?"

"I answered a call on your private number since Gypsie transferred that line to my office phone. It's a staff member at Serenity Springs. I put the woman on hold. Do you want me to kick the call back to you in here or would you rather take it in my office?"

Josiah looked at Gypsie and then refocused on Jeremiah. "I'll grab it in your office. You and Gypsie can finish my speech."

Josiah left his office and made his way to Jeremiah's. A warning bell went off inside his head as he closed the door and made timid steps toward the phone on the desk. It felt like the room was spinning slowly, and the air was stiff and thick. He picked up the phone with a trembling hand and pressed it against his ear.

"This is Josiah Bishop."

"Mr. Bishop, my name is Meredith Glanville, social service director at Serenity Springs Rehabilitation and Mental Health Center. Regretfully, I have some unpleasant news to report about your wife."

Josiah swallowed the huge lump in his throat. "Just tell me."

"Mrs. Bishop has left the facility, sir. We don't know when she left or how she was able to exit the premises without our knowledge. But she's gone, and most of her belongings are too. I assume she hasn't reached out to you since you didn't notify us."

"No, I haven't spoken to my wife since last night. Apparently, she left the center after our phone conversation."

"We aren't sure about anything at this time, sir. Our chief of security and his team are investigating the situation as we speak. I'll update you as soon as more information is available."

"I would appreciate that."

"It's our obligation to keep you informed, although Mrs. Bishop hasn't broken any laws by leaving. She entered treatment at Serenity Springs on a voluntary basis. Residents that seek care at our facility on their own free will may leave at any time. But, of course, they place themselves and their guarantors at great financial risk."

"I know."

"Our staff is still very concerned about Mink, though. We'll even accept her back into treatment here if she returns voluntarily within twenty-four hours of the time we discovered her missing."

"That's good to know. In the meantime, what can I do to help you find my wife?"

"You could contact her relatives and friends to see if she's reached out to any of them. And let us know if she calls you."

"I'll do that. Thanks again."

"You're welcome. Good luck, Mr. Bishop."

Josiah hung up the phone and immediately loosened the knot in his tie. He found it nearly impossible to take in enough air no matter how deeply he inhaled. Suddenly, Jeremiah's office felt like the Sahara Desert. Every inch of Josiah's skin was drenched profusely with perspiration. A sudden pain on the left side of his chest caused him to lose his balance and stumble forward. It was as if someone had driven a sharp dagger into his heart with unbelievable force.

Even as the world seemed to be spinning recklessly on its axis with the speed of light as dimness enveloped the room, Josiah remained cognizant. He clutched his heart with one hand and leaned forward onto Jeremiah's desk for support. He gasped for the tiniest bit of oxygen while tears rolled down his cheeks against the excruciating chest pain. He tried to call out for help, but unfortunately, his dry, cottony mouth and the shortage of air robbed him of his ability to utter a sound.

Vivid images of Gem and Treasure's smiling faces danced through his psyche. *God, please don't let me die! Have mercy on me for my daughters' sake, please! Help me, Lord!*

Something was terribly wrong. But God was merciful, allowing Josiah to have a split second of clear thinking even as a veil of darkness began to cover him gradually. He reached inside his pocket and removed his cell phone. Panting for every breath, he managed to steady his shaking hand enough to press the number 3 on his speed dial list. Josiah silently prayed that his lifeline would answer soon as sweat dripped from his brow, blurring his vision. Another piercing pain struck his chest, and all of the air instantly swooshed from his lungs. Josiah fell forward, knocking over a framed picture that crashed into a sterling silver clock. A loud clattering noise bounced off all four walls, rising above the phone ringing in his ear.

"Man, why are you calling me? Why didn't you just walk your lazy ass back to your office?"

"Uh . . . huh . . . uuugh . . ."

"JoJo? *JoJo!* What's going on, man?"

Trying like hell to stay on his feet and on the right side of consciousness, Josiah leaned even farther on the desk. A granite paperweight shaped like the state of Georgia toppled over noisily.

"JoJo! JoJo!"

Chapter Forty-one

"What's wrong, Jeremiah? You're scaring me."

"Something ain't right. JoJo sounds like he's sick or something." He rounded the desk in a hurry. "Stay here."

Gypsie totally ignored Jeremiah. She took off running behind him and slammed the door shut. She sprinted down the hall on his heels.

They entered Jeremiah's office within seconds and closed the door.

Josiah stumbled toward them, but collapsed to his knees, holding his chest with sweat and tears trickling nonstop down his face. His body began to jerk violently as if he were having a seizure.

"Oh my God!" Gypsie screamed.

Jeremiah was on his knees by his brother's side in a flash. He snatched Josiah's shirt open, sending buttons flying around the room in all directions. Then he started massaging his brother's chest while he cradled him in the crook of his arm. "Dial 911! I think he's having a heart attack!"

Gypsie dashed toward Jeremiah's desk, but Josiah reached out and tugged on her skirt. He wrapped his arms around her legs, holding her in place. He shook his head frantically.

"Let go of me, Josiah! I'm trying to help you."

"N-no . . . n-no . . . ." He continued to shake his head and wheeze for air.

"JoJo, you need medical attention, bruh. Let Gypsie go so she can call an ambulance."

"N-no . . . n-no . . . uuugh . . . no . . . no . . . no . . . ambulance . . ."

"Okay, we won't call an ambulance, but you're going to see Ship *right now*. Let's go, bruh."

Josiah released Gypsie and wrapped his arms around Jeremiah's neck. He began to sob miserably like a helpless baby. His body tremors grew more intense, and his sweat-soaked shirt clung to his skin.

Gypsie kneeled next to them and caressed the top of Josiah's head gently as tears fell freely from her eyes. She had no idea what was wrong with him, but she silently thanked God that he didn't have a heart attack. The fact that he was able to breathe, speak, and cry was proof of that. But even though it appeared that Josiah was nowhere near the grave, he was definitely experiencing some type of sudden illness. Gypsie would bet her last dollar that it was an emotional episode that had *everything* to do with the phone call from Serenity Springs. More specifically, Mrs. Mink Bishop had done something to break her husband's heart *once again*.

"I can't get him up, Gypsie. He's too heavy. I think he's having a mental breakdown. What am I supposed to do?"

Jeremiah's voice fretting through tears and panic snatched Gypsie back to the current situation. The heartbreaking sight of two grown men on the floor bawling their eyes out unleashed more emotions from her heart. She couldn't control the waterworks cascading down her cheeks. Josiah's whimpers mixed with Jeremiah crying and cursing Mink to hell and back were pushing Gypsie closer and closer to the edge. But even in the midst of fear and shock, she somehow pulled herself together. Josiah needed her, and she refused to let him down.

"I'm going to call his doctor, J. What's his name?"

"Our homeboy, Ship, is our doctor. His number is on my iPad on the left side of my desk. My password is T-W-I-N-B and the number 2. Scroll through my contacts and find Davion Ship. Please hurry, baby girl."

Gypsie followed Jeremiah's instructions. She found Dr. Ship's name, but there were three different numbers listed for him. "Which number, J? There's more than one."

"Try the one with the 770 area code. I think that's his cell phone. When you get him on the line, tell him who you are and give him the entire rundown on what's going on with JoJo. Tell him I said he needs to drop whatever he's doing and get to city hall ASAP."

Again, Gypsie did as she'd been told. She held Jeremiah's desk phone receiver to her ear as it rang on the other end.

"This is Davion Ship."

"Um, Dr. Ship, my name is Gypsie Robinson. I'm Mayor Josiah Bishop's administrative assistant. His brother, Jeremiah, insisted that I call you because . . ."

Mink breathed a sigh of relief when she saw the row of public phones along the wall near the Delta Airlines reservation counter. She rushed over, pulling the handle on her rolling suitcase and carrying an overstuffed duffle bag. She dropped her bags and grabbed a phone. When she raised the receiver to her ear, her other hand paused in midair, inches away from the number keys. Mink didn't know who to call. Leaving drug rehab in the middle of nowhere without a plan was the stupidest thing she could've ever done. And she had done lots of stupid shit since she'd been in the grips of heroin. But all of her drug madness had taken place in or around Atlanta, which made it easy for her to return to Josiah's open arms like a little, lost puppy whenever she crashed.

The very thought of Josiah caused Mink's heart to rip right down the middle. She figured that someone from the Serenity Springs staff had notified him about her disappearing act by now. He was probably pissed. And he had every right to be. Mink knew Josiah had sunk over $15,000 in cash into her treatment this time around. Her ongoing bill was gnawing a hole through his health insurance plan too. But what the hell could she do about it now? She had left Serenity Springs like a teenage runaway, and she had no intention to go back.

"I'll make you understand, JoJo." Mink pressed the phone's receiver to her chest and cried. "Because you love me, you'll understand why I left that awful place. It wasn't right for me. Bad people . . . very bad people . . ."

Mink inserted several quarters into the coin slot and dialed Josiah's private line at city hall. The phone rang several times before the call rolled over to voicemail. Frustrated, she dialed his cell phone and got the same result after the fourth ring. Mink hung up without leaving a message, only to dial a number that she hadn't dialed in a very long time. But desperate times called for desperate measures. Plus, they owed her as far as Mink was concerned. Actually, they owed her *a lot* after all the pain they'd caused her.

"Hello?"

"Daddy, it's me, Mink."

The sounds of the estranged father and daughter breathing filled in the moments of tense hush. It felt like the hands of time had turned back almost two decades. Once again, Mink was that very frightened and timid 15-year-old girl, reaching out to her father for love and understanding. She had needed him back then, and she damn sure needed him now. Her heart ached at the memory of how her father had disappointed her all those years ago.

Mink hoped he would show her a speck of compassion today.

"Daddy, are you still there?"

"Yes, I'm here. What can I do for you, Mink? Go ahead and tell me what kind of nonsense you've gotten yourself into this time."

Mink sniffed and dried her tears with her forearm. "I need to come home for a little while. Things are kind of complicated for me right now. But if—"

"Save it, Mink. You can't come here. I won't allow you to come to this house and drive your mother and me crazy like you've done Josiah. And I thought you were in rehab somewhere up in the mountains in Montana anyway."

"I was, but those people are crooks. There were more drugs in that facility than I came across on the streets. So, I got the hell out of there."

"You left, huh?" Major Sinclair laughed, and the roughness in his tone caused Mink to flinch. "So why didn't Josiah fly up to the mountains and take you back to Atlanta? Better yet, why didn't he send for you?"

Mink didn't have a truthful answer, so she didn't respond. She just continued to cry quietly.

"Just as I thought. You took off without his knowledge. Damn it, Mink! What the hell is *wrong* with you? You haven't learned a goddamn thing since you were 15. Wasn't *that* enough? You should be thanking God every single day that you ended up with a good husband like Josiah after what you and that . . . that . . . *son of a bitch,* Ethan, did to this family!"

"Calvin, who are you talking to, babe?"

Mink's heart palpitated when she heard the familiar voice in the background. "Is that Mom? I want to speak to her, *please.*"

"Who's on the phone, Calvin? You sound upset."

"Let me speak to Mom, damn it!"

"I will *not*. Her health is too fragile for your drug fool-
ery. The doctor finally stabilized her blood pressure, and
her sugar is under control. Do you think I'm going to let
you bring her world crumbling down and cause her to
stroke out? I'll be damned. Go back to rehab, girl, and
don't call this house again until you complete treatment
and you're off of that stuff."

Mink's heart dropped to her belly when the dial tone
hummed in her ear.

Chapter Forty-two

"How is he, Ship?"

"I injected him with a sedative, so he's pretty mellow right now. From everything his assistant told me over the phone, I figured he was having an anxiety attack, so I came prepared." Ship removed the stethoscope from around his neck and placed it on Josiah's desk. "But what the hell is going on, J? How come my boy flipped out like that? Is the reelection campaign that damn stressful?"

"Nah, man, that ain't the problem. It's that dope fiend wife of his. I swear that trick is going to be the death of my brother. And I'll probably die right along with him. But I'll take her ass out first. Then I'll close my eyes and drop dead."

"What's her deal now? I thought she was away in rehab."

"I don't have a clue. The only thing I know is someone from the treatment center that JoJo tucked her ass away in called him. They must've told him some pretty heavy shit because he bugged out before he got a chance to give me the rundown. But I've got an idea about what's going on." Jeremiah frowned and massaged his temple.

"What?"

"I think Mink did an abracadabra on him."

Three quick knocks at the door ended the conversation abruptly. Rev and Myrlie rushed inside Josiah's office with worried expressions on their faces.

"Hello, Reverend and Mrs. Bishop."

Rev extended his hand and grabbed Ship's in a friendly shake. "It's good to see you."

"I'm so glad you came to take care of my baby, Ship. Where is he?" Myrlie asked.

Jeremiah hugged his mother. "He's resting in my office, Ma. Ship said he's going to be fine."

"Why did you leave him alone, son?" Rev asked.

"I didn't. Gypsie is with him. And anyway, as I said, he's asleep." Jeremiah turned back to Ship. "What should we expect for the rest of the day and even tomorrow?"

"I made a referral for JoJo to see one of my colleagues in the privacy of his home first thing in the morning. His name is Saidu Kabbah. He's a psychiatrist."

"*Psychiatrist?* My baby ain't crazy!"

"No, ma'am, he's not. But as a physician, I recommend that JoJo speak with a mental health professional about his feelings and concerns. He may even need medication to offset future anxiety attacks and depression. I trust Dr. Kabbah to take good care of him. He's the best in his field of expertise."

"Something terrible must've happened to my child. Who or what upset your brother, J?"

Rev wrapped his arm lovingly around his wife's shoulders. "Calm down, Myrlie Anne. Let the boy explain what's going on."

"The truth is I don't know what's going on. A staff member from Mink's treatment center called JoJo and whatever the woman said to him caused him to have a major emotional shakeup. I was so scared that I freaked out. If it hadn't been for Gypsie, JoJo and I would have a joint appointment with that shrink tomorrow. That girl saved the day."

"Yeah, thank God Gypsie was here. If she hadn't called me, JoJo would've been carried out of city hall on a gurney. The incident would be all over the news by now. That wouldn't have been a good look for him."

"Thanks for showing up, Ship. You came through for my son."

"JoJo is my lifelong friend, sir. Some of my fondest childhood memories took place in your home or at your church. Nothing could've kept me from coming here to help my boy. I just hope he'll overcome this." Ship turned to Jeremiah. "I left Dr. Kabbah's address and phone number on your desk. He's expecting JoJo at his crib in the morning at nine o'clock sharp."

"Cool. I'll drive him there. Thanks, man."

"No problem." Ship reached out and gave Jeremiah a man hug. "Take your parents down the hall to see your brother. He should be able to walk out of here in two or three hours, but he can't drive until Dr. Kabbah gives him clearance. I'll check in with you later to see how he's doing."

"JoJo, it's your mama, baby. Rev and I came to see about you."

"He's sleeping, Myrlie Anne. That shot Ship gave him knocked him out cold, so he can't hear you."

Myrlie reached down and stroked Josiah's cheek with the gentleness that only a mother possessed in the palm of her hand. And her firstborn son secretly basked in the warmth of her touch. The familiar scent of the hand cream she'd used since he was a little boy was like a balm for his troubled spirit. The combination of the softness of Gypsie's lap, where his head lay comfortably, along with his mother's caress and his father's voice was better than anything the doctor had ordered.

Rev was wrong. Josiah was very much awake and aware of everything going on around him. He was playing possum to avoid a conversation with his parents. He knew they were concerned about him and had billions of questions to ask about his nervous breakdown, but he wasn't ready to face them or answer any of their questions yet. Hell, he hadn't even told Jeremiah that Mink had left Serenity Springs. He would fill him in before the end of the day, though. And Gypsie deserved an explanation as well. So, Josiah would come clean to them at the same time as soon as his parents left. He wasn't looking forward to the conversation, but what other choice did he have?

"Let's go, Myrlie Anne. We can check up on JoJo later. J will take good care of him, won't you, son?"

"You know I will."

Rev reached out and placed his hand on Gypsie's shoulder. "God bless you, child, for all you do for my son and granddaughters. I don't know where they'd be without you. If I had a million dollars, I'd give it to you, but I don't. Don't worry, though. God's got a special blessing for you. Just you wait and see, baby. Just you wait and see."

"So, what's your next move?"

"I honestly don't know, J." Josiah looked up at Gypsie and smiled after she placed a plate of food on the table in front of him. "Thank you."

"You're welcome," she softly replied before she left the kitchen.

"I think it's time for you to cut your losses, bruh. It's been almost three years now. This ain't about love and commitment or family anymore. It's about survival . . . *your* survival. What more can Mink do to you other than stab you in the heart or blow your fucking brains out? It's a wrap, JoJo. Just accept it."

"You're right. I've done all I can do to help her, and then some. And God knows I love her, but one of us has to stay alive to raise Gem and Treasure. Mink is back on drugs and no doubt doing any and everything she can to cop a fix, so that leaves *Daddy* to take care of them."

"Correct. And I don't even want to think about what kind of shit Mink will try to pull you into when she crashes back down to earth this time. End this thing *now* before it kills you, JoJo."

"I hear you. I have to live for my girls because their mom is out there digging her grave. I'll call CoCo in the morning so she can start my divorce proceedings."

Josiah and Jeremiah's conversation shifted to the campaign and city hall matters over a late dinner Gypsie had prepared. Life and business had to go on, no matter what. Josiah couldn't allow Mink's unexpected departure from drug treatment and his breakdown to steer him off course. Gem and Treasure needed their father to take care of them, and his political allies were counting on him to win his second term in office. But even with all of that in mind, Josiah couldn't stop thinking about Mink. Regardless of the horrible things she'd done to him and the girls over the past two and a half years, he still loved her to death, and he was very concerned about her well-being.

Although Josiah's head was screaming it was time to let Mink go and move on, his heart was begging him to give her one more chance. Divorcing his wife of almost nine years, the mother of his adorable daughters, would be much easier said than done. He had vowed before God to love and cherish Mink for better, for worse, for richer, for poorer, in sickness and in health . . . until death. But *whose* death? Would he have to die to be free of Mink's addiction?

"Are you going to eat that?"

Josiah snapped out of his trance and stared at Jeremiah's hand holding a fork above his succulent salmon filet. "Nah,

man. Go ahead. That damn shot Ship gave me is messing
with my appetite."

"Thanks. Gypsie put her foot in this food." Jeremiah
helped himself to Josiah's salmon and half of his loaded
baked potato as well. "I would prefer you to lose your
appetite any damn day instead of your mind. You scared
the shit out of me. And poor Gypsie damn near pissed
her panties when you dropped to your knees, bruh. We
thought you had a heart attack."

"I felt like I was having one too. I really thought I was
gone, man. But then I thought about my princesses. God,
I love those little girls. I can't leave them here without a
daddy to take care of them and protect them from man
whores like *you*." Josiah laughed at his jab at his brother.

"With Mink out on the dope prowl again, if you die,
Uncle J-slash-the godfather wouldn't have a choice but to
raise Gem and Treasure. And they would definitely grow
up to be nuns under my watch. That's exactly why your
ass better end this bootleg marriage with their druggie
mama once and for all so *you* can raise them."

"I will, J. Trust me."

Chapter Forty-three

"How did it go, bruh?"

"It's all good." Josiah stuffed the prescriptions of Xanax and Zoloft Dr. Kabbah had given him into his breast pocket. He had no intention whatsoever to have either filled because he wasn't going to take them. He didn't need any "nut pills." His anxiety attack was a one-time experience, and a speedy divorce from Mink would cure his depression. But he would follow Dr. Kabbah's advice to contact the psychologist he'd recommended and start individual and family therapy with the girls as soon as possible.

"So you're cool?"

"Yeah, J, I'm cool. I ain't crazy. I just had an anxiety attack when I found out Mink had left treatment like a thief in the night. I didn't see it coming. The girls and I were just in Montana with her, and everything was fine. We had a good time as a family. And it seemed like Mink had transformed back to the girl I fell in love with in college. I wonder what happened to make her fall off the wagon again."

When they reached the SUV, Jeremiah pressed a button on the key fob to unlock the doors. After two high-pitched chirps, he climbed behind the steering wheel, and Josiah hopped in the passenger seat. Jeremiah started the engine and drove off once they'd secured their seat belts.

"I'm not trying to hurt your feelings, but . . . um . . . Why do you think something had to happen to drive Mink back to drugs? She was in *rehab*. Plus, in the past, things between you two have been ice cream and chocolate cake, but she still slipped back out."

"Yeah, I know, but it was different in Montana. We reconnected, J. It felt like old times. I swear I was in heaven."

Jeremiah smirked and shook his head. "Good sex doesn't equal reconciliation. And it damn sure can't erase trust issues, infidelity, a broken heart, or chronic addiction. Sure, your marriage to Mink can be repaired, but it should start with her full recovery from drugs and alcohol. Then you two will have to spend the next six years in couple's therapy. And don't forget about my nieces. At some point, you'll need to bring them into the mix with family therapy."

"I know."

"*You know?* So what are you saying, JoJo?" Jeremiah shot him a sharp side eye. "Are you seriously considering taking that route? Please don't tell me you've changed your mind about cutting Mink off."

Josiah remained quiet. The heat from Jeremiah's gaze was burning a hole through the side of his face, but he ignored him. After his session with Dr. Kabbah, he felt the need to regroup and make a mental adjustment. He still planned to move forward with the divorce, but he didn't want to move too hastily.

"JoJo, don't be stupid, dude!" Jeremiah yelled and hit the steering wheel. "Mink ain't going to do right no matter how much you help her. She *can't*. Your love cannot fix her, bruh. No disrespect intended, but the chick is emotionally challenged on top of her love affair with smack. I knew she was cuckoo the first day I met her. You were too blinded by her phat ass and pretty face to notice back then, but I know you realize she's crazy as hell today. Get out now before Mink's bullshit destroys you."

"I'm going to, J. As soon as the election is over I'll file for divorce."

At least I think will.

Gypsie was surprised to find Josiah at home when she and the girls arrived. She couldn't recall the last time he'd been home so early. It wasn't even five o'clock yet.

"Daddy! Daddy! Daddy!" Treasure ran into the den and jumped on her father's lap.

"Hey, princess. How was school?"

"I made an A on my spelling test, and I named all the months of the year in front of my whole class."

"That's great. Daddy is so proud of you." Josiah kissed his baby girl's cheek.

"Tell your father your good news, my brightest Gem," Gypsie coaxed from the entrance of the den.

"I got an A- on my solar system test. I only missed *one* question. I forgot how to spell Uranus. But I made an A, 100, on my math test because Miss Gypsie helped me study really, really hard."

"Come here, sweetie." Josiah placed Gem on his lap next to Treasure after she crossed the room.

The girls giggled when he started tickling them and kissing them alternately on their cheeks.

"I'll go and put dinner on the table," Gypsie announced softly. "I picked up a bucket of crawfish, a carton of fried shrimp, and Cajun potato salad from the Bayou Shack. It's what the girls asked for. I hope you don't mind."

"It sounds good to me. Do you need any help?"

"No. I got it. You guys get washed up."

Gypsie entered the kitchen and washed her hands. She removed three plates from the cabinet and walked to the center island where she had placed the food when they'd first arrived. As she began to remove the food from its containers and prepare plates, her mind flashed back to the scene in Jeremiah's office yesterday. The thought of Josiah dying and leaving Gem and Treasure while Mrs. Bishop was missing disturbed Gypsie a great deal. Those poor little girls would be devastated without their father. They loved him endlessly, and so did *Gypsie*. And for the first time, she had to admit to herself that she wanted him—*all of him*.

Of course, she'd never confess her flaming lust for Josiah to a living soul, not even Tianji. But Gypsie was tired of being a Goody Two-shoes, prim, proper, and prudish little girl where he was concerned. To hell with Mink! If she wanted to keep her husband, she needed to reenter rehab so she could get clean and sober and then hurry her ass back to the A and act like a *real* wife should. If she didn't, Gypsie couldn't promise herself that she'd continue to keep the scene PG-13 between her and Josiah. No, she wouldn't make the first move under any circumstances, but if he ever touched her intimately again, it would *go down* absolutely, unequivocally, and beyond a shadow of a doubt. For the first time in Gypsie's life, she would let go and roll with the flow and allow Josiah to make love to her without regrets. She would give herself to him completely, if only for one night.

"I'm ready."

Gypsie trembled when Josiah's warm breath caressed the back of her neck. And his velvety bass timbre struck a melody so deep within her feminine core that it unlocked the floodgates. He may have been ready for dinner, but Gypsie had a burning desire to become his dessert.

She turned around from the center island ever so slowly to face Josiah. He was standing much too close for her good sanity. The scent of his cologne and the sight of his toned pecs and abs bulging underneath his form-fitting wife beater nearly caused her to drool. She glanced at the girls who were already seated at the kitchen table. Thank God they were present to serve as a safeguard. Otherwise, Gypsie's raging hormones and raw sexual need may have kicked her ass and driven her to violate Josiah from his wavy head of hair to the tips of his toes.

"Have a seat, and I'll serve you and the girls before I go upstairs to shower."

"Aren't you going to eat with us?"

I'm not hungry for food. What I want ain't on the Bayou Shack's menu. "No. I . . . um . . . I'm still stuffed from a late lunch."

Gypsie turned around without another word and finished her task. When she did an about-face with a plate of food in each hand, she smiled at the sight of Josiah and the girls sitting at the table talking and laughing. Mrs. Bishop had no idea how truly blessed she was. God had given her the best husband any woman could ever wish for, and her two daughters were as close to perfection as children could be. If heroin could make a chick skip out on a fine brotha like Josiah and awesome little girls like Gem and Treasure, it had to be a mighty powerful drug.

Josiah growled and stretched his long legs in bed as he flipped through television channels. It was way past midnight, but he wasn't sleepy. His mind was flooded with all kinds of thoughts about Mink. Where was she? Was she all right? How much lower in her addiction had she sunk?

Dr. Kabbah had advised Josiah to try to the best of his ability to avoid those types of thoughts because they would only lead to anxiety and depression. He had forced him to realize he had no control over Mink, her addiction, or her behavior. But although Josiah had accepted that fact, he still wished he could somehow save his wife from her demons so their family could be restored. He loathed the very thought of becoming a single father. And how would his girls deal with the fact that their mommy would never live with them again? He erased those dismal thoughts from his mind and flipped to his favorite premium channel, hoping to catch a good movie.

"Ah, shit!" Josiah's eyes bucked, and an instant erection sneaked up on him at first sight.

He quickly turned to CNN when he saw a gorgeous, curvy woman in her birthday suit straddling a fully-clothed cowboy while he sucked her nipples and groped her ass. A spicy scene like that was the last thing a man in his predicament needed to see late at night while he was alone in bed. Josiah would never get used to sleeping solo after being married for so many years. He would die before he ever admitted it to Jeremiah, but he wasn't built for the single life. A brotha like him needed a woman in his world. And it had nothing to do with sex, home-cooked meals, or housekeeping. He simply enjoyed being emotionally connected to a gorgeous, intelligent woman. Josiah was a one-woman-commitment kind of guy. But unfortunately, he had committed his life to the wrong woman. Yet, he still loved her.

He turned off the TV and rolled over onto his stomach. He closed his eyes and envisioned his family in happy times when his world seemed perfect. Without warning, tears filled his eyes, but he refused to let them fall. He had cried an ocean over the past two and a half years, and he'd be damned if he would shed a tear tonight. Instead of crying, he prayed for Gem and Treasure, his parents, and Jeremiah. He asked God to bless the rest of his family members on his mother's and father's sides, as well as his church family and every employee at city hall.

The poor, the homeless, and the wrongfully incarcerated made Josiah's prayer list too. Then he paused with a heavy heart.

"And, God, wherever Mink is, please watch over her and keep her safe. Amen."

Chapter Forty-four

"Come in!" Norm M. barked.

The older woman slowly entered his office, seemingly nervous, rubbing her hands together. Norm M. ignored her obvious hesitance because she'd been ordered not to disturb him as he prepared for a meeting in one hour with Meryl Streep, her agent, and Medallion's East Coast legal team. Contract negotiations were always tricky and cutthroat with award-winning A-list thespians. And Miss Streep was far from the exception. To be frank, she was the *extreme*.

"This better be an emergency, Ethel. You know how important my next meeting is."

"I know, Mr. Murchison, but this um . . . um . . . *situation* requires your immediate attention, sir. No one else seemed to be able to handle it."

"Well, what the hell is it? Did the stock market crash? Is the country at war? Spit it out already, for Christ's sake!"

"You see, there's a—"

The office door popped wide open with a loud bang. "Surprise! What's up, Mr. Norman M.?"

"Mink, what the hell are you doing here?" He jumped up from his chair and felt dizzy immediately.

"You told me to call you from time to time, but I thought I'd do you one better." Mink sashayed toward Norm M. with her arms spread apart wide.

He stood in place like a statue with his mind spinning all over the place as Mink hugged him. Then she placed a kiss on each of his cheeks. Her next words faded into the background as Norm M. wondered how the hell she had traveled from Montana to New York City—and why. He'd only been in town a little over a week, and his comeback plan was progressing smoothly. A major distraction like Mink could snatch the rug from under his feet, and he didn't need that, and he sure as hell didn't want it. Life was too good right now.

Norm M. had been cocaine and alcohol free since arriving in the city, and it felt damn good. Despite his busy schedule, he had carved out time every evening to attend a Narcotics Anonymous meeting. He'd even asked a young guy with seven years of drug abstinence to be his sponsor. Mink's untimely and unwanted appearance didn't fit into his series of positive moves. As a matter of fact, Norm M. was pretty sure her pop-up visit meant trouble for him.

How the hell had she been released from treatment before she completed the six-month program? And why was she standing in the middle of his office in New York instead of being at home in Atlanta with her husband and little girls? Norm M. smelled a rat, and it stunk to the high heaven. He also smelled cheap liquor on Mink's breath. It seemed like she'd bathed in it.

"Ethel, you're dismissed," Norman M. spoke in a calm voice. He freed himself from Mink's arms.

"Yes, sir, Mr. Murchison."

"Close the door and hold all my calls unless it's Ms. Streep or someone in her camp."

"Of course, sir."

"You shouldn't be here, Mink," Norm M. said the minute they were alone. "Your time at Serenity Springs isn't up yet, so I assume you checked out early."

"I did. So what? You, of all people, know how corrupt that place is. The entire staff is shady, especially *Greg*.

He didn't do one damn thing you told him to do for me. I hate that dirty, low-down motherfucker!"

"I'm sorry about Greg, Mink. I really am, but there's nothing I can do about it."

"I know that. Hell, there was nothing *I* could do about it either. That's why I kicked rocks."

"I understand why you left the facility, but why did you come to *New York?*"

Mink walked over to the love seat on the other side of the room and plopped down. "I didn't have anywhere else to go."

"Why didn't you go home?"

"JoJo don't want to see me. I wasted all his money on treatment and left early *again*. He probably filed for divorce as soon as he found out I broke camp. I bet he took out a restraining order against me too, so I can't go anywhere near my babies." She started crying.

Norm M. walked over and rubbed Mink's shoulder. "Hush now. Don't cry."

"I am such a fuckup! I just can't get my life together."

"Yes, you can. You just need to try, Mink. I mean *really* try."

"I don't think I can be fixed, Norm M. Maybe I'm one of those people who is irreparably broken. My flaws are just too damn deep and ugly. I feel like I've screwed up my life to the point that there ain't no hope for me. And, oh my God! I've caused JoJo and my beautiful babies so much pain. They'll never forgive me."

"They *will* forgive you eventually, Mink, but you need to give them a reason to. That's why *today* you need to concentrate on your addiction. Drugs are no good for you. Go back to treatment because that's where you should be, my dear. I'll have Ethel book you a first-class flight back to Montana today."

Mink shook her head as tears streamed down her face. "I can't go back there. Serenity Springs isn't a good environment for me."

"Where would you like to go then?"

"I was hoping I could hang out with you here in the Big Apple for a minute. That is, until I can figure out my next move."

"That's not a good idea, Mink." He folded his arms across his chest. "Besides, I'll only be here for a few more weeks before I return home to LA."

Mink jumped up from the love seat smiling as she stood near Norm M. "I only need a few weeks. That'll give me time to find another treatment facility and check myself in."

"Mink, you need to go back to Mon—"

"By then, JoJo will have cooled off too. Then he'll pay the deposit for my admission. Yeah, he always pays whatever cash amount is required for my treatment—*always*. And he'll hook me up with his insurance too."

Norm M. rolled his eyes to the ceiling in annoyance. "Mink—"

"*Please* let me stay. I'll get it right this time, and JoJo and my girls will be so proud of me. And that bastard, Jeremiah, and the rest of my haters can kiss my ass. Then I—"

"Mink!"

"*What?*"

Norm M. couldn't speak right away because his words had gotten lost somewhere in Mink's insanity. He was having a hard time grasping her total disconnection from reality. She was beyond delusional. She'd left treatment, wasting her husband's money once again, and now, she expected him to shell out more cash for her to throw away at another rehab center. The woman was crazy! And she was trying desperately to pull him into her madness. All kinds of warning signs started flashing through his brain.

"Come on, Norm M.," Mink purred as she grabbed his crotch and massaged it gently. She seductively smiled as she palmed his penis and stroked the length of it up and down, nice and slow. "I promise to make it worth your while. Every day I'll work on getting into treatment, and I'll work on *you* every damn night."

The decision of good sense versus good sex started yanking Norm M. back and forth like a tug-of-war rope. He'd only slept with Mink once, but he would never forget the experience. The woman was an expert under the sheets. A few nights at his Manhattan apartment wouldn't hurt. And damn it! How could he deny her anything while his dick hardened and throbbed in the palm of her soft hand?

"One week," he whispered hoarsely. He held up his index finger for emphasis. "You have one week to find a rehab center, check in, and notify your husband."

Mink pressed her pouty lips against Norm M.'s open mouth and continued stroking his stiff dick through his pants. "Thanks, babe."

"You're welcome, but I have a few rules, Mink."

"*Rules?*" She frowned and released his penis from her grasp. "What kind of rules?"

"No drugs of any kind or alcohol."

"Say what?"

"You heard me. I haven't had a drink or used coke since I left Serenity Springs. If you're going to be a guest in my home, I insist that you refrain from all substances as well."

Mink sucked her teeth. "Fine."

"During the day, you'll actively seek treatment, and you *will* attend NA meetings with me every evening, Monday through Friday, at seven o'clock without fail. I'm serious, Mink."

"Okay! Okay! Okay! What else? I'm sure you've got a long-ass list of other rules."

"That's it." Norm M. checked his watch before he walked to his desk. "I have a very important meeting in thirty minutes, so you'll have to leave now. I expect to see you *on time* at the NA meeting this evening." He sat down, scribbled something on a notepad, and tore the page out. He offered it to Mink. "This is the address."

"You're serious about this shit, huh?"

"I sure am. I'm enjoying my fresh new start at life, and I won't allow you or anyone else to sidetrack me, Mink. For the first time in years, I don't feel like a failure. I've finally gotten my thunder back, and it's all because I went to treatment. Now that I'm no longer snorting coke and I've started working the twelve steps of NA, my life has new meaning."

Mink slowly approached Norm M.'s desk. She snatched the piece of paper from his hand. "I'll be there at seven, but I need money to catch cabs all over this big-ass city. I'm going back to my motel room to take a nap."

Without hesitation, Norm M. reached inside his pocket and removed his wallet. Quickly, he pulled out a few bills and handed them to Mink. "I'll see you at the meeting. I'll take you back to your hotel afterward to retrieve your things."

"Yeah . . . whatever . . ."

Chapter Forty-five

Treasure ran toward her father and Gem with her shiny silver halo bouncing up and down on her head. "Daddy, look at how much candy I got! I *love* Reese's Peanut Butter Cups."

"I like Sour Patch Kids, and I have a bunch of them," Gem said excitedly. She opened her bag wide so Josiah could take a look inside.

"You'll have to visit the dentist soon if you eat all that candy. It'll give you a tummy ache too."

"Okay. I'll just eat a little bit tonight and save some for tomorrow."

"I will too," Treasure said, following her big sister's lead.

"Good," Josiah laughed.

"Bye, Daddy." Gem waved.

"Where are you going, little girl?"

"Treasure and I want snow cones."

"Uuuugh!" Josiah growled. "Your mommy would spit fire if she knew you two were eating so much sugar."

Treasure cocked her head to the side. "But *Miss Gypsie* said we could eat junk food today if we promise to eat healthy food tomorrow and all the other days."

"Did she now?"

"Yes, Daddy," Gem confirmed with a nod. "And we promised to eat broccoli, Brussels sprouts, spinach, and lots of fruit, starting tomorrow."

Josiah couldn't contain his laughter. "Well, if you two have already struck a deal with Gypsie, I won't interfere. Enjoy your snow cones."

"Yesss!"

"Thank you, Daddy." Treasure wrapped her arms around his long legs and squeezed. "You're the best daddy in the whole world."

Josiah's smile lingered on his face even after his daughters left him and ran through the swarming fellowship hall. They made a mad dash to the snow cone line with the wings on their matching angel costumes flapping. The church's October holiday party was a big hit. There were over one hundred lively children in attendance, enjoying tasty food, fun games, and great prizes. Parents and guardians looked on attentively. The assortment of costumes, ranging from popular superheroes to Disney princesses, made the party much more festive.

Love may have tainted Josiah's opinion, but he thought Gem and Treasure were the cutest little angels ever. As a matter of fact, no one could tell the proud father that his daughters weren't the most gorgeous children at the party.

Despite the chaos ripping its way through Josiah's life with Election Day approaching and Mink's mysterious disappearance from rehab, Gem and Treasure were still living in peace and contentment. They were so joyful and carefree, but their daddy couldn't take credit for their happiness. *Gypsie* was responsible for that. The woman was a special gift from God. She was a solid rock in his girls' lives. Without her, Josiah dreaded to even think about how jacked up their world would be. Yes, Gypsie represented peace in the midst of the storm.

Josiah suddenly felt an unexplainable urge to seek her out amongst the lively children and attentive adults in the crowded fellowship hall. As his eyes swept around the room, he noticed Nelson, his driver, holding a baby while watching two little boys play with a race car set on the floor close by. After staring for a few moments, he recognized the three children from the giveaway event at the community center. He had made arrangements for Nelson to transport the children and their mother to the party, but he hadn't expected him to babysit them once they arrived.

Just then, Ms. Mayes appeared and reached out for her daughter. When Nelson handed the child over, he did so with a smile and a gleam in his eyes. He and the woman appeared quite comfortable and even friendly with each other. To the naked eye, they looked more like a couple than two strangers who'd just met today. Josiah sent himself a mental memo to question Nelson about his interaction with Ms. Mayes and her children as soon as possible.

"Are you having a good time?"

The smooth tone of Gypsie's voice was just too damn sexy. It was arousing, soothing, and damn near erotic. The stiffening of the member between his thighs was a natural response to her sultry sound combined with the subtle scent of her perfume. He turned slowly to his right to face her, hoping his body wouldn't betray him any more than it already had by being so close to her while he battled through another day of forced celibacy. The moment his eyes took Gypsie in, Josiah knew he was in trouble. She was an overdose of temptation in her gypsy costume, head scarf, theatrical makeup, and all.

"Other than the noise, I'm enjoying myself," I finally answered. "What about you?"

"I can handle the noise as long as the kids are happy. Gem and Treasure are having a blast, so I'm cool."

"We're going to have a hell of a time getting them to settle down at bedtime because of the excess sugar they've consumed. A little birdie told me *you* gave them the green light on the junk food."

Gypsie laughed hysterically and held up both hands in surrender. "Guilty as charged. But I've got to teach those two about the girl code. We girls have to stick together. We can't tell our secrets and give up info to *boys,* even when they try to pressure us. That's when our girl super-powers are supposed to kick in and make us strong so we can resist the heat."

"Resist the *heat,* huh?"

"Yeah," she shot back with a seductive smile that almost caused Josiah's knees to buckle.

"That's a skill *boys* need to learn as well." *Especially this boy because I'm burning up right now in hot lust looking at your fine ass. Damn, I want you!*

"I guess boys need to learn to resist the heat too, but I can't help them with that because it's against the girl code."

Josiah heavily exhaled as he watched Gypsie sashay away from him, laughing, with her curvy hips and tight, round ass swaying from side to side. The sight was pure torture to a brotha in his current situation. But by the grace of God, he would resist the heat at any cost.

Mink returned the smile of the short, husky dude with the black skull cap on who had been staring at her the entire meeting. For the second night in a row, he had been making all kinds of friendly gestures to get her attention, and she had made a conscious effort to ignore him each time. He wasn't her type. Mink had never been attracted to short and beefy guys. And his reddish complexion with freckles splattered across his hairless, baby face turned her completely off. Those two gold teeth in the front of his mouth were pretty disgusting, and those man boobs were too. Mink wrinkled her nose and turned her head, pretending to be interested in the NA meeting all of a sudden. The chick sharing her experience, strength, and hope about her journey from crack addiction to drug abstinence had become long-winded. She was rambling all over the damn place.

"Excuse me," Mink whispered in Norm M.'s ear and tapped his thigh. "I have to tinkle."

He turned his long legs to the side to allow her to ease past him and continue down the row of folding chairs occupied by other druggies. The conference room in the run-down, roach-infested hotel was wall-to-wall crammed with some of New York City's weirdest-looking junkies. There were bikers rocking spiked-out leather gear, Wall Street suits with their noses in the air, teenagers of all races, and a village of rugged thugs, which included the fat, freckled-face dude who had been eyeballing Mink.

As soon as she exited the conference room, leaving the smell of stale coffee brewing and human musk behind, she spotted a tall, white chick with fuchsia and lime-green hair. She was headed toward the double glass exit doors, clutching a pack of Newports in her hand. Mink remembered her from the meeting the night before, and since the girl had shown up again, she decided to introduce herself. What was the harm in making friends during her brief stay in the city?

"Hey, you," Mink called out, power walking behind her. "My name is Mink, and I'm new to the Big Apple."

Miss Crayola Head whipped around to face Mink when she got outside in the cold night air. "You talking to me?" She lit a cigarette, took a long drag, and released a cloud of smoke into the air.

Sarcastically, Mink looked all around her. "Yeah. I saw you last night and then again tonight, so I thought I'd say hello."

"My name's Kyleigh, and I'm two weeks out of a nine-ty-day treatment program after spending a year in the slammer. This is my last chance at life, and I'm trying my best not to fuck it up. Been in and out of treatment programs since I was 15. I lost my kids, my old man, and my pride, so, I ain't got nothing else to lose. I just want to get rid of my meth and booze demons once and for all. What's your story?"

"Um, can I bum a cigarette?" Mink asked.

"Sure." Kyleigh handed Mink a cigarette and lit it for her the moment she secured it between her lips.

"Thanks."

"No problem."

"Like I said, my name is Mink. I just got out of rehab in Montana after a little over thirty days. I'm in the city hanging out with a friend for a minute, trying to figure out my next move."

"What's your pleasure?"

Mink frowned. "Huh?"

Kyleigh tossed her cigarette butt to the pavement and stomped it out with the heel of her boot. "What's your drug of choice?"

"Oh . . . I'm a recovering heroin addict, but I think I've got a grip on it now. I just need to work on some personal issues, then my life will be back to normal."

"We're *addicts*, Mink. You and I will *never* be normal. Yeah, we can live drug free as long as we work a program, but we'll never be like regular people. That's just—"

Kyleigh stopped talking for some strange reason without warning. Her eyes widened as she stared at someone behind Mink. Mink glanced over her shoulder to see why she had spazzed out.

Chapter Forty-six

"What's up, ladies?"

The fat, red dude with freckles was standing behind them, grinning his face off. Mink was kind of surprised it was him because his soft and even voice didn't match his husky appearance. His tone was boyish, almost feminine. He pulled a half-smoked cigar from the breast pocket of his leather jacket and lit it.

"Um, I-I . . . I'm going back in-inside," Kyleigh stammered. "It was nice meeting you."

"Yeah, the same to you."

Mink watched Kyleigh scurry back inside the building like she had seen a ghost or some other scary being. She shook her head, thinking she was just another paranoid addict acting impulsively.

"I'm Rizz," the guy said, offering Mink his hand.

Hesitantly, she reached out and quickly shook his hand and released it. "I'm Mink."

Rizz nodded. "I ain't ever met a chick with a boss name like *Mink*. You ain't from around here. Where you from, ma?"

"I was an army brat, so I've lived all over the world. But Maryland is home for me, although I've spent the last fifteen years in the Deep South."

"Let me guess. You're from the 305. Yeah, you look like one of them Miami chicks with all that long, pretty hair. But it's *yours* too. Rizz knows real hair. And you rocking that bronze tan on that yellow, butter-soft skin. Mmm-mmm, you a 305 dime."

Mink smiled and shook her head before she took a long drag on her cigarette. "Wrong," she shot back, exhaling smoke through her nostrils. "I lived in Atlanta."

"Word?"

Mink nodded. "Yeah."

"Okay. You juicy enough to be a peach. What did you do down in the A? I bet you were one of them video chicks, right? You got a dancer's body. So, you could've been a pole princess."

"Fuck you. I'm an educated woman with a master's degree in business. I sold millions of dollars in commercial real estate during my career. How come niggas think the only thing pretty women can do is shake their asses or lay on their backs for a living? I'm out."

Mink dropped her cigarette on the ground and stomped off toward the entrance of the building. She didn't get very far, though, because Rizz reached out, grabbed her wrist, and gently pulled her back. In the blink of an eye, they came face-to-face. The sudden closeness made it possible for Mink to take in Rizz's facial features. Deep brown, almond-shaped eyes shaded by curly lashes softened the face of the asshole that had insulted her. Sincere regret was present in those eyes too.

"I'm sorry. I didn't mean to offend you, ma. What I was trying to say was you're beautiful, and your body is perfect like the chicks in them rap videos and the ones who dance at the strip clubs. Forgive me for the fucked-up way I said it."

"Apology accepted. And thanks for the compliments."

"Every word came from my heart. So, what's a pretty, intelligent woman like you doing hanging out with a bunch of drug addicts?"

"I'm trying like hell to stay off the needle. I've been clean for a minute, but I want to maintain. What about you?"

"I ain't no addict, yo. I took a case for my brother. The cops found some of the drugs I had been holding for him at my crib, so I had to do what I had to do to keep my son from going into the system. Thank God it was just a little bit of weed. I was lucky because I didn't have no priors, and I passed the piss test. But the assistant DA was still trying to stack time on me. So, the lawyer my brother had hired for my defense worked out a deal for me. I got probation, a fine, community service, and six months in Narcotics Anonymous. I ain't mad, though, because my son didn't get taken, and my brother dodged major time in the pen."

Voices captured Mink's attention before she had a chance to respond to Rizz's drug saga. The meeting was obviously over because she recognized faces of some of the attendees exiting the building. Norm M. was among them, and he didn't look too pleased to see Mink standing outside talking to a stranger and fellow junkie. He cut his eyes at her as he walked in her direction and talked to a man walking beside him at the same time.

"I've got to go," Mink said dryly.

Rizz looked toward the front of the hotel. "You here with somebody?"

"Yeah . . . kind of. I'll tell you about it some other time. I'll see you around."

"Hey, drop by my job so we can hang out, if you can. I work at the Gentle Beast Pool Hall and Grille on West 124th Street in Harlem from eleven to five, Monday through Saturday. Everybody knows me, so just ask for Rizz."

Norm M. was just two feet away on his approach with a nasty expression on his face, so Mink didn't utter a word to Rizz in response. She simply stuffed her hands inside her coat pockets and nodded. Still silent, she followed Norm M. down the sidewalk where he waved down a cab.

The moment they were seated in the back of the yellow midsize car and the door slammed shut, Mink became fidgety as hell as a pair of gray eyes sliced through the darkness and shot daggers at her.

"You are not to associate with any of the people in NA outside of the meetings unless it's your sponsor. Not everyone in that room is there for the right reason. Most come by force. Either a judge, their employer, or an insistent loved one has led them to NA."

Mink sucked her teeth. "What difference does it make why they come? The important thing is they show up, right?"

"Bullshit. The desire to be clean and sober is the most important thing. So, no matter if the court, a boss, or a nagging spouse issues an ultimatum to a drug addict like you and me, they will not recover unless they really want to."

"That's not true. Your family members and a judge twisted your arm into rehab, and now, look at you. You're clean and working the program."

"That's because at some point during the process, I began to want it for myself. I got serious. And since I've been in New York, my life has gotten better each day I've stayed clean. I'm done with the bullshit, Mink. Drugs and alcohol are a thing of my past. I want to live, and I want to live large."

"You ain't the only one who wants to live, Norm M. I want to live too. Hell, *everybody* wants to live."

"If you really want to live, then I suggest you spend the rest of your days here searching for another long-term treatment program, attending meetings, and keeping your distance from the city's undesirables. You only have a few days, my dear."

"What if I can't find another rehab facility to take me?"

Norm M. looked at Mink through narrowed eyes. "That's not my problem. We agreed that you would be a guest in my home for one week, and you'd live by my rules during your visit. Nothing has changed. If you haven't handled your business by your scheduled date of departure, I will buy you a one-way ticket home to Atlanta."

"*Damn!* It must be my lucky day. I'm surprised to see you, ma. Welcome to the Gentle Beast. What can I get for you? My man, Percy, our bartender, can mix all kinds of nonalcoholic drinks. Just name it." Rizz wiped down the countertop with a wet rag and nodded toward an empty bar stool.

"Shit, I need a *real* drink. Let me get a double shot of Hennessy." Mink plopped down on the bar stool.

A puzzled look crept across Rizz's face. "Hey, I thought recovering addicts didn't drink or use any type of drugs. Plus, it ain't even noon yet, ma."

"Well, if your life was as fucked up as mine is, you'd be drinking, snorting, smoking, and shooting up too. I just can't catch a damn break."

"Chill, ma. Let me get you that drink, and then you can tell me all about it."

After several double shots of Hennessy over a hard-to-believe recap of the last three years of her life, Mink was sloppy drunk. She was barely able to balance her body on the stool at the bar without flopping and nearly falling off. So, since business at the Gentle Beast was kind of slow, Rizz decided to leave work early to give Mink a ride home. But first, he needed her accurate address. The story she had told about living in a penthouse apartment on Park Avenue with some big Hollywood movie producer she'd met in Montana was bullshit. Like a typical dope fiend,

Mink knew how to lie her ass off. Rizz thought her little tale was funny as hell while she was rambling it off as she threw back drink after drink. But now, the humor was gone.

"Yo, ma, where do you live? I mean like *for real*." He picked up Mink's purse from off the ground and tried to tuck it underneath her arm, but she was too wobbly to stand up straight and carry anything.

"T-take me . . . me to P-park Avenue, ba-baby," she slurred. "I-I told you . . . you that's w-where I . . . I . . . I'm s-staying."

Rizz's frustration spiked. There was no bigger turn-off than a good-looking chick slurring and stumbling around under the influence. Women in this condition often got raped out here in these streets.

"Hey, I'm about to take you to my crib and let you sober up over some black coffee. Then you can tell me where you really live, and I'll take you there. Cool?"

Mink threw her head back and giggled as Rizz guided her down the busy sidewalk. "Cool."

Chapter Forty-seven

"Watch your step, ma." With a tight arm wrapped around Mink's drooping shoulders, Rizz pulled her up the last two steps leading into the apartment building. They crept down the hall and stopped in front of the third door on the left. "Just lean back against the wall while I unlock the door."

"Okay."

This goddamn pocketbook! Rizz grumbled internally at the designer bag when the straps interfered with unlocking the door. Rapper Don Trip's "Open Your Eyes" blasting from the apartment two floors above their heads had so much bass in it, the whole damn building was vibrating. Once the door was unlocked, Rizz entered with Mink stumbling close behind.

"I got to pee!" she squealed and started spinning around in a circle like a little kid.

"Yo, don't piss on my floor, ma. The bathroom is straight down the hall, last door on the right."

Rizz stood in the middle of the living room floor, wondering if it was a mistake bringing Mink to the crib in her condition. Shit, she was a stranger and a heroin addict at that. And although she was fine as hell, she had an insane imagination and a weak-ass relationship with the truth. After a few minutes, Rizz walked down the hall and stopped outside the closed bathroom door. Mink was running the faucet on the sink.

Rizz banged on the door. "Yo, are you good in there, ma?"

"I'm fine. I'm just freshening up a little bit. Um . . . Rizz?"

"Yeah, baby?"

"Didn't you say your brother served customers out of your spot?"

"Hell nah!" Rizz barked through the closed door. "I said I used to hold some stuff for him from time to time until a bitch he was dealing with got mad at him for cheating on her and snitched me out. Anyway, how come you wanna know about Brett?"

The water stopped running all of a sudden, and the door opened. Mink stepped out into the hallway topless. A pair of red lace boy shorts was the only item of clothing on her body. The rest of her clothes, including her boots, were in a pile on the bathroom floor. Rizz's heart began to pound wildly at the sight of her smooth butterscotch breasts topped by hardened nipples.

Mink leaned in and kissed Rizz fully on the mouth. "I was hoping I could get a little taste of something to take the edge off."

"Nah, baby, my brother don't bring drugs up in here no more. And you don't need to mess with any of that shit no way, ma. I thought you wanted to stay clean."

"I just need one small hit, Rizz, and I won't ever bother you again. I swear. And if you hook me up, I'll fuck you real good. Ain't a bitch alive that can put it on you like Mink." She followed up her offer with another open-mouthed kiss.

"Ma, I like you. You fine as hell, but I ain't about to play middle man between you and my brother over some goddamn smack."

"*Please,* help me out just this one time, Rizz. I swear I'll do you right. Let me suck your dick." Mink dropped to her knees.

Rizz didn't waste any time snatching her up and pressing her back against the wall. "I wanna get down with you, girl, but I ain't gonna fuck around with Brett and his work. Plus, there's something I need to tell you about me. You see, I—"

"I don't give a fuck! I've got condoms and money, so let's make this shit happen!"

Like a desperate, out-of-control dopehead, Mink stripped out of her panties and grabbed Rizz by the back of the head. Her kisses were wild and sloppy with lots of tongue and saliva.

"Yo, stop! Stop it!" Rizz snatched away from Mink. "I'm trying to keep it real with you! I ain't . . . I mean . . . Damn it, I'm a *female*."

Mink froze and stared at Rizz for a few silent seconds. Then she smiled. "Bullshit."

"I swear to God. I'm a woman just like you, but I'm gay. I came out back in my teens when I was in high school over twenty years ago."

"But you said you have a son."

Rizz nodded. "I do. I did a little experimenting fourteen years back and ended up pregnant with my son, Tyriq. He's 13 now, and I ain't been with a man since."

"Damn!" Mink folded her arms across her bare breasts as her eyes traveled up and down Rizz's body, from the black skull cap on her head to her Tims boots.

"Yeah, just what I figured. You don't wanna fuck with me no more, huh? You're 'strictly dickly' like a whole lotta other bitches claim until they experience a woman."

Rizz studied Mink's face carefully as she seemed to be seriously considering a dip in the lady pond. If she decided to dive in, Rizz was going to make sure every second was worth her while. She would treat her body so good that she'd never think about a dick again. Then maybe something solid could develop between them.

Rizz was sure she could help Mink get back on her feet since she was educated and all. And they could attend NA meetings together so she could stay clean. Yeah, Mink was possibly the woman Rizz had been wishing for since her last relationship. They could be good together and take care of each other. The possibility of wife and wife for life sounded good to Rizz.

Quietly and without another thought, she reached out and pulled Mink's naked body snuggly against hers. She plunged her tongue between her partially open lips in a rough kiss. The taste of Hennessy greeted her exploring tongue as her hands squeezed and rubbed Mink's bare ass cheeks. Rizz ended the kiss and pulled back to look into Mink's eyes for a sign that Mink wanted this moment as much as she did. After a brief pause, she smiled with satisfaction and watched Mink's eyes roll to the back of her head when her right hand left her butt to explore her hot, wet pussy with two fingers. Rizz entered Mink's slick slit before she began to strum the full length of her hard clit. Their lips connected again in another passionate kiss.

"Aaahhh . . ." Mink moaned into Rizz's hungry mouth.

"C'mon, ma, let's go to bed."

Mink rolled over in bed and stared at the snoring body lying next to her.

Rizz? Oh, shit! No, I didn't! Nooo!

Yes, she most definitely had. Drunk out of her mind and itching for a fix, she'd had sex with Rizz, hoping to persuade her to hook her up with her drug-dealing brother. Now that she had slept the alcohol off and her head was clear, Mink felt nauseated as she recalled all the things she had allowed Rizz to do to her. Then bile rose up in her throat and threatened to spill from her mouth when a memory of her going down on Rizz filled her headspace. Mink jumped up from the bed butt-ass naked and scrambled toward the door with her hand clamped over her mouth.

"Hey, where're you going, ma?"

Rizz's hoarse voice brought Mink's sprint to a screeching halt. "I'm going to the bathroom." She laughed nervously. "I've got to pee."

When the room fell silent again, Mink took that as her cue to rush to the bathroom. She closed the bedroom door quietly and hurried up the hall. Once inside the bathroom, she shut the door, locked it, and hovered over the commode. Retching terribly, Mink's body jerked as the contents of her belly oozed from her mouth and splashed into the water in the toilet bowl below. Through ragged and dry breaths, she continued to shake and heave over the commode, but no more vomit came forth.

Reluctantly, Mink looked in the mirror. Her soul wept at the reflection staring back at her. She didn't even recognize the weary face. It wasn't Mrs. Josiah J. Bishop, mother of Gem and Treasure Bishop and first lady of Atlanta, Georgia. No, the woman she saw was a complete stranger, the remnants of someone she used to know. Filled with raw emotions brought on by memories of her past life with Josiah and the girls when they were happy and content, tears filled Mink's eyes. She missed her family, but she was in no condition to reach out to them right now. They were much better off without her because she hadn't changed one bit. The hands of addiction were still wrapped tightly around her neck, choking the life out of her. Yet, her love affair with heroin was very much alive.

Mink stepped away from the mirror and turned on the shower. She adjusted the water spray to the warmest temperature her hand could stand. Then she rummaged through the large drawer below the sink and found a blue, well-worn shower cap and tucked her long hair underneath it. Before she stepped inside the bathtub under the hot water spray, she grabbed a burgundy towel and a matching washcloth from the wicker shelf. Finally, Mink pulled the shower curtain in place to hide behind it to try to scrub away her guilt, depression, and shame as tears trickled down her face.

"'Bout time your ass came out—"

"*Aaahhh!*" Mink screamed at the male stranger walking down the hallway toward her. She tightened the knot on the towel above her breasts and backed away from the tall, lanky dude, scared out of her mind.

"Chill out, girl. I'm Brett, Rizz's brother. You must be one of her friends."

Relieved, Mink doubled over, taking in deep gulps of air as she nodded her head frantically. She was too shaken up to speak. The long, hot shower had relaxed her and allowed her to push all disheartening thoughts to the far recesses of her mind, but Rizz's brother had popped up out of left field and scared the shit out of her.

"I didn't mean to scare you, baby. I just swung by to check up on my li'l sister. We got keys to each other's spot, so we pop in on each other all the time. I didn't know she was entertaining a hottie."

Mink stood up straight and immediately checked Brett out. He wasn't all that good-looking, but he wasn't necessarily a monster either. He was a thin redbone, well over six feet with a sandy-brown mustache-and-beard combo and cornrows. He was rocking facial freckles just like Rizz. That rugged, bad-boy vibe was oozing from his pores. Yeah, "dope boy" was written all over his face. Just the thought of it made Mink smile.

Chapter Forty-eight

Brett may have been a tenth-grade dropout and a common street hustler, but he was a long way from stupid. The chick sitting on the passenger's side of his black, pimped-out 2005 Cadillac DeVille was up to no good. One minute after introducing herself, she dropped the towel from her naked body and slid into her clothes in front of him in the hallway of his sister's apartment like he was her longtime bae. Then she asked him for a ride home. When he insisted that she wake Rizz up to tell her goodbye and he was giving her a ride to her place, she came up with a bullshit excuse so quick that his head was still spinning. His sister wasn't too damn tired to wake up and see her friend off. Nah, this Mink chick had crept out on Rizz. And she didn't even leave a note.

"So, where do you live?"

"I ain't going home right now. I want to hang out with you." Mink smiled suggestively and placed her hand on Brett's lap close to the monster imprint on his inner thigh.

He licked his lips and returned her smile. "I stopped by Rizz's spot on my way home after I made my last drop for the day, so now, I wanna chill at the crib with some Jamaican food, a bottle of Cîroc, and some kush. You down with that?"

"I could definitely eat, and I like Cîroc. But you ain't got nothing harder than weed?"

"How hard you talking about? You want some blow, or you like that brown sugar?"

"Brown sugar."

"Damn, girl. You got money?"

"Yeah, I got a little bit of cash, and *anything else* you want."

Brett looked in his rearview before he crossed over into the left turning lane. "Okay, baby, I got you."

Norm M. was seething as he rode the elevator up to the twelfth floor. Mink had not checked in with him all day, and she hadn't bothered to show up for NA that evening. Instinct told him she had hooked up with some bad character, more than likely the overweight, black guy he'd seen her talking to last night, and she was some-where getting high. How had he been so stupid to allow her into his home after she'd left Serenity Springs before completing the treatment program? Good sex wasn't an excuse for stupidity, and Norm M. felt very stupid at the moment.

He exited the elevator when it stopped on his floor, and the doors opened. Removing his keys from the left pocket of his overcoat, he walked down the quiet hallway toward his apartment. As soon as he unlocked the door and entered the dark living room, his house phone rang. He flipped on the light and hurried over to the coffee table.

"Hello?"

"Mr. Murchison, this is Sheldon at the concierge's desk. There's a young lady here named Mink Bishop who wishes to visit you. Should I allow her upstairs or would you prefer to come down and escort her up?"

Norm M. closed his eyes and pinched the bridge of his nose in annoyance. "Please allow Mrs. Bishop upstairs, Sheldon. She's visiting me for a few days. Please make a note of that. Thank you."

"I sure will, sir. Mrs. Bishop is on her way up."

After he hung up the phone, Norm M. went and stood by the door to wait for his troublesome houseguest. He was still upset with the dumb mistake he'd made by allowing Mink to spend a week at his apartment. His better judgment told him to rescind his hospitality and send her on her way before she did something crazy that would turn his world upside down. He wouldn't survive another scandal at this point in his life. The Meryl Streep movie was in the preparatory stages, he and Tawny had set a January thirtieth wedding date, and he would be back in LA two days before their little boy's fifth birthday. Life was good, and Norm M. wanted it only to get better.

As if he sensed Mink's presence on the other side of the door, he released the locks, turned the knob, and pulled. "Where have you been?" he snapped the instant she crossed the threshold.

"I've been running around the city, checking out drug farms. Ain't that what you told me to do?"

The booming sound of the door slamming shut rattled Mink. She spun around and glared at Norm M. as her hands roamed up and down her arms, which were folded over her chest. That's when he noticed her glossy eyes and jittery body language. He felt instant rage.

"You look *terrible*. Have you been drinking and drugging with that loser you met last night?"

"Nooo!"

"Then why weren't you at the meeting? He wasn't there either. And look at you," he growled, snatching one of Mink's arms and yanking her toward him. "You're high."

"Let go of me! Who the fuck do you think you are?" She wiggled her arm free from his hold.

"*I'm* the person who has provided you with a warm bed, food, and cab fare since you landed on my doorstep. I must've been a fool to let you stay here. What the hell was I thinking? You're nothing but a pathetic heroin addict."

Mink shot Norm M. a heartless grin. "You weren't saying that last night when I was licking your asshole. Nah, motherfucker, I was your baby then."

"Well, you're not anything to me anymore. Your gig is up, Mink. You may sleep in the guestroom tonight, but I want you out of here tomorrow. I'll give you money for a bus ticket to Atlanta and a few extra dollars for food on your trip. But make no mistake about it. You are no longer welcome here. When I return home from work tomorrow, I expect you to be gone."

Josiah looked up from his phone and smiled at Nelson singing along with Charlie Wilson on the radio as he cruised down I-75 South. "What's up with you, my man? You've been mighty happy since the party at the church the other night. What's going on?"

Their gazes met briefly in the rearview mirror. Nelson's smile was so animated that his deep cheek dimples made a rare appearance.

"I'm *always* happy. You know that."

"That may be true, but you've got this glow today that I've never seen before. Does it have anything to do with a certain single mother with three well-behaved kids that you transported to the party at my request?"

Nelson grinned bashfully. "Could be or could be not. But she *is* a nice lady, and she's got some good children. They asked if I could pick them up for church Sunday, and, of course, I said yes. Since I'm a deacon and all, it's my godly duty to help all souls any way I can."

"Yeah, I hear you, *Deacon*." Josiah chuckled but only for a moment because his cell phone rang. He swiped the answer icon and pressed it to his ear. "This is Josiah Bishop."

"Hey, son, it's your father-in-law."

"Major, how are you, sir?"

"Roxie and I are well. How are *you*, son? Have you heard from that daughter of mine yet?"

Sighing deeply, Josiah mumbled, "No, sir, I haven't. I've thought about hiring a private investigator to track her down, but I have no clues to give anyone even to begin a search. I'll just continue to pray that Mink is safe and that she'll soon come to her senses and call me."

"And when she does call you, what do you plan to do, Josiah? Are you going to race halfway across the country, bring her home, and spend thousands of more dollars on another drug treatment facility?"

"Honestly, I have no idea what I'll do. What would *you* do if you were in my shoes, sir?"

"I would keep her away from my daughters and administer tough love. Mink needs to hit rock bottom without a lifeline to rescue her. For once, Josiah, allow her to help herself. If my daughter really wants to be free of her heroin addiction, she'll seek the treatment she needs without any assistance from you or anyone else."

"I'll keep that in mind, Major."

"You do that. It's the best thing you could ever do for Mink."

Josiah nodded in agreement because he was too overwhelmed by emotions to say anything. He sniffed and fought back the tears threatening to spill from his eyes. He knew his father-in-law's advice was on point, but it was going to be hard to turn his back on Mink completely. Regardless of all the terrible things she had done because of her addiction, he still loved her very much, and he wanted her to get clean so she could return home to him and their girls.

"Kiss my beautiful granddaughters for me and tell them their nana and papa love them very much. I'm praying for you and those sweet, beautiful girls."

"We appreciate your prayers."

"And just in case I can't get through to you Tuesday night, congratulations on your reelection, Mr. Mayor."

The thought of victory brought a smile to Josiah's face although election night wouldn't be quite the same without Mink there to celebrate with him and the girls. "Thanks for the vote of confidence, Major. It means a lot to me. Thank you for calling. We'll talk again soon."

"I want to talk to my little princesses next time."

"I'll be sure to make that happen, sir."

"Bye, Josiah."

"Goodbye."

Chapter Forty-nine

Norm M. laughed. "Yes, Evan, we'll swim with the dolphins when we go to Catalina Island for your birthday."

Mink stopped outside the slightly cracked bedroom door and peeped inside. Norm M. was sitting on the bed, FaceTiming his son on his iPad. Hearing the child's excited voice caused a vision of Gem and Treasure to float through her mind. But it quickly disappeared when her empty stomach tumbled and growled like it was about to burst. Then her body trembled when a sudden chill swept all around her. Seconds later, she experienced a hot flash. The old familiar withdrawal symptoms were wreaking havoc on her body. She had spent every dime in her purse on heroin when Brett took her to his friend, Oscar's, house to score a fix. Now, her high was fizzling out, and she was irritable as hell.

After refusing to eat any of the Jamaican food they'd picked up at a restaurant in Queens, Mink had made love to a syringe containing an ounce of heroin at the kitchen table in front of Brett, Oscar, and a white guy whose name she couldn't remember. She'd reinforced her high with a few quick shots of Cîroc afterward before wobbling into the living room and collapsing on the sofa. And she'd remained there, enjoying her cloud nine experience even as the nameless white dude removed her tights and panties and fucked her while Brett and Oscar watched.

Mink wrapped both arms around her waist to ward off the icy sensation attacking her body. Her mouth was desert dry, and she was weak from hunger. Depression was weighing her way down because Norm M. wanted her out of his apartment, and she had nowhere to go. That's why she had come to his bedroom. She was prepared to beg him for forgiveness and an extension on her visit. And if she literally had to kiss his ass, she wasn't above that either.

Mink tapped lightly on the cracked door and poked her head inside the room when Norm M. ended his video call. "Can I come in?"

"What do you want, Mink?"

"I'm sorry I didn't go to the meeting this evening, but I got caught up at a treat—"

"Save it, Mink. I don't believe a damn thing you say. The truth of the matter is, I don't care where you were, who you were with, or what you were doing. Just pack your things tomorrow and leave. Go home to your husband and children, my dear. Check in at a rehab center and work the program."

Mink was speechless; she felt defeated, realizing there was nothing she could say to turn her situation around. Her addiction had caused her to burn yet another bridge and lose another friend.

Norm M. stood from the bed, walked to the other side of the bedroom, and removed a framed picture of a boat at sea from the wall. Surprisingly, the picture had been hiding a safe. After entering a code on the keypad, the small metal door opened. Mink's eyes nearly bulged from their sockets when she saw a few stacks of money and a crystal jewelry box. There were some folders stuffed with documents inside as well. Norm M. removed some money from the safe. Mink quickly lowered her head as if she hadn't seen anything when he turned around to face her.

"This should cover your cab fare to the bus station and a ticket to Atlanta." He handed Mink the money. "The extra is for food and incidentals along the way."

"Thank you," Mink whispered as she accepted the money.

"You're welcome. I'm going to bed now. I have a very busy day tomorrow. Good night."

Realizing she had been dismissed, Mink exited the room without a word.

Mink hadn't slept one hot second last night because she was so worried and frustrated over her current situation. Also, her withdrawal symptoms had been more severe than ever before because she hadn't used heroin for several weeks. The initial high after a period of abstinence was insane, but the meltdown was like plummeting slowly into the pit of hell. When she finally crashed all the way down the previous night, she was nauseated, agitated, and extremely depressed. Worst of all, she was wide awake although she was physically and emotionally exhausted. Mink was craving a taste of that brown sugar, and she couldn't shake it.

So, as soon as Norm M. left for work this morning, she called Brett and begged him to bring her another fix, which she planned to pay for with her bus ticket money. She would figure out where she was going to live and how she would eat and support her habit later. At the moment, Mink's only concern was getting high.

She dragged her body into the living room, picked up the telephone from the coffee table, and pressed the star key and the number 3 on the speed dial. It was the direct line to the concierge's desk. Mink's body uncontrollably shook as she held the receiver to her ear and waited for someone to answer her call.

"Good morning. This is Ginger. How may I help you?"

"Um, this is Mink Bishop. I'm visiting with Mr. Murchison on the twelfth floor for a few days."

"Yes, ma'am. Your name is on his visitation list. What can I do for you, ma'am?"

"I . . . um . . . ordered some breakfast from a restaurant. The deliveryman should arrive soon, so please let him upstairs."

"Sure thing, Mrs. Bishop. Is there anything else I can help you with?"

"No. I'm good."

The constant switch between hot flashes and chills with nausea on top was taking its toll on Mink. The taste and smell of the drug she worshipped had filled her imagination, making her salivate like a rabid dog. She had a hard time standing still as she watched the unidentified white guy from the day before counting the money she had given him.

He flipped through the bills one final time before he looked up at Mink and smiled. He gave Brett a nod. "It's all here. Give her the shit so we can get the hell out of here."

Brett dropped the small brown paper bag on the coffee table, and Mink snatched it up right away with shaky hands. While she tied the elastic band around her arm and prepared to fill her veins with dope, Brett started walking around Norm M.'s apartment, touching the expensive furniture and décor.

"*Damn!* That bitch wasn't lying. This cracker is ballin'!"

"Let's go, Brett. I got moves to make," the white dude grumbled.

"Chill, man. I'm just looking around." Brett headed down the hall toward the back of the apartment.

"Hey, man, I'm out!" Mr. Anonymous yelled. "I didn't come here for this shit."

Through low eyes, Mink watched Brett's friend walk out the door, slamming it behind him. Her fresh high caused her to giggle like a fool and fall sideways on the sofa. The warm and fuzzy sensation coursing through her body made her feel like she was soaring weightlessly through the air. She felt no pain, but she heard Brett running from room to room, rambling. Mink wondered what the hell he was doing, but at the same time, she really didn't give a damn. Her mind and body were in a zone, unable to connect with the real world around her. The constant craving that ruled her existence had been satisfied, even though it was only temporary. But it was the best feeling in the world while it lasted.

"Yo, this cracker's got paper," Brett said, returning to the living room carrying a laptop, a pair of sterling silver candleholders, and two designer watches.

Mink sat up, shaking her head lazily as drool slid down her chin. "W-what . . . What are you doing? That's Norm M.'s stuff. Go . . . Go put it back."

"Fuck you, girl. That motherfucker won't even miss this shit. He's got money to replace it anyway." He stuffed the watches in his pocket and walked toward an antique display case.

The front door opened all of a sudden, and Norm M. walked into his apartment and froze when he saw Brett. "What the hell is going on here? Mink, who is this man?"

"Norm M., you . . . You're home sooo early," she whined as her head bobbled up and down.

"What are you doing with my property, you hoodlum?"

"Just relax, man," Brett said in a low and eerie voice. "Mink invited me here."

"This is not Mink's apartment, and those aren't her things! I'm calling the police."

Brett stepped in front of Norm M., blocking him when he tried to reach for the phone. "You don't wanna do that, old man."

Norm M. attempted to push past Brett, but he wasn't strong enough. Brett dropped all of the items in his hands on the floor, except one of the candleholders. He raised it high in the air and brought it down forcefully against the side of Norm M.'s head, causing him to slump to the floor.

"*Uuuuuugh!*"

Mink opened her mouth to scream, but no sound came forth. She watched in horror as Brett kneeled over Norm M., bludgeoning his head repeatedly, sending blood and inner flesh splattering all over the sofa, coffee table, and carpet. Warm, red liquid splattered on Mink and Brett too as the foul odor of human membrane filled the air. The crunching sound of his skull shattering nearly sent Mink into cardiac arrest. The whole scene unfolding before her eyes was gruesome. She covered her mouth with bloodstained hands when Brett finally stopped bashing Norm M.'s head.

The stench of death crept slowly into the room with a choking effect. Even though she was as high as the sun in the sky, Mink knew Norm M. was dead beyond a shadow of a doubt. She couldn't speak or moan or even cry silent tears. She was numb and in shock. The only thing Mink could do was rock back and forth with her arms wrapped tightly around her shivering body. Brett grabbed her by the wrist and almost pulled her off the sofa. Their faces were so close together that she could smell his rotten breath.

"We gotta get rid of these bloody clothes and get the fuck outta here. But we can't walk out at the same time, though. You leave first and walk the few blocks down the street to that little café on the corner. I'll meet you there in a little while. My friend, Kuwasi, will come and scoop us up. I'll wear some of his clothes outta here." Brett pointed to a lifeless Norm M. lying flat on his face on the carpet in a pool of his own blood. "Go change your clothes." He stood up and took off his jacket.

Mink just sat there staring at Norm M., shaking her head in disbelief. Finally, tears began to fall from her eyes and streamed down her face. "He's dead? Is my friend dead? He didn't deserve to die. Why did you have to kill Norm M.?"

"Look, bitch, that old white dude was about to call the police on me, so I did what I had to do to stop him. Now, stop wasting time and let's go."

Mink wiped her eyes, smearing blood and mucus across her face. Then she leaned over and removed Norm M.'s wallet from his back pocket. The heinous murder that had just been committed fled her brain space when she saw several big bills of cash. Mink snatched the money out in a hurry and stuffed it in her bra before she let the wallet drop to the carpet.

Chapter Fifty

"Oh, I'm sorry. I thought you had turned in early."

Josiah aimed the remote control at the TV and turned it off. He offered Gypsie a faint smile. "I did, but I couldn't sleep."

"I was reading, but I couldn't concentrate. I guess I'm overly excited about the election. We've only got two more days."

Josiah held up two fingers. "Just *two* more days. Are you excited or worried? Tell me the truth, Gypsie."

"I'm not worried at all because I know you're going to win. What I'm feeling right now is excitement." Gypsie walked farther into the den and sat down in the recliner across from the sofa where Josiah sat. "Are *you* nervous, Mr. Mayor?"

"Maybe. If I am, does that make me a punk?"

"I would never describe you as a punk. You're one of the bravest men I know. In spite of everything going on in your personal life, you keep right on moving. You work hard for the citizens of Atlanta, you maintain a much-needed voice in your law firm, and you're the world's greatest father, hands down. I think you're quite a special guy, Josiah Jacob Bishop."

"You're a special woman. Look at the way you take care of Gem and Treasure while you balance managing me at work. And you're so selfless. I wouldn't be able to do all the things I do if it weren't for you. My debt to you is steep, girl. I don't know how I'm going to repay you."

"You don't owe me anything. Just win Tuesday night and win big. Then I want you to approve a *long* vacation for me after you're sworn in for your second term."

Gypsie smiled, and Josiah had to fight his libido to stay seated instead of crossing the room to pick her up and caveman her ass upstairs to his bedroom. He used the few moments of silence after her vacation request to regroup before he answered her.

"You deserve some time off. How does two weeks sound?"

"It sounds cool, but *three* weeks would be even better." Gypsie stood up, maintaining her breathtaking smile. "Think about it, boss."

"I'll consider it, but I don't think I could live without you for three weeks. Hell, two will be hard enough."

"You'll manage, I guarantee it. Good night."

"Good night, Gypsie. Sleep well."

Josiah watched her until she disappeared out of sight. And oh, what a sight she was. How the hell could she look so damn good in baggy sweatpants and an oversized tee? Josiah released air from his cheeks and turned the TV back on. He flipped through the channels until he saw a basketball game. The Golden State Warriors were playing the Dallas Mavericks. Josiah was a ride-or-die Atlanta Hawks fan, and he was friends with some of the players. So he really didn't have a dog in the fight. He just wasn't sleepy, and he still loathed the thought of sleeping alone. Josiah reclined comfortably on the sofa and decided to throw his support behind Stephen Curry and his crew.

With only two days until the election, Connor was grinding like crazy on Sunday night, organizing the poll watchers list to monitor each voting precinct in the city. He was also making sure all volunteer attorneys in the campaign knew their specific assignments in the event of any sign of voter suppression. It was quiet and still at city hall because Connor was the only member of the mayor's staff with obsessive-compulsive disorder and was stressing over the upcoming election. No other city government employee besides him wanted to spend Sunday evening working at the office.

As usual, Connor decided to check all of the news channels before he left for the night. He turned on the small TV on his desk and flipped to CNN first. Tired from a long and busy day, he thought his eyes were doing some tricky shit when a still shot of Mink captured on videotape appeared on the screen. Connor rubbed his eyes a few times and refocused on the image. He even increased the volume so he could better hear. And to his utter dismay, Don Lemon said the two words he didn't want to hear—*Mink Bishop*.

Josiah's staff didn't call Connor the drama king behind his back for nothing. He represented his title with full honor the moment he heard that Mink was a "person of interest" in connection with the grisly murder of a Hollywood movie producer found dead in his apartment in New York City. Dramatic to the highest degree, Connor grabbed two handfuls of his red hair and screamed like lightning struck him.

"If you know the whereabouts of this woman or you have seen her, please contact the New York Police Department immediately. And if you can identify either of these men, authorities ask that you contact the NYPD at 212 . . ."

"Aye, slow the fuck down and relax, Connor. I can't understand a damn thing you're saying. I've told you about panicking like a little-ass girl."

"She *murdered* someone! Mrs. Bishop . . . I just saw her on CNN. Don Lemon said it. He wouldn't lie. The mayor's wife is wanted for suspicion of murder in New York. It's her, J! I swear to God it is. They showed her picture on TV. It was a still shot of her on some video footage. This is bad, J! It's really, *really* bad. What the hell are we going to do?"

Jeremiah jerked the steering wheel sharply to the left and whipped across the median on I-75 North. He jutted into the interstate traffic heading in the opposite direction to the sound of horns blaring and screeching tires.

"*Fuck!*" He banged the heel of his hand on the steering wheel. "Meet me at JoJo's house ASAP. Hit up Geisel, Pennington, and um . . . um . . . What's his name?"

"Who? Seth Benedict?"

"Yeah. Call all of them and tell them to get their asses over to the mayor's house right now. They don't need to know why. Just tell them I said hurry the hell up. And do *not* call JoJo and tell the others not to contact him either. I'll see you in a minute."

"Okay. What about—"

Jeremiah hung up on Connor, and as soon as he did, his cell phone rang. He ignored it, though, because he didn't recognize the number. When the call rolled over to voicemail, he pushed a button on the dashboard and barked, "Call Rev."

The doorbell rang, startling Josiah fully awake. He sat up on the sofa and looked around the dark den. The basketball game was in the final few minutes of the fourth quarter, and the Warriors were slaying the Mavericks unmercifully. When the chime of the doorbell rippled through the house again, Josiah realized he hadn't been dreaming. Someone was really at his door after eleven on a peaceful Sunday night.

Mink!

Immediately, sheer panic caused a sharp pain to slice through Josiah's chest. Refusing to have another meltdown, he closed his eyes, took in a deep breath, and released it gradually in short puffs as Dr. Kabbah had suggested he do whenever he experienced anxiety. He repeated the anti-stress technique a few times before he jumped up and ran to the front door. Within seconds, he had deactivated the alarm, disengaged the locks, and opened the front door wide. The person standing on the stoop looked traumatized.

"*Connor?*"

The senior aide was totally flushed, redder than a fire engine when he walked past Josiah, shivering as if he were freezing. Connor offered no greeting or even a gesture of acknowledgment upon entering his boss's house. He just stood like a statue in the foyer with his back to him.

"What the hell is go—"

"JoJo, are you okay?" Jeremiah asked, bursting into the house.

"Yeah, I'm cool. Why wouldn't I be?"

"We've got problems, bruh . . . *major* problems. Where's Gypsie?"

"Here I am," she called out, tying the belt on her bathrobe on her way down the stairs.

"Good. You need to be in on this too. The rest of the gang is en route."

"Will somebody please tell me what the hell is going on?" Josiah yelled after he closed the front door.

Before anyone could respond to him, the house phone started ringing at the same time as Jeremiah's cell phone. Connor's phone buzzed too, adding to the noise. No one made any moves to answer the phones.

"J, Conner, one of y'all better start talking to me right now!"

"Connor, you're on front door duty. Watch out for the media. Let's go to the den and talk, JoJo. Gypsie, come with us."

Apparently, Connor's brain finally returned to earth because he nodded his agreement to Jeremiah's instructions. He turned around and marched like a robot to the front door while his boss and coworkers left the foyer, walking toward the den.

Josiah's cell phone was vibrating on the mantle when Jeremiah entered the den with his brother and Gypsie right behind him. They all sat down. Jeremiah chose the recliner while Gypsie sat next to Josiah on the sofa. The tension in the room was thick, and it sounded like thousands of phones were ringing all at once. It was driving Josiah crazy.

"Just tell me, J. Give it to me straight. This is about Mink, ain't it?"

"Yeah, it's Mink, man."

"Oh God. Is she dead?"

Gypsie reached over and placed her hand on top of Josiah's hand and squeezed.

"Nah, *she* ain't dead, but some rich guy she was hanging out with in New York City is. And she may have killed him. The police are on a manhunt for Mink and two dudes, JoJo. They think she may have played a part in beating the man to death in his Park Avenue apartment. It's all over the news."

Josiah lowered his head before he looked at Jeremiah again. "Damn."

Chapter Fifty-one

"I can't believe this shit! My little girls are going to be devastated by this. No school for them this week. Mama and Rev said they'll be here early in the morning. They can hang out with them."

Josiah was on the brink of tears as he flipped from CNN to MSNBC. Some local news stations were even airing special late-breaking reports about Mink. And every damn phone in the house was ringing off its hook.

"Who wants coffee?" Gypsie asked, entering the room carrying a tray with a carafe and mugs on top.

"None for me," Jeremiah answered.

Josiah shook his head and waved his hand. "No, thank you."

Pennington removed the tray from Gypsie's hands and placed it on the coffee table. "I'll have some."

Connor rushed into the den looking like he'd just escaped from a mental institution. "News cameras are at the guard shack, asking for access, J. Geisel just called and told me. She's on her way down the street."

"Good. As soon as she gets here, we can start composing her statement. We'll do just like we did last time."

"No, we won't." Josiah stood up with his hands in his pockets and started pacing in front of the fireplace. "I'm going to address the public this time. Mink is my wife, and my reelection bid is on the line. This time, the people who elected me to serve them need to hear from *me*. I have nothing to hide."

"JoJo, think about what you're saying, man. Those reporters are going to be all over you like hungry lions. They'll eat you up like a raw steak."

"I ain't scared, J. Let them bring it on. I'm tired of this nightmare I've been living. It's time to set myself free. No more ducking and dodging. I'm going to put the truth out there, and whatever is supposed to happen Tuesday night will happen. And regardless of whether it works out in my favor, I'm going to accept it."

"Hello, everybody." Geisel walked into the room.

Everyone returned a greeting in one form or another.

"Have a seat," Jeremiah offered. Then he turned to his brother. "Okay, Mayor Bishop, your team is here. Tell us what you want us to do."

"Geisel, I need you to round up the press. I want them all there. Let them know I'll be holding a press conference to address Mink's situation tomorrow morning at ten o'clock sharp at city hall."

"Yes, sir."

"Connor, contact my ground troops, more specifically, my lieutenants. Assure them that everything is cool. I don't want anyone to freak out over this."

"I'm on it."

"Pennington, reach out to your NYC sources. Find out anything you can about the deceased. I need to know about his connection to Mink. How did they meet? Was he an addict too? Dig deep."

"Done."

"J, get some high-ranking brass from the NYPD on the phone for me. They know Mink is the first lady of Atlanta by now. As soon as I speak to them, Seth, Gypsie, and I can start working on my speech."

"Good morning, everyone, and thank you for coming. I promise to be as brief as possible, but as the son of a Pentecostal preacher, my sense of time can be a little iffy."

A soft hum of laughter spread throughout the wide-open area filled with globs of journalists from local and national media outlets. TV cameras, photo cameras, video monitors, and microphones were everywhere. Josiah exhaled as he took it all in through bright lights. He was filled with a myriad of emotions. Fear, shame, and deep sadness were just a few. But he took comfort in knowing Jeremiah was just two feet behind him on his right and Connor on his left. Geisel, Seth Benedict, and Pennington were right behind them, showing their support. Josiah smiled at Gypsie and Rev who were seated front and center, surrounded by dozens of his key allies. When the laughter fully subsided, Josiah continued.

"I stand before you today not as the mayor of the great city of Atlanta or a political candidate or even as an attorney at law. I *am* all of the above, but I won't address you under the influence of any of those titles this morning. Right now, I'm just a man . . . A man who puts his pants on one leg at a time just like the next man. I hurt, I have fears, I get angry, and, yes, I make mistakes. I'm not perfect. No one is. And because no human being is without flaw, we *all* make bad decisions sometimes.

"Unfortunately, my wife, Mink Sinclair Bishop, decided to leave a drug rehabilitation facility in Montana three weeks ago without completing her treatment program. I don't know why she left because she didn't inform me or the healthcare professionals and members of the support staff at the center. Only Mink and God know why she chose to discontinue treatment. After leaving Montana, my wife found her way to New York City somehow where she was the guest of a gentleman who was found dead in his apartment last night. His name was Norman Allen Murchison, and he was brutally murdered.

"Detectives at the New York Police Department believe that . . . um . . . Mink, m-my . . . My wife may be responsible for Mr. Murchison's untimely death, or she has some knowledge of how he met his demise. But because Mink's whereabouts at this time are unknown, the circumstances surrounding the death of the deceased remains unresolved due to a lack of information.

"My family and I wish to express our heartfelt condolences to Mr. Murchison's family and friends. I understand he leaves a fiancée, his 4-year-old son, and two brothers to mourn his passing. Each of them is in my sincerest thoughts and prayers, and I intend to reach out to them later today.

"As far as my wife is concerned, I hope she'll turn herself in to the New York authorities and cooperate with their investigation. That's the only right thing to do. Mr. Murchison's family deserves answers regarding his death so that they can have closure. And I think Mink can play a major role in the process. I don't believe she killed Mr. Murchison. She has no violent tendencies whatsoever, but active addiction can cloud one's judgment. Therefore, she may very well be involved in this crime in some way."

Josiah paused and looked directly at the row of TV cameras in front of him. "Mink, honey, if you can see me and hear my voice, please call me. I'm worried sick about you. Let me know you're okay. I can help you. Just call me, and I'll come wherever you are and take you to the New York authorities. Regardless of whether you had anything to do with Mr. Murchison's death, it's important that you speak to the investigators and tell them everything you know. Please, Mink, call me. I love you, and I'm here for you."

Mink traced Josiah's handsome face with her fingertip over the dusty television screen. It was hard to see him through the heavy flow of tears spilling from her eyes.

The pain in his voice ripped her heart to shreds. After all she had put him and their little girls through and despite all of the terrible things she'd done, he still loved her. Why else would he go on national TV on the eve of his reelection bid and beg her to contact him? And why did he even give a damn about what could happen to her at this point? It was all because of *love*—a love that Mink didn't deserve, but one that her selfish greed wanted and her heart longed for.

Her breath hitched in her throat when Josiah turned and walked away from the cameras. Mink wanted to watch him and relish in the soothing sound of his voice just a little while longer. God, she missed him and her babies so much, but they didn't know that because her actions said otherwise.

As the CNN cohosts at their studio began to discuss her and her possible involvement in Norm M.'s murder, pictures and video footage of Mink at various times during Josiah's tenure as mayor flashed across the screen. The most recent family portrait they had taken reminded her of the happy times. She smiled through her tears when she saw herself dressed in an emerald-green, designer pantsuit, brightly smiling as she held the Bible at Josiah's mayoral swearing-in ceremony. Gem was an energetic toddler dressed in pink, squirming in Rev's arms while Myrlie cried tears of joy as she looked on with pride. Jeremiah was right there next to Mink, rocking 4-month-old Treasure in the crook of his arm.

Mink turned away from the outdated TV and flopped facedown on the bed. Unable to hold it in any longer, she began to wail into one of the lumpy pillows at the top of the bed. How had she downgraded from political wife, a stay-at-home mom, and first lady of Atlanta to a drug addict, fleeing the law? She had definitely sunk from sugar to shit. Brett had her held up in some fucking roach motel in the heart of Buffalo, hungry and itching for substance relief. A can of Pringles potato chips and a bottle of wine were the only things that had hit her belly since his friend, Kuwasi, had dumped them there early Saturday morning with the understanding that he was done with them. Dude said the long drive upstate, and a wad of cash was his limit.

"Please, Mink, call me. I love you, and I'm here for you."

Mink clamped her hands over her ears when Josiah's plea replayed in her head. She couldn't call him and tell him where she was. He would fly to Buffalo and drag her back to New York City. Although she didn't kill Norm M., she was responsible for his death. A fucking hood rat would come to that conclusion after hearing the whole story. So, no matter what, Mink would catch a case if she were to turn herself in. That's why reaching out to Josiah wasn't an option. Her only hope was to trust Brett to make some things happen. He was out now working on a plan to get them up to Niagara Falls and across the border to Toronto, Canada. His homeboy, a dude named Lucky, was supposed to be helping them out with some more cash and fake passports.

Chapter Fifty-two

"Yo, girl, wake up. I got food, liquor, and some other shit we need."

Mink sat up on the bed, trembling and raking her fingernails across the dry skin on her chin and neck. She had cried herself to sleep, twitching through a tug-of-war between hot flashes and chills. She didn't know how long she'd been snoozing when Brett returned to the motel room carrying a bunch of bags. He was almost unrecognizable with a completely bald head and no facial hair.

The aroma of food drew Mink out of bed. She walked over and grabbed the greasy brown paper bag Brett had placed on the dresser. When she opened it, the scent of grilled onions and peppers and seasoned beef kissed her nose, further stirring her hunger. Mink was starving to the point that it felt like her belly was chewing itself. She reached inside the bag and removed an oblong sandwich wrapped in foil. There were three other sandwiches inside with two containers of fries and a small bowl of coleslaw for each of them.

"I bought a gallon of vodka. It's cheap, but we gotta watch our money. I bought some beer too." He handed Mink a spoon for her coleslaw.

She was too busy stuffing her face to say thank you, so she gave Brett a quick head nod. After a few bites of her Philly cheese steak sandwich, Mink rambled through the bigger brown paper bag and lifted the huge bottle of vodka out.

"*McCormick?* What the hell?"

"Yo, we ain't exactly rolling in dough. Most of that money Kuwasi gave us went toward this here room. So, you better drink that shit and pretend like it's some Grey Goose VX, girl."

Mink wrinkled her nose and rolled her eyes. Brett didn't have any money, but *she* did. That $713 she'd lifted off Norm M. was in her bra. Her mama had taught her very early on that a girl should always set a little nest egg aside for a rainy day, and that's exactly what Mink had done. Her secret stash belonged to her, and it was for drugs. The cheap-ass vodka Brett had bought would get her through the night, but tomorrow, she was going to find some heroin or coke somewhere. It wasn't going to be hard either because they were in the hood for sure.

Settling on the bed with her food and the big bottle of bootleg vodka, Mink resumed eating. In between bites, she took long swigs of liquor, bringing on a slow buzz. It wasn't heroin, but she would make do until tomorrow.

Then Brett tossed a plastic bag on the bed, and it landed near Mink's thigh.

"What's this?"

"You need to change your look, yo."

Mink placed her food aside and screwed the top back on the vodka so she could check out the stuff in the bag. There was a pair of scissors, a box of hair dye, some false eyelashes, and a fake gold grill.

"Damn, nobody will recognize me with all this shit." Mink ran her fingers through her long, thick mane.

"Don't start acting all sentimental over your hair. Black women make me sick with that shit. You ain't got no choice but to cut it off. Lucky said your face is all over the news, social media, and every search engine on the internet. You a rock star, Mink Bishop."

"Yeah, I know. I watched the news earlier today."

"So, you're really married to the mayor of Atlanta?"

Mink nodded as she opened the vodka bottle again. She took it straight to the head for a big gulp. "Yep, that's me."

"Damn, girl! How the hell did you—"

"Don't ask me that. Just don't. You wouldn't understand."

"All right. I won't ask. Anyway, I hit Rizz up for some help, but she's trippin'. She cussed me out and told me she wasn't fucking with me no more because she ain't about to lose her son because of my bullshit. Plus, she's pissed because she thinks we fucking."

"Why didn't you tell her it wasn't like that between you and me?"

"I did, but she wasn't trying to hear it. She sounded like she was in love with you." Brett raised his eyebrows at Mink. "Is the pussy that sweet?"

"Hell yeah."

Brett laughed as he turned on the TV and flipped to BET. Then he grabbed a beer from a bag on the dresser and took a seat at the foot of the bed. Mink watched him in silence as she finished off her food. When her thoughts drifted to Josiah and her babies, she opened the vodka bottle again and started gulping it down fast. She needed to shush the damn crying baby and escape the pain and sorrow that was gnawing a hole in her heart. Numbing her senses with drugs and alcohol was the only way she knew how to cope.

"*Mom-eeeee!* I want my mom-eeeee!"

"Daddy! Daddy! Come quick! Mommy is on TV!"

All four adults in the kitchen looked at each other for a hot second. Then they hopped up from the table and took off running with Josiah leading the way. Treasure was

jumping up and down, screaming and crying hysterically
for her mommy. Gem was just standing in front of the
television, staring at the pictures of Mink flashing across
the screen, showing no emotion at all.

"Who left the damn TV on that channel?" Jeremiah
roared.

Gypsie quickly grabbed the remote control and turned
the television off.

"I did," Josiah confessed, rocking his upset baby girl in
his arms. "I forgot to turn it back to Nickelodeon."

Myrlie leaned down and wrapped her arms around
Gem. "There ain't no need for cussing and fussing. It was
a mistake."

A heavy cloud of tension lingered in the den. Treasure's
soft whimpers were heartbreaking. The spirit of Mink
was a powerful negative force on her family. No matter
how near or far away she was from them in the flesh, her
actions continued to bring them grief.

"I'll take them upstairs for their baths now," Gypsie
said softly and reached for Treasure.

"Nooo!" She squeezed her daddy's neck tight and shook
her head. "I want to see my mommy on TV again!"

"I'll give them their baths and read to them before I put
them to bed, Gypsie. You and J will have to start the conference call with the team without me. I'll join in later."

"Okay."

"Come on, Gypsie and Mama. Let's finish eating."

Josiah and his daughters headed for the staircase
while the others returned to the kitchen.

Mink stepped out of the shower and started drying her
body with a dingy, stained white motel towel. Just one
peep at her reflection in the mirror caused tears to pud-

dle in her eyes once again. It was going to take some time for her to get used to her new makeover. She'd bawled like a spoiled brat earlier this morning after Brett helped her cut her hair down to a tiny, curly Afro, three inches from her scalp. The sandy locks of her hair were still on the dresser because she didn't have the heart to throw them away.

Mink had always worn her hair long and natural because she hated chemicals. Other than shampoo, conditioner, and organic oils, an electric straightening comb on occasion had been the only other hair-care essential she'd ever used. The generic-brand cranberry-red hair dye she'd colored her new Afro with this morning was her virgin hair's intro to harsh chemicals. It looked awful against her butterscotch skin and coppery eyes, she thought for the hundredth time as she raked her fingers through her short curls.

Mink wrapped the towel around her body, opened the door, and padded out of the bathroom on bare feet.

"What the fuck?"

"Sorry! Sorry! Sorry!" The maid dropped the dust rag and held up both hands. Her long ponytail swung from side to side as she shook her head. "I knock on door. No answer. Sorry! Sorry! Sorry! I go!"

"Yeah, your taco-eating ass better get the hell out of here!"

Clearly frightened, the maid bent down and picked up the rag from the floor. Her eyes darted back and forth between Mink's frowning face and the cleaning caddy she'd placed on the dresser while she tidied the room. She placed the can of furniture polish and the bottle of glass cleaner inside of the caddy. Then, in a rush to leave, she knocked the empty box of hair dye and some of Mink's hair off the dresser and on to the floor.

"Bitch, get your clumsy ass out of my goddamn room! You're up in here knocking shit over like you got Tourette's or something. Get out!" She yanked the door wide open. "And learn to speak English!"

"Sorry! Sorry! Sorry!"

Mink slammed the door and locked it. Then she reached for the security chain, but it was broken. Sucking her teeth, she walked over to the dresser and picked up the vodka bottle. After she removed the top, she killed the corner she'd saved after her breakfast binge. Who knew cheap vodka and a Waffle House all-star special would taste so good together?

Now that she had a little alcohol buzz, it was time for Mink to get dressed so she could hit the streets. That smack was calling her name, and she was going to answer the call just as soon as she made herself presentable. But she couldn't do that until Brett got back. He had gone to the liquor store and one of those no-contract cell phone places. He was scared to use his phone to call his friend, Lucky, again, because the police were probably keeping tabs on all of his kinfolks and friends since several anonymous callers had identified him and the white dude. Once he got an untraceable cell phone, Brett was supposed to find a dollar store to buy Mink some lotion, hair moisturizer, and a tube of red lipstick. There wasn't enough time to pack toiletries before they left Norm M.'s apartment. It was a miracle she'd been able to bring as many clothes and shoes as she had.

"Jesus," Mink whispered when she thought about her poor friend.

She had never meant for Norm M. to get caught up in her bullshit, and she damn sure hadn't expected him to get killed. But crime and misfortune usually came along with chronic drug addiction for the addict as well as the people around them. No one was exempt.

Antsy and impatient, Mink slid into a black bra and a matching pair of boy shorts. Her body tremors and nausea were becoming hard to ignore. And that nagging itch was driving Mink crazy. She couldn't stop scratching her dry skin. Brett needed to hurry up so she could finish getting dressed and go handle her business. If he didn't return soon, Mink's impulsiveness was going to drive her to do something stupid. . . . Like she always did.

Chapter Fifty-three

Election Day

"Some people are just stupid," Connor whispered.

Gypsie nodded quietly in agreement.

"As much as JoJo has done to improve this damn city, I can't believe some people have decided to stay away from the polls today. It's really fucked-up."

"His numbers are still strong in every one of the predominantly black areas. Our volunteers have been busy since seven o'clock this morning, giving voters rides to the polls," Nelson chimed in. "The phone lines are busy because folks are still calling."

Connor eyed Jeremiah directly. "Do you think we should tell him about the low turnout in some of our stronghold areas?"

"What good will it do him?" He shook his head. "Nah, man. He's already dealing with enough, so he doesn't need to know about it."

"What don't I need to know?"

Everyone sitting around the conference table at Josiah's campaign headquarters turned around at the sound of his voice. He had caught them off guard because they'd left him in the main area with dozens of volunteers. At first, no one said a word as he walked farther into the room.

"What's up, JoJo?"

"You tell me. You and the team are in here huddled up, whispering about something you apparently don't want me to know." He took a seat at the conference table next to Connor. "So, y'all want to keep secrets from me, huh? What's the big secret, Geisel?"

She turned her head and looked at Jeremiah without parting her lips.

Josiah smiled at Seth Benedict, his deputy chief of staff. "My man, Seth, talk to me."

The silence was his reply.

"Voters in traditionally Democratic affluent areas are not voting, sir," Connor blurted out to Jeremiah's anger.

"Connor, you run your mouth like a little bitch!"

"He has a right to know!"

"I decide—"

"Whoooa! Are you two serious right now?" Josiah barked. "Let's talk like grown-ass men. I'm glad Connor gave me a head's-up on the low voter turnout. Actually, *you* should've been the one to tell me, J. You know I ain't weak like that. Bad news has never broken me. How come folks aren't voting, though?"

Everybody cast their eyes on the bigmouthed drama king.

"They don't like Lomax because he's a Republican. But they aren't sure if you're up to leading the city another four years because of your family issues. It's dumb because you have been a great mayor in spite of everything you've been through. It's a damn shame that some people are too full of shit to see it."

Josiah patted Connor's shoulder. "It's just an election. If I lose for whatever reason, it won't be the end of my life. I'll go back to my law firm and resume my duties there. And every one of you, as well as the rest of my staff, will receive excellent letters of recommendation from me to assist with finding suitable employment. Life will go on for all of us regardless of the results of the election tonight. I will be fine, so don't worry about me. As long as my daughters are healthy and sane, I'll be just fine."

Mink jerked and gasped when Brett banged hard on the door. She jumped up from the chair, cursing him out under her breath. He'd been gone all morning, and now it was late in the afternoon. She was hungry and experiencing grave withdrawal symptoms. Her Waffle House breakfast and the cheap vodka had kept her running to the bathroom vomiting and shitting until her stomach was empty and aching.

"What the hell did you do with your key?" Mink shouted as she turned the doorknob and yanked it open.

"Police! Step back and get down on your knees! Do it now!" one of the three uniformed officers yelled with their firearms aimed at her.

Mink shuffled backward, stumbling with her hands in the air before falling awkwardly to her knees. She was afraid to look up to see what was going on, but she heard doors opening and slamming shut and stuff being thrown around. It sounded like one of the officers was reporting every move to someone on a radio. Mink was too damn shocked and sick to her stomach to cry. It seemed like the chaos was unfolding in slow motion, but her mind still couldn't quite grasp it.

"Get up slowly with both hands on your head."

Mink did exactly what the officer had ordered. When she stood up, she looked into the faces of two white male officers and a redbone female, rocking a short do like Halle Berry back in the day. Dressed only in a black bra and panties, Mink shivered when a sneaky chill wrapped around her body. The sista in uniform stepped forward as her fellow officers kept their guns trained on their suspect.

"Are you Mink Sinclair Bishop?"

Finally, reality slapped Mink dead in her face. Tears sprang forth from her eyes. She swallowed hard and nodded her head. "Yes, ma'am."

As the policewoman Mirandized her and clamped the cold steel cuffs on her wrists, Mink's stomach began to churn and growl. She dry heaved a few times, causing saliva to seep from the right corner of her mouth and drip down the side of her chin.

"I want you to sit down on the bed while I find a pair of pants or a skirt and a shirt for you to put on. I'll release the cuffs and assist you getting dressed, but don't move or do anything stupid. Do you understand?"

Staring at the officers holding the guns, Mink whispered, "Yes, ma'am."

Five minutes later, all three officers and their suspect exited the motel room, and a pair of plainclothes cops entered to wait for Brett to return. He was in for a big, unpleasant surprise.

Mink held her head down, attempting to hide her face from a group of people standing in the motel's parking lot. For some strange reason, she looked to her left as they approached the blue and white police cruiser. Standing no more than five feet away was the petite Hispanic maid Mink had been so mean and condescending to just for the hell of it. The woman quickly lowered her eyes to the pavement before she turned and walked away.

The victory party crowd went wild when Josiah started moon walking down the Soul Train line to Michael Jackson's "Billie Jean." His little dance partners, Gem and Treasure, were busting their own moves to energetic handclaps and cheers. Before the trio reached the end of the line, the deejay killed the music.

"Ladies and gentleman, we have an update!" Jeremiah announced over the microphone. "With 48 percent of all precincts reporting, Mayor Bishop has 26,791 votes, and Dendrick Lomax has 25,643!"

Deafening cheers and applause shook the building. Grateful for even a slight lead, Josiah picked Treasure up and spun around in a circle. Her high-pitched squeal mixed in with the music, which the deejay had cranked up again, and the loud victory chants. Josiah's supporters had more confidence than he did. They were already claiming a win, although it wasn't time for the fat lady to sing yet.

"Josiah," Gypsie whispered in his ear. She'd suddenly appeared in his personal space undetected like a ghost. "You're needed in the office right away."

Quietly, Josiah placed Treasure on her feet and guided her to the table where his parents were seated with some church members. Gem followed them. "I need to check on something in the back, so you two stay here with Nana and Papa."

"Yes, Daddy," Treasure said.

Gem took a seat next to Rev. "Okay."

Following Gypsie toward the office, Josiah's heart began to race a hundred miles a minute. He didn't know what to expect. Had some new results come in, putting him behind Lomax? He got the answer to his question the moment they entered the office. There was a breaking news report on TV from a local news channel. Mink had been found and arrested at a motel in Buffalo, New York. The Erie County Sheriff's Department had processed her and contacted the NYC authorities who had already flown upstate to receive their most popular fugitive of the week and transport her to NYPD Central Booking.

"I need to get to New York. Mink needs me. I have to get her an attorney and—"

"I'll book a flight for you ASAP. I'm sure there's a red-eye I can get you on."

"Nah, Gypsie," Josiah said softly with his eyes still fixated on the TV. "I'll fly up in the morning. Win or lose, I want to finish out the night dancing, eating, and having a good time with my girls, my parents, and the rest of the people I care about."

"I ain't saying shit!" Mink hugged her body tighter against the tremors and chills. "I know my damn rights! I'm married to an attorney-turned-politician. Don't forget that shit. Y'all might as well take me back to my cell because I ain't telling y'all a goddamn thing until I get a lawyer. My husband will get me one soon. You can believe that."

The older detective of the two interrogating Mink scowled at her. She knew by his beet-red face and flaring nostrils that he was frustrated because she was refusing to answer any of their questions. But she didn't give a damn. Although she felt responsible for Norm M.'s death, Brett had beaten the life out of him with that damn candleholder. Mink wasn't about to take the blame for that or anything else she hadn't done.

"Brett Searcy said *you* killed Norman Murchison. He claims the whole setup was your idea. He told us he had never laid eyes on the victim until the morning you invited him and his friend, Corey Slade, over to the Park Avenue apartment to rob Murchison and murder him."

"That's a motherfucking lie! I called and asked Brett to bring that white dude to Norm M.'s apartment to—" Mink started laughing. Rocking back and forth in the plastic chair, she scratched her chin and neck roughly and narrowed her eyes at both men sitting across the table from her. "You motherfuckers think y'all slick. My lips are sealed until I get a lawyer, but I'll tell you this for free. I didn't kill Norm M., and I didn't set him up to be killed. Brett acted alone. I swear to God he did. Now, I want to make my phone call."

Chapter Fifty-four

"Hello?"

"JoJo, it's me."

There was a moment of silence on the line while Josiah tried to bring his emotions under control. "Are you okay?"

"I'm in a damn cage, JoJo. How okay can I be?"

"Well, at least I know where you are." *I'm not going to cry. I'm not going to cry,* Josiah chanted silently. "I know you didn't kill Mr. Murchison, but I need to hear you say it."

"I did not kill Norm M., and I didn't set him up either. I had no idea that fool was going to try to steal some of his shit and beat him to death. See—"

"Be quiet, Mink. This call is being monitored. You can tell me everything when your lawyer and I visit you tomorrow."

"Oh, hell yeah! I knew you would get me one of them expensive celebrity lawyers to make this shit go away. These people don't know who the hell they're fucking with. I'm *Mink Bishop*, Josiah Bishop's *wife*. So, what time will you and my lawyer get here tomorrow?"

"My flight will leave Atlanta at nine o'clock in the morning and arrive in New York shortly after eleven. I'll go straight to your lawyer's office to confer with him and his team, and then he and I will visit you at two o'clock sharp. Everything has already been set up."

"Thank God because I can't take it in here. You got to get me—"

"Mink, the judge hasn't set a bond for you yet. Your first court appearance isn't until Friday."

"*Friday?* Uh-uh, JoJo, I can't stay in this shit hole until Friday. I'm ready to get the hell up out of here."

Sighing, Josiah said, "You can't. You'll have to wait and allow the process to play out. I've got to go now."

"Why? What are you doing that's so important you can't talk to your wife?"

"It's election night, so I'm hanging out with the girls, the rest of the family, and friends. I won, by the way."

"Oh, that's good. I knew you would. So, how much do you think my bond is going to be? I hope you won't have to put our house up. I love our home. Remember when we first bought it?"

"Yes, I remember, Mink. Anyway, I'm hanging up now. My supporters are partying without me. I'll see you tomorrow."

"You mean to tell me you'd rather party with—"

Josiah leaned back in his chair and looked up at the ceiling after hanging up on Mink. He didn't want to hear another word of her bullshit. Out of anger and frustration, heavy teardrops escaped from the corners of his eyes. Mink was so fucking selfish. The reelection bid her drug addiction could have very well ruined for him meant nothing to her. Hell, her daughters obviously weren't important to her either because she didn't even ask about them. Mink, Mink, Mink . . . Everything was all about *her*. No one and nothing else mattered. Josiah hated to admit even to himself, but Mink was like poison. She was a dangerous woman. Because of her, a man was dead, Treasure was emotionally fragile, and he had damn near had a heart attack.

Josiah wiped his eyes dry and sat up straight in the chair. It was *his* night, damn it! He had busted his ass to win a second term as mayor while working for the citi-

zens of Atlanta and taking care of his daughters. If anyone deserved a strong drink and a couple of spins on the
dance floor, it was him. So, he left the office and returned
to the big room in the headquarters where the music was
still pumping, and folks were dancing. There was plenty
of good food, and the bar was still open. Electricity was
in the air, and Josiah wanted to enjoy every minute until
the end.

"Hell nah! I ain't pleading to a damn thing. I didn't kill
nobody and—"

"Shut the hell up, Mink!" Josiah slammed his palm
hard on the table. He leaned over and through gritted
teeth, growled, "Your bloody fingerprints were all over
the dead man's back pocket and wallet, which means
you removed it and took cash from it *after* he had been
assaulted. What you should've done was called an ambulance and the police. But because you chose to rob a
severely beaten dead man instead of reporting the crime,
you now look guilty of accessory to murder and aiding
and abetting—at the very least."

"Your husband is right, Mrs. Bishop," Attorney Cassius
Wyatt confirmed. "It's your word against Brett Searcy's.
He said you killed Mr. Murchison, but the evidence indi-
cates otherwise. Your fingerprints were nowhere on the
murder weapon or any of the stolen items recovered from
the stolen duffle bag found in the motel room in Buffalo.
Therefore, I'm confident I can successfully defend you
against the murder charge and armed robbery. But the
conspiracy, accessory to murder, and aiding and abetting
charges will be much harder to beat."

"So, what does that mean?" The sound of Mink's fingernails scraping against her scalp, chin, and neck was
annoying as hell.

"I'm sorry, but you're going to serve some time in prison, Mrs. Bishop. I'll do my damnedest to try to get the charges reduced to the minimum based on your cooperation with the DA to help nail Searcy's ass, but you'll serve some time in the end."

"For what? I didn't do anything."

"Mink, you participated in a drug deal. That's a crime of possession. Corey Slade, the guy who sold you the drugs, has already confessed and made a deal with the prosecution. He's going to testify to the fact that when he left Murchison's apartment, you were on the sofa and Brett Searcy was in the back rummaging. You can't deny it because video footage confirms that Corey Slade left the apartment building twenty-nine minutes before you did and Searcy left sixteen minutes after you, carrying the duffle bag found in the motel room in Buffalo."

"So, I bought some drugs. Okay, I'll plead to that. What else?"

Mink's attorney cleared his throat. "You witnessed a murder, and instead of reporting it to the authorities, you chose to leave the scene of the crime with the murderer, who, by your own admission, didn't threaten or force you to do so. And then you assisted him in flight and stayed in hiding with him until the Buffalo authorities apprehended you as a person of interest in the murder and armed robbery committed in New York City. You committed a long list of misdemeanors too, but you only need to be concerned with the heavy stuff."

For the first time since Josiah and his law school buddy, Cassius, had arrived at the jail, Mink seemed cognizant. The reality of the seriousness of her situation had finally struck her like a powerful bolt of lightning. Josiah saw it in her eyes the moment realization finally settled in, and with the realization came a heavy flow of tears.

"I didn't kill my friend, and I didn't call Brett and that white dude over to his apartment to kill him either. I just wanted some drugs. I never meant for Brett to kill Norm M., but I was too high to stop him, JoJo. I swear to God. And the only reason why I went with that asshole to Buffalo and hid out with him in that motel was because I didn't know what else to do. The police were going to find Norm M.'s body soon, and I knew they would blame me for his murder. I was scared, so I ran away with Brett."

"I believe you, Mink, but Cassius is going to have one hell of a time convincing a judge and a jury that you bear no guilt at all in the case."

"I think I can debunk the conspiracy charge because according to Murchison's administrative assistant, he left his office on a whim that day because, by mistake, he'd left a DVD he needed at his apartment. He told everyone he would be back in less than an hour."

Mink's eyes lit up. "I had no idea Norm M. was coming home in the middle of the day. I was surprised to see him. So, if I didn't know ahead of time he was going to be at his apartment, how could I have set him up for Brett to kill him?"

"You couldn't have," Josiah answered.

"That's true. As I said, I believe I can squash that charge. Accessory to murder and aiding and abetting are on a whole other level, especially since y'all ran and hid out together like Bonnie and Clyde. I'll do my best, though, Mrs. Bishop. Now, let's talk about your first appearance before the judge."

Between the crying baby and the out-of-control with-drawal symptoms, Mink felt like she had one foot in the grave and the other one in a pile of shit. And the fact that she was facing the possibility of ten to fifteen years in prison was messing with her head too. Every woman on lockdown had witnessed her at her worst, but she was too depressed to give a flying fuck. Because she couldn't keep any food or liquids on her stomach, Mink had vomited in the middle of the floor in the dining hall. A lot of hungry inmates were pissed the hell off with her for ruining their delicious dinner of Spam sandwiches, stale potato chips, and applesauce. And as if puking up an entire meal wasn't enough, Mink fainted before she could make her way out of the dining hall and back to her cell.

Even in semiconsciousness, Mink had heard the inmates cursing and complaining out loud about how disgusting she was for emptying her belly in the middle of the floor. Some were accusing her of pretending to have fainted. If only they'd known how terrible she'd felt, they would've shut the hell up and finished eating the slop on their plates.

That was the last thought Mink had before her stomach churned and complete darkness covered her again.

Chapter Fifty-five

"Ethan, it's Mink. I've been calling you for three days. Didn't your sister give you my messages?"

"Yeah."

"Well, why didn't you call me back? I've been waiting by the phone all this time."

"Mink, we just settled in the city, and I'm preparing for college. Things are a little complicated right now."

"I know, but I've got enough money for my flight to Oklahoma and some extra for a cheap motel room for a few days. I'll find a job as soon as I get there so when I move into the apartment with you and your roommates, I'll be able to chip in on the bills. And I'll work up until the day I have the baby. I hope I can come soon because my parents have already made an appointment at the clinic on base for me to have an abortion."

"That might be the best thing for you. An abortion, that is."

"No, Ethan! Why would say that? Don't you still love me?"

"Damn it, Mink, I don't know! I mean, everything was cool while I was in Germany, but things are different here. I'll start college in two weeks, and you're only fifteen. How am I supposed to take care of you and a baby?"

Mink recoiled like she'd been doused with ice water. She couldn't believe the change in Ethan's attitude since he'd left Germany. The pain in her heart was unbearable. *"Ethan, you told me you loved me, and you wanted this baby. It was your idea for me to leave Germany and move to Oklahoma so we could get married and raise our baby together."*

"Things have changed, Mink, so get over it! My parents don't want us together, and they never did. And they don't want a black grandbaby."

"Ethan! How could you do this to me? I believed in you. I thought you really loved me."

"Well, you thought wrong because I don't! Now, stop calling me!"

"Noooo! Please don't make me! Please, Daddy! I don't want to do it! I want my baby! Noooo!"

"Wake up, Mrs. Bishop. You're having a bad dream. Everything is okay now. Open your eyes, sweetie. Wake up."

Mink's eyes fluttered open and focused on the woman standing above her cot. Through tear-filled eyes, she made out her face. She had the most beautiful blue eyes, and her straight, blond hair was pulled back into a loose ponytail.

"I'm Libby Jordan, the nurse practitioner on call here. You're in the jail's infirmary. Tell me what happened in the dining hall this afternoon."

"My stomach was upset, but I was hungry. So, I ate dinner and drank some water. It made me feel worse. I tried to run when my stomach started bubbling, but I wasn't fast enough. I threw up and passed out."

"Your body is responding to the absence of drugs. I saw the track marks on your arms. How long have you been addicted to heroin, and when was the last time you used it?"

"I've used on and off for almost three years now, but I haven't had anything but alcohol in my system in four days."

"Would you like to speak with a counselor and attend NA meetings while you're here?"

"No. I'm leaving Friday. My husband is going to pay my bail to get me out of here, regardless of how high it is."

"Okay. I'm going to run an IV to get some fluids and nutrients in your body and keep you in here overnight for observation. Hopefully, you'll feel better in the morning."

"When are you coming home, Daddy?"

"Tomorrow night, sweetheart."

"Are you going to bring surprises for Treasure and me?"

"Of course, I'll bring special treats for my two favorite girls."

"Thank you, Daddy. I love you."

"Daddy loves you more. Now, put Miss Gypsie back on the phone."

"Okay."

"Hello?"

"Hey, Gypsie. How are the girls doing with home studies?"

"Gem is doing well. Treasure is struggling because she's not happy. She's missing her friends. I'm going to call their parents to see if we can get the gang together for a play date."

"That's a good idea."

"I thought you would approve."

Cassius walked into his office with an iPad in his hand. Jack, his, paralegal followed him inside and closed the door.

"Mink's lawyer just walked in, so I've got to hang up now. I'll check in with you and the girls this evening."

"Okay, Josiah. We'll talk later."

He ended the call and put his cell phone on vibrate before he placed it inside his breast pocket. "What's going on, Cash Money?"

Cassius sat behind his desk. "We just left the district attorney's office, trying to come to an agreement on the case. It's not looking too good for your wife, JoJo."

"I'm listening."

"The DA wants Searcy's ass bad, and he has no problem sacrificing Mink to get him. He's willing to throw everything out the window on her except the aiding and abetting charge. If Mink will plead guilty to that and cooperate with the DA, he assured me she'd only serve seven years."

"And if she refuses?"

Cassius exhaled out loud with obvious displeasure. "He'll go after her for accessory to murder and aiding and abetting a felon. That means she can do twenty-five to life, JoJo. No less. I expect him to ask the judge for the highest bail possible. And Mink can forget about leaving the state of New York before her trial. No judge will allow her to leave the state. The worst of it is I can't guarantee you a win. I'm a damn good defense attorney. Shit, I'm the *best*, but this case is complicated."

"Damn!" Josiah rubbed both hands down the length of his face. "Mink is so freaking stubborn and explosive. And to top it off, she's a chronic, hard-core heroin addict. I can't imagine her humbling herself to take the plea deal."

"Why not?"

"Because she's selfish as hell! She'll expect me to bail her out, rent a place for her to stay in up here while she awaits trial, and bankroll her defense. I can't do that, Cassius. It would break me, and that's not fair to my little girls. And what if she violates the terms of her bond? I'll lose even more. I can't risk it, man, I just can't."

"Then don't."

Cassius and Josiah looked at Jack after he spoke up for the first time.

"Tell your wife she doesn't have a choice but to take the deal. If she refuses, make it clear to her that she's on her own. That's what my family had to do with my cousin. We stepped back and let him hit rock bottom when he kept dragging us through the mud with his cocaine addiction. And when no one was around to help him, he had to help himself. Now, he's been clean and sober seventeen years. Dude is married with three great kids and pastoring a church in Harrisburg, Pennsylvania."

"I'll give it my best shot to convince Mink to take the deal, but if she decides to go to trial and fight, she'll do it without my help. As her husband and the father of her children, I'll give her all the emotional support I can. But I can't invest any more money or resources, especially not on a legal gamble. I'm all tapped out."

Cassius stood up. "Let's roll. Jack made a three o'clock appointment for a client-attorney meeting with your wife at the jail. I'll explain the terms of the plea deal, but you've got to persuade her to take it."

After giving Mink a very thorough and detailed run-down of the plea deal the DA had offered her, Cassius stood from the table and looked down on her with sympathy in his eyes. "I'm going to leave you and JoJo alone to talk. I'll see you in court in the morning."

Mink wiped her eyes and blew her nose on her husband's monogrammed handkerchief before she nodded her head. "Fine."

A teary-eyed Josiah stared at his wife from across the table. He felt like a failure and less than a man because he hadn't been able to save her from herself. She was his soul mate, his babies' mama, and his partner for life. He'd sworn to protect her and take care of her until death, but he had fallen short, and it was sucking his soul out of his body.

"Mink, the plea deal is your best option. Believe me. It really is." He reached across the table to hold her hand.

"It's the best option for *who?*" She snatched her hand from Josiah's grip. "You want me to spend seven years of my life in prison away from you and my babies like I'm off on a goddamn extended vacation? Fuck that! If you were a *real* man and a *devoted* husband, you would stand by my side and fight for me! I am your *wife,* JoJo! Whatever happened to love and cherish in sickness and in health 'til death do us part, huh? Who are you trying to get rid of me for? Some bitch you've been fucking while I was trying to get my life together? You're a dirty, low-down motherfucker! You ain't shit!"

"Mink, I have been faithful to you our entire marriage, and I've supported you 110 percent through your drug bullshit. You have no idea how much money I've shelled out on rehab centers, therapy, and medications for *you,* Mink." He wiped tears and mucus from his face with his palm. "When Treasure cries for her mommy, I comfort her. I attend school meetings when other children tease Gem because you're on drugs. I have done everything I can do for you, and I've given you my all. There is nothing more I can do or give, Mink."

"You ain't broke, nigga. Put up the house! Hell, take out a loan. You're supposed to do any and everything in your power to help me. I'm your *wife!*"

Josiah shook his head with tears streaming down his face. "I'm sorry, but I can't do it. I can't."

"Well, don't bring your black ass to court tomorrow then. If you ain't coming with your checkbook ready to bail me out, don't show up at all. I don't want to see your face if you ain't willing to make the sacrifice to pay my lawyer to take me to trial and fight for my innocence! You know damn well I didn't do anything wrong. Humph, but you want me to take a goddamn plea deal. Get the fuck out of here!"

Josiah stood up, pushed his chair under the table, and walked toward the door.

"That's right! Take your raggedy, selfish, cheap ass home! Run on back to Atlanta where you belong! You care more about your voters than you care about your own damn wife. I gave up my career so you could rise in politics, and you pay me back by letting me go to prison for seven motherfucking years. I hate your punk ass! I hope you die!"

Once he made it outside the room and closed the door on Mink's vulgar rant, Josiah broke down. Regardless of the pain in his heart, he knew he had done right by Mink. She hated him now, but one day, she would have to confess to herself if to no one else that she had married a faithful and loving man who had done his best to honor his wedding vows to her and had committed his life to raising their two children. She would realize someday. He knew she would.

Chapter Fifty-six

Mink jumped in her seat when the van door slammed closed.

The woman sitting next to her laughed. "Don't be scared, honey. The sound of gates and doors closing and jingling chains is a normal thing in this world. If things don't go your way with the judge today, you'll get used to it."

"This is my first and last time in jail, so I'm not trying to get used to being caged and shackled like a wild animal."

"I felt the same way my first time. I wasn't ever coming back either. But after I served my five years and got back home, I started doing the same ole shit again. Drinking, drugging, and stealing to support my crack habit—that's what I did. Now, I'm looking at ten years unless God has mercy on me."

Out of the six women on the van being transported to the courthouse, Mink was the only one dressed in civilian clothes instead of one of those god-awful, orange jumpsuits. So, quite naturally, she was feeling a sense of pseudo self-superiority when the truth of the matter was . . . She was no better than any of her fellow inmates. However, she felt like a queen amongst paupers in a brand-new navy business suit. She'd lost a lot of weight since the last time Josiah had shopped for her, so the skirt and single-breasted jacket were loose as were the flesh-tone pantyhose. The only thing he'd purchased for her court appearance and brought to the jail that fit was the shoes. The navy, size-8 Spectator Pumps looked perfect on Mink's feet.

"You look like a little girl. How old are you, chile?" After a period of silence, the veteran inmate sitting next to Mink decided to strike up a conversation with a younger woman on the other side of her.

"I'm 23."

"Damn! You're a baby." She laughed and gave the young woman's shoulder a friendly slap. "I'm Patsy. What's your name?"

"Angelica."

"You don't look like you could hurt a flea. What'chu in jail for, girl?"

Angelica's eyes watered, and she swallowed a few times. "I helped my boyfriend and his boys rob a bank."

"Say what?"

Every woman on the van looked at Angelica. Even the guard who was driving and the one in the passenger's seat turned around and peeped at her for a hot second.

"I wasn't actually with them when they did it. I was a teller at the bank, and I set the whole thing up to go down on my day off."

"Do you have a lawyer, baby girl?" a fat white lady sitting on the back row asked.

"No, not a real one. The court appointed me one. I couldn't put my mama and my stepdaddy through all the drama and let them spend their retirement on an attorney for me when I knew exactly what I was doing. I did something stupid for a man who don't give a damn about me. He snitched me out the first opportunity he got. His ass could've gotten away with the robbery if he hadn't been so damn greedy. But because he got caught, he told on me and all his boys. None of that matters, though, because I helped plan the robbery, so I'm guilty."

"What's your lawyer's plan?" Patsy wanted to know.

"He allowed me to make the decision based on his professional opinion. So, I'm going to plead guilty to accomplice to armed robbery and pray to God the judge will be lenient with me because it's my first offense ever. Hopefully, I'll get fifteen to twenty-five years. But if the security guard who got shot dies, I'll catch an accessory to murder charge too. They got me on accessory to attempted murder right now, but it could change. Hell, if he dies, I could get life."

Mink's heart dropped to her stomach. "How is that possible? You said you weren't even there, so you couldn't have shot anyone."

"It don't matter," the white lady blurted out. "Her actions contributed to everything her old man and his buddies did. They couldn't have robbed the bank without her input, and the security guard would not have caught a bullet if they hadn't been robbing the goddamn bank. So, she's guilty of everything that happened by association and deed."

"That's exactly how my court-appointed attorney explained it to me. So, what's the use in fighting it? I'm going to put on my big-girl panties and own my shit. Hopefully, the judge will take my first-time offender status into consideration. And I'll keep praying for that security guard."

Mink reclined her head and kept her mouth shut for the rest of the ride to the courthouse. While the other women discussed their charges and personal lives, she thought about her life since becoming addicted to heroin. She couldn't remember a single time she had taken responsibility for her actions. No matter what she did, it was always someone else's fault in her twisted mind. Josiah had made it easy for her by paying globs of money for treatment and allowing her to come back home with little to no consequences. All she'd ever had to do was apologize and promise never to shoot up again. But she never kept that promise.

"Okay, ladies, you are to exit the van one by one and line up in a single file. Do not move unless given the order to do so. You are not to speak to each other or any-one else. Do not look around or make direct eye contact with free members of society. If your attorney is present, you will be allowed to speak with him or her by permis-sion only after the proper credentials are presented. Do you understand?"

"Yes, sir."

Mink spotted Cassius, his paralegal, and Josiah as soon as she and the other shackled inmates exited the elevator. They all nodded at her, but she kept walking without acknowledging them as she'd been told. Deep in her heart, Mink knew Josiah would show up at court even though she had acted a damn fool on him the day before. It was just his nature to always be in her corner, support-ing her and loving her although she didn't deserve it.

Shortly after the inmates sat down on a bench fac-ing the courtroom, Cassius and Josiah approached both guards and presented their credentials. Josiah's were temporary because they had been issued through Cassius's law firm as a visiting attorney from Georgia.

"Bishop," the guard who had driven the van called out, "your attorneys are here."

He walked over to the bench and released Mink from the other inmates, but she remained handcuffed with her hands in front of her. He escorted her to a small room with a heavy metal door and a Plexiglas window. Cassius and Josiah were right behind them.

The two bailiffs on post outside the room verified both attorneys' credentials before one of them opened the door.

Right outside the room, Mink turned to Cassius. "I would like to speak with Attorney Bishop alone please."

He looked at Josiah for his approval.

"It's fine."

"You have seven minutes," one of the bailiffs said and then locked them inside the room.

Mink sat down on a short bench attached to the wall, and Josiah sat on one just like it across from her.

"I'm so sorry for how I treated you yesterday, JoJo. You didn't deserve it just like you don't deserve to put your life on hold for me any longer. I'm going to take the plea deal because I left here, running away from a senseless murder that I had caused. It's my fault Brett killed Norm M. If I had kept my ass in Montana and worked the treatment program like I was supposed to, he would still be alive. I really screwed up, JoJo!" Mink doubled over and sobbed.

"It's okay, Mink. I'm going to visit you—"

She held up her hands that were still cuffed together and shook her head. "No, you're not. Don't ever come up here again. Don't even write to me. You are going to divorce me and go on with your life. I mean it, JoJo. You're a young, successful, good-looking man who's been living in hell for almost three years. It's time for you and those little girls I've neglected and traumatized to enjoy life without me floating in and out like a fucking ghost. I want you to send those divorce papers as soon as you get home, and I'm going to sign them. And you might as well have sole custody of the girls. I can't do anything for them, so I don't deserve parental rights anymore. Prepare those papers and send them too. Do it soon. Do you hear me?"

"Mink, you're just talking crazy now. You don't want to sever ties with me and the girls."

"Yes, hell, I do! And you should want me to. Wake up, JoJo. You've been married to me all this time, and I've been married to *drugs*. While you were faithful to me and loved me, I didn't give a fuck about you. I didn't even love myself. Now, it's time for a good woman to love you and take care of your needs. Pick someone who'll love my babies like her own. Lord knows I didn't love them enough to do right by them. I was a terrible mother."

"What am I supposed to tell Gem and Treasure?"

"Tell them the *truth*. Don't hold nothing back when you tell them either. I know they won't understand right now, but they will one day when they're older and more mature. Tell them everything about drugs and what they did to me. Nah, tell the how I *allowed* drugs to fuck up my life. Talk to them about boys, sex, peer pressure, and loving themselves. Don't let my beautiful babies turn out like me. They'll probably need therapy. Shit, I'm going get me some too as soon as I get settled at Rikers Island. I've got emotional issues I never told anyone about, including you, but it's okay because I need to deal with my demons and not anyone else. And when the NA people come to the prison, I plan to throw myself into the program and work it like nobody's business."

"Mink, I love you, and I will until I die. Let me be there for you. I love you."

"No! Your love has hindered me. You've been my enabler, JoJo. I never really tried to get my shit together because you didn't require me to. As long as I knew you were going to be there to take me back and love me, I didn't give recovery my all. Now, I don't have a choice because the next seven years I'll have to stand on my own two feet and help my damn self. So, if you really love me, I want you to leave now. There's no need for you to go into the courtroom with me because I have an attorney thanks to you. Go home to our little girls and forget about me. Pour all the love in your heart for their mommy over them every day. Promise me, JoJo."

Sniffling and wiping his eyes, he whispered, "I promise."

"You were a wonderful husband, but I was too damn stupid to appreciate you. I used you and took advantage of your love. I'm going to pray that your next woman will treat you like a king. And she better treat Gem and Treasure like little princesses too."

The bailiff banged on the door and held up one finger.

"Go on now, JoJo. I'll be expecting those divorce and custody papers soon. I don't want you to prolong the process. Take care of my babies like you've always done, and start taking care of yourself."

Epilogue

Six months later . . .

"Little divas, I'm home!"

Gypsie hung her umbrella on a wall hook and walked farther into the dim house. Surprised that Gem and Treasure hadn't come running down the stairs yet, she headed for the den, flipping the foyer light on along the way. The den was empty, but there was a note on the coffee table, written in bright red crayon, directing her to the formal dining room.

"What the hell?" Gypsie snorted and walked in the direction of the one place in the house where they spent very little time.

The moment she crossed the threshold, the scene before her made her heart go pitter-patter. The candlelit table was set for two with fine china, sterling silver flatware, and crystal stemware. Snow-white linen always added a touch of class to any occasion. And a fine-ass, chocolate brotha dressed in a pair of relaxed-fit jeans and a plain black T-shirt never failed to make her lust spike so high that she felt weak in the knees. Damn, he smelled good.

Is this Negro playing Luther?

"Hey, you. Have a seat, and I'll pour you a glass of wine."

"Josiah, what's going on? Where are the girls?"

"They're with J for the entire weekend. Aren't you going to sit down?"

"Oh yeah." Gypsie was so nervous and shocked that she didn't even realize she was still standing. "Thank you," she whispered after Josiah made sure she was comfortable in her chair before he took his seat.

"The family therapist released Gem and Treasure today. She expects them to flourish and adapt to any given environment in society. According to her summary, they have the tools to make good decisions and develop healthy, lasting relationships."

"That's great. I'm happy for my little divas. I love those girls to death."

Josiah poured wine into Gypsie's glass and his. "What about their daddy? How do you feel about him?"

"I think Gem and Treasure have a wonderful daddy who loves them very much."

"Gypsie, let's stop playing games. You know I want you, and you want me too, but we've been dancing all around our feelings because of circumstances. Initially, I was married to Mink, and after the divorce, I still wasn't emotionally available."

"And now?"

"I'm ready to love again and be loved. I've worked my way back from a very dark place, Gypsie, and you were a shining light all the way through."

"Maybe what you feel toward me is gratitude for taking care of the girls, Josiah."

"Nah, baby. What I feel for you has nothing to do with Gem and Treasure. I got *grown-folks'* feeling for you." Josiah reached over and took Gypsie's hand in his. "I want you in my life as more than just my AA and my daughters' caretaker. Let me love you the way you deserve to be loved, and you give that same kind of love right back to me. I want to wine and dine you and take you places you've never been before. There are so many things I want to experience for the first time with you.

And when the time is right, I want to make love to you all night long until you beg me to stop and then start all over again at sunrise."

"I want that too, Josiah."

"Good." He leaned in and kissed Gypsie's lips softly. "You need to turn in your two-week notice Monday morning." He kissed her again.

"I can do that, but I need a letter of reference for my job search."

"No problem."

Josiah wrapped both arms around Gypsie's waist and pulled her closer. Then he went all the way in for a deep and passionate kiss with a promise of better things to come over the weekend and for the rest of her life.

What about the girls? a loud voice screamed inside Gypsie's head. Reluctantly, she broke the kiss and looked into Josiah's lust-filled eyes. "How are we going to explain our new relationship to Gem and Treasure?"

"We'll be honest, direct, and open with them. That's the best way. When J brings them home Sunday evening, you and I will sit them down and tell them the truth."

"Which is?" she smiled.

"I'll simply remind them that their mother and I are no longer married. Then I'll say something like Daddy and Miss Gypsie really like each other a lot, and we're boyfriend and girlfriend now."

Gypsie tried to hold back her laughter, but she failed. "Are you serious, Josiah?"

"I'm very serious. It's going to work too. You'll see. By the time we go on our Disney World vacation, we'll be one happy family."

"We're going on vacation? You, the girls, and I are going to Disney World?"

He kissed her cheek. "Yeah."

"When?"

"We'll fly down to Orlando next month as soon as they get out of school for the summer. I think a week at the Walt Disney Resort will be a good way for us to unwind and have some fun after all we've been through over the past year. Don't you think?"

"As long as I'm with you, we can go camping in the backyard." Gypsie leaned in and gave Josiah a hot, wet kiss.

"Girl, if you keep playing with me, I'll have to call J and tell him to keep Gem and Treasure until *next* Sunday."

"Go ahead. I dare you."

"Mmm, Josiah, mmm, mmm, mmm . . ."

Slow and easy, he stroked Gypsie deeply, filling her tight, juicy goodness to capacity. Each time he pulled out and reentered, her pussy hugged his dick unmercifully. His throaty groans of pleasure echoed throughout the room, mixing with the sound of raindrops tapping against the windowpane.

Lazy, rainy-weather loving had never been this damn sweet. It felt so good that Josiah wanted to take a nap in the pussy and dream about it. The sting of Gypsie's fingernails digging into the flesh on his back brought a little pain to his pleasure as she wrapped her legs around his waist, causing his hardness to sink deeper into her slick walls and tap her G-spot. Each time his swollen head touched that secret place, she moaned sensually in his ear and sang his name.

Gypsie may have been a petite woman, but she had some powerful hips that bucked and grinded in perfect coordination with Josiah's aggressive strokes. And that little hip-roll action she hit him with each time his tongue latched on to hers in a sloppy kiss was about to make him prematurely nut if he wasn't careful. He couldn't let that happen, though, until he made her body do that familiar happy dance underneath him while her honey rained all over his dick.

She was on the brink of explosion. Josiah could tell by the way her inner muscles had begun to clench and release him uncontrollably. And when he looked into her eyes, only the whites showed as they blinked repeatedly and rolled to the back of her head. Gypsie's hips started pumping wildly. Josiah doubled down on his strokes and picked up speed.

"Oh, Josiaaah!" She pressed her palms against his shoulders and humped him hard. "Mmm . . ."

Surrendering to sexual euphoria, Josiah released warm semen inside Gypsie's womb in response to her shudders and soft purrs. He kissed her passionately as he willed the room to stop spinning long enough for him to catch his breath. Weak and satiated, he rolled off of her body and pulled her on her side to face him. Hair tousled and beads of sweat dotting her nose, Gypsie had never looked more radiant in Josiah's eyes. He studied her face covered with a post-orgasmic glow. Her eyelids were low, and her breathing was choppy.

There was so much he wanted to say to her, but now wasn't the time because she was falling asleep before his eyes. Josiah smiled, satisfied that he had loved Gypsie to exhaustion. Their first time together had far exceeded his highest expectation—and then some. Good things always came to those who waited.

Josiah's cell phone rang unexpectedly. He reached over on the nightstand and picked it up. It was Jeremiah.

"What's up, J?"

"We just passed the guard shack."

"Damn. Okay."

"You don't want your little girls, man?" Jeremiah chuckled.

"Yeah, I want them. I'll see y'all in a minute."

Gypsie's eyes popped wide open when Josiah hung up the phone.

"I thought you were asleep."

"I was, but now I'm up. Gem and Treasure need to take baths and prepare for school tomorrow."

Josiah sat up and threw his legs over the side of Gypsie's bed. "Let me take care of the girls, baby. You need your rest for round two in my bed later tonight." He kissed her forehead. "Go back to sleep. I'll see you later."

"What about the conversation with the girls?"

"We can do it tomorrow, next week, or next year. It doesn't matter because you and I are in this forever. Okay?"

"Okay."